THE NAIVE AND
SENTIMENTAL LOVER

"John le Carré's superb and disturbing thrillers
placed him in the company of the foremost novel-
ists writing today. This latest book bears the stamp
of his distinctive talent . . . Sad, funny, captivating
and stunningly fertile, it is the most satisfying
novel I have head this year."

—*Sunday Express*

"Comic and touching . . . This novel is solid,
brilliant and marvelously good reading."

—*Book World*

"Splendid, original . . . Le Carré shows how en-
dowed he is with the art of storytelling."

—*The Times*

THE
NAIVE AND
SENTIMENTAL
LOVER

John le Carré

BANTAM BOOKS
TORONTO • NEW YORK • LONDON • SYDNEY • AUCKLAND

THE NAIVE AND SENTIMENTAL LOVER

*A Bantam Book / published by arrangement with
Alfred A. Knopf, Inc.*

PRINTING HISTORY
Knopf edition published January 1972
Bantam edition / November 1978
9 printings through September 1988

Cover type design by R. D. Scudellari

*Bantam Books are published by Bantam Books, a division of
Bantam Doubleday Dell Publishing Group, Inc. Its trademark,
consisting of the words "Bantam Books" and the portrayal of
a rooster, is Registered in U.S. Patent and Trademark Office
and in other countries. Marca Registrada. Bantam Books,
666 Fifth Avenue, New York, New York 10103.*

PRINTED IN THE UNITED STATES OF AMERICA

KR   18 17 16 15 14 13 12 11 10 9

For John Miller
and Michael Truscott,
at Sancreed, with
love.

Haverdown

1

Cassidy drove contentedly through the evening sunlight, his face as close to the windshield as the safety belt allowed, his foot alternating diffidently between accelerator and brake as he scanned the narrow lane for unseen hazards. Beside him on the passenger seat, carefully folded into a plastic envelope, lay an Ordnance Survey map of central Somerset. An oilbound compass of the newest type was fastened by suction to the walnut dashboard. At a corner of the windshield, accurately adjusted to his field of view, a copy of the Estate Agent's particulars issued under the distinguished title of Messrs. Grimble and Outhwaite of Mount Street W. was clipped to an aluminium stand of his own invention. *For the attention of Mr. Aldo Cassidy* ran the deferential inscription; for Aldo was his first name. He drove, as always, with the greatest concentration, and now and then he hummed to himself with that furtive sincerity common to the tone-deaf.

He was traversing a moor. A flimsy ground mist shifted over rhines and willow trees, slipped in little puffs across the glistening hood of his car, but ahead the sky was bright and cloudless and the spring sun made emeralds of the approaching hills. Touching a lever he lowered the electric window and leaned one side of his head into the rush of air. At once rich smells of peat and silage filled his nostrils. Over the reverent purr of the car's engine he caught the sounds of cattle and the cry of a cowhand harmlessly insulting them.

"It's an idyll," he declared aloud. "It's an absolute idyll."

Better still it was a safe idyll, for in the whole wide beautiful world Aldo Cassidy was the only person who knew where he was.

Beyond his conscious hearing, a closed-off chamber of his memory echoed to the awkward chords of an aspiring pianist. Sandra, wife to Aldo, is extending her artistic range.

"Good news from Bristol," Cassidy said, talking over the music. "They think they can offer us a patch of land. We'll have to level it of course."

"Good," said Sandra his wife, and carefully rearranged her hands over the keyboard.

"It's a quarter of a mile from the largest boys' school and eight hundred yards from the girls'. The city authorities say there's a fair chance that if we do the levelling and donate the changing rooms, they'll put up a footbridge on the by-pass."

She played a ragged chord.

"Not an ugly one, I hope. Town planning is *extremely* important, Aldo."

"I know."

"Can I come?"

"Well you *have* got your clinic," he reminded her with tentative severity.

Another chord.

"Yes. Yes, I've got my clinic," Sandra agreed, her voice lilting slightly in counterpoint. "So you'll have to go alone, won't you? Poor Pailthorpe."

Pailthorpe was her private name for him, he could not remember why. Pailthorpe the Bear, probably; bears were their most popular fauna.

"I'm sorry," said Cassidy.

"It's not *your* fault," said Sandra. "It's the Mayor's, isn't it? After all," she added speculatively, "he *runs* the town, doesn't he?"

"Naughty Mayor," said Cassidy.

"Naughty Mayor," Sandra agreed.

"Spank him," Cassidy suggested.

"Spank, spank," gaily said Sandra, wife to Aldo, her face in combat with its shadows.

He was a fair-haired man of thirty-eight and quite handsome in certain lights. Like his car he was groomed with loving elegance. From the left-hand buttonhole to the breast pocket of his faultless suit ran a thin gold chain of obvious usefulness whose purpose was nevertheless undefined. Aesthetically it perfectly answered the subdued pin stripe of the cloth behind it; as a piece of rigging it joined the head of the man to the heart, but there was no telling which end if either held the mastery. In both build and looks he might have served as an architectural prototype for the middle-class Englishman privately educated between the wars; one who had felt the wind of battle but never the fire of it. Heavy at the waist, short in the leg, a squire always in the making, he possessed those doggedly boyish features, at once mature and retarded, which still convey a dying hope that his pleasures may be paid for by his parents. Not that he was effeminate. True, the mouth was well advanced from the rest of the face and quite deeply sculptured under the lower lip. True also that as he drove he was guilty of certain affectations which pointed in the female direction, such as brushing aside his forelock or putting back his head and wrinkling his eyes as though a sudden headache had interfered with brilliant thoughts. But if these mannerisms meant anything at all, then most likely they reflected a pleasing sensitivity towards a world occasionally too shrill for him, an empathy as much parental as childish, rather than any unwelcome tendencies left over from public school.

Clearly he was no stranger to the expense account. An untaxable affluence was legible in the thickening of the lower waistcoat (for his safety and comfort he had unfastened the top button of his trousers) and in the widths of white cuff which isolated his hands from manual labour; and there was already about his neck and complexion a sleek rich gloss, a tan almost, *flambé* rather than sun-given, which only balloon glasses, Bunsen burners, and the fumes of *crêpes suzette* can faithfully reproduce. Despite this evidence of physical well-being, or perhaps in contrast to it, the outward Cassidy possessed in some devious way the power, even the authority to disturb. Though he was not in the slightest degree pathetic there was something to him which caught the eye and demanded help. Somehow he managed to convey that the encroachments of the flesh had not yet killed the magic of the spirit.

As if in recognition of this protective rôle which Cassidy unconsciously imposed on his environment, the interior of the car was provided with many important adaptations designed to spare him the distressing consequences of collision. Not only had the walls and ceiling and doors been generously upholstered with additional layers of quilt; the steering wheel, the child-proof door handles—already deeply recessed in succulent cavities of felt—the glove compartment, brake lever, even the discreetly concealed fire extinguisher, each was separately encased in handstitched leather and padded with a pleasing flesh-like substance calculated to reduce the most drastic impact to no more than a caress. At the rear window a sun-proof canopy, electrically operated and bordered with small silk balls, hung poised to defend at any time the good man's neck against an overzealous sun or his eyesight against the harmful dazzle of alien headlights. As to the dashboard it was a veritable medicine chest of preventive physic: from blinker lights to ice-alert, from reserve battery to reserve oil supply, from safari petrol tank to auxiliary cooling system its switches anticipated every catastrophe known to nature and the manufacturing industries. Cassidy's was a car that conveyed rather than transported; a womb, one might even have thought, from whose padded, lubricated interior the occupant had yet to make his entry into the harder world.

"How far to Haverdown, do you mind?"

"Eh?"

"Haverdown." Should he spell it? Most likely the fellow was illiterate. "Haverdown. The great house. The manor."

The lolling mouth opened and partially closed, voicelessly mimicking the name; a grimy arm struck towards the hill. "Straight on up over look."

"And is it far, would you say?" Cassidy enquired loudly, as if addressing the deaf.

"Won't take you more than five minutes, will it, not in *her?*"

"Thanks a million. Good luck to you old son."

In the mirror the yokel's brown face, frozen into an expression of comic incredulity, watched him out of sight. Well, thought Cassidy, the fellow has seen something of the world today and two shillings won't make him drunk.

All nature, it seemed, had turned out for his procession. In cottage gardens romping peasant children put aside their ancient games and turned to stare at him as he glided by. How *pastoral*, he thought; how rude, how vital. From trees and hedgerows buds of varying shades of green were bursting forth with seasonable energy, while in the fields wild daffodils mingled with other flowers he could not identify. Leaving the village, he began climbing a hill. The high banks gave way to sloping wooded glades. Below him farms, fields, churches, and rivers faded into far horizons. Lulled by such a delightful prospect he abandoned himself to the contemplation of his quest.

My pleasurable quest, as the favoured after-dinner speaker called it, my *very pleasurable* quest.

"A quest for *what?*" a nagging voice enquired inside him. "A quest *towards,* or a quest *from?*"

With an airy shake of his head, Cassidy brushed aside such pedantries. Nonsense, he told his inward audience, I have come to buy a house. Inspect it, cost it, buy it. And if I have not informed my wife, that is my own affair.

"Shall you stay all night?" Sandra remarked very casually. The piano practice temporarily interrupted, they were finishing their evening meal.

"We may not get going till five or so," Cassidy replied, avoiding the direct answer. "It depends when the Mayor's free." A clause of conciliation: "I thought I might take a book to read. If you could find me one."

Slowly, hand in hand with his cultural advisor, Cassidy the aspiring reader paraded the ranks of Sandra's bookshelves.

"Now," she mused, very earnest. "What do Pailthorpes read when they go gallivanting in Bristol?"

"It's got to be something I can manage when I'm a bit tight," he warned. They both laughed. "And not—" recalling a previous selection "—*not* Jane Austen."

They settled for non-fiction, a *straight* book suitable to a tired Pailthorpe of little fantasy.

"Sometimes," said Sandra playfully, "I wonder whether you ever really see these people at all."

"I don't," said nimble Cassidy, volleying at the net. "She's a blonde and she's eight feet tall."

"*Sexy,*" said Sandra, wife to Aldo, kissing her loyal man. "What's her name?"

Haverdown.

He hoped he had pronounced the word correctly. Such things can make a difference when one arrives in a new neighbourhood.

Haverdown.

Was the *a* long or short? To have or to haver?

A pigeon was barring his approach. He sounded his horn. Prudently it withdrew.

And the *down*: what did *down* mean? A country gentleman should know his derivations. *Down* as in descent, or *down* as in the rolling downs in England? A happy repartee occurred to him, as with the exaggerated gesture of those enjoying their own company the ready wit raised his eyebrows and smiled in quiet academic superiority. Or *down* like duck-down, fluff? Answer me that if you please Messrs. Grimble and Outhwaite of Mount Street W.

Haverdown.

It was a pretty name for all that, though names of course meant nothing in such cases. Stately too. Not Hall or Court or Grange, not Haverdown Manor even. Just Haverdown: a sovereign concept, as his Oxford tutor would have said, requiring no qualification. *Haverdown.* A man might well choose it as a title if such a thing were ever asked of him. "You know young Cassidy of Haverdown? Remarkable fellow. Flourishing business in London, gave it all up, came down here. Two years later made a going thing of farming. Knew damn all about it when he began, total duffer. Mind you they do say he's a bit of a financial wizard. Locals adore him of course. Generous to a fault."

About to consult the mirror in order light-heartedly to put a face to his baronial image, Cassidy veered sharply. *The entrance is marked by a Pair of finely pointed stone gateposts surmounted by ornamental Beasts dating from the sixteenth Century.* Directly before him, two disintegrating griffins, glumly clutching armorial shields, rose into the green darkness of a beech tree. Their feet were manacled to the plinth and their shoulders hunched from fatigue. Intently, Cassidy examined their scrolled shields. An eroded diagonal cross formed the central theme, feathers or recumbent serpents filled the upper triangle. He frowned in perplexity. Feathers were Wales, that much he knew; but was not the cross Saint Andrew? And was not Saint Andrew Scotland, hence the golf course?

Shifting gears, he set off along the drive. Patience. In due course he would research the matter, it would be an occupation for the winter months. He had always fancied himself as something of a local historian, browsing in county libraries, inspiring local digs, sending postcards to learned vicars.

"Perhaps," said Sandra, wife to Aldo, as they made ready for bed, *"next* time you go, I could come?"

"Of course you can," said Cassidy. "We'll make a special trip."

"An ordinary trip will do," said Sandra and put out the light.

Briefly the coppice closed round him. Over a carpet of bluebells he caught a glint of water between the trees. The drive returned him to the sunlight, passed a derelict cottage, skirted a rusted iron fence. Now a broken signpost drunkenly divided the approach. Tradesmen left and visitors right. I'm both, Cassidy thought gaily and took the right fork. Tulips lined the verges, poking their heads between the nettles. Lot of stock there, if only he could get at the weeds in time. The pond was overgrown. Dragonflies switched across the unbroken surface of the lily leaves, bullrushes almost obscured the boathouse. How fast was nature to reclaim her own, Cassidy reflected in growing exhilaration, how inexorable, how maternal was her will!

On its own grass plateau, between a ruined chapel and the picked skeleton of a fruithouse, Haverdown rose suddenly before him.

An Historic and Scheduled FORTIFIED MANOR HOUSE AND KEEP thirty Miles from Bath (Padding-

ton one Hour forty minutes) Haverdown is a *GEN-
TLEMAN'S RESIDENCE FULLY EQUIPPED FOR
IMMEDIATE OCCUPATION WITH FIVE LOOSE
BOXES AND FORTY ACRES OF GOOD GRAZ-
ING.* The style is part Tudor part Earlier with restora-
tions dating Chiefly from the Georgian period at which
time the original Keep was substantially rebuilt under
the genius of *LORD Alfred de Waldebere.* His many
fine Additions include a Fine Curved Staircase in the
Style of adam and a number of Fine *ITALIAN BUSTS*
of great Value which are included in the Asking price.
Since Earliest Times Haverdown has been the Home
and Fortress of the de Waldebere family.

THE GEORGIAN PORTION. Perfectly sited on a
natural Spur the distinguished south Face discreetly
Masters some of the finest Scenery in Somerset. The
elevations are of old Brick, mellowed by Time and
weather to a pleasing russet Hue. The centre block
is crowned by a Shallow pediment of Bath stone. Eight
freestone Treads worn by the feet of ages lead to a fine
imposing curved Portico carried by six Individual Pil-
lars. To the West, between the Chapel and the Fruithouse, a superb Cupola in need of Minor Repair
offsets the symmetry. The Pigeon croft is in its unspoilt
Original condition providing ample Space for heating
unit, Guesthouse or *GENTLEMAN'S STUDIO RE-
TREAT. In rear GARDEN* cast-lead cupid in *TRA-
DITIONAL POSE,* valued separately see annexe.

THE EARLIER PORTION consists of fine battle-
mented *TOWER* with Original steps and Bellchamber
adjoining to a Row of tudor Almshouses. Central to
these stands the castellated Great Hall and Refectory
with fine basements under and *OLD MOAT ROUND.*
In the Great Hall, surely one of the finest in the West
of england, a Minstrel Gallery dating from the reign of
King Edward the 1st comprises the principal Feature.
From here according to local lore, journeying Musi-
cians paid their tribute to *SIR Hugo de Waldebere* the
first Recorded Owner of Haverdown until the Year
1261 when he was Outlawed for felony. The House
passed to his younger Son whereafter no Tenancy is
recorded until 1760 when Lord *ALFRED* returned
from Foreign Parts to rebuild the Home of his Forebears, probably after Catholic Persecutions had tem-

*porarily dispersed them. The Gardens are conceived
on the CLASSICAL English Pattern of containing Nature without undue Formality and are in need of upkeep all enquiries*

>*SOLELY THROUGH ABOVE NAMED
REFER JR/P MR. GRIMBLE*

Carefully replacing the prospectus in its stand and de-
taching a light cashmere overcoat from its ingenious
hanger beside the rear window, Cassidy happened to
glance backwards past the baby seat and the silk balls of
the blind, and was subjected to a remarkable hallucination.
The drive had vanished. Thick walls of green, pierced
with dark tunnels, had closed upon his route and cut
him off from the outside world. He was alone in a magic
cave of dark green; at the pantomime, his father's guest;
in childhood, thirty years ago. . . .

Afterwards, he was well able to explain this optical illusion. A strand of vapour, he assured himself, such as lay
upon the moor, had settled below the level of his immediate vision, and by some trick of light assumed the colour
of the foliage. It had been raining (as indeed it had) and
the moisture on the drive, aided by the low sun, had set
up a green shimmer which gave it the appearance of high
grass. Or he himself, by the quick movement of his head
after the long drive, had transposed upon his own vision
images from other places . . . a natural coincidence therefore, such as mirages are made of.

Nevertheless, for an instant, and perhaps for much
longer in terms of the interior experience of Aldo Cassidy,
he had the sense of being caught up in a world that was
not as controllable as the world he was accustomed to: a
world, in short, capable of dismaying metaphysical leaps,
and although a second examination soon restored the
drive to its rightful position in the scheme of things, its
agility, or rather the remembrance of it, caused him to
remain seated for a moment while he collected himself. It
was with some distrust, therefore, as well as a lingering
sense of disconnection, that he finally opened the door and
cautiously lowered one well-shod foot on to the capricious
surface of the earth.

"And enjoy yourself," Sandra his protective spouse had warned him at breakfast in her army officer voice. "Don't let them *browbeat* you. Remember it's *you* who are doing the giving."

"I'll try," Cassidy promised with an English hero's smile.

His first impression, far from pleasurable, was that he had stepped into an air raid. A fierce evening wind had come up from the east, battering his eardrums and crashing like gunfire into the elms. Above him, recklessly swirling rooks dived and screamed at his intrusion. The house itself had already been hit. It groaned from every door and casement, waving its useless limbs in outrage, slapping them in agony against its own defenceless walls. At its base lay the débris of masonry and tiles. A fallen cable passed close over his head and ran the length of the garden. For one disgusting moment Cassidy fancied, looking up at it, that he saw a dead pigeon hanging from its frayed binding, but it was only an old shirt left behind by a careless gypsy and wound upon itself by a careless wind. Odd, he thought, recovering his composure: looks like one of mine, the kind we wore a few years back, striped, with stiff collars and a generous width of cuff.

He was extremely cold. The weather, which had looked so gentle and inviting from within the car, now assaulted him with a quite unnatural venom, inflating his thin coat with barbarous draughts and lashing at the cuffs of his tailored lightweight suit. Indeed so sudden and so fierce was the first impact of reality upon his internal reveries that Cassidy was actually tempted to return then and there to the safety of his car, and it was only a late assertion of the bulldog spirit that stayed his hand. After all, if he was to spend the rest of his life here he might as well start getting used to the climate. He had driven, by his own standards, a long way, a hundred miles or so; was he seriously proposing to turn back for a mere breeze? Resolutely fastening his collar he embarked in earnest upon the first phase of his inspection.

He called this process *taking the feel of the place*. It was one he had rehearsed often and which involved the sampling of many intangible elements. The setting for instance: is it hostile or amicable? Does it offer seclusion, which is desirable, or isolation, which is not? Does it embrace the occupant, or expose him? Was he—a vital question—born here, is *that* a feasibility?

Despite the cold, his initial impressions were not unfavourable. The park, which clearly provided the view from the principal windows of the house, had a lush pastoral quality which was distinctly soothing. The trees were deciduous (a rare advantage since he secretly found conifers too bleak) and their great age imbued them with a fatherly gentleness.

He listened.

The wind had dropped and the rooks were slowly settling. From the moor, where the sea fog still clung, the rasp of a handsaw vied with the grumbling of livestock. He examined the grazing. Good fencing there, ample space for ponies provided there was no yew to poison them. He had read somewhere, probably in Cobbett, whose *Rural Rides* he had studied for School Certificate, that yew poisoned ponies, and it was one of those aimless cruelties of nature which had remained impressed upon his memory.

Palominos, that was the word.

I shall have palominos. No need for shelter, the chestnuts will provide the shelter. The Welsh variety is best: hardy beasts, he had heard from all sides, self-sufficient and cheap to run. The right temperament too: townsmen could manhandle them without danger of reprisal.

He sniffed the air.

Woodsmoke, damp pine, and the indefinable mustiness that is fostered by neglect. I find no fault with it.

Now at last, quite coolly in his outward manner, he turned to the house and gave it his critical attention. A deep silence had fallen over the hilltop. In the trees nothing stirred. The shirt hung motionless from its cable. For long minutes he remained as if in prayer, his gloved hands loosely linked over his stomach, his shoulders well back, his fair head a little to one side, a survivor mourning his lost comrades.

Aldo Cassidy in the twilight of his thirty-ninth spring surveyed the elegant wreck of a dozen English generations.

The light was dying even as he stood there. Red shafts glinted from the buckled weather vane, touched what little glass remained in the sash windows, and were gone. A rock, he thought, with a gush of proud Victorian purple. A mountain peak against the evening sky, unscalable and immutable, an organic outcrop of English history. A rock, he repeated, his romantic heart pounding with half-remembered lines of English poetry; broken from the earth, whose name is England. A rock, fashioned by the hand of centuries, hewn by God's masons, guarded by His soldiers.

What would I not give to have been born of such a place? How much bigger, how much braver could I not be? To draw my name, my faith, my ancestry, even my profession perhaps from such a monument of heroic ages: to be a crusader still, serving not brashly but with humble courage a cause too evident to be defined? To swim in my own moat, to cook in my own refectory, to dine in my own Great Hall, to meditate in my own cell? To walk in my own crypt among the shell-torn standards of my forebears; to nurture tenants, counsel wayward servants, and till the earth in pleasingly dilapidated tweeds?

Gradually a vision formed before the dreamer's inner eye.

It is Christmas evening and the trees are bare against the early sunset. A solitary figure, no longer young, dressed in costly but unobtrusive habit, is riding through the long shadows of the chestnut avenue. The horse, well conscious of its precious burden, is docile even in sight of home. A lantern is beckoning in the portico, merry servants hasten to the door. "Pleasant ride then, Mr. Aldo?" "Not bad, Giles, not bad. No no I'll rub him down myself, thank you. Good evening, Mrs. Hopcroft. The celebrations well advanced I trust?"

And within, what then? No children, grandchildren tugging at his hand? No amiable lady in a long tweed skirt woven on the premises, no *Eve*, descending the Fine Curved Staircase in the Style of *adam*, holding a bowl of potpourri in her unhardened hands? No Sandra, younger by a dozen years, piano-less, free of her private darkness, unquestioning of Aldo's male sovereignty? Born to the gracious life, fresh to him, witty, varied, and adoring? *"Poor love you must be frozen through. I lit a fire in the library. Come, let me help you with your boots."*

There was no within. Cassidy on such occasions concerned himself resolutely with exteriors.

It was all the more surprising to him, therefore, chancing to look irritably upwards at a flock of doves whose restless fluttering had disrupted his reflections, to notice a faint but undeniable curl of woodsmoke rising from the western chimney stack and a real light, very yellow like an oil light, swinging gently in that same portico through which, in his imagination, he had that minute passed.

"Hullo lover," a pleasant voice said. "Looking for someone, are we?"

2

Now Cassidy prided himself on his aplomb at moments of crisis. In business circles he had a reputation for thinking on his feet and he considered it fairly won. "Deft" they had called him in the *Times Business News* during a recent take-over battle. "That gentle trouble-shooter." The quality derived not least from a refusal to recognise the extent of any peril, and it was backed by a solid understanding of the uses of money. Cassidy's first response therefore was to ignore the strangeness of the address and to give the man good evening.

"Jesus," the voice said, "is it?"

His second was to walk casually to his car, not by any means in order to escape but rather to identify himself as its owner and therefore, by definition, as a potential purchaser of substance. He also had in mind the agents' particulars on their aluminium stand which gave the proof, if such were needed, that he was not a wilful trespasser. He felt very badly towards the agents. It was the agents after all who had sent him, they who had given him the clearest assurances that the house was unoccupied, and they who would tomorrow pay very dearly for that error. "It's an Executors' sale, old boy," Outhwaite had croaked to him on the telephone in the fatuous tone of conspiracy which only estate agents seem to acquire. "Offer them half and they'll cut your arm off." Well, Cassidy would see who lost an arm after this adventure. Backing out of his car with the duplicated pages prominently displayed in his free hand, he became uncomfortably conscious of the fixity of his interrogator's gaze represented by the unwavering beam of the lantern.

"This is *Haverdown*, isn't it?" he asked, speaking up the steps and using the shorter *a*. His tone was precisely pitched. Puzzled but not dismayed, a dash of indignation to preserve his authority: the respectable citizen is disturbed in the conduct of his lawful business.

17

"I expect so, lover," the lantern replied not altogether playfully. "Want to buy it do we?"

The speaker's features were still hidden by the lamplight, but from the position at which the head was measured against the lintel of the door Cassidy was able to guess a person of his own height; and from the width of the shoulders, where he could define them against the interior darkness of the house, of his own build as well. The rest of his information, as he ascended the Eight freestone Treads worn by the feet of ages, was gained by ear. The man was of his own age too, but more confident, good at addressing the troops and coping with the dead. The voice, moreover, was remarkably compelling. Dramatic even, he would say. Tense. Balanced on a soft beguiling edge. Cassidy detected also—for he had a quick ear for social music—a certain regional deviation, possibly in the Gaelic direction, a brogue rather than an accent, which in no way affected his good opinion of the stranger's breeding. *The cross of Saint Andrew and the feathers of Wales:* well here, if he was not mistaken, was the harp of Ireland. He had reached the top step.

"Well I'd like to consider it certainly. Your agents, Grimble and Outhwaite sent me"—slightly moving the mimeographed sheets to indicate that the evidence was in his hand. "Did they get in touch with you by any chance?"

"Not a word," the lantern replied evenly. "Not a peep, not a funeral note."

"But I made the appointment almost a week ago! I do think they might have rung you or something. I mean don't *you?*"

"Phone's cut off, lover. It's the end of the world out here. Just the moo cows and the chickadees. And wild rooks, of course, seeking whom they may devour, the buggers."

It seemed to Cassidy more necessary than ever to preserve the line of his enquiry.

"But surely they could have *written* after all," he protested, anxious to insert between them the spectre of a common enemy. "I mean really these people *are* the end."

The answer was quite a while in coming.

"Maybe they don't know we're here."

Throughout the whole course of this exchange Cassidy had been the subject of minute scrutiny. The lamp, playing slowly over his body, had examined first his handmade shoes, then his suit, and was now engaged in deciphering the crest on his dark blue tie.

"Jesus, what's that?" the soft voice asked. "Indians?"

"A dining club actually," Cassidy confessed, grateful for the question. "A thing called the Nondescripts."

A long pause.

"Oh *no,*" the voice protested at last, genuinely shocked. "Oh Jesus, what a terrible bloody name! I mean what would Nietzsche make of that, for Christ's sake? You'll be calling yourselves the Filthy Cameldrivers next."

Cassidy was not at all used to such treatment. In the places where he spent his money even his signature was an unnecessary formality, and in the ordinary way of things he would have protested vigorously against any suggestion that his credit or his person—let alone his dining club—was in doubt. But this was not the ordinary way: instead of a surge of indignation, Cassidy was once more overcome by the same uncommon feeling of disconnection. It was as though the figure behind the lamp were not a separate figure at all, but his own, mysteriously reflected from the depths of the liquid twilight; as though his swifter, freer self were examining, by the light of that unusual lantern, the features of his pedestrian other half. And after all, the Nondescripts *were* a rather seedy lot; he had thought so more than once of late. Brushing aside such bizarre inventions, he finally managed a show of heat.

"Look here," he said quite strongly. "I don't want to intrude, I can perfectly well come back another time. Assuming you *want* to sell of course," he added, to give extra sting.

The voice did not hurry to console him.

"*You're* not intruding, lover," it said at last, as if passing a considered verdict. "You're *gorgeous,* that's my view. In the first position. No fooling. We haven't had a bourgeois for years."

The beam descended. In the same moment a ray of red sunlight, reflected from the upper window of the chapel, broke like a tiny dawn over the interior of the porch and provided Cassidy with a first sight of his examiner. He was, as Cassidy had already suspected, very handsome. Where Cassidy curved, his examiner went straight. Where Cassidy was weak, his examiner was resolute; where concessive, zealous; where Cassidy was fluid, the other was rock, and where he was pale and fair, his examiner was dark and sudden and eager. From a handsome face dark eyes shone with the greatest animation; a Gaelic smile, at once predatory and knowing, illuminated its features.

So far so good. Still seeking, however, to assign him to one of the social categories into which the world is naturally divided, Cassidy transferred his concentration to the man's attire. He wore a black coat of the kind favoured by Indian gentlemen, midway between a dinner jacket and a military blazer, but cut with a decided oriental flair. His feet were bare and his lower body was encased in what appeared to be a skirt.

"Good Lord," Cassidy said involuntarily, and was about to offer some further apology such as: "Oh my God, you were in the middle of your bath"; or: "Oh look here this is monstrous of me I've got you out of bed," when the lantern turned sharply away from him and shone upon the car.

There was no need for the lantern at all—the pale coachwork stood out excellently against the half-light, a safety factor which Cassidy was well aware of—but the examiner used it all the same, less to observe, perhaps, than to stroke the pure outlines in slow caressing movements of the beam, much as a moment earlier he had studied its owner.

"Yours is it, lover?"

"Yes it is actually."

"Your very own? All of it?"

Cassidy laughed easily, presuming a veiled reference to hire purchase, a form of payment which (since he had no need of it) he considered one of the ills of his generation.

"Well yes. I think it's the only way really, don't you?"

For some while the examiner made no reply but remained in deepest concentration, his body motionless, the lantern swinging gently in his hand, his eyes intent upon the car.

"Jesus," he whispered at last. "Jesus. There's a hearse for a Nondescript."

Cassidy had watched people admire his car before. He had even encouraged them. He was perfectly capable, on a Saturday morning for instance, returning from shopping or some other semi-recreational errand, and finding a small group of enthusiasts gathered along its elegant length, of offering them some account of its history and properties, and demonstrating from a stationary position some of its more unusual modifications. He considered this democratic open-heartedness to be one of his most likeable characteristics: life had wrought its distinctions true enough, but when it came to the fellowship of the road Cassidy counted himself little better than the next man. His host's interest however was of a different sort. Once again it appeared to be an examination in principle, a fundamental questioning of certain unstated values which were inherent in the car's existence, and it only added to Cassidy's unease. Did he consider it vulgar? Was it inferior to his own? The upper classes, he knew very well, had strong views on the display of wealth, but surely the car's *specialness* put it beyond the reach of such superficial charges? Somebody has to own it, after all. Just as they have to own Haverdown, ha, ha. Perhaps he should say something, offer some deprecatory phrase? There were several which in other circumstances he might have ventured: "It's only a toy really . . . well I think of it as a sort of man's mink coat . . . of course I couldn't begin to run it without the Company . . . present from the taxpayer I'm afraid . . ." He was still considering such a move when he felt his left arm seized in a grip of unexpected force.

"Come on, lover," the voice said, beguiling. "Get your cork out, I'm freezing."

"Well, if you're sure it's not inconvenient—" Cassidy began as he almost stumbled over the rotting threshold.

He never discovered whether it was convenient or not. The heavy door had closed behind him. The lantern had gone. He was standing in the total blackness of an unknown interior with only his host's friendly grasp to guide him.

Waiting for his eyes to grow accustomed to the light, Cassidy endured many of the hallucinations which afflict the temporarily blinded. He found himself first in the Scala Cinema at Oxford, edging past rows of unseen knees, trampling apologetically on unseen feet. Some were

hard, some soft; all were hostile. There were seven cinemas at Oxford in the days when Cassidy was privileged
to receive his higher education, and he had got round
them nicely in a week. Soon, he thought, the grey rectangle will open before me and a dark-haired girl in period
costume will unbutton her blouse in French to the appreciative whistles of my fellow academics.

Before any such delight was afforded him, however,
he was abruptly translated to the Natural History Museum
in South Kensington whither one of his stepmothers had
threatened to consign him as a punishment for self-abuse.
"You're no better than an animal," she furiously assured
him. "So you'd best go and join them. For ever." Though
his vision was by now clearing, he found much evidence
to support the nightmares: prickly upholstery redolent
of cinemas, the pungent smells of moulting fur and forma-
lin, the amputated heads of elks and wildebeests which
glared down on him in the glazed terror of their last
agony, looming mammoth shapes draped in white dust
covers.

Gradually, to his relief, more familiar images reassured
him of human habitation. A grandfather clock, an oak
sideboard, a Jacobean dining table; a stone fireplace
armed with crossed muskets and the pleasingly familiar
crest of the de Waldeberes.

"My goodness," said Cassidy at last in what he hoped
was a voice of awe.

"Like it?" his companion asked. Retrieving the lantern
from Cassidy knew not where, he carelessly flicked the
beam over the uneven flagstones.

"Superb. Quite superb."

They were in the Great Hall. Chinks of grey light
marked the tall outlines of the shuttered windows. Pikes,
assagais and antlers adorned the upper levels; packing
cases and mouldering books were strewn over the floor.
Directly before them hung a gallery of dense black oak.
Behind it stone arches mouthed the openings to dismal
corridors. The smell of dry rot was unmistakable.

"Want to see the rest?"

"I'd adore to."

"The whole thing? Warts and all?"

"From top to bottom. It's fabulous. What date is the gallery by the way? I should know but I've forgotten."

"Oh Jesus, some of it was made from Noah's Ark, no kidding. So they tell me anyway."

Laughing dutifully Cassidy could not fail nevertheless to detect, above the familiar smells of antiquity, the fumes of whisky on his host's breath.

Ha la, he thought with an inward smile of recognition. Les aristos. Slice them where you will, they're all the same. Decadent, devil-may-care . . . but actually rather marvellous in an other-worldish way.

"Tell me," he asked politely, as they once more turned a corner into darkness, "is the furniture for sale too?" His voice had acquired a new Englishness as he offered it for the aristocrat's consideration.

"Not till we've moved out, lover. Got to have something to sit on, haven't we?"

"Of course. But later?"

"Sure. Have what you like."

"It would only be the smaller things," said Cassidy cautiously. "I've quite a lot already, actually. *Put by,* you know."

"Collector, eh?"

"Well a bit, certainly. But only when the price is right," he added on the same defensive note. *If there's one thing your English gentleman does understand, it's the value of money.* "I say do you think you could shine that light a little higher? I can't see a thing."

The corridor was lined with portraits of gentle soldiers and murderous civilians. The beam revealed them only capriciously, and this was unfortunate, for Cassidy was sure that, given the chance, he could have identified in their varied features traces of his eccentric escort: the brilliant erratic smile for instance, the pirate's eyes lit from within, the crop of black hair that fell so nobly over the powerful brow.

The lantern descended what appeared to be a short staircase, leaving him again in the deepest darkness.

"It's interminable," Cassidy said with a nervous laugh, and then: "I'd never have done this alone. I'm rather afraid of the dark to be honest, always have been. Some

people don't like heights, I don't like the dark." In point
of fact, Cassidy did not care for heights either, but there
seemed no point in spoiling the analogy. "Have you been
here long?" he asked, receiving no absolution for this
confession.

"Ten days."

"I meant your family."

The beam shone briefly on a rusted iron coat hanger,
then sank to the floor. "Oh Christ . . . for ever, man, for
ever."

"And it was your father who . . ."

For an uncomfortable moment Cassidy feared he had
again trodden upon too delicate ground: a recent death,
after all, is not a subject one discusses in the dark. There
was quite a delay before he had his answer.

"My uncle *actually*," the soft voice confessed,
and gave a small revealing sigh. "But we were very
close."

"I'm sorry," Cassidy murmured.

"He was gored by a bull," his guide continued in a
more cheerful tone which reinforced the brogue. "So at
least it was quick. None of your ugly lingering, I mean,
the peasants dropping in with gruel."

"Well that's some consolation," said Cassidy. "Was he
old?"

"Very. And I mean that bull—"

"Yes?" said Cassidy, puzzled.

The lantern appeared to shake in a sudden paroxysm
of grief. "Well the bull was *terribly* old himself. I
mean it was kind of death in slow motion. Come to think
of it, I don't know how they caught each other up."

Comedy had evidently dispelled tragedy, for now a wild
boyish laughter rose to the unseen roof, the beam swayed
merrily in time to its peals, and a strong hand descended
on Cassidy's shoulder.

"Listen it's great to have you. Great. You're doing me
a power of good, and that's the honest truth. Jesus, I've
been so bored: reading John Donne to the chickadees.
Imagine. Great poet, mind, but what an audience. The
way they look at you. Jesus. Listen I've had a wee drink,
you don't mind that now?"

Very much to his surprise, Cassidy felt a definite tweak
on what the law courts call the upper thigh.

"Like a drop yourself now and then, eh?"

"Indeed yes."

"Specially when you're lonely, or down on your luck a mite?"

"And at other times too, I promise you."

"Don't do that," the stranger said shortly, with a sudden change of humour. "Don't promise a thing."

They descended two stairs.

"Who the hell do you meet round here anyway?" he resumed in his jocular tone. "Even the bloody gypsies won't talk to you. You know, Christ, it's class, class all the way."

"Oh dear," said Cassidy.

The hand still guided his shoulder. As a rule Cassidy did not like to be handled, particularly by men, but the contact disturbed him less than he might have expected.

"What about all those acres?" he asked. "Don't *they* keep you busy any more?"

The smell of woodsmoke which Cassidy had hitherto admired for its rural fragrance became suddenly oppressive.

"Ah, fuck the acres. Who the hell wants land any more? Form-filling . . . rabies . . . pollution . . . . American air bases. It's over, I'm telling you. Unless you're in mink of course. Mink are great."

"Yes," Cassidy agreed, somewhat confused by this idiosyncratic description of the farmer's problems. "Yes I hear mink can make a *lot* of money."

"Hey listen. You religious at all?"

"Well half and half . . ."

"There's this fellow in County Cork calling himself the one true living God, have you read about him? J. Flaherty of Hillside, Beohmin. All over the papers it was. Do you think there's anything in it at all?"

"I really don't know," said Cassidy.

Obedient to his companion's whim, Cassidy allowed himself to be brought to a halt. The dark face came very close to his and he was suddenly aware of tension.

"Only I wrote to him see, challenging him to a duel. I thought that's who you might be."

"Oh," said Cassidy. "Oh no, well I'm afraid I'm not."

"You've a trace of him though, all the same, you've definitely a spot of divinity in you, I could tell it a mile off."

"Oh."
"Oh yes."

They had turned a second corner and entered another corridor even longer and more derelict than the first. At its far end red firelight was playing on a stone wall and whorls of smoke were curling towards them through the open doorway. Seized by a sudden sense of lassitude, Cassidy had the eerie feeling of walking through an adverse tide. The darkness was dragging against his feet like currents of warm water. The smoke, he thought, the smoke has made me dizzy.

"Bloody chimney's bunged up. We tried to get the fellow to fix it but they never come, do they?"

"It's the same in London," Cassidy agreed warming to his favourite topic. "You can ring them, write to them, have an appointment, it makes absolutely no difference. They come *when* they want and charge *what* they want."

"Bastards. Jesus, my grandfather would have flogged the lot of them."

"You can't do that these days I'm afraid," said Cassidy loudly, in the voice of one who also yearned for a simpler social order. "They'd be down on you like a ton of bricks."

"I'll tell you this for nothing, it's time we had another bloody war. Listen, they say he's about forty-three years of age."

"Who?"

"God. This fellow in Cork. That's a bloody odd age for him to choose, don't you think so? I mean let's have him young or old, that's what I said to him see, who the hell thinks he's God at forty-three? Still, when I saw the car, then you . . . well you can't blame me can you? I mean if God *was* going to run a car, well that Bentley of yours . . ."

"How *is* the servant problem round here?" Cassidy enquired, cutting him short.

"Bloody awful. All they want is fags, telly, and fucks."

"I suppose they get lonely. Like you."

Cassidy was now quite recovered from his initial nervousness. His companion's racy tones, echoing ahead of him, were for all their quaintness pleasantly reassuring; the firelight was now definitely closer and the sight of it, after their inward journey through the successively darker chambers of the enormous mansion, gave him further cheer. His composure however was barely won before it was violently intruded upon by a new and wholly unannounced phenomenon. A sudden waft of tinny music issued from a side doorway and a girl crossed their path.

Cassidy in fact saw her twice.

Once silhouetted against the smoky firelight at the end of the corridor, and once in the direct beam of the lantern as she stopped and turned her head to look at them, at Cassidy first and then in cool question at the torchbearer. Her stare was straight and by no means welcoming. She held a towel over one arm and a small transistor radio in her hand. Her copious auburn hair was banked on top of her head as if to keep it out of the wet, and Cassidy recognised, as they briefly exchanged glances, that she was listening to the same programme which he had been playing in the car, a selection of Frank Sinatra's music on the theme of male solitude. These impressions, fragmented as they were by the wandering beam of the lantern, the flickering of the firelight, and the clouds of woodsmoke, did not by any means run consecutively. The girl's appearance, her fractional hesitation, her double glance were but flashes upon his heightened consciousness. She was gone in a moment, vanishing into another doorway, but not before Cassidy had observed, with the helpless detachment which often accompanies a wholly unexpected experience, that she was not only beautiful but naked. Indeed, so utterly improbable was the apparition, so irreconcilable its effect upon Cassidy's beleaguered fantasy, that he would have discounted her altogether—fed her at once into his ever-ready apparatus of disbelief—had not the beam of the lantern firmly pointed him the proof of her terrestrial existence.

She had been walking on tiptoe. She must have been quite used to going barefoot, for each toemark was drawn separately in round spots on the flagstone like the print of a small animal in the snow.

3

Long ago in a great restaurant an elderly lady had stolen Cassidy's fish. She had been sitting beside him at an adjoining table facing into the room, and with one movement she had swept the fish—a sole Waleska generously garnished with cheese and assorted seafoods—into her open tartan handbag. Her timing was perfect. Cassidy happened to look upwards in response to an inner call—a girl probably, but perhaps a passing dish which he had almost ordered in preference to his Waleska—and when he looked down again the fish had gone and only a pink sludge across the plate, a glutinous trail of cornflour, cheese and particles of shrimp, marked the direction it had taken. His first response was disbelief. He had eaten the fish and in his distraction not even tasted it. But *how* had he eaten it? the Great Detective asked himself. With his fingers? His knife and fork were clean. The fish was a mirage: the waiter had not yet brought it, Cassidy was looking at the dirty plate left by a guest who had preceded him.

Then he saw the tartan handbag. Its handles were clamped tight together, but a telltale pink smear was clearly visible on one brass ball of the clasp. Call the waiter, he thought: "This lady has stolen my fish." Confront the thief, summon the police, demand that she open her handbag.

But her posture of spinsterly composure as she continued to sip her apéritif, one hand curled lightly in her napkin, was too much for him. Signing the bill he quietly left the restaurant, never to return.

Following the lantern into the smoke-filled drawing room, Cassidy underwent the same symptoms of psychic disarray. Had the girl existed, or was she the creation of his lively erotic fantasy? Was she a ghost? A de Waldebere heiress, for instance, murdered in her bath by the reckless Sir Hugo? But family ghosts do not leave footprints nor carry transistor radios, and are certainly not constructed of such eminently persuasive flesh. Assuming then that the girl was real and that he had seen her, should he as a matter of protocol venture some casual comment suggesting he had not? Imply that he had been studying a portrait or an architectural feature at the critical moment of her appearance? Ask his host whether he was all alone here or who looked after him?

He was still wrestling with the problem when he heard himself addressed in what he took to be a foreign language.

"Alc?"

To compound Cassidy's sense of unreality he had the strong impression of being cut off by fog, for the enormous fireplace was emitting billows of cannon smoke over the stone floor and heavy palls already hung from the rafters overhead. The same fire, which seemed to consist entirely of kindling wood, provided their only source of light, for the lantern was now extinguished and the windows, like those in the Great Hall, were firmly shuttered.

"I'm awfully sorry. I don't think I understand."

"*Alc,* lover. Alcohol. *Whisky.*"

"O thank you. Alcohol. Alc." He laughed. "Yes indeed I'd love an alc. It's quite a long drive from Bath actually. Well *fussy,* you know. All those narrow lanes and side turnings. *Alc.* Haha."

Mistress? Lecherous housemaid? Incestuous sister? A gypsy whore slunk in from the woods? Fiver a bang and free bath after?

"You want to try walking it." Glass in hand, the tall figure rose massively at him out of the smoke. If we were the same size, thought Cassidy, how are you now bigger? "Eight bloody hours it took us, with all God's limousines damn near running us into the hedge. It's enough to turn a man to drink, I'm telling you." The brogue was even stronger. "Still *you* wouldn't do that would you, lover? Carve us into the ditch, and not even stop to set the bone?"

A call girl perhaps, sent down by disgraceful agencies? Question: how can you call a call girl when your phone's cut off?

"Certainly not. I'm a great believer in defensive driving."

"Are you now?"

The dark eyes seemed, with this question, to invade still further Cassidy's unprotected consciousness.

"Look my name's Cassidy," he said as much to reassure himself as to inform his host.

"Cassidy? Jesus that's a lovely native name if ever I heard one. Hey, was it you robbed all those banks then? Is that where you got your money from?"

"Well I'm afraid not," said Cassidy silkily. "I had to work a little harder for it than that."

Emboldened by the aptness of his retort, Cassidy now undertook an examination of his host as frank as that which he himself had recently undergone. The garment which encased his dark legs was neither a skirt nor a bath towel nor yet a kilt, but a very old curtain embroidered with faded serpents and ripped at the edges as if by angry hands. He wore it off the hip, low at the front and higher at the back like a man about to bathe himself in the Ganges. His breast under the black jacket was bare, but garnished with clusters of rich black hair which descended in a thin line down his stomach before opening again into a frank pubic shadow.

"Like it?" his host enquired, handing him a glass.

"I beg your pardon?"

"*Shamus* is the name, lover. *Shamus*."

Shamus. Shamus de Waldebere . . . look him up in Debrett.

From the direction of the doorway Cassidy heard Frank Sinatra singing about a girl he knew in Denver.

"Hey Helen," Shamus called over Cassidy's shoulder. "It's not Flaherty after all, it's Cassidy. *Butch* Cassidy. He's come to buy the house now poor Uncle Charlie's dead and gone. Cassidy me old friend, shake hands with a very lovely lady, lately of Troy and now reduced to the abominable state of—"

"How do you do," said Helen.

"Matrimony," said Shamus.

She was covered, if not yet fully dressed.

Wife, he thought glumly. I should have known. The Lady Helen de Waldebere, and all doors closed.

There is no established method, even to a formalist of
Cassidy's stamp, of greeting a lady of great family whom
you have just met naked in a corridor. The best that he
could manage was a hog-like grunt, accompanied by a
watery academic smile and a puckering of the eyes, designed to indicate to those familiar with his signals that
he was a short-sighted person of minimal libido in the
presence of someone who had hitherto escaped his notice. Helen on the other hand, with looks and breeding
on her side and time to think in the dressing room, displayed a stately composure. She was even more beautiful
dressed than not. She wore a housecoat of devotional simplicity. A high collar enfolded her noble neck, lace cuffs
her slender wrists. Her auburn hair was combed long like
Juliet's and her feet were still bare. Her breasts, which
despite his simulated myopia he could not help remark-
ing, were unsupported, and trembled delicately as she
moved. Her hips were similarly unbound, and with each
balanced stride a white knee, smooth as marble, peeped
demurely through the division of her robe. English to the
core, thought Cassidy to his relief, what an entry; what a
dash she'd cut in trade. Switching off the wireless with a
simple movement of her index finger and thumb, she
placed it on the sofa table, smoothed the dust cover as if
it were the finest linen, then gravely shook his hand and
invited him to sit down. She accepted a drink and apologised for the mess in a low, almost a humble tone. Cassidy
said he quite understood, he knew what it was to move,
he had been through it several times in the last few years.
Somehow, without trying, he managed to suggest that
each move had been for the better.

"My God, even moving the *office*, when one has secretaries and assistants, even one's own workmen, it takes
months. Literally *months*. So what it's like here . . ."

"Where is your office?" Helen asked politely.

Cassidy's opinion of her rose still higher.

"South Audley Street," he said promptly. "West One.
Just off Park Lane, actually. We went in there last spring."
He wanted to add that she might have read about it in
the *Times Business News* but modestly he forebore.

"Oh how *very* nice." Chastely rearranging her skirts
to cover her peerless thighs, she sat down on the sofa.

Towards her husband she showed a greater reserve.
Her eyes seldom left his face and Cassidy did not fail to

notice their darting expression of concern. How well, as always, did he understand a pretty woman's feelings! A drunken husband was liability enough. But who could tell what other blows her pride had suffered in the last months, the fights with lawyers, the towering death duties, the painful partings from family retainers, the tattered keepsakes in the silent desk? And how many potential purchasers in that time had swept brutally through the treasured chambers of her youth, mouthed their gross objections, and left without a word of hope?

I will ease her burden, he decided; I will take over the conversation.

Having concisely rehearsed the reasons for his unheralded arrival, he laid the blame squarely at the door of Grimble and Outhwaite:

"I've nothing against them, they're very good people in their way. I've dealt with them for a number of years and I shall go on dealing with them no doubt, but like all these old firms they get complacent. Slack." Under the velvet, the steel showed. "I mean to take this up with them in quite a big way as a matter of fact."

Shamus, who had crossed his legs under the curtain and was leaning back in an attitude of critical reflection, merely nodded with energetic approval and said, "Attaboy Cassidy," but Helen assured him that his visit was perfectly convenient, he was very welcome at any time and it made no difference really:

"*Does* it Shamus?"

"None at all, lover," said Shamus heartily. "We're having a ball."

And resumed, with a complacency amounting almost to pride of ownership, his study of his unexpected guest.

"I'm so sorry about the smoke," said Helen.

"Oh it's quite all right," said Cassidy restraining himself with difficulty from wiping away a tear. "I rather like it actually. A wood fire is one of the things we just can't buy in London. Not at any price I'm afraid."

"It's all my own fault," Shamus confessed. "We ran out of firewood so I sawed up the table."

Shamus and Cassidy laughed loudly at this good joke and Helen after a moment's doubt joined in. Her laugh, he noticed with approval, was modest and admiring; he did not care for women's humour as a rule, fearing it to be directed against himself, but Helen's was different, he could tell: she knew her place and laughed only with the men.

"Now there's a terrible thing about mahogany." Leaping to his feet, Shamus wheeled away to where the bottle stood. "It just won't bloody burn like the lower-class woods. It positively resists martyrdom. Now I count that very bad manners indeed, don't you? I mean at a certain point we should all go gentle into that good night, don't you think so, Cassidy?"

Though the question was facetious, Shamus put it with great earnestness, and waited motionless until he had his answer.

"Oh rather," said Cassidy.

"He agrees," said Shamus, with apparent relief. "Helen, he agrees."

"Of course he does," said Helen. "He's being polite." She leaned across to him. "It's weeks since he met a soul," she confided in a low voice. "He's been getting rather desperate, I'm afraid."

"Don't give it a thought," Cassidy murmured. "I love it."

"Hey Cassidy, tell her about your Bentley." Shamus' brogue was all over the words: the drink had brought it to full flower. "Hear that, Helen? Cassidy's got a Bentley, a dirty big long one with a silver tip, haven't you lover?"

"Have you really?" said Helen over the top of her glass. "Gosh."

"Well not new of course."

"But isn't that rather a good thing? I mean aren't the old ones *better* in lots of ways?"

"Oh absolutely, well in my judgment anyway," said Cassidy. "The pre-sixty-three models were a *much* superior job. Well certainly this one has turned out pretty well."

Before he knew it, with only the smallest prompting from Shamus, he was telling her the whole story, how he had been driving through Sevenoaks in his Mercedes—he'd had a Merc in those days, very functional cars of course, but no real handwriting if they knew what he meant—and had spotted a Bentley in the showroom of Caffyns.

"In Sevenoaks, hear that?" Shamus called. "Fancy buying a Bentley in *Sevenoaks*. Jesus."

"But that's half the fun of it," Cassidy insisted. "Some of the very finest models come from as far away as India. Maharajahs bought them for safaris."

"Hey, lover."

"Yes?"

"You're not a maharajah yourself by any chance?"

"I'm afraid not."

"Only in this sort of light you can't always see the colour of a person's skin. Are you a Catholic then?"

"No," said Cassidy pleasantly. "Wrong again."

"But you are holy?" he insisted, returning to an earlier theme. "You do *worship*?"

"Well," said Cassidy doubtfully, "Christmas and Easter, you know the kind of thing."

"Would you call yourself a New Testament man?"

"Please go on," said Helen. "I'm riveted."

"Or would you say you were more in favour of the barbaric and untrammelled qualities of the Ancient Jews?"

"Well . . . neither or both I suppose."

"You see this fellow Flaherty in County Cork now—"

"*Please,*" said Helen, directing a second quelling glance at her husband.

Well, Cassidy had had this feeling that the car was *right*, he couldn't explain it really, and so in the end he'd stopped and gone back to take a second look. And anyway to cut a long story short this young salesman hadn't pushed him at all but recognised one of the breed, so to speak, and in ten minutes they'd done the deal. Cassidy wrote out a cheque for five thousand pounds dated that same day and drove away in the car.

"Goodness," Helen breathed. "How *terribly brave*."

"Brave?" Shamus repeated. "Brave? Listen he's a lion. You should have seen him out there on the terrace. He frightened the hell out of me. I'll tell you that for nothing."

"Well of course I did have the weekend to stop the cheque," Cassidy admitted a little injudiciously, and would have gone on with a great deal more of the same thing— the Automobile Association's report for instance which had been one long paean of technical praise, the car's

genealogy which he had only stumbled on months after
he had bought her—if Shamus, suddenly bored, had not
suggested that Helen show him round the house.

"After all, if he's a compulsive buyer, maybe he'll buy
us too, eh: I mean Jesus, we can't pass over an opportunity like this. Now Cassidy have you brought your
cheque book? Because if you haven't you'd best get in
that grey bedpan and hurry back to the West End and
fetch it, I'm telling you. I mean we don't show the house
to just *anyone*, don't you know. After all, if you're not
God, who *are* you?"

Once more Cassidy's seismographic spirit recorded
Helen's reticence and understood it. The same worried
glance troubled her serious eyes, the same innate courtesy
prevented her from putting her anxiety into words. "We
can hardly show it to him in the dark, darling," she said
quietly.

"Of course we can show it to him in the bloody dark.
We've got the lamp haven't we? Christ, he could buy the
place by Braille if he felt like it, couldn't you, lover? I
mean look here, Cassidy's quite clearly a *very influential
person* and *very influential persons* who can wander round
Sevenoaks signing cheques for five thousand pounds don't
bloody well like having their time wasted, Helen, that's
something you have to learn in life—"

Cassidy knew it was time for him to speak. "Oh now
look here *please* don't worry. I can perfectly well come
another time. You've been so good already—"

In an effort to make his intention real, he rose falter-
ingly to his feet. The woodsmoke and the whisky had had
more effect on him than he knew. His head was dizzy
and his eyes were smarting.

"I can *perfectly* well come back another time," he
repeated foolishly. "You must be tired out, what with all
the packing and making do."

Shamus was also standing, leaning his hands on Helen's
shoulders, and his dark, inward eyes were watching Cassidy intently.

"So why don't we make a date for next week?" he suggested.

"You mean you don't like the house," Shamus said in a
flat, menacing tone, more as a statement than a question. Cassidy hastened to protest but Shamus rode him
down. "It's not good enough for you, is that it? No cen-

tral heating, no poncy fittings like you've got in London-town?"

"Not at all, I merely——"

"What do you want for Christ's sake? A tart's parlour?"

Cassidy in his day had handled scenes like this before. Angry trade unionists had beaten his rosewood desk, deprived competitors had shaken their fists in his face, drunken maids had called him fat. But finally such situations had remained within his control, occurring for the greater part on territory he had already bought, among people he had yet to pay. The present situation was altogether different, and neither the whisky nor his misted vision did anything to improve his performance.

"Of *course* I like the house. I thought I'd made that abundantly clear, as a matter of fact it's the best I've seen for a long time. It's got everything I've been looking for ... peace ... seclusion ... garage space."

"More," Shamus exhorted.

"Antiquity ... what else do you want me to say?"

"Then come on with you!"

A brilliant, infecting smile had replaced the brief cloud of anger. Grabbing the whisky bottle in one hand and the lantern in the other, Shamus beckoned them brightly up the great staircase. Thus for the second time that evening Cassidy found himself conveyed, not altogether against his liking, upon a compulsory journey that seemed to his swimming consciousness to alternate with each new step between past and future, illusion and reality, drunkenness and sobriety.

"Come, Flaherty!" Shamus cried. "God's house has many mansions, and me and Helen will show you the whole bloody lot, won't we, Helen?"

"Will you follow me?" Helen asked with an air hostess' charming smile.

Sir Shamus and Lady Helen de Waldebere. It was symptomatic of Cassidy's confused state that he never stopped to consider whose heritage was actually for sale. Having cast Shamus as a kind of grounded cavalry officer drinking away the humiliations of a horseless existence, he vested in Helen the fortitude and dignified resignation which properly accompany the evanescence of a Great Line; and never asked himself how it had come about within the probabilities of a conventional union that the two of them had passed their childhood in the same house. Even if he had hit upon the question, Helen's bearing would only have added to his bewilderment. She was in her element: the young chatelaine had stepped lightly from her portrait and was showing them her domain. Whatever restraint she had felt in the drawing room was swept aside by her transparent devotion to the task. Solemn, wistful, informative by turn, she guided him with loving familiarity through the labyrinth of mouldering corridors. Cassidy kept close behind her, led by the smell of baby soap and the contra-rotations of her firmly rounded hips; Shamus followed at a distance with the bottle and the lantern, moving on the edge of their discourse or calling after them with harsh ironic jokes. "Hey Cassidy get her to tell you about Nanny Higgins having it off with the vicar at the Servants' Ball." In the Great Hall he found a pike and fought a shadow duel with his father's ghost; in the planthouse he insisted on presenting Helen with a flowering cactus, and when she accepted it he kissed her for a long time on the nape of her neck. Helen, in her serenity, took it all in good part.

"It's the waiting and the worry," she explained to Cassidy while Shamus was chanting Gregorian plainsong in the crypt. "It's so frustrating for him."

"Please," said Cassidy. "I do understand. Really."

"Yes, I think you do," she said casting him a look of gratitude.

"What will he do now? Get a job?" Cassidy asked, in a tone which recognised that, for such as Shamus, employment was the final degradation.

"Who would have him?" Helen asked simply.

She took him everywhere. In hanging dusk with the first stars breaking they patrolled the crumbling battlements and marvelled at the empty moat. By the light of the lantern they stood in awe before worm-eaten four-posters and delved in dust-filled priest holes, they caressed mildewed screens and tapped on panelling honeycombed by beetles. They discussed the problems of heating and Cassidy said small-bore piping would do the least harm. They worked out which rooms could be sealed off with little alteration: how the rewiring could be run behind the skirting boards and how an electrolyte circuit worked perfectly as damp course.

"It turns the house into a dry battery," Cassidy explained. "It's not cheap but then what is these days?"

"You know an *awful* lot about it," said Helen. "Are you an architect by any chance?"

"I just love old things," said Cassidy.

Behind them, hands clasped, Shamus was chanting the *Magnificat*.

4

"You're a lovely man," Shamus says quietly, offering him a drink from the bottle. "You're really a lovely perfect man. Tell us, do you have any theories on the general nature of love?"

The two men are on the Minstrel Gallery. Helen stands below them, gazing through the window, her eyes upon the long view of the chestnut walk.

"Well I think I understand how you feel about the house. Let's put it that way, shall we?" Cassidy suggests with a smile.

"Oh but it's worse for *her*, though, far."

"Is it?"

"Us men, you know, we're survivors. Cope with anything really can't we? But them, eh, them."

She has her back to them still: the last light from the window shines through the thin housecoat and shows the outline of her nakedness.

"A woman needs a home," Shamus pronounces philosophically. "Cars, bank accounts. Kids. It's a crime to deprive them of it, that's my view. I mean how else are they fulfilled? That's what I say."

One black eyebrow has risen slightly and it occurs to Cassidy, but not with particular force, that Shamus is in some way mocking him, though how is not yet clear.

"I'm sure it'll work out," says Cassidy blandly.

"Tell me, have you ever had two at once?"

"Two what?"

"Women."

"I'm afraid not," says Cassidy very shocked; not by the notion, which he has quite often entertained, but by the context in which it is expressed. Could any man blessed with Helen think so base?

"Or three?"

"Not three either."

41

"Do you play golf at all?"

"Now and then."

"How about squash? Would squash be a game you play?"

"Yes, why?"

"I like you to keep fit that's all."

"Shouldn't we go down? I think she's waiting."

"Oh, lover," says Shamus softly as he takes another pull from the bottle. "A girl like that'll wait all night for the likes of you and me."

"Couldn't you give it to the National Trust?" Cassidy asked loudly in his boardroom voice as they descended the rickety staircase. "I thought there was some arrangement whereby they maintain the house and let you live in it on condition that you open it to the public so many days a year."

"Ah, the buggers would stink the place out," Shamus retorted. "We tried it once. The kids peed on the Aubusson and the parents had it off in the orangerie."

"You have to pay something for upkeep as well," Helen explained with another of those appealing glances at her husband that were so sadly eloquent of her distress.

Pee-break, Shamus called it. They had left Helen in the drawing room staunching the smoking fire and now they stood shoulder to shoulder at the edge of the moat, listening to their own water trickling over the dry stones. The night was of an alpine majesty. With shaggy splendour the black house rose in countless peaks against the pale sky, where powdery swarms of stars followed the moonlit ridges of the clouds like fireflies frozen into the eternal ice. At their feet a white dew glistened on the uncut grass.

"The heaventree of stars," said Shamus. "Hung with humid nightree fruit."

"That's beautiful," said Cassidy reverently.

"Joyce. Old girl friend. Can't get her out of my hair. Hey, lover. Watch out for frostbite for God's sake. Nip it off in a jiffy, I warn you."

"Thanks," said Cassidy with a laugh. "I will."

Shamus sidled closer. "Er . . . tell us," he enquired con-

fidingly. "Er do you think it'll do you? The house I mean
. . . will it suit you at all?"

"I don't know. I hope it will, I'll have to have a survey
of course. Get a quantity surveyor in too, probably. It'll
cost a bomb to put straight."

"Hey lover, listen."

"I'm listening."

Long pause.

"What do you want it for?"

"I'm looking for a bit of tradition, I suppose. My father
was a self-made man."

"Oh my *God*," Shamus drawled and, as if to show that
the revelation had quite put him off, stepped quickly out of
reach. "Big place all the same isn't it, for a weekend
hideaway? Twenty bedrooms or more . . ."

"I suppose it is."

"Not probing you know. Do what you like with it as far
as we're concerned, provided you pay the price. Still you
can always let a few floors I dare say."

"If I had to, yes."

"Rent out the land too, eh? Local farmer'd take it off
your hands no doubt."

"Yes I suppose he would."

"I've always thought it'd make a good school actually."

"Yes, or a school."

"Or a hotel for that matter."

"Possibly."

"Hey, what about a casino? Now there's a thought.
Some of those wicked London hostesses, eh? Get a few of
the holy fathers in for a flutter."

"I wouldn't want that," said Cassidy shortly. He was
perfectly sober but the whisky appeared to be affecting his
movements.

"Jesus why ever not?"

"I just wouldn't want it, that's all."

"Oh now for the love of God," Shamus declared in a
tone of exasperation. "Don't go telling us you're a bloody
Puritan. I mean listen, we're not giving Haverdown to the
Ironsides, lover, not even if we're crying out for a crust of
bread."

"I don't think you quite understand me," said Cassidy,
hearing himself at a distance.

Safely buttoned, he was gazing back at the great house
and the one pink window shivering with firelight. While

he watched, he saw Helen's perfect outline slip silently across it as she gravely went about her domestic duties.

"We seem to feel rather differently about these things. I'd like to put the place on its feet, certainly. I'd also like to keep it as it was."

Once more he felt Shamus' eyes watching him intently in the darkness, and he pitched his tone high to avoid the encroaching sentiment.

"I mean by that, I'd like to do some of the things that you might have done if . . . well if you'd had the chance. I expect that sounds rather silly to you, but I'm afraid that's the way I feel."

"Listen," said Shamus suddenly. "Ssh."

They stood very still while Cassidy strained his ears for an unusual rustic sound—the boom of a bittern perhaps, or the snarl of a natural predator—but all he could hear was the creaking of the house and the drowsy rustle of the treetops.

"I thought I heard someone singing," said Shamus, softly. "Doesn't matter really, does it. Maybe it was just mermaids." He was standing perfectly still, and the aggression had gone out of his voice. "Where were you?"

"Never mind."

"No, go on. I love it!"

"I was only trying to tell you," said Cassidy, "that I believe in continuity. In preserving the quality of life. Which I suppose in your book makes me rather a fool, does it?"

"You lovely gorgeous lover," Shamus whispered at last, still staring into the night.

"I don't follow you," said Cassidy.

"Ah, fuck it. Helen! Hey, Helen!"

Seizing the lower folds of his black jacket he darted bat-like in wide zigzags over the lawn until they reached the portico.

"Helen!" he shouted as he burst into the drawing room. "Get this! A most fantastic incredible epoch-making thing has happened! We are *redeemed*. Butch Cassidy has fallen in love with us. We're his *first married couple!*"

Helen was kneeling at the fireside, her hands folded in her lap, her back straight, and she had the air of someone who had taken a decision in their absence.

"He didn't get frostbite either," Shamus added, as if that were the other part of his good news. "I looked."

"Shamus," Helen said, into the fire. "I think Mr. Cassidy should go now."

"Balls. Cassidy's far too pissed to drive a Bentley. Think of the publicity."

"Let him go, Shamus," Helen said.

"Tell her," he said to Cassidy, still breathing heavily from his run. "Tell her what you told me. Out there, when we were having a pee. Helen, he doesn't *want* to go, do you, lover? You want to stay and play, I know you do! And he *is* Flaherty. I know he is, I love him, Helen, honest!"

"I don't want to hear," said Helen.

"Tell her! It's nothing filthy, honest to God, Helen. It's Cassidy's Good Housekeeping testimonial. You tell her, go *on!*"

Sweat had formed on his brow and his face was red from the exertion of the run.

"Nothing more nor less than a papal blessing," he insisted, still breathing heavily. "Cassidy admires us. Cassidy is *deeply moved*. You and me are the backbone of his Empire. The flowers of bloody England. Virginal roses. *Beaux sabreurs*. Buchan-babies. He's Flaherty, Helen, and he's come to buy Paradise. *It's true!* Tell her, for Christ's sake Cassidy, get your cock out of your mouth and *tell* her!"

Seizing Cassidy by the shoulder he forced him roughly to the centre of the room. "Tell her what you'll do with the house when you've bought it!"

"Goodbye Cassidy," Helen said quickly. "Drive carefully."

"Tell her!" Shamus insisted through harsh breaths. *"Tell her what you'll do with the house! Damn it man, you came to buy it didn't you?"*

Acutely embarrassed—not to say menaced—by the vehemence of Shamus' demand, Cassidy endeavoured to recall the main lines of his thesis.

"All right," he began. "If I buy the house I promise to, well, try and keep it in your style. Fit for a great English family with a past. . . . To honour it. I'd try to do with it whatever *you* would have done if you'd had the money. . . ."

The silence was absolute save for the long rasps of

Shamus' breathing. Even the water dripping from the ceiling fell soundlessly into its enamel pan. Helen's eyes were still lowered. Cassidy saw only the golden outline of the firelight on her cheek and the one quick movement of her shoulders as she rose, went swiftly to her husband, and buried her head in his breast.

"Please," she whispered. *"Please."*

"That was beautiful, lover," Shamus assured him with a bright diagonal nod of his head. "Really beautifully put. I'll tell you another thing. The maharajah is a fan of the great James Joyce. He quoted a whole chunk to me out there, you want to hear him."

"That was you," Cassidy protested. "That wasn't me, that was you."

"And he heard mermaids singing, Helen, and he knows the English poets back to front—"

"Shamus," Helen pleaded. *"Shamus."*

"Cassidy, listen. I've got a great idea. Spend the weekend with us! Come hunting! We can mount you."

"I'm afraid I don't ride. Otherwise I'd like to."

"Never mind! Listen, we love you, we don't care about things like that, nor does the horse! And besides you've a great leg for a boot, lover, hasn't he, Helen? Truth."

"Tell him, Shamus," Helen said quietly. "Tell him or I will."

"And in the evening—" his enthusiasm for his new friend was rising with every image "—come the evening we'll play mah-jongg, and you shall read poetry to us and tell us all about the Bentley. No need to dress up, black tie will do. And we'll dance. Nothing grand, just twenty couples or so, the County and a few earls to stiffen them, don't you know, and when finally the last coach has teetered drunkenly down the drive—"

"Shamus!"

The next moment she had crossed the room and was standing before Cassidy, arms down and hair straight like a child sent to say goodnight.

"And we'll have the Montmorencys in!" Shamus shouted. "Cassidy would love the Montmorencys! They've got *two* fucking Bentleys!"

Very softly, her hazel eyes gazing bravely into his, Helen began speaking.

"Cassidy, there's something you've got to hear. We're squatters," she said. "Voluntary squatters. Shamus doesn't believe in property, he says it's a refuge from reality, so we go from one empty house to another. He's not even Irish, he just has funny voices and a theory that God is living in County Cork disguised as a forty-three-year-old taxi driver. He's a writer, a marvellous, wonderful writer. He's altering the course of world literature and I love him. And as for you," standing on tiptoe she put her arms round his shoulders and leaned the length of her body against him. "As for Cassidy, he's the sweetest man alive, whatever he believes in."

"What does he *do*, for Christ's sake?" Shamus cried. "Ask him where he gets it all from!"

"I make accessories for prams," Cassidy replied. "Foot brakes, canopies, and chassis."

His mouth had gone quite dry and his stomach was aching. Music, he thought; someone must make music. She's holding me for dancing and the band won't play and everyone's looking at us saying we're in love.

"Cassidy's Universal Fastenings. We're quoted on the Stock Exchange, fifty-eight and sixpence for a one-pound share."

Helen is in his arms and the nestling movement of her breasts has told him she is either laughing or weeping. Shamus is taking the cap off the whisky bottle. All manner of visions are crowding upon Cassidy's troubled mind. The dance floor has given way. The soft hair of her mound is caressing him through the thin stuff of her housecoat. Swiss waterfalls alternate with tumbling castles and plunging stock prices; two-plus-two Bentleys lie wrecked along the roadside. He is in Carey Street on the steps of the Bankruptcy Court being pelted by infuriated creditors and Helen is telling them to stop. He is standing naked at a cocktail party and the pubic hair has spread over his navel, but Helen is covering him with her ball dress. Through all these intimations of catastrophe and exposure, one instinct signals to him like a beacon: she is warm and vibrant in my arms.

"I'd like to ask you both to dinner," Cassidy says. "If you promise to wear real clothes. Or is that against your religion?"

Suddenly Helen is pulled from his grasp and in her place Cassidy feels the wild heart of Shamus thumping through the black jacket; smells the sweat and woodsmoke and the fumes of whisky buried in the soft cloth; hears the dark voice breathing to him in love.

"You never wanted to buy the bloody house in the first place, did you? You were having a little dream, weren't you, lover? Truth?"

"Truth," Cassidy confesses, blushing very deeply. "I was pretending too."

Moved by a single instinct they turned to look for Helen but she had gone, taking her wireless with her. Its far strains just reached them through the doorway.

"Poor kid," said Shamus suddenly. "She really thought she owned the place."

"I expect she's getting her shoes," said Cassidy.

"Come on. Let's give her a ride in the Bentley."

"Yes," said Cassidy. "She'd like that, wouldn't she?"

5

Setting off for London early next morning in the euphoria of a painless hangover, Cassidy recalled each incident of that miraculous night.

First, to overcome a certain common shyness they drank more whisky. God alone knew where Shamus had it from. He seemed to have bottles in every pocket and to produce them like a conjuror whenever the action flagged. Hesitantly at first but with growing enthusiasm they re-enacted the brighter moments of what Cassidy called their little misunderstanding, and they made Shamus talk some more Irish for them, which he did very willingly, and Helen said it was amazing, he'd never even been to Ireland but he could just put on accents like clothes, he had the gift.

Next they made Cassidy take off his braces and they all played billiards by candlelight. There was one cue, which they shared, and one ball and one candle, so Shamus invented a game called Moth. Cassidy liked games and they agreed it was very clever of Shamus to make one up on the spot. Shamus pronounced the rules in a sergeant major's voice which Cassidy (who was by way of being a mimic himself) could still perfectly remember:

"To play Moth, you puts the candle on the centre spot, 'ere. You then 'its the ball round the candle in a clockwise direction, and I mean clockwise. Scoring will take place in the following manner. One point for each complete circuit of the candle, five points penalty for each hinfringement of the natural borders of the table. 'Elen, kick orf."

There was a men's tee for Shamus and Cassidy and a ladies' tee for Helen. Helen won by six points, but secretly Cassidy reckoned himself the victor, because Helen twice hit the ball off the table and they hadn't counted it; but he didn't mind because it was only fun. Besides, it was a men's game; a female victory was only chivalrous.

After Moth, Shamus went and changed, and Helen

49

and Cassidy sat alone on the Chesterfield finishing their whisky. She was wearing a black dress and black leather boots and Cassidy thought she looked like Anna Karenina in the film.

"I think you're a wonderful gallant man," Helen told him. "And Shamus was absolutely *awful*."

"I've never met anyone like either of you," Cassidy assured Helen truthfully. "If you'd told me you were the Queen of England I wouldn't even have been *faintly* surprised."

Then Shamus returned looking very spruce indeed and said *"Take your hands off ma girl"* in a Wild West voice and they all got into the Bentley and drove to the Bird and Baby, which was Shamus' name for the Eagle and Child. The plan was to eat there, but Helen explained privately to Cassidy that they probably wouldn't eat there because Shamus didn't hold with first places.

"He likes to work his way into an evening," she said.

Shamus wanted to drive but Cassidy said unfortunately the car was only insured for him, which wasn't quite true but a sensible precaution, so Shamus sat in front with Cassidy and when Cassidy changed gear Shamus put his foot on the clutch for him so that Shamus could be co-pilot. "Wife-swapping" Shamus called it. The first time this happened they went into reverse at fifteen miles an hour but Cassidy managed to get his own foot on the clutch and no damage was done to the gearbox. Shamus was not car-minded, but he was very appreciative.

"Jesus," he kept saying, "this is the life, hey Helen can you hear me back there? . . . To hell with writing, from now on I'm going to be a big fat Gentile bourgeois. . . . Got your cheque book then, Cassidy? . . . Hey where's the cigars?"

All this in a non-stop monologue of breathless praise which made Cassidy wonder how a man who so clearly coveted property could have found the courage to renounce it.

Sure enough they had not been in the bar ten minutes before Shamus made for the door.

"This place stinks," he said in a very loud voice.

"Absolutely stinks," Helen agreed.

"The landlord stinks too," Shamus said and one or two heads turned to them in surprise.

"The landlord is a prole," Helen agreed.

"Landlord, you're a lowlander and a sheep-shagger and you come from Gerrard's Cross. Goodnight."

"Never hold him back," said Helen. They were walking to the car, going ahead in the hope that Shamus would follow. "Promise you never will."

"I wouldn't even try," Cassidy assured her. "It would be an absolute crime."

"You really feel for other people don't you?" said Helen. "I watch you doing it all the time."

"Why *Gerrard's Cross?*" asked Cassidy, who knew the place only as a desirable semi-rural dormitory town on the western fringes of Greater London.

"It's where the worst proles come from," she said. "He's been there and he knows."

"Chippenham," Shamus called from behind them.

At Chippenham railway station, they drank more whisky at the buffet. Shamus had a passion for terminals, Helen said, he saw all life as arrivals and departures, journeys to unnamed destinations.

"We have to keep moving," she said. "I mean don't you agree, Cassidy?"

"God yes," said Cassidy, and thought—the analyser in him thought—yes, that's what's exciting about them, they share a mutual desire for somewhere to go.

"The ordinary hours just aren't enough for him," Helen said. "He needs the night as well."

"I know," said Cassidy. "I can feel."

The platform ticket machine was out of order but the collector was Scottish and let them through for nothing because Shamus said he came from the Isle of Skye, and that Talisker was the best whisky in the world and that he had a friend called Flaherty who might be God. Shamus christened the collector Alastair and took him with them to the buffet.

"He's completely classless," Helen explained, while Shamus and Alastair at the other end of the bar discussed the similarities of their professions in rich Scottish accents. "He's a sort of Communist really. A Jew."

"It's fantastic," said Cassidy. "I suppose that's what makes him a writer."

"But you're like that too aren't you," Helen said, "deep down? Don't you have to get on with your workmen and that kind of thing? *They* don't put up with any side, surely?"

"I hadn't thought of that," said Cassidy.

The train arrived while they were drinking, next stop Bath, and suddenly they were all standing in a first-class compartment, waving to Alastair through the window.

"Goodbye Alastair, goodbye. God, look at him," Helen urged. "What a face in that lamplight, it's immortal."

"Fantastic," Cassidy agreed.

"Poor little sodder," said Shamus. "What a way to die."

"You know," said Helen later, when they had closed the window, "Cassidy really *notices* things." Using her arms to help, she lifted her long legs on to the cushions. "He's got a real *eye*, if only he'd use it," she added drowsily and was soon asleep.

The two men sat on the opposite bench passing the bottle and regarding her in the light of their separate experience. She lay on her side in a pose as classical as it was effortless, knees drawn and overlapping, Goya's Maja, naked and fully clothed.

"She's the most beautiful wife I've ever seen," Cassidy said.

"She's pissed," said Shamus, drinking. "Absolutely ossified."

"*Shamus* says," said Helen drowsily, "I'd be a whore if he ever let me off the lead."

"Oh my God," said Cassidy, as if that were a very shallow view.

"I wouldn't, would I, Cassidy?"

"Never."

"I would," said Helen, and turned over. "He beats me too, don't you, Shamus? I wish I had a *gentle* lover," she reflected, talking to the cushions. "Like Cassidy or Mr. Heath."

"You know," Cassidy said still contemplating her long body, "I don't care whether you own Haverdown or not. That house will belong to you for ever."

"For ever is now," said Shamus and drank some more whisky.

"Shamus," Cassidy began, as dreams and visions pressed upon him.

"What is it, lover?"

"Nothing," said Cassidy, for love has no language.

At Bath station, where the fresh air reminded Cassidy that he had drunk a great deal of neat whisky, Shamus underwent one of those sudden changes of humour which had made him such unnerving company at Haverdown. They were standing on the platform and Helen was gazing at a pile of mailbags, weeping silently into Cassidy's handkerchief.

"But what's the matter?" Cassidy insisted, not by any means for the first time. "You must *tell* us, Helen, mustn't she, Shamus?"

"They were stitched by prisoners," she cried at last, and resumed her weeping.

"For fuck's sake," Shamus shouted furiously, and rounded on Cassidy. "And you: stop curling your fingers round your cuff like that. Christopher Robin's dead, right? D'you hear that, Helen? *Dead*."

"Sorry," said Cassidy and the incident was forgotten.

Meals, in Cassidy's world, were sacrosanct. They were truces for conviviality or silence; time out, when neither passion nor hostility was allowed to mar the devout communion.

They ate at a place called Bruno's, on a slope, because Shamus was in his Italian mood and would speak no English, and because slopes (as Helen explained) have tension, a view which Cassidy found extremely profound. Bath stank, Shamus said. Bath was the lousiest city in the world. Bath was toytown, halfway between the Vatican and the Wind in the Willows, designed by Beatrix Potter for rural proles.

"Shamus is a terrific innocent really," Helen told him. "Of course anyone is a terrific innocent who is looking for love all the time, don't you agree?"

Astonished by the depth, let alone the urbanity of this observation, Cassidy agreed.

"He hates sham. He hates it more than anything in the world."

"That's absolutely what *I* hate too," said Cassidy stoutly, and glancing surreptitiously at his watch, thought: I must ring Sandra soon or she'll wonder.

At Bruno's also they played another Shamus game called Fly, which he had invented specifically to disconcert rural proles and uncover sham. Shamus selected the victim as he entered. He chose mainly the younger managerial type of person whom he consigned at once to certain arbitrary categories: Gerrard's Crossers, bishops, publishers, and, in deference to Cassidy, pram manufacturers. These, he said, were the basic components of the Many-too-Many, the compromisers for whom freedom was a terror; these were the backcloth for the real drama of life. The purpose of the game was to demonstrate the uniformity of their responses. As soon as Shamus gave the word the three of them must stare at the prole's fly, Shamus fixedly, Helen with fluttering coyness, and Cassidy with an artful embarrassment that was particularly effective. The results were varied but gratifying: a furious blush, a hurried descent of the right thumb along the telltale seam, a hasty gathering of the jacket. In one case —submerged poof, Shamus declared, typical of the pram trade these days, *real* pooves were not submerged—the victim actually retreated altogether with a distracted apology about car lights and returned minutes later after what must have been an exhaustive check.

"What would *you* do, lover," Shamus asked Cassidy quietly, "if we gave *you* the treatment?"

Not knowing what answer Shamus wanted, Cassidy took refuge in the truth.

"Oh I'd bolt," he said. "Absolutely."

There was a small silence while Helen played with her spoon.

"But what *should* I do?" Cassidy asked, suddenly confused. "What do you *want* me to do?"

"Flash it," said Helen promptly, very much to Cassidy's consternation, for he was not used to wit in women, nor coarseness either, even of the harmless, mannish kind.

"But then you don't know any better, do you?" Shamus said at last and gently reached for his hand across the table. "You've never seen the bloody daylight, have you lover? Jesus, I remember now, you're Flaherty."

"Oh no I'm not," Cassidy assured him modestly.

"He thinks all the time," said Helen. "I can tell."

"Who *are* you?" Shamus asked, still holding Cassidy's hand and watching his face with an expression of great puzzlement. "What have you got?"

"I don't know," said Cassidy, putting on a shy expression. "I'm sort of waiting to find out I suppose."

"It's the waiting that kills you, lover. You have to go and get it."

"Look at Alastair," Helen exhorted. "Alastair's been waiting for a train all his life. They come and go but he never hops aboard, does he, Shamus?"

"Maybe he *is* God at that," said Shamus, still studying his new friend.

"Not old enough," Helen reminded him. "God's forty-three. Cassidy's much younger, aren't you, Cassidy?"

Finding no immediate answer to these questions, Cassidy shrugged them off with a rueful, world-weary smile calculated to suggest that his problems were too profound to be resolved at a single sitting.

"Well anyway I'm very proud to be with you. I really am."

"We're very proud to be with Cassidy," said Helen after a slight pause. "Aren't we, Shamus?"

"Estatica," said Shamus in homemade Italian, and kissed him.

6

And it was at Bruno's still, just before they left for other treats, that they first touched upon the subjects of Shamus' new novel, and of Shamus' reputation as a writer. This moment was most vivid in Cassidy's recollection.

Helen talking.

"I mean honestly, Cassidy, it really is so, *so* fantastic you've no idea. I mean God, when you see the muck that *does* get well reviewed and you read this, just read it, it's ridiculous that he should worry at all. I mean I *know*."

"What's it about?" Cassidy asks.

"Oh God, *everything,* isn't it, Shamus?"

Shamus' attention has been drawn to the next table, where a blond lady from Gerrard's Cross is listening to a disguised bishop talking about The Dustbin of Ideas, which is Shamus' metaphor for politics.

"Sure," he says vaguely. "Total vision," and shifts his chair into the aisle the better to observe his quarry.

Helen resumes.

"I mean he's put his entire life into it: me and . . . well everything. I mean just the dilemma of the artist, the way he *needs* real people, I mean people like you and me, so that he can match himself against them."

"Go on," Cassidy urges. "I'm absolutely fascinated. Honestly. I've never, sort of . . . *met* this before."

"Well, you know what Henry James said, don't you?"

"Which bit exactly?"

"Our doubt is our passion and our passion is our doubt. The rest is the madness of art. That's Shamus, honestly, isn't it, Shamus? Shamus, I was talking about Henry James."

"Never heard of them," says Shamus.

The bishop, having taken the Gerrard's Crosser's hand, is apparently summoning his courage for a kiss.

"And then the identity thing," Helen continues, returning to Cassidy. "You know, who *are* we? Actually *that*

57

part of the book's rather like Dostoevsky, not a crib of course, just the sort of *concept*, isn't it, Shamus?" Still distracted, Shamus ignores her. "I mean honestly the symbolism just on this one level alone is incredible and there are so many levels, I mean I've read it half a dozen times at least and I haven't got them all yet."

"Follow, Cassidy?" Shamus enquires, over his shoulder. "Got the meat of it, have you, lover?"

Bored, finally, by the rutting habits of the Many-too-Many he pulls in his chair and helps himself to the menu, which he now reads, moving his lips in a caressing Italian murmur. "Jesus," he whispers once, "I thought *cacciatori* was a parrot."

Helen lowers her voice.

"It's the same with suffering. Look at Pascal, look at, well, anybody . . . We've *got* to suffer deeply. If we don't how *on earth* can we overcome suffering? How on earth can we create? How? That's why he simply hates the middle classes. And I mean do you blame him? They compromise the *whole* way along the line. With life, with passion, with, well . . . everything."

She is interrupted by Shamus' applause. He is clapping quite loudly and a lot of people are watching, so Cassidy changes the subject to politics: how he is thinking of standing as a candidate, how his father was a devoted parliamentarian, retired now of course, but still passionately wedded to the Cause, how Cassidy believes in enlightened self-help rather like the old-style Liberals . . .

"Meeow," says Shamus, and, losing interest, begins writing on the back of the menu, but privately, withholding his Art.

"He writes on *anything*," Helen whispers. "Envelopes, old bills, it's fantastic."

"I was a writer once," Cassidy confesses, "but only in advertising."

"Then you know what it's like," says Helen. "You've been down there in the pit."

They watch him, head bowed in the candlelight, still writing on the menu.

"How long does it take him to finish one?" Cassidy asked, still watching him.

"Oh God years . . . *Moon* was different of course,

being his first. He just sort of romped through it in four months. Now, well he's . . . *conscious*. He demands more of himself. He knows what he has to do to . . . justify his success. So naturally it takes longer."

"*Moon?*" Cassidy repeated in bewilderment, and the thing was out.

Before addressing herself to Cassidy's heresy, Helen cast a fearful glance across the table to make certain Shamus was still busy with the menu. Her voice sank to a whisper.

"You mean you didn't *know?*"

"Know what?"

"*The Moon by Day*. That was Shamus' first novel. Shamus *wrote* it."

"Good Lord! . . ."

"Why?"

"But that was a *film*. I remember!" Cassidy was very excited. "A *film*," he repeated. "All about university, and being in our prime and how rotten it was to have to go into commerce . . . and about this undergraduate and his love for this girl, who was all he had ever dreamed of, and—"

Helen waited, pride and relief reflected equally in her solemn eyes.

"I was his love," she said. "I was the girl."

"Good Lord," Cassidy repeated, his exhilaration gathering. "He really *is* a writer! Good *Lord*. And it was all *him?*"

He gazed at Shamus, studying his profile in the candle-light, and watching with a new respect how the master's pencil slipped smoothly across the menu.

"Good Lord," he said yet again. "That's *wonderful*."

The revelation was of great significance to Cassidy. If there had been, until that moment, any tiny cloud of reservation in his mind concerning his new-found friends, then it was on this very matter of credentials; for while Cassidy was far from being a snob, he had not for several years been comfortable in the presence of the unsuccess-ful. And though not by nature cynical, he had never quite managed to overcome the prejudiced belief that the renun-ciation of property was a gesture reserved to those who had nothing to renounce. To learn therefore in a single stroke that Shamus was not merely a household name—

the title had been much in circulation during Cassidy's
last year at Oxford, and he even remembered a nagging
envy for a contemporary who had made his name so soon
—but that his eccentricities were backed by solid achievement, this was a matter of great and rare joy to Cassidy
which he was quick to impart to Helen:

"But we've *all* heard of him! He was brilliant, everyone
said so. I remember my tutor raving about him . . ."

"Yes," said Helen. "Everyone did."

At this point Cassidy recalled that it was now eighteen
years since he had left Oxford.

"What's he been doing since?"

"Oh the usual things. Film scripts, television . . . even a
ghastly pageant, once. For Abingdon if you please."

"Novels?"

"The ghouls all wanted him to write *Moon* again," she
said. "Son of Moon, Moon at Easter, Moon Rides Out. . . .
Well of course he wouldn't do that would he? He wouldn't
repeat himself."

"No," said Cassidy doubtfully.

"You see he won't be vulgar. He refuses *absolutely*. He's
got that kind of integrity. Virtue," she added glancing at
him, and Cassidy somehow knew that virtue, the word as
well as the concept, was a part of their profound complicity.

"I'm sure he has," he said reverently.

"So in the end he just put a bomb under the whole lot."
With a show of brightness, Helen opened her hands, revealing the obvious solution. "Just took off. Like Gauguin,
except that I went with him of course. That was . . . years
ago."

"But good God, what happened to all the publishers and
people, the ghouls . . . didn't they come after him?"

Helen dismissed the question.

"Oh I told them he was dead," she said carelessly.

It was right that Cassidy should pay; patronage formed a
large part of his aspiring soul, affording not only protection and justification for his wealth, but also the pleasure of a public sacrifice. Calling for a settlement, using
the practised gesture of the rich—which consists of passing
an imaginary pencil over an imaginary writing pad—he
discreetly summoned his cheque book from an inner

pocket and waited in a slightly crouched position to pounce upon the bill and conceal its total before Shamus (should he prove to be that kind of guest) had a chance to object.

"God I envy him," he said, but following the waiter with his eyes.

"It needs courage at first of course," said Helen. "To be free. But then courage is what he's got. And gradually . . . you realise, well you don't need money, no one does. It's just a complete trick."

Still waiting, Cassidy shook his head at his own absurdity.

"What good did it ever do *me?*" he asked.

"We even gave up our flat in Dulwich."

"What," said Cassidy sharply. "All to be free?"

"I'm afraid so," Helen admitted a little doubtfully. "But of course we'll be *rolling* once the new book comes out. It's fabulous, it really is."

The bill came and Cassidy paid it. Far from disputing Cassidy's rôle of host, however, Shamus seemed quite unaware that the transaction had taken place. He was still busily writing on the menu. They sat and watched him, too tactful to disturb the flow.

"It's probably about Schiller," said Helen in a low aside.

"Who?"

Still waiting for her husband's mood of inspiration to pass, Helen explained.

Shamus had developed a *theory*, she said, which he had worked into his latest book. It was based on someone called Schiller who was a terrifically famous German dramatist actually but of course the English being so insular had never heard of him, and anyway Schiller had split the world in two.

"It's called being *naive,*" she said. "Or being *sentimental.* They're sort of different kinds of *thing*, and they interact."

Cassidy knew she was putting it very simply so that he could understand.

"Which am I?" he asked.

"Well Shamus is *naive*," she replied cautiously, as if remembering a hard-learned lesson. "Because he lives life and doesn't imitate it. Feeling is knowledge," she added rather tentatively.

"So I'm the other thing."

"Yes. You're sentimental. That means you long to be *like* Shamus. You've left the natural state behind and you've become . . . well part of civilisation, sort of . . . corrupt."

"Isn't *he*?"

"No," said Helen decisively.

"Oh," said Cassidy.

"What Nietzsche calls innocence, that's what you've lost. The Old Testament is terrifically innocent, you see. But the New Testament is all corrupt and wishy-washy and that's why Nietzsche and Shamus hate it, and that's why Flaherty is such an important symbol. You have to *challenge*."

"Challenge what?" asked Cassidy.

"Convention, morals, manners, life, God, oh I mean everything. Just everything. Flaherty's important because he *disputes*. That's why Shamus challenged him to a duel. *Now* do you understand?"

"Is that what Schiller says?" Cassidy asked again, now thoroughly confused. "Or the other one?"

"And Shamus," Helen continued, avoiding his question, "being *naive*, part of nature in fact, longs to be like *you*. It's the attraction of opposites. He's natural, you're corrupt. That's why he loves you."

"Does he?"

"I can tell," said Helen simply. "You've made a conquest, Cassidy, that's all there is to it."

"What about you, then," Cassidy enquired, only partially succeeding in hiding his gratification. "Which side are you on? Shamus' or mine?"

"I don't think it works for women," Helen replied at last. "I think they're just themselves."

"Women are eternal," Cassidy agreed as finally they got up to leave.

In return, at the pub, he told her about his accessories.

That conversation alone, in retrospect, would have made his evening unforgettable.

Even if he had never set eyes on Helen before walking into the saloon bar; if he had never seen her again after he left it, if he had simply bought her a double whisky and chatted to her in the garden, he would have counted his visit to Bath—that timeless exchange would stand for all time—among the most amazing experiences of his life.

The pub was higher up the hill—the slope of tension as Cassidy now thought of it—a leafy place with a verandah and a long view of the valley lights. The lights reached to the edge of the earth, melting together in a low haze of gold before joining the descending stars. Shamus had made straight for the public bar and was playing dominos with the naive classes, so the two of them sat outside looking into the night with eyes made wide by wisdom, mutely sharing the infinite vision. And for a moment, it seemed to Cassidy, a kind of marriage was made. For a moment, he would swear, before either one of them had spoken a word, Cassidy and Helen discovered secretly in the motionless night air a joining of their destinies and their longings, of their dreams and their enchantments. So strong was his sense of this, in fact, that he had actually turned to her in the hope of catching in her devout expression some evidence of the shared experience, when a gust of coarse laughter, issuing from inside the pub, reminded them of their companion.

"Shamus," Helen sighed, but not at all by way of criticism. "He does so adore an audience. We all do really don't we? It's no more than the warmth of human contact, when you think about it."

"I suppose it isn't," said Cassidy, who had never supposed till now that any excuse could be found for showing off.

"Ever since I've known him," she said dreamily, "he's been the complete enchanter. When we were rich it was the maid, the garage man, the milkman. And when we decided to be poor again it was . . . just anyone. Proles, Gerrard's Crossers, he magicked them all. It's the loveliest thing about him."

"But it's always been *you*," Cassidy suggested. "Rich or poor, you were his real audience, weren't you, Helen?"

She did not immediately accept the notion, but seemed to dwell on it as if it were new, and perhaps a fraction facile for her reflective nature.

"Not always. No. Just sometimes. *Sometimes* it was me. At the beginning perhaps." She drank. "In the beginning," she repeated bravely.

"But you must help him *enormously* with his work,"

said Cassidy. "Doesn't he lean on you an awful lot, on your knowledge, Helen? Your *reading?*"

"A bit," Helen said, in the same airy, questionable tone. "Now and then, sure."

"Tell me: what did you *read* at Oxford? I'll bet you're *covered* with degrees."

"Let's talk about you," Helen suggested modestly. "Shall we?"

And that was how it happened.

Deliberately, to begin with, he had emphasised the human aspect of his products, the *mother appeal* as they called it in the trade. After all, there was not a reason on earth for her to be interested in the technical side: none of his other female customers was. Cee-springs, suspension, braking mechanisms: you might as well talk to a woman about pipe tobacco as try to explain all that to her. So he had begun by telling her in simple narrative terms, albeit apocryphal, how the idea had come to him in the first place. How he had been walking one Saturday morning, in the days when walking was about the only recreation he could afford—he had just started in advertising though he had always been a meddler, if she knew what he meant, gadget-minded so to speak, handy with a screwdriver if she followed him—and he was vaguely thinking of a drink before lunch ("Thank you," said Helen. "Just a single will be lovely") when he spotted a mother trying to cross the road.

"A *young* mother," Helen corrected him.

"How did you know?"

"Just guessed."

Cassidy smiled a little ruefully. "Well, you're right actually," he confessed. "She *was* young."

"And pretty," said Helen. "A *pretty* mother."

"Good *God* how did you—"

"Go on," said Helen.

Well of course, said Cassidy, there were no zebra crossings in those days, just the studded lines with Belisha beacons at either end, and the traffic was pretty well nonstop: "So she began probing."

"With the pram," said Helen at once.

"Yes. Exactly. She stood on the curb sort of *testing the*

water with this baby, lowering the pram into the road and pulling it out again while she waited for the traffic to stop. *And all there was between that kid and the traffic was this . . . this one footbrake.* Just a rickety bit of rodding with a rubber grip on the end," he said, meaning the foot-brake still.

"Rodding?" Helen repeated, unfamiliar with the word.

"Low-grade alloy," Cassidy replied. "Virtually no stress. Metal fatigue ratio zero."

"Oh my God," said Helen.

"Well that's what I felt."

"I mean, Christ, risk your own neck if you must, but not well, God, not a child's."

"You're absolutely right. That's *precisely* what I say. I was horrified."

"You felt responsible," Helen said gravely.

Yes that was precisely what he had felt. No one had put it to him like that before, but it was true: he had felt *responsible*. So he didn't have a drink, he went home and did a spot of thinking. Responsible thinking.

"Where's home?" asked Helen.

"Oh Christ," said Cassidy, hinting at the long road and unrevealed hardships. "Where was anywhere in those days?"

And Helen nodded to show that she too understood the vagaries of an aspiring male life.

"I just thought for a moment it might have been your own wife you were watching," she said casually, not at all in the tone of someone *accusing* him of marriage, but merely recognising his state and taking it into account.

"Oh Lord no," said Cassidy, as if to say that even if he had a wife and that wife had a pram, he would certainly not waste time watching her; and plunged on with his story. So anyway, he'd had this idea: if he could build a brake, a really unbeatable, multi-systemed brake, that functioned on any pram—a brake that stayed the *hub* rather than just well Christ let's face it *dragged along the road* like your old chariot brake—

"A *disc brake*," Helen cried. "You invented the disc brake! Cassidy!"

"That's an extremely good *analogy*," said Cassidy after a slight pause, not quite certain whether analogy was what he meant.

"It was *your* idea," Helen said. "Not mine."

"Of course it was only prams," he reminded her. "Not grown-ups."

"Are children more important?" Helen demanded. "Or adults?"

"Well," said Cassidy very surprised. "I hadn't thought of it that way, I must say."

"I had," said Helen.

Having fetched replenishments from the bar, Cassidy returned to Helen on the verandah and continued his narrative.

So anyway: over the next few days he had done a spot of research. Nothing explicit of course, nothing that gave the show away, just taken a few soundings among reliable people he happened to know. Vital question: would a quality footbrake be universally acceptable? A twin-circuit system, for instance; something one could attach to the hubs?

"You made your mark early, didn't you?" Helen said. "Like Shamus."

"I suppose that's true," Cassidy conceded.

Be that as it might, quite soon he came up with his answer. If he could build a brake that *really* held, a one-hundred-per-cent safety brake, based on a hub-retarding principle, then he would stir up such publicity, get so much support from the Road Safety League, the Royal Society for the Prevention of Accidents, not to mention the public media, "Woman's Hour" and all the other goof programmes, that he could get the financing and clean up a fortune overnight, just on the patent alone.

"And perform a fantastic service for society," Helen reminded him.

"Yes," Cassidy said reverently. "That above all. And once it caught on, of course, I took on chaps, we expanded, grew, diversified. A *lot* of people came to us with their problems and before long . . . Look here, am I being pompous?"

Helen did not immediately reply. She looked at her drink and then through the French doors at Shamus, and finally at Cassidy with the long, frank, fearless look of a woman who knows her mind.

"I tell you this," she said. "If ever I need a pram, which I never will if Shamus has anything to do with it, it's going to be one of yours."

For a moment neither spoke.

"Do you really mean never?" Cassidy asked, embarrassed but feeling he knew her well enough.

"Well *really*," she said laughing. "Can you *imagine* Shamus going through all that? Wife and two veg, that's what he calls it. God he'd go raving mad in a week! How can an *artist* be tied to that?"

"God, you're so right," said Cassidy, and once more covertly examined his watch.

Give it ten minutes and I'll make that call.

From there it had been but a step to the technical exposition. How they had expanded to become their own customer. (*What a brilliant idea,* said Helen. *You take the profit twice!*) How they had repeatedly ploughed back profits into research, exploring ever deeper the application of these same safety principles, until Cassidy's name had become a byword, from the great hospitals to the individual housewife, for comfort and safety in your world of infant transportation. Heaven knows, he had spared her nothing. From fluid flywheels and dual braking circuits he passed with hardly a breath to the intricacies of a twin-jointed push bar and the variable suspension. Helen never faltered. He could tell by the steadiness of the sombre eyes that she took in every word; nothing, not even the universal joint, clouded their perfect comprehension. He drew for her, sketched on paper napkins until the bar was like a drawing board: gravely she sipped her drinks and gravely nodded her approval.

"Yes," she said. "You thought of everything."

Or: "But how did the competition take it?"

"Oh, the Japs had a shot at copying us as usual."

"But they couldn't," Helen said, not as a question at all but as a positive statement there was no gainsaying.

"Afraid not," Cassidy replied obligingly, preferring the spirit of the truth to the truth itself. "They put their best chaps on to it. Total failure."

"Then how did *you* take it?"

"*Me?*"

"The sudden wealth, the fame, the recognition of your talents . . . didn't you go a *little* bit mad, Cassidy?"

Cassidy had met with this question often, and answered it, in his day, in many different ways, according to his mood and the requirements of the audience. Sometimes, principally within the hearing of his wife, he insisted that he was inviolate, that a natural sense of Values was too strong an answer to mere materialistic temptation, that the act of making money had shown him also its futility, he was impervious. At other times, to close male acquaintances, or strangers in railway compartments, he confessed to a deep and tragic change, a frightening loss of appetite for life.

"There's no *fun* any more," he would say. "Having money takes all the joy out of achievement."

While occasionally, in moments of great apprehension, he flatly disowned his money altogether. The British tax system was confiscatory; no honest man could keep more than a fraction of what he earned, whoever did so was on the fiddle, more should be done to control them. But in Helen's mouth the question was new, and fundamental to their relationship. Therefore, having rapidly considered many alternatives, he shrugged lightly and said, in a moment of the nicest inspiration, "A man is judged by what he looks for, Helen. Not by what he finds."

"Christ," said Helen softly.

For a long while she gazed at him with an expression of the greatest intensity. Cassidy, indeed, had difficulty in meeting it; he found his eyes drifting, or closing with the smoke of her cigarette. Until, taking a draft of whisky, she broke the spell.

"Anyway," she said, indicating an obstruction to some unspoken proposition. "How did your wife take it?"

This question also he had faced on more than one occasion. Where does she shop *now?* Did you buy her a fur coat? Once again he found the greatest difficulty in replying. Get rid of her, was his first thought. I am divorced; I am a widower. My wife died a lingering and tragic death; she recently eloped with a great pianist. The reappearance of Shamus mercifully absolved him.

It was some time now since Shamus had paid them much attention. Already at dinner his first effusive interest in Cassidy had given way to a more general interest in his fellow man, and Helen had explained that, since he went out very little as a rule when he was working, he had to cram a lot of experience into a very short period of time.

"It's being an artist," she said as they went indoors.

"He has to live terrifically intensively otherwise he just stands still."

"Which is hopeless," Cassidy agreed.

Whatever else Shamus might have been doing he was not standing still. He had a girl with him and his arm was round her waist, her upper waist as it were, his hand was cupped comfortably over her left breast and he was not at all steady on his feet.

"Hey Cassidy," he said. "Look what I got for you."

Alas, the offer is no sooner made than it is withdrawn. Two men appear from somewhere and quietly detach the nice girl from his grasp, someone in authority suggests they take a spot of fresh air, and suddenly they are playing games on a grass traffic circle, leapfrogging over posts under the gaze of a startled young policeman.

"Anyway," said Helen, as they made their way towards the next pub, "she was miles too young for Cassidy."

"Yes," said Cassidy loyally, not wishing to wound *anyone* with his private appetites, "she was."

Sequence, in Cassidy's recollection, had by now become blurred. It remained blurred for the rest of the evening. The journey to Bristol, for instance, left no clear imprint on his memory. He assumed they had a free lift—a lorry driver named Aston played a misty part, and Cassidy's suit next morning smelt strongly of diesel oil. They went there, he remembered clearly, because Shamus needed water, and he had heard from reliable sources that Bristol was a port.

"He can't survive without it," Helen explained.

"It's the sound," said Cassidy. "The lapping sound."

"*And* the permanence," Helen reminded him. "Think of undulating waves, going on for ever."

Shamus insulted Aston and called him a sodder, probably because Aston was a Methodist, and disapproving of drink. Whatever the reason, the ride ended in dissent, and Cassidy distanced himself from it. The beer hall on the other hand made a vivid impression. He perfectly remembered every white contour of the barmaid's *décolleté*—she wore a Bavarian costume which lifted the milky balls almost to her throat—and he remembered the accordion player's astonishment when Shamus, to the great pleasure of the crowd, sang all the verses of the *Horst Wessel lied* in a slow, romantic lilt.

But it was from Bath, not Bristol, that Cassidy, after a last examination of his costly gold watch, finally made that brief sojourn into a world which, in all other respects, he had for several hours rigorously banished from his thoughts.

7

A new pub, not on a slope but part of a Vatican outbuilding; the public bar because the saloon was filled with Gerrard's Crossers.

Helen and Shamus were playing darts, Smoothies versus Bumpkins, Bumpkins were all right because they were still one with nature. Shamus had drawn a pig on one side of the blackboard and a bowler on the other.

"Lovers, I am *not* asking you to vote," he assured them. "I am teaching you to read."

Helen's turn. She missed the board and nailed the poor box to the panelling. A peal of laughter shook the bar.

"Excuse me," Cassidy said confidentially to the landlord. "Have you a telephone I could use?"

"These your friends, are they?"

"Well, in a way you know."

"I don't want trouble. I like fun but I don't want trouble."

"That's all right," said Cassidy. "I'll pay for breakages."

"Mind you, I'll say this. He's a lovely boy. They don't come like him often do they? And she's a lovely girl. I haven't seen a pair like that for quite a while."

"He's a very famous television writer," Cassidy explained, intuitively adjusting Shamus' talent to the mass audience. "He's got three serials running at the moment. He's worth an absolute bomb."

"Is he though?"

"You ought to see his Bentley. It's a two-plus-two, dove grey with electric windows."

"Well I'm blessed," the landlord said. "There's not many of them about is there?"

"It's unique. Here, care for one yourself? Anything you like. How about a gold watch?" he suggested, mixing with the men.

"A *what?*"

"A Scotch," said Cassidy in a lower tone.

71

"That's all right son, I'll just take a shilling's worth off you, thanks. Cheers."

"Cheers," said Cassidy. "Through here is it?"

From Bath he can dial direct.

"Hi," he says. "How was the clinic?"

Sandra wife to Aldo (of Cassidy's General Fastenings) is not a quick girl. Sound takes longer to reach her, particularly on the telephone.

"All right. Where are you?"

"Just in the pub. Heather bearing up?"

It may, of course, be the other way round: that her voice takes longer to carry the distance. That she has already answered me, but the words are clogging the line. *Ay'm sorry, sah, there is a traffic jam on the M4 telephone route. Will you tray later?* That there are too many husbands apologising to too many wives on cheap rates shortly before closing time. Or that an atomic bomb has fallen, never impossible: *hurry back and shoot the children.* Alternatively that the Russians have—

"Who with?" the earpiece demands suddenly.

She has her father's military instinct for monosyllables. Montgomery's five basic questions, who, why, when, where, how? And my *God* the chaps respected him.

"The Corporation," says Cassidy. *The Corporation is with me, in full-bottomed wigs, and furs and chains, we have just given a five-year contract to the Pied Piper.* "The Corporation, the people who run the city. Great chaps, you'd love them. We only finished an hour ago."

Winged words, flying but not settling. He musters still greater enthusiasm.

"Listen it's all falling into place. The land is *absolutely* central, it needs *very* little levelling, and the boys in the Corporation assure me that the moment we raise the first twenty thousand they'll come through with the footbridge. Free. They really *believe* in it, I'm astonished."

Silence. Does *she* believe in it? For Christ's sake, Sandra, this is our meeting point. What does it matter whether it's true or not? Say *yes*, admire the achievement. What the hell?

"There's one fellow here's a contractor, in heavy machinery, all that sort of stuff. He'll level the place free and

give us a cost quotation on labour for building the changing rooms."

Silence.

"They really have risen to it in a *big* way." But Sandra
has not. Sandra has been cut off. Sandra has gone deaf;
her mother has switched me through to an extension.

"Sandra?"

In the bar, the jukebox is playing a low tune. In the
earpiece, a well-bred dog is barking. Sandra has several
dogs, all are large and classically entitled. Encouraged by
this sign of life, Cassidy himself rallies.

"They actually showed me a drawing, heart . . . well
one *like,* you know. Off the peg, of course, but well *great,*
really. Just right for kids. A *fun* bridge."

"Shut up Mummy," says Sandra. "Sorry it was Mummy,
fussing about the dogs."

"Sandra, aren't you pleased?"

"What about?"

"The bridge. The playing field. For God's sake . . .
"Hullo? ?"

"Don't shout."

"Are you still speaking?" the operator enquires.

"Did Hugo see the specialist?" Cassidy demands suddenly, selecting in his anger a contentious point.

A rustle in the earpiece. Her impatience sigh, unlike her
sigh of frustration, is not so sharp. The impatience sigh
begins with a liquid click in the roof of the mouth and is
followed by a decision not to breathe, like a hunger strike,
in fact, but done on air, not food.

"Just because a man can afford rooms in Harley Street,"
she begins, speaking off-key but with large emphasis for
the sake of the untutored, "just because there are people
around prepared to pay *twenty guineas* in order not to
stand in a queue, it does *not* mean that a specialist is *any*
better than a *perfectly* ordinary decent doctor who doesn't
care about money."

"So you haven't taken him?" Cassidy says. The witness
has condemned herself out of her own mouth.

"Pieces of eight," says Shamus.

He was standing in the doorway wearing a brown peaked
cap and carrying a mynah bird on one finger. He had

tucked one leg under his black coat and was pretending to be Long John Silver while he supported himself against the lintel.

"Pieces of eight, pieces of eight," he said, talking to the bird.

"Time," the landlord shouted from the bar, and rang a ship's bell, dong, dong.

"Goodnight," said Cassidy, into the telephone.

"Is that all you're going to say?" Sandra demanded. "I'd have thought it was hardly worth ringing up."

"Goodnight and thank *you*," said Shamus, taking the receiver from him and speaking in his Italian accent. " 'Ullo, 'ullo, 'ullo?"

Cassidy recovered the receiver but the line was dead. He put it back on its cradle.

"Hullo, Shamus," he said at last, smiling. "Have a pint."

They were still in the back room. The sounds of revelry came from all sides, but the back room was quiet all the same; an adding machine and several wholesale boxes of sweets lay on the baize-covered table.

"Was that the bosscow?" Shamus asked.

"The *what?*"

"Your wife. Bosscow. Queen of the herd."

"Oh I see. Well, just checking up," said Cassidy. "Can't have her going out with the lodger, eh?"

The noise in the bar became suddenly deafening, but neither raised his voice.

"What's the trouble?"

The mynah was also watching Cassidy. Its feathers were almost lost against the black of Shamus' jacket, but its eyes were jet bright.

"It's my little boy," said Cassidy. "Hugo. He broke his leg in a skiing accident. The bone won't seem to mend."

"Poor little bugger," said Shamus not moving.

"Anyway, the specialists are looking after him."

"Sure it's not your leg?" Shamus asked.

In the saloon, someone was playing the piano, a whole tune straight the way through.

"I don't quite understand."

"Work on it, lover, you will."

"I meant to tell you actually," Cassidy said carelessly, with an attempt at movement. "I've got a house in Switzerland, a chalet. Quite modest but surprisingly comfortable for two. Place called Sainte-Angèle. It's empty most of the year. If you like tense slopes you might try that one some time."

No laughter.

"I just mean, if you ever want a place to work, to get away from it all, I'd be delighted to lend it to you for nothing. Take Helen."

"Or a substitute," Shamus suggested. "Lover."

"Yes?"

"You should have been angry with me. For barging in on that call and fucking it up. That was *very* rude."

"Should I?"

"You should have *hit* me, lover. I mean I rely on discipline. I believe in it. That's what the fucking bourgeoisie is for: to inhibit rude sodders like me."

Cassidy laughed awkwardly. "You're too strong for us," he said. Feeling in his pocket for small change, he made to open the door.

"Hey, lover."

"Yes?"

"Ever killed anyone?"

"No."

"Not even physically?"

"I don't understand," said Cassidy.

"I'll bet the bosscow does," said Shamus. "Hey, lover."

"Well?" Testily, as becomes a tired man with a crippled son.

Shamus flung out his arms. "Give us a cuddle, lover. I'm *starving*."

"I've got to pay for the call," said Cassidy.

Arms still outstretched, Shamus remained in the open doorway staring at Cassidy in astonishment while he completed his transactions at the bar; until, without waiting for the promised embrace, he swung away into the grimy crowd.

"All right you lousy filthy stinking hayseeds," he yelled. "Button your smocks, Butch Cassidy's in town!"

"Time," the landlord said quickly. "And I mean it."

After the pub, the taxi. From Bath or Bristol? No matter. They had missed the last train so Shamus ordered a radio cab in his Italian accent while they all squashed into the

telephone booth. Shamus sat in the front so that he could
talk to the driver, who was an old man and rather tickled
to be driving drunken gentry. Quite soon the radio caught
Shamus' fancy.

"Listen to her," he urges them, turning up the volume.

They all concentrate.

"Come in Peter One . . . Control calling . . . Peter Two
. . . party of four at the station, no luggage, they'll sit
three up at the back. Party waiting now, Peter Three.
Come in Peter One, Control calling . . ."

To Cassidy she sounds as bossy and inexpert and strident
and periodic as any other female announcer, but Shamus is
entranced.

"She's not your daughter is she?" he asks the driver
reverently.

"Not likely. She's fifty in the shade."

"She's terrific," says Shamus. "That lady is in the first
position. Believe me."

"She really is," Cassidy agrees, about to doze off. Helen's
head has fallen on to his shoulder and she has threaded
her fingers through his hand and he is very pleased to
agree to anything when suddenly they hear Shamus talking
into the microphone in his Italian voice.

"I want-a you," he is whispering fervently. *"I love-a
you and I want-a you. I-a long for you.* Is she dark?" he
asks the driver.

"Darkish."

"Come to bed with me," Shamus breathes back at the
microphone. "Fuck me."

"Here, steady," says the driver. On a tense slope, they
all wait for the reply.

"She's calling the police," says Cassidy.

"She's packing her bags," says Helen.

"What a woman," says Shamus.

In a tone of incipient hysteria, the radio speaks. "Peter
One . . . Peter One . . . who is that?"

"Not Peter One. Peter One is dead. My name is
Dostoevsky," Shamus insists, dextrously adjusting to the
deeper Russian tone. "I have just murdered Peter One
without a spark of regret. It was a *crime passionel*. I
want you all for myself, I love you. One night with you is
worth a lifetime in Siberia." The radio pops but finds no
words. "Listen I am also Nietzsche. I am no man. I am

dynamite. Don't you understand—" very thick Russian—
"that immoralism is a necessary precondition of new
values? Listen, we will found a new class together. We will
engender a world of innocent, murderous, beautiful boys!
We—"

The driver gently takes the microphone. "It's all right,
dear," he says kindly. "I've got a funny, that's all."

"Funny?" the radio screams through the interference.
"You call that funny? Bloody foreigner murdering my
drivers in the middle of—"

The driver switches her off. "She'll murder *me* in the
morning," he says, not much worried.

Shamus has fallen asleep. "Lot of woman there, boy,"
he whispers.

"I wish we could play Moth again," says Cassidy.

"Moth was super," says Helen, and gives his hand another friendly squeeze.

On the last leg home they stopped the Bentley at a phone
box and put through a call to Flaherty so that Shamus
could again test the sincerity of his conviction. "A man is
what he *thinks* he is," Helen explained, quoting the master. "That's what Shamus means by faith."

"He's absolutely right," said Cassidy.

Cassidy booked the call because he had a Post Office
credit card and Shamus, amazingly, had the number written neatly in the margin of a cutting from the *Daily Mail*.
"It's Beohmin village pub," he explained. "He's there
most evenings." FLAHERTY FOR GOD the cutting read.
They squeezed in all three together and closed the door
for comfort. Alas, Flaherty was not available. For five
minutes perhaps they listened to the number ringing out.
Cassidy was secretly quite glad—after all, it could have
been embarrassing—but Shamus was hurt and disappointed, returning to the car ahead of them and climbing
into the back without a word. For a long while they drove
in silence; while Helen, sitting beside her husband now, consoled him with kisses and small attentions.

"Sodder," Shamus declared at last, in a cracked voice.
"Shouldn't even *need* a fucking telephone."

"Of course he shouldn't," Helen agreed tenderly.

"Hey look," said Shamus, sitting up straight, watch-

ing the unnatural moonlight scatter over the hedges.
"Kolynos headlights!"

"They're iodine quartz," said Cassidy. "Halogen. The
latest thing."

"Meeow," said Shamus and went back to Helen.

Back at Haverdown—after a pause for refreshment—they
had a horse race. Shamus was Nijinsky, Cassidy was Dob-
bin. The start was unclear to him, and for once he forgot
who won, but he had the clearest recollection of the
thunder of their six feet as they galloped down uncarpeted
back staircases, and of Shamus doing his butler voice while
he charged a locked door.

"'Ere's my lady's bedroom!" He charged it again.
"Merry bloody England, let's knock the bugger down!"

"Helen . . ." whispered Cassidy. "He'll smash himself to
pieces."

But the door it was that smashed and suddenly they
were flying, crashing into bare mattresses that smelt of
lavender and mothballs.

"Shamus, are you all right?" Helen asked.

No answer.

"Shamus is dead," she declared, not in the least alarmed.

Shamus was underneath them, groaning.

"Sounds like a broken neck," she said.

"It's a broken heart you fool," said Shamus. "For when
they butcher my masterpiece."

She was already undressing him as Cassidy left the room
to make himself a bed on the Chesterfield. For a while he
lay awake listening to the bucking of the bed as Helen
and Shamus once more consummated their perfect relationship. The next moment Helen was waking him with a
gentle shaking of his shoulder and he heard the transistor
again playing cremation music from the pocket of her
high-necked housecoat.

"No," said Helen quietly, "you can't say goodbye to him
because he works in the mornings."

She had brought a complete breakfast on a mother-ofpearl tray: a boiled egg and toast and coffee, and she carried the lantern because it was still dark. She was very neat and wore no make-up. She might have slept twelve hours and been for a country walk.

"How is he?"

"His neck's stiff," she said cheerfully. "But he likes a bit of pain."

"For the writing?" Cassidy said, being of the clan now, and Helen nodded yes.

"Were you warm enough?"

"Fine."

He sat upright, partially covering his bare paunch with the overcoats across his lap, and Helen sat beside him watching him with motherly indulgence.

"You won't leave him will you Cassidy? It's time he had a friend again."

"What happened to the others?" Cassidy said, his mouth full of toast, and they both laughed, not looking at his tummy. "But I mean why *me?* I'm mean *I'm* not much good to him."

"Shamus is *very* religious," Helen explained after a pause. "He thinks you're redeemable. Are you redeemable, Cassidy?"

"I don't know what he means." Helen waited, so he went on. "Redeemable from what?"

"What Shamus says is, any fool can *give,* it's what we take from life that matters. That's how we discover our outlines."

"Oh."

"That means . . . our identity . . . our passion."

"And our art," said Cassidy, remembering.

"He doesn't like people throwing up the struggle whether their name is Flaherty, or Christ, or Cassidy. But you *haven't* thrown up the struggle, have you Cassidy?"

"No. I haven't. I feel sometimes . . . I'm just beginning."

Very quietly, Helen said, "That's the message *we* got." She took the tray to the far end of the room, the ship's lantern lighting her face from below. *Caravaggio,* Cassidy thought, remembering Mark's postcard from Rome.

"I told him your remark about money."

"Oh . . ." said Cassidy, not knowing which remark, but wondering somewhat nervously whether it was to his credit.

"A man is judged by what he looks for, not by what he finds."

"What did he think of it?"

"He's using it," she said simply, as if there were no higher accolade. "Do you know Shamus has written his own epitaph?" she continued brightly. *"Shamus who had a lot to take*. I think it's the most super epitaph that's ever been written, don't you?"

"It's wonderful," Cassidy said. "I entirely agree. It's beautiful." Adding: "I'd like it for myself too."

"You see Shamus *loves* people. He really does. He's the difference between paddling and swimming. He's like Gatsby. He believes in the light at the end of the pier."

"I think that's what I believe in too," said Cassidy, trying to remember who Gatsby was.

"That's why he loved your remark about money," Helen explained.

She saw him to the car.

"He'll even believe in Flaherty if Flaherty will only give him a chance."

"I thought he wanted to kill him."

"Isn't that the same thing?" said Helen, giving him a very deep look.

"I suppose it is," Cassidy conceded.

"Give my love to London."

"I will. Helen."

"Yes?"

"Can I give you some money?"

"No. Shamus said you'd ask. Thanks all the same." She kissed him, not a goodbye kiss but a kiss of gratitude, swift and accurate on the blank of the cheek. "He says you're to read Dostoevsky. Not the works, just the life."

"I will. I'll start tonight." He added, "I don't read much, but when I do I really like to take my time."

"He'll be up in a week or two. As soon as he's finished the book, he'll come up and see all the managers and agents and people. He likes to be alone for that." She laughed resignedly. "He calls it charging his batteries."

"The ghouls," said Cassidy.

"The ghouls," said Helen.

The early sun sprang suddenly through the monkey puzzle trees, raising the brickwork of the mansion to a warm, flesh pink.

"Tell him to ring me at the firm," said Cassidy. "We're in the book. Any time, I'll always take the call."

"Don't worry, he will." She hesitated. "By the by, you remember last night you offered Shamus a Swiss house to work in?"

"Oh the chalet. Yes. Yes, of course. Tense slope. Ha."

"He says he might take you up on that."

"Goodness," said Cassidy gratefully, "that would be wonderful."

"He can't promise."

"No, of course."

A moment's silent plea: "Cassidy."

"Yes?"

"You won't rat, will you?"

"Of course not."

She kissed him again without fuss, on the mouth this time, the way sisters kiss brothers when they're no longer worried about incest.

So Cassidy left Haverdown with the taste of her toothpaste on his lips and the smell of her simple talc in his nostrils.

8

Bohemia.

That was his first thought and it sustained him all the way to Bath. I have visited Bohemia and got away unscathed. It was many years since he had met an artist. At Oxford in his time there had been an old house near the river that was reputed to contain a number of them and sometimes, passing on his way to the Scala Cinema, he had seen their clothes hanging from the iron balcony, or a great quantity of empty bottles sprawling out of their dustbins. On Sundays, he had heard, they congregated in the George Bar, their men in earrings and their womenfolk smoking cigars, and he imagined them saying amazing things to one another about their private parts. At public school there had been a painting master known as Whitewash, a soft man in later middle age who had worn butterfly collars and made the boys sit for each other in gym shorts, and one Wednesday Cassidy had been to tea with him alone but he had hardly spoken a word, just smiled sadly and watched him eat hot muffins. Apart from these sparse experiences, his knowledge of the breed was negligible, though he had long counted himself an honorary member.

Stopping in Bath he went to his hotel to collect his luggage and pay the bill, and found himself glancing in furtive excitement at the daylight shining on the scenes of their revel. Rotten little town, he told himself. Prole-ridden Vatican. And vowed never to return.

He had signed in as Viscount Cassidy of Mull.

"Enjoy your stay my lord?" the cashier enquired with a little more intimacy than Cassidy considered needful.

"Very much indeed, thank you," he said and gave two pounds to the porter.

The process of ratting therefore, which Helen had so accurately anticipated, did not begin until round about Devizes. For the first hour of the drive, before his hangover had entered the retributive phase, Cassidy remained confused but still elated by his encounter with Helen and Shamus. He had little idea of what he felt; his mood seemed to change with the landscape. On the highroad to Frome where blue plains reached to either side of him, a child-like innocence gilded all he saw. His whole future was one long adventure with his new friends: together they would bestride the world, sail distant seas, mount the sky on wings of laughter. In Devizes where the rain began and a dull sickness overtook his gastric system, he remained moderately enchanted, but the sight of the morning shoppers and mothers with prams gave him food for thought. By the time he reached Reading his head was aching terribly and he had convinced himself that Helen and Shamus were either a dream or a pair of fakes posing as celebrities.

"After all," he argued, "if they're who they say they are, why should they be interested in me?"

And later: "I am one of a row. People like me have no part in the life of an artist."

Reconstructing Helen's *tour d'horizon* of Shamus' argument on the relationship between the artist and the bourgeois, he found it frail, confused, and poorly reasoned.

I'd have put it better, he thought, if I'd held that opinion: a lot of hot air actually.

By the time he reached the outskirts of London he had come to certain useful conclusions. He would never hear from Helen or Shamus again; they were probably confidence tricksters and he was lucky to get away with his wallet; and whether they reappeared or not, they belonged with certain other phenomena to that area of Cassidy's world which for the general peace was best not revisited.

He would have dismissed them then and there, in fact, if a small incident had not forcibly reminded him of Shamus' disagreeably personal perceptions.

Parked in a lay-by, he was checking the pockets of his car for compromising souvenirs when he came upon a crumpled sheet of paper stuffed into a glove pocket. It was the menu from Bruno's restaurant in Bath on which, in his simplicity, he had believed that Shamus was writing immortal prose. Down one side of the back, done in pencil, was Shamus' portrait of Cassidy with words written at the side and arrows to show what feature they referred to. "Baby cheeks, good at blushing; noble brow, furrowed by vague agonies; eyes shaggy and very, very shifty." Over the top of the head in capitals was the word WANTED and underneath a further description of Cassidy.

NAME: Cassidy, Butch. Also known as Hopalong, Christopher Robin, and Paul Getty.
CRIME: Innocence (cf, Greene: a leper without his bell).
FAITH: First Church of Christ Pessimist.
SENTENCE: Survival for life.

The other side of the menu contained a letter, addressed to LOVER.

Dear Lover,
I hope you are well. I am. Thank you very much for a lovely nosh. Twice or thrice had I loved thee before I knew thy face or name. So forgive nasty drawing, can't help the Eye but the Heart's yours for the asking. Love, love, love

> P. Scardanelli, alias
> Flaherty, alias Shamus

What a *very* undergraduate communication thought Cassidy indignantly; how very embarrassing. Sighing, he threw the menu away. Talk about submerged proof...
Ever killed anyone lover? a voice asked from inside him. Switching on the wireless, he turned south for Acton. Art is all very well, he thought, but sometimes it goes a damn sight too far.

His business in Acton was brief and useful. A wholesaler named Dobbs, notoriously difficult but an influential connection, had been objecting to the new leather-look strollers and was flirting with a rival manufacturer. Cassidy had never much cared for strollers, which he regarded as an unhappy cross between your mere pushchair and your full-scale baby carriage, but they were a useful stand-by in the spring when demand was capricious. Rightly he calculated that a personal visit would end the dispute.

"Well I didn't expect Himself I will say," Dobbs confessed nervously. "What's happened to the rep then, horse?"

He had lost a lot of hair, Cassidy noticed; the second marriage is wearing him out. He was a very wasted man, always perspiring, and scandal attached to him.

"I like to check on these things myself, that's all. Where a valued customer complains," Cassidy said not without a certain sternness, "I like to look into it personally."

"Now look this isn't a complaint, Mr. Cassidy. The stroller's a very elegant job and your chassis does it credit, course it does. The making of it in fact. I sell a lot of them, swear by them, course I do, horse."

"A complaint's a complaint, Andy, once it gets into the pipeline."

"It's the *folding* they don't like, Mr. Cassidy," Dobbs protested not with any real conviction. "They're doing their stockings on the links."

"Let's take a look shall we, Andy?"

They climbed the wooden steps to the warehouse and examined links.

"Yes," said Cassidy, kneeling to caress a particularly well-turned example, "I see what you mean."

"Here, watch your trousers," Dobbs cried. "That floor's filthy."

But Cassidy affected not to hear. Stretching himself at full length on the unswept floorboards he ran a devoted hand along the underpart of the pram, touching with his fingertips the nipples, threads, and couplings of his earliest and most fruitful patent.

"I'm very grateful to you, Andy," he said as they returned to the office. "I'll have my people look into it right away."

"Only they do their nylons on them you see," Dobbs repeated feebly as he brushed down Cassidy's suit. "They did on the last lot anyway."

"Know what one nylon said to the other, Andy?" Cassidy asked casually as he unloaded the crate of sherry he had ready in the trunk. Sherry, they said, was what he drank.

"What's that then?"

"There's a fellow feeling between us," said Cassidy. Their laughter covered the flurried transaction. "It's an Easter present," Cassidy explained. "We're shedding a bit of the profits from the last financial year."

"It's very decent I must say," said Dobbs.

"Not at all. Thanks for putting us on to that link."

"I get worried sometimes," Dobbs confessed, seeing him back to the Bentley. "I just think I've been forgotten."

"I understand," said Cassidy. "How's the wife then?"

"Well, you know," said Dobbs.

"I know," said Cassidy.

Changing his mind, he went to the cinema. He liked best those films which praised the British war effort or portrayed with Fearless Honesty the Intimate Sex Life of Scandinavian Teenagers. On this occasion he was fortunate enough to find a double bill.

Sandra was out. She had left a *quiche Lorraine* on the kitchen table and a note saying she had gone to her meths drinkers' clinic. The hall smelt of linseed oil. Dust sheets and painters' ladders reminded him uncomfortably of Haverdown. Adding or subtracting? He tried to remember. The mouldings, he knew, were inferior and must be taken down. The fireplace perhaps? They had bought one at Mallets a month or two ago, pine, eighteenth century, three hundred quid and fine carvings over. The fireplace was a *feature*, their architect assured them, and features, God alone knew, were what their house most needed.

Her mother was in her room. From several flights above, he heard the mellifluous tones of John Gielgud reading Héloïse and Abélard on her gramophone for the blind. The sound moved him at once to a trembling fury. *Idiot, braying idiot*, she can see perfectly well when she wants to.

Very softly he went to the nursery and by the glow of the uncurtained window tiptoed to Hugo's bedside, picking his way through the litter of toys. Why had he no night light? Cassidy was convinced he was afraid of the dark. The boy slept as if dead upon the blankets, his plastered leg shining palely in the orange light and his pyjama jacket open to the waist. On the floor beside him lay the egg whisk which he used for frisking up his bubble bath. One by one Cassidy fastened the pyjama buttons, then gently laid his open palm on the child's dry brow. Well, at least he was not overheated. He listened, studying him intently through the speckled twilight. Against the sleepless boom of traffic the boy's breath came and went in small, regular sips. Nothing wrong there apparently, but why did he suck his thumb so? A child of seven doesn't suck his thumb, not unless he's deprived of love. Inwardly, Cassidy sighed. Hugo, he thought, oh Hugo, believe me son, we all go through it. Kneeling now, he minutely examined the outer surface of the plaster, searching for the telltale ridges which might betray a second parting of the fractured bone within; but the light from the window was not enough, and all he could make out were graffiti and pictures of houses done in felt-nibbed pens.

A lorry climbed the hill. Quickly standing, he drew the curtain and closed the window against the pollution of its engine. The boy stirred, laid his forearm across his eyes. A key turned in the front door.

"Hi traveller," Sandra called.

A prepared speech, reaching for modern humour.

"Hullo," said Cassidy.

Her footsteps stopped.

"Is that all you've got to say?" she asked, still from the hall.

"What else am I supposed to say? You said hi, I said hullo. I think he should see a specialist, you don't."

He waited. She could stand like that for minutes at a time; the loser was the first to move. Losing, Sandra, wife to Aldo, went slowly upstairs to her mother.

London

9

My dear Mark.

The letter hung on him like a damp cloud. Flat, non-visual; an after-lunch letter, reaching for sustenance he did not want. A letter of the liver, rather than the heart.

The paper was headed 12 Abalone Crescent, but he wrote from South Audley Street for peace. Cassidy's office was not unlike Cassidy's car: a mahogany bastion against the non-negotiable hazards of terrestrial existence. In Audley Street he was neither Aldo nor Cassidy, but *Mister Aldo*, a Christian name treated with Christian respect. In Audley Street no foot was laid upon the ground, no door closed upon its frame but cunning pads reduced the impact. Even the several telephones on his rosewood desk had been disarmed; instead of the raucous woman's scream which from childhood had so unsettled him, the instruments emitted only a grateful purr of sexual contentment, inviting not anger, not panic, but a caress along their white, submissive spines.

Well old son how are you? I must say I envy you down there in the rural quiet of Dorset, what with all the bustle and hectic tear which more and more seems in these competitive days to be the lot of the honest merchant striving for his crust! The weather at least continues balmy (which means not daft but warm and pleasant!) but all else is activity, form-filling, and an ever-tougher struggle with foreign competition. Sometimes I fear one is inclined on reaching home to wonder whether the game is worth the candle. Even my poor efforts in the direction of doing something for the less fortunate of the community seem doomed to failure—you would be appalled at the greed and selfishness of vested local interest when asked to collaborate in a scheme to help and aid their young. Even the Bristol

Corporation, of whom I had the highest hopes, have suddenly turned tail and left us back at square one. However, soldier on, as the school motto says. We are making a great effort for the Paris Trade Fair, incidentally: if ever you come into the firm which as you know I don't want to force on you, the Foreign Desk could well be an attractive slot for you to begin at, provided always that your French comes up to scratch. . . .

A bundle of solicitors' documents caught his eye, green borders and pink ribbon. Without a pause he made a second paragraph and wrote:

Well Mark, you have probably read that we here in Commerce are all deeply worried about inflation. I thought you would be reassured to know that the Chilren's Trust, of which you and Hug are equal beneficiaries, is made up of a wide spread of equities and gilt-edged, and should be well protected from the present kind of madness. I only mention this in passing.

Having read through what he had written, Cassidy sighed, laid down his gold pen, and stared absently through the lace curtains at the pageant of smartly dressed pedestrians and shining limousines. Did Mark *care* about equities? Did he know about them? Was it even desirable that he should? Vaguely, not at all a memory man when it came to the detail of his early life, Cassidy tried to establish whether he himself had been informed about such things at the age of eleven. At eleven, most likely he was still boarded with an Aunt Nell, a gross, noisy lady with a bungalow near Pendeen Sands. Had *that* child studied the financial pages? Was the lady of a sort to encourage him to study them? He remembered only her undergarments as she waded out to sea, dragging him after her to certain death: soiled petals pink and black, flapping over sunless thighs. If he was not with Aunt Nell, he was with the Spider, a discarded mistress of his father's who kept him in bed to protect him from germs.

No. His case had no relevance to Mark's.

A deep sense of malaise informs the national scene. Everyone is counting his own chickens while the poli-

ticians exhort us to the Dunkirk spirit. Last night, the Prime Minister urged the nation to work harder for its money. Few believe that his speech will make any difference. The unions have turned their faces firmly against reconciliation. Only a showdown can result.

He put down the pen.

Ridiculous.

Tear up the letter.

Here I sit, bored stiff and what do I do? Summarise the leading articles of the *Financial Times*. Business has corrupted me: I have no relationship with my son.

A few years back he would have drawn him bears and piglets—he even kept a set of Swiss crayons handy in his desk for that very purpose. But Mark had outgrown piglets, and it was very difficult to know what else was likely to give him pleasure. Perhaps money, after all, was the answer. A promise of security never came amiss. Even if he doesn't understand in detail, the *notion* will remain with him; comfort him on dark nights when the parental world bewilders him.

Mummy will have told you that she and Heather Ast are trying to open a second all-night clinic for down-and-outs. Heather has found a disused Oxfam warehouse on the southern edge of Hampstead Heath, where many of these poor wretches spend the night sleeping fitfully under old newspaper. Heather, as you know, has suffered a great blow in her life after her husband walked out on her for no good reason. Your mother is helping to bring her round. . . .

Hearing a lighter tread on the warm pavement outside, he looked up again hopefully, but his vigilance was rewarded by a redhead, and redheads alarmed him. Also, she had a determined walk; to hear it was to know already she was not easily deflected. A heel-to-toe walk, requiring a good rotary action of the elbows and a vindictive moral purpose.

Cassidy sighed. Sandra's walk.

Should he ring her?

Much of their relationship was conducted on the telephone. It was a conceit of Cassidy's, indeed, that with time all they would need for a successful marriage was two functioning telephone boxes. . . .

No, this was not an occasion for the telephone.

Send her flowers, then?

"Dear love please forgive me, it was well meant, I only want your happiness, Aldo."

Or the bullying tone? "Smile or get out."

Or beg?

"Sandra, you're making holes in my heart. *Please, please, please* . . ."

Please whom? What can she do that will please *me* any more?

> *As to myself, well I must confess that I have not had much time for anything but the papers on my desk and that bane of human existence, the telephone. . . .*

As to himself, *what?*

Glumly, the unfinished letter still before him, he made the reckoning. Four weeks had passed since his visit to Haverdown. He had conducted meetings, read the trade press, composed A Word From Your Chairman on the forthcoming Paris Trade Fair, taken out new policies for private medication, retirement, and sudden death, sat with accountants over the April figures for the outgoing financial year, drafted speeches for the Annual Informal Meeting of Shareholders. He had lunched with high officials of certain charities, to whom—tentatively—he had offered large sums upon obscure conditions. He had dined with the Nondescripts and repeated, with considerable success, his nice joke about what one nylon had said to the other. He had dismissed a works foreman on suspicion of industrial espionage and by adroit diplomacy averted a walk-out. He had opened a spares depôt in Amsterdam and fought and won a savage battle with the Exports Credit Guarantee Department. He had attended a matinée spectacular in one of the smaller Soho theatres, and continued his long and costly correspondence with Somerset House about his genealogy. The discussion turned on a Cassidy who had fought at Marston Moor in Cromwell's great charge against Prince Rupert's Horse; but it appeared that the effort had exhausted him for he had never been heard of since. After six years, it now seemed to

Cassidy, the correspondence threatened to become as long and fruitless as the Civil War itself. He had taken the Bentley to Park Wards and left it there while the mechanics respectfully pursued an illusory rattle in the offside door. He had played golf with his competitors and squash with his graduate trainees. His competitors had sneered at the quantity of his clubs and the graduates said "Sorry sir" and told him how Oxford had changed. He had dictated letters to his secretary, Miss Mawdray, and quizzed her youthful shape over the rim of his unnecessary spectacles. (These spectacles were not at all to be compared with those of Sandra's mother. Cassidy's spectacles were there to give him power; Mrs. Groat's to advertise her frailty.)

His frown deepened.

There, he would admit, certain pleasurable tremors had been recorded on the Cassidy seismograph. Miss Mawdray was a trim, desirable girl, dark like Sandra but taller, with a swimmer's body and a great passion for Greece. On Fridays she wore a poncho with goat's wool tassels, and on Tuesdays she read him his horoscope, knees pressed together like little buttocks, the tips of her ears pointing through her long brown hair.

"What beastliness have you got lined up for me this week, Angie?" he had asked her yesterday morning, burying his lust in an attitude of fatherly indulgence, and listened attentively to her bold prophecies from a newspaper below his station. She had recently acquired an engagement ring, but resisted all enquiries about its origin. Fellow's probably married, Cassidy concluded with lofty disapproval; these girls are all the same nowadays.

Worse still, she had taken the day off.

On one other occasion only during this entire period had Cassidy been conscious of *impact*. Attending an ordinary meeting of his manufacturing association the distinguished member had launched, for no reason he could now determine, a searing and undeserved attack on the Board of Trade. The speech was widely considered to be out of place and for several days he had contemplated suicide. Happily, good sense prevailed and he treated himself to a great luncheon instead. He had discovered a new

restaurant in Lisle Street where they made *mille-feuilles*
with a chocolate cream, and he had two helpings with his
coffee.

What have I felt? he asked himself, gazing morosely out
of the window. What have I *learned?* In what way had
he benefitted mankind? More important still, in what way
has mankind benefitted *me?* The answer: nothing. A
vacuum. Cassidy lives in a vacuum. Poor Cassidy. Poor
Bear. Poor *Pailthorpe* Bear.

And it is probably in order to fill this vacuum, Cassidy
reflected, that I have now sinned. Grossly sinned. Mother,
against Heaven and against Thee. Against Sandra, and
(he would confess) against his own flesh too. . . .

It was too much for him. Banishing the shameful memory of his most recent and provocative marital transgres-
sion, Cassidy resumed his tribute to wise fatherhood.

*Hugo is in the pink, though of course he looks forward
very much to joining you at Hearst Leigh next year. The
other day I took him to the cinema. We rang the manager
first and he was very good and arranged for a Bath chair
in the aisle. We saw* High Noon. *Hugo loved the shooting but got very impatient with the love scenes.*

Hugo: "Is he killing her?"

Me: "No. They're hugging."

Hugo: "Why don't they shoot their guns instead?"

Me: "They will when they've finished hugging."

Collapse of all around.

*Actually, he is quite reconciled to his plaster leg, and
I really think it will be a great disappointment to him
when they remove it! Though at times, of course, particularly when the weather is as fine as it is now, and the
Elderman girls are out playing on the Heath, he gets a
bit fractious, and Father is called in to play the big bogey
man. . . .*

"Come in!"

A knock at the door. His stomach froze in panic. Tele-
gram from Sandra? I HAVE LEFT YOU FOR EVER SUPPER
IN THE FRIDGE SANDRA?

Visit from an Inland Revenue Inspector: spot check
sir, if you don't mind, here's my warrant.

Her mother, Mrs. Groat, has called, tapping her way down the corridor with her fake white stick. Hullo darling, giggle, giggle, I'm afraid she's dead, isn't she?

It was Meale, an overqualified trainee, hovering at the threshold. A goatish, unappetising boy poached from Bee-Line, their principal competitor. An author of endless schemes; charmless but thrusting. Large in the field of business studies. New. Well, Cassidy would be fair to him. Meale had had few advantages of the undefinable sort and Cassidy must make allowances. Nor did he begrudge Meale his betterment. Where would Cassidy be, after all, if he had not insisted on taking the most that the market would stand? Also, he was a distraction, and distraction was what Cassidy needed.

Affecting a small *moue* of surprise, the Chairman and Managing Director woke from his weighty deliberations.

"Ah, who's that? Meale. Good morning, Meale, sit down. Not there, over here. Coffee?"

"No thank you sir." ·

"*I'm* having some."

"Well thank you very much. I wondered whether you had had a chance to read my projection programme sir."

Manners first, Meale, manners first, I expect you to drink with me.

"Sugar?" Cassidy enquired pleasantly.

"Yes sir."

"And milk?"

"Afraid so, sir."

To the box: "Coffee, Miss Orton, will you? Milk and sugar, and the usual for me."

Switch her off. Adjust spectacles. Finger confidential papers. Squint at costly reproduction chandelier. And not find it in his heart to disappoint any man who came to ask his counsel.

"I *like* it, Meale. I think it's *good*, and I think it's *right*."

"Do you really, sir?"

"Yes. Jolly *good*. You ought to be *jolly* pleased with yourself. I am. I mean pleased with you, ha ha, not *me*."

A hiatus; a cloud of discontent, suspicion, "I say—" reaching once more for Miss Orton's provoking little button "—you don't prefer tea do you?"

"Oh *no* sir!"

"Ah."

Rearrange the hands in judicial-benevolent posture, see our photograph in *The Times* eighth March this year: *Swift but Sound. Aldo Cassidy en poste in his Audley Street Premises.*

"So let's go ahead with it, shall we, Meale?"

The door closed.

Nothing.

Not even a depression on the black hide chair to mark where the grateful boy had sat. Or—hm hm—perhaps had not sat? Not visited, not spoken?

With a low-burning smile of winsome superiority, Dr. Aldo Cassidy, D. Phil. and bar., Fellow of All Souls and the Chairman and Managing Director's most frequent familiar, put the proposition relating to the unvisit of the man Meale:

"There are philosophers, dear boy, and no doubt psychiatrists and mystics as well, who loudly refute any notion of a distinguishing line between our wishes and their external counterparts. That being so, dear boy: does their doctrine not also extend to people? Thus: if those we meet are unmet by an act of forgetfulness, does it not follow, dear boy, that those we retain are kept in being by acts of *remembering?* Our acts? And this is turn being so—I fear I overburden the thesis?—and this in turn being so, does not such a system impose upon each one of us a most distressing responsibility for his creations? Hm? Hm? I mean what if *you* forgot *Sandra*, would *she* exist?"

Losing the thread, Cassidy drained his cold coffee and continued, in his literary persona, his *tour d'horizon* of the domestic scene.

Well Mark, the restoration work here at home continues slow but sure. The marble fireplace for the hall is pretty well in situ (*Latin fourth declension or is it fifth?!*) *and Mr. Mud the Mason has succeeded, not without some stern encouragement from Mummy, in getting the mantelpiece level without breaking the supports underneath. He wanted, if you please, to cut, physically cut, a piece out of the carved pine pillar, but Mummy caught him in the act and he was duly contrite!*

Here at home.

He cast a sodden gaze round his room. Once, *this* had been his home. My *dulce domum,* my sanctuary, my refuge. His compensation for all the disagreeable rooms of his childhood. Here I administered, I dispensed, I praised; and here he received in return that glow of motherly security which no woman of Cassidy's acquaintance had come within shouting distance of providing. Once, even to approach the building had been to know peace. The brickwork, with its dull, dark red of internal flesh; the frilly wooden gables painted cream, like anonymous lifted petticoats awaiting his penetration; the glistening brass plate on the rosewood front door, brighter than any woman's smile, all these things had tantalised him with favourable sensations of purchase, conquest, and expansion. "You've go so *much,*" they said to him. "And you handle it so *well.*" While Miss Mawdray's murmured "Good morning, Mister Aldo," issuing, it seemed, from the depths of her youthful breasts, had reminded him of the many assets he had yet to turn to cash. Here—whatever else he left behind at 12 Abalone Crescent—*here* in this sweet deep casket, seven hours a day and five days a week, he was at peace. He could recline or sit upright. He could scowl, smile, take a drink or a bath with equal privacy and, thus cossetted, freely deploy his many God-given talents of leadership, drive, and charm.

And now it is my prison. *Pitiful* Cassidy. *Abject* Toad. *Poor* Pailthorpe.

We should have stayed in Acton, he thought, yawning after his heavy luncheon—Boulestin wasn't bad actually, he must go there more often, they were one of the few places that looked after you if you went alone—we should never have become a public company. We were pioneers then; merchant adventurers, dreamers, strivers. Lemming, the chief lieutenant, now a portly man, was then a greyhound, lithe, swift, and tireless. Faulk, his advertising manager, today a balding, flagrant queen, was in those days the sharp-tongued visualizer of unlikely stunts. Now, with recognition behind them and public audits before them, a slackening of pace, a settling of the commercial digestion as it were, had tacitly replaced their youthful frenzy. Six months ago, he himself had been the first to praise this mellowing. *Retrenching* he had called it in a lengthy interview; *steadying down* and by his own deport-

ment set the tone. *The battle is over, we have entered
the smoother waters of a long and prosperous peace,* he
had assured his shareholders at last year's meeting. Great.
And when you have retrenched? And when you have
settled down? Then what do you have? The memory, and
damn all else. "Remember the night we welded up that
first prototype?" Cassidy would say to Lemming at the
Christmas party. "In that old bike shed round behind
the toyshop? Remember how we ran out of juice and had
to knock your missus out of bed, eh Arthur?"

"Lord alive," Lemming would reply, drawing on his
cigar while the young ones waited for his words. "And
wasn't she bloody mad, and all?"

Oh, how they laughed at yesterday.

*Must rush now. Promised to pay my fortnightly visit
to Grandpa, then home to Mummy. Wonder what she's
got for supper, don't you? Hey Mark—I had a thought:
isn't it funny to think that one day, sitting at this very
desk, you may be writing these very same words to your
beloved son? Well, cheerio. Remember that life's a gift
and not a burden, and that you are still barely at the stage
of opening the wrapping.*

Dad

*P.S. Incidentally, did you read the extraordinary case of
this Irishman Flaherty, in County Cork, who goes round
claiming he is God? I am sure there is nothing in it but one
never knows. I imagine you missed it, I know you only
get the* Telegraph *down there, despite your mother's letter
to Mr. Grey.*

"Take your time," he told the driver.

Cassidy's feelings about his father varied. He lived
in a penthouse in Maida Vale, a property listed among
the assets of the Company and let to him rent free in
exchange for unspecified consultative services. From its
many large windows, it seemed to Cassidy, he followed
his son's progress through the world as once the eye of
God had followed Cain across the desert. There was no
hiding from him; his intelligence system was vast, and
where it failed, intuition served him in its place. In bad
times, Cassidy regarded him as undesirable and made elaborate plots to kill him. In good times he admired him

very much, particularly his flair. When younger, Cassidy had made copious researches about Old Hugo, interviewing lapsed acquaintances in clubs and browsing through public records; but facts about him, like facts about God, were hard to come by. In Cassidy's early childhood, it appeared, Old Hugo had been a minister of religion, most likely in the nonconformist cause. By way of corroboration, Cassidy could point to the Cromwellian connection and certain memories of a pine pulpit on a cold day, Old Hugo wedged into it like an egg into an egg cup and the tender child alone on a forward pew a mute Christ among the elders. With time however—a very variable factor in Old Hugo's incarnations—the Lord had appeared to His shepherd in a dream and counselled him that it paid better to feed the body than the mind, and the good man had accordingly put aside the cloth in favour of the hotel trade. The source of this information, not unnaturally, was Old Hugo himself, since no one else except God had been party to the dream. Often, he insisted, he regretted his divinely inspired decision, at other times he recalled it as an act of courage; and occasionally, lamenting his misfortunes, he deeply resented the years he had wasted on the Word.

"There I was, trying to teach those cretins wisdom, and what did I get? Four old nellies and a lollipop man."

At some point in his life, he had also been a Member of Parliament, though Cassidy's enquiries of the Clerks of the House of Commons had failed to confirm the claim; and he had stood in no election that any Party Headquarters could recall. Nevertheless, the initials M.P. followed him everywhere, even on his bills; and were done in heavy ink on the nameplate below his doorbell.

It was a day for buying the Savoy Hotel.

"You can't go wrong," Old Hugo insisted. "What's a hotel, then, tell me that?"

"You tell me," said Cassidy admiringly, for he knew the answer too well.

"Bricks and mortar, food and drink, that's what a hotel is. Your basic elements, your basic facts of life. Shelter and sustenance; what more do you want?"

"It's perfectly true," said Cassidy, secretly wondering as always in these conversations how, if his father knew so much about business matters, he had managed to be penniless for twenty years. "There's a lot in what you say," he added with obedient enthusiasm.

"Forget fastenings. Fastenings are dead. So's prams. All dead. Look at the pill. Look at Vietnam. Are you going to tell me, son, that this world of ours today is a world in which men and women are going to breed their babies the way your mother and I did?"

"No," Cassidy agreed pleasantly, "I suppose not," and wrote him a cheque for a hundred pounds. "Will that do you for a bit?" he asked.

"Never forget," his father remarked, reading the words as well as the figures. "The sacrifices I made for you."

"I never could," Cassidy assured him. "Truly."

Carefully arranging his dressing gown over his bald white knees, Old Hugo shuffled to the window and surveyed the misted rooftops of Dickensian London.

"Tipping," he burst out in sudden contempt, seeing perhaps, among the chimney pots, descending generations of unpaid waiters, Cypriots from the Waldorf in Yarmouth, Anglo-Saxons at the Grand Pier in Pinner. "Tipping's *funk*, that's what tipping is. I've seen it time and again. Any fool can tip if he's got ten bob and a waistcoat."

"It's just that I know you need a little extra now and then."

"You'll *never* pay me off. *Never.* You've got assets no man can put a price on, least of all you. Where do they come from? They come from your old man. And when I'm judged as judged I shall one day surely be, as surely as night follows day, son, make no mistake about it, I shall be judged *solely and exclusively* on the many wonderful talents and attributes I have passed on to you, although you're worthless."

"It's true," said Cassidy.

"Your education, your brilliance, your inventiveness, the lot. Look at your discipline. Look at your religion. Where would *they* be if I hadn't done you right?"

"Nowhere."

"A delinquent, that's what you'd be. A pathetic delinquent, same as your mother, if I hadn't paid those boys down at Sherborne a towering fortune to put virtue and patriotism into you. You've got all the opportunity in the world. How's your French?"

"Good as ever," said Cassidy.

"That's because your mother was French. You'd never have *had* a French mother if it hadn't been for me."

"I know," said Cassidy. "I say you don't know where is do you?"

"Well keep it up," Old Hugo urged. His bloodless palm described a magisterial arc, as if it would stop the sun from moving. "You can get anywhere with languages," he informed the cosmos. "Anywhere. Still say your prayers do you?"

"Of course."

"Still kneel down and put your hands together like a little child then?"

"Every night."

"Like hell you do," Old Hugo retorted stoutly. "Say the prayers I taught you."

"Not now," said Cassidy.

"Why not?"

"I don't feel like it."

"Don't feel like it. Christ. Don't feel like it."

He was drinking, steadying himself on the steel window frame.

"Hotels," he repeated. "That's your line. Same as it was mine; your manners alone are worth five thousand a year, you ask Hunter. Don't *feel* like it!"

Hunter was a source, now dead. Cassidy had met him secretly in the National Liberal Club, but learned nothing. Both father and son had attended his funeral.

"They're *your* manners," said Cassidy courteously.

The old man nodded approvingly and for a while seemed to forget his son altogether, giving himself wholly to his profound contemplations of the London skyline.

"There's a man in County Cork who says he's God," said Cassidy, with a sudden smile.

"It's a con," Old Hugo replied, with that prompt certainty which Cassidy adored in him. "The oldest con in the world."

Discovering the cheque still in his hand Old Hugo reread it. That's all he reads, thought Cassidy, it's all he's ever read, evening papers and cheques and a few letters diagonally, to get their drift.

"You hang on to her," Old Hugo said at last, still reading the cheque. "You'd have been a delinquent if you hadn't married a bitch."

"But she doesn't *like* me," Cassidy objected.

"Why the hell should she? You're a bigger bloody liar than I am. *You* married honesty, not me. Live with it and shut up."

"Oh I've shut up all right," said Cassidy with some spirit. "We haven't spoken for a week."

The old man rounded on him.

"What do you mean, *haven't spoken to her for a week?* Jesus, I went months with your stupid mother. *Months.* All for *your* rotten sake, because I'd given you life. You wouldn't *exist* without me. Hear?" He returned to the window. "Anyway, you shouldn't have done it."

"All right," said Cassidy meekly, "I shouldn't have done it."

"Bitch," Old Hugo declared at last, dully, but whether he meant Sandra or some other lady, Cassidy could not tell. "Bitch," he murmured yet again, and leaning the vast lilac torso as far back as it would go, poured the rest of his brandy into it as if he were filling a lamp.

"And keep away from the queers," he warned, as if they too had let him down.

Kurt was Swiss, a neutral, kindly man dressed in cautious greys. His tie was dull brown and his hair was dull honey, and he wore a pastel-shaded ruby on his pale, doctor's hands, but the rest of him was cut from slate, off-season skies, and his shoes were trellised in matt grey leather.

They sat in a plastic office beside a plastic globe, discussing great climbs they would make this summer, and studying brochures for rucksacks, crampons, and nylon ropes. Cassidy was very frightened of heights but he felt that now he owned a chalet he should come to grips with the mountains. Kurt agreed.

"You are made for it, I can tell by your shoulders you see," he said, his eyes appraising them with pale pleasure. Kurt and Cassidy would start on the smaller ones and work upwards. "Then maybe one day you climb the Eiger."

"Yes," said Cassidy, "I would like that."

Cassidy would pay, he said, if Kurt would do the arranging.

A small silence intervened. Time for business? Kurt's job had never been defined for Cassidy, but his function was undisputed. He handled money. Money as an end, a commodity, a product. He received it in England and returned it abroad, and somewhere over the Channel he took a small commission for defying tiresome English laws.

Time for a drink.

"You would like a kirsch?"

"No thank you."

"Got to get in training."

"Yes," Cassidy said. And laughed shyly, trying to anticipate the Alpine consummation. He can't want *me*, he thought; he's just *generally* queer, it's nothing local I'm sure.

"How is it?" Kurt enquired, lowering his voice to match the intimacy.

"Well. . .you know. Up and down. Down at the moment actually. She's learning the piano again."

"Ah," said Kurt. A short deprecating *ah*. A puppy has messed on my Wilton. "She is competent?"

"Not very."

"Ah."

A tiny Swiss light winked from his desk. He blew it out.

"It's just . . ." Cassidy went on. "It's just, we never talk. Except about charities and things. How about *my* charity . . . ? You know."

"Sure," said Kurt. The smile slit the pale cushions of his jaw. "My God," he remarked equably. "The piano huh?"

"The piano," Cassidy agreed. "How is it with you, Kurt?"

"Me?" The question puzzled him.

In Switzerland, Cassidy thought, they have a lot of suicides and divorces, and sometimes Kurt seemed to be the explanation for them all.

Kurt had a silver ballpoint pen. It lay like a polished bullet on his fibreglass desk. Lifting it, he peered for a long time at the tip, examining it for engineering defects.

"Thank you I am fine."

"Great."

"Is there another way I can help you, Cassidy?"

"Well if you could manage five hundred?"

"No problem. At ten to the pound okay? We rob you a few centimes."

"I'll give you a cheque," said Cassidy and wrote it out to cash, using Kurt's pen.

"You know," said Kurt, "I don't like to criticise your government but these are crazy regulations."

"I know," said Cassidy.

Old Hugo left cheques open, ready for immediate presentation, but Kurt folded them, handled them the way a card player handles cards, assuming them into the palm and emitting them through the finger and thumb.

"Then why don't you change them?" he asked.

"We should, shouldn't we? It's the silly English thing, I'm afraid. Regulations are part of our tradition. We make them, then we fall in love with them."

The expression held Kurt still for several chronometric seconds. "Fall in love?" he repeated.

"Figuratively."

Kurt saw him to the door. "Please give her my regards."

"I will. Thanks. I say, I don't know whether you read the English papers but there's a southern Irish man who's announced he's God. Not the new Christ, apparently. God."

Kurt's frown was as faint as a pencil line after the rubbing out.

"Southern Ireland is Catholic," he said.

"That's right."

"I am sorry. I am evangelical."

"Goodnight," said Cassidy.

"Goodnight," said Kurt.

For an hour, perhaps longer, he took taxis to places. Some smelt of Old Hugo's cigars, some of the scent of women he loved but had never met. It was dusk by the time he approached the Crescent and the lights were on in the houses either side. Stopping the cab he walked the last hundred yards and the Crescent was like the night they had first seen it, a treasure chest of pastel doors and antique coaching lamps, bound books, rocking chairs, and happy couples.

"You can have any one of the three. This one, this one, this one."

"Let's have them all," said Sandra, holding his hand as they stood in the rain. "Lorks, Pailthorpe—" using their game words and giving his hand a squeeze "—whoever will we get to fill so many rooms?"

"We'll found a dynasty," said Cassidy proudly. "We'll be the Greeks, the Minoans, the Romans. Masses of little Pailthorpes, fat as butter. So."

Woollen gloves she wore, and a woollen headscarf soaked through, and the rain lay on her face like tears of hope.

"Then there won't *never* be enough rooms," she said proudly. "Cos I'm going to have litters of them. Ten at a time like Sal-Sal. Till you trip over them on the stairs. *So.*"

Sal-Sal was a Labrador bitch, their first, now dead.

She had drawn the curtains early, as if she were afraid of each day's dying. When she was young she had enjoyed the evenings, but now the curtains made an early night of them, and the twilight was left outside. The house stood in darkness, a dark green column, six floors of it, one corner stuck like a prow on to the pavement and chipped at handlebar height where the tradesboys passed. He hardly noticed the scaffolding any more, it had been there so long. He saw the house like a face under the hair of it, changing only where the masons changed it as they replaced the wooden lintels with hand-turned stone.

We'll make it perfect. We'll make it just as it would have been in the eighteenth century.

And if you do decide to go into the Church, said Sandra, *we'll let it to a boys' club for peanuts.*

Yes, Cassidy agreed, *we will. So.*

Ducking under the scaffolding he unlocked the front door and stepped inside. Bundles of Oxfam clothing in the hall, a plastic lifeboat for putting pennies in.

Music.

She was practising a simple hymn; just the tune, no attempt at harmony.

The day Thou gavest, Lord, is ended.

He looked for Heather's coat. Gone.

Christ, he thought; not a witness, not a referee. It'll take them a month to find our bodies.

"Hi," he called up the stairs.

The music continued.

Sandra had her own drawing room and the piano was too large for it. It stood between her doll's house and a crate of bric-à-brac she had bought at Sotheby's and not yet unpacked, and it looked as though it had been dropped there from above like a lifeboat and no one knew where to sail it. She sat very upright before it, manning it alone, one light burning for help and the metronome ticking out a signal. On its bow, where it finally tapered to a halt, stood a pile of dusty circulars about Biafra. From under the words "Biafra the Facts," a black baby, terribly emaciated, screamed soundlessly into the crystal chandelier. Sandra wore a housecoat and her mother had put up her hair for her as if to say it wouldn't be needed any more that night. There was a hole in the wall behind her, jagged like a shell hole. Builders' dust sheets covered the floors, and a very big Afghan hound watched her from the depths of a Queen Anne winged chair.

"Hi," he said again. "What gives?"

Her concentration deepened. She was a slight, hard-bodied girl with brown, male eyes and, like the house, she wore a wistful, uninhabited look which somehow discouraged trespass and yet lamented loneliness. Something had been planted there and withered. Regarding her, and waiting for the storm to break, Cassidy had the uncomfortable feeling that that something was himself. For years he had tried to want what she wanted, and found no external reason to want anything else. But in all those years he had never quite known what she wanted. Recently, she had acquired several small accomplishments, not for herself, but to pass on to her children before she died. Yet her children wearied her, and she was frequently unkind to them in little spiritual ways, the way children are unkind to one another.

The darkness falls at Thy behest.

"You're getting on fine," Cassidy volunteered. "Who's teaching you?"

"No one," she said.

"How was trade?"

"Trade?"

"Down at the clinic. Many turn up?"

"You call that trade?" she asked.

The day Thou gavest, Lord, is ended.

"No one turned up," she said.

"Perhaps they're cured," he suggested, his voice slowing to the rhythm of the music.

The darkness falls at Thy behest.

"No. They're out there. Somewhere."

The metronome ticked slowly to a halt.

"Shall I wind it up for you?"

"No thank you," she said.

The day Thou gavest, Lord, is ended.

Awkwardly, not wishing to disturb the Afghan, he balanced one buttock on the winged chair. It was very uncomfortable and the original embroidery pricked his tender skin.

"So what did you do?"

"Baby-sat."

"Oh. Who for?"

The darkness falls at Thy behest.

"The Eldermans."

She spoke with an infinite patience, in sad acceptance of an unfathomable mystery. The Eldermans were the doctor and his wife, a hearty, treacherous couple and Sandra's closest allies.

"Well, that was nice," said Cassidy, genially. "Go to the flicks did they? What did they see?"

"I don't know. They just wanted to be together."

Very stiffly, she played a descending scale. She finished very low and the Afghan growled in discomfort.

"Sorry," said Cassidy.

"What for?"

"About Hugo. I just got worried."

"Worried what about?" she asked, frowning. "I don't think I understand."

The day Thou gavest, Lord, is ended.

In his heart, Cassidy was prepared to confess to anything—human crimes had no logic for him, and he readily assumed he had committed them all. Outward confession, however, was painful to him, and offensive to his notions of deportment.

"Well," he began reluctantly, "I deceived you. I took him to a specialist. I pretended I was taking him to *High Noon* and instead I took him to a specialist." Receiving not even a reply, let alone absolution, he added more crisply, "I thought that was what we've been quarrelling about for the last eight days."

The darkness falls at Thy behest.

With a noise like slopping water the Afghan began chewing at her forepaw, trying to get at something deep in the skin.

"Stop that!" Sandra bellowed; and to Cassidy: "Are we quarrelling? I'm sure we're not."

The Afghan paid her no attention.

"Oh well that's fine," said Cassidy. And being close to anger, let the hymn soothe him, both lines.

"Where's Heather?" he asked.

"Out with a boyfriend."

"I didn't know she had one."

"Oh, she has."

The day Thou gavest, Lord, is ended.

"Is he nice?"

"He cherishes her."

"Oh well that's fine."

The hole in the wall gave into what was once a study. The plan was to link the two rooms, which they agreed had been the original architect's original intention.

"What did the specialist *say?*" she enquired.

"He took another set of X-rays. He'll ring me tomorrow."

"Well let me know, won't you?"

"I'm sorry I deceived you. It was . . . emotion. I care very much for him."

She played another slow scale. "Of course you do," she said, as if accepting the inevitable. "You're very fond of your children. I know you are. It's perfectly natural, why apologise? Have you had a *good* year?" she asked politely. "Spring's the time you count your money, isn't it?"

"Useful," Cassidy replied cautiously.

"You mean you've made a lot of profit?"

"Well, before tax, you know."

Folding away her music she went to the long window and stared at things he couldn't see.

"Goodnight darling," her mother called reproachfully from upstairs.

"I'll be up in a minute," Sandra said. "Did you buy an evening paper?"

"No, no I'm afraid not."

"Or hear the news by any chance?"

He thought of telling her about Flaherty but decided

against. Religion was one of the subjects they had agreed not to discuss.

"No," he said.

She said no more but only sighed so finally he asked: "What news?"

"The Chinese have launched their own satellite."

"Oh my Lord," said Cassidy.

The political world meant nothing to either of them, Cassidy was convinced of it. Like a dead language it provided the opportunity for studying at one remove the meaning of their own. If she talked America she was objecting to his money and Cassidy would reply in kind with a reference to the falling value of the pound; if she talked world poverty she was harping upon their early days when a slender budget had forced upon them an attitude of selfless abstinence. If she talked Russia, a country for which she professed the profoundest admiration, he knew that she longed for the plainer, passionate laws of a more vigorous sex life, for a never-never land in which his own sophistries could once more be subjugated to urges he no longer felt for her.

It was only recently however that she had entered the field of Defence. Uncertain of her meaning he selected a jovial tone.

"Was it yellow?"

"I don't know what colour it was I'm afraid."

"Well I'll bet it was a flop," he said.

"It was a complete success. Jodrell Bank has confirmed the Chinese bulletin."

"Oh Lord well that'll stir things up I suppose won't it?"

"Yes. I forgot how much you enjoy sensation."

She had moved closer to the window. Her face so near the glass seemed to be lit by darkness and her voice was as lonely as if she were talking of lost love. As if the day Thou hast given her, Lord, was ended.

"You do realise don't you that the Pentagon assessment of war risk foresees an annual rise of two per cent per annum?" With the tip of her small finger she drew a triangle and crossed it out. "That gives us fifty years at the most."

"Well, not *us*," he said still striving for a cheerful note.

"I meant civilisation. Our children in case you'd forgotten them. It's not much fun is it?"

Under the piano, two cats who had till then slept peacefully in each other's arms woke and began spitting.

"Perhaps it'll change," he suggested. "Perhaps it'll go down again; it might. Like the stock market."

With a shake of her dark hair she dismissed all chances of survival.

"Well, even if it doesn't there's not much we can do about it, is there?" he added injudiciously.

"So let's just go on making money. It'll be nice for the children won't it, to die rich. They'll thank us for that, won't they?" Her voice had risen a key.

"Oh no," said Cassidy, "I don't mean that at all. God, you make me out to be a sort of monster . . ."

"But you don't propose to *do* anything do you? None of us does."

"Well . . . there are the boys' clubs . . . the playing fields . . . the Cassidy Trust . . . I mean I'm sorry they haven't *happened* yet, but they will, won't they?"

"Will they?"

"Of course they will; if I go on trying hard enough. And you encourage me enough. We got jolly close to it in Bristol, after all."

If you believe in God, he argued, surely you can believe a few simple lies like mine? Sandra, you *need* faith, scepticism ill becomes you.

"Anyway," she said. "The war will hardly be averted by a playing field, will it? But still."

"Well what about you? Biafra . . . the meths boys . . . Vietnam . . . Oxfam . . . look at that Greek petition you signed . . . you must be doing *some* good. . . ."

"Must I?" she asked of the misted window as the tears began running down her childish cheeks. "You call that *doing?*"

Somehow he had crossed the room, squeezed past the piano, and taken her unfamiliar body in his arms. Bewildered, he held her as she wept, feeling nothing but a sadness he could not change and an emptiness he could not fill, like the hunger of the screaming child on the piano.

"Take him to any specialist you like," she said at last, rolling her head on his shoulder as the tears still fell. "I don't care. Take him to the whole lot. It's you that's sick, not him."

"It's all right," Cassidy whispered, patting her. "The specialist was no better than John Elderman. Truly. Just a silly old dodderer, that's all he was. John will look after him. John will. He'll do just fine, you'll see."

For a while longer he held her until, gently releasing herself, she walked from the room, drawing her skirts after her like chains. As she opened the door, the sound of her mother's radio swept in past her, dance music from between the wars. The animals watched her leave.

Next morning trying at breakfast to keep the shadow from Sandra's eyes, he invited her to accompany him to Paris for the Trade Fair.

"It's only business," he said, "but we might get a *bit* of fun."

"Fun is what we need," said Sandra, and kissed him absently.

10

Waiting.

A time for flowers.

"In *principle* I'm all for it," Lemming insists piously.
"No one more so, I dare say. But it's the details that
worry me, to be frank, the details."

And it was the details which, with the cunning of an
old campaigner, he was now proceeding to assault.

A Monday, balmier if possible than the last Monday,
balmier than the Monday before that; Mister Aldo's prayer
session, all present and correct; a day when waiting is to
dream; to believe in Nietzsche and J. Flaherty.

"Nice buttonhole, Mister Aldo," said Faulk.

"Thank you, Clarence."

"Get it off a barrow?" asked Lemming coarsely.

"Moyses Stevens," said Cassidy, reminding Lemming of
his membership of the Many-too-Many. "In Berkeley
Square, or haven't you heard of them?"

The topic however is not flower shops but the Paris
Trade Fair, now two weeks away. Lemming loathes the
French more than any living thing, and next to the French
he loathes exports, which he regards as synonymous with
the most reckless managerial malpractice. A golden sunlight is falling in strips across the liquid surface of the
eighteenth-century table and the dust rises through it in
tiny stars. Miss Mawdray, dressed like a summer flower, is
serving coffee and fruitcake and Lemming's lugubrious
monologue is an offence against the beauty of the day.

"Take your new prototype all-aluminium chassis right?
Now I admire that chassis. Properly handled I believe
that chassis is going to sweep your home market. But
what *I'm* saying is this: it's not going to sweep *any*
ruddy market while it's lying in pieces all over the work-
shop floor."

And slaps the table, not too heavily, leaving pads of sweat on Mrs. Croft's Antiquax.

"Oh come on," Cassidy protests. "Of course it will be ready, they've been tinkering with that thing for months; don't be bloody silly."

Lemming's piety, Lemming's objectivity, Lemming's status do not take kindly to this rebuke, so he pulls back his chin and puts on his Trade Union Leader Voice.

"I am assured *both* by Works *and* by the Engineers," he announces in a fighting, ungrammatical statement approved by fourteen committees, "that they see no hope *whatever* at this point in time of putting together that chassis prior to last date of shipment. Thanks, dear."

And takes some more fruitcake from Miss Mawdray's ample store.

The rose in Cassidy's buttonhole smells of paradise, and freckled girls in green, arboreal overalls. *"And you can throw this in for me," says Gaylord Cassidy, the well-known West End beau, signing a cheque for other purposes. "I'll fetch you a pin," says the freckled girl in green.*

"Well that settles it," pipes queer Clarence Faulk, much under Lemming's influence these days, and does a *thing*, as he would say, with his hair. Kurt's thing, a sudden limp-wristed correction to an arrangement which only exists in the mirror. "Oh I *am* sorry Mister Aldo, I interrupted you."

"Did you?" says Cassidy. "I don't think so. Mr. Meale, what have *you* got there?"

"A rather depressing report on the sealed absorbers I'm afraid, Mister Aldo. It seems *they've* shown up badly on the testing floor too."

"Better let's have it," says Cassidy with an encouraging smile. "Take your time now." For Meale is still inclined, in conference with the great, to gabble his words and lose the sense.

Meale takes a deep breath.

"The Cassidy Easy-Clean Shock Absorber," he begins, starting rather quaintly with the title, "housed in its own PVC container and designed for all strollers and small carriages. Patent pending, fifty shillings, trade only." He stops. "Shall I read it *all?*" he asks in some embarrassment.

"If you please, Meale."

If you please Meale. Your voice, Meale, is not half as offensive as you suppose and a great deal more congenial than the voice of the prole Lemming or the sodder Faulk. There is hope in it you see, Meale. There is life, there is tomorrow, Meale. Continue with our blessing.

"The action of the spring, confined to an airtight case, has caused overheating and in one instance actual combustion. Subjected to a simulated velocity equivalent to five m.p.h.—that is, the maximum allowable pedestrian rate—the spring was observed to burst *through* the housing, whereupon a rapid deterioration of the plastic also ensued. . . ."

Whereupon, Meale, it was a free spring, burst as you rightly suggest from its unnatural housing. A bouncing jolly, vibrant spring, a liberated spring with a life to lead and a heart to give.

"Miss Mawdray."

"Yes, Mister Aldo."

Caught, you bitch.

Cassidy might have tweaked her, she turns so sharply. She had her back to him. Was stooping, generously stooping, bless the child, to freshen Meale's cup, a treacherous operation considering his own was empty, and her breasts had nudged perilously downwards almost to his neck, when Cassidy's summons recalls her to loyalty. Is that the cause of her surprise? Is that the reason she has turned to him full face, full chest, skirt tautly rucked across her pelvis, eyebrows finely raised, tongue slack upon the lip? Was there an unconscious note of urgency in his voice, of jealousy not withheld, as he saw the sunlight narrow between the two lush tips and the callow boy's hard shoulder? *Only teasing Mister Aldo.*

"Miss Mawdray—forgive me Meale—Miss Mawdray, the mail. That was *all* the mail. You're sure?"

"Yes, Mister Aldo."

"There was nothing . . . personal. No personal material?"

Like a rose, for instance?

"No."

"You've checked in the package room?"

"Yes Mister Aldo."

Back. Back to waiting. We have time to wait, time to wait.

"Well that rules the spring out, doesn't it?" said Lemming with satisfaction, jabbing one overpaid finger at Meale's report.

"Not entirely," said Cassidy. "Meale, will you continue?"

Slowly Meale, we have all the time in the world.

Waiting.

Waiting, he languished like an Edwardian girl, in flower gardens of his own remembering. Walked in morning parks and watched the first tulips open to the restive sun; wore other roses in his buttonhole, slept in the Savoy under the pretext of a charitable errand, bought Sandra several expensive gifts, including a pair of long black Anna Karenina boots and a plain, wrapover housecoat which became her adequately but not more. Waiting, he dawdled guiltily outside bookshops, teetering but somehow never daring; till one day he sent Angie out to buy a copy and put it in a drawer of his desk, and locked the drawer against his own invasion. Waiting, he took Hugo to the zoo.

"Where does *Heather* live?" Hugo asked as they rode on the waterbus under hanging beeches. He was sitting on Heather's lap, his broken leg dangling negligently between her large thighs.

"In Hampstead," said Heather. "In a teeny-weeny flat next to a milkshop."

"You ought to come and live with *us*," said Hugo, reprovingly, "because you're my friend, aren't you Heather?"

"I almost *do* live with you," said Heather, and cuddled him closer against her soft, loose body, while she munched a red apple from a bag.

She was a warm, blond creature, fortyish, once the wife of a publisher. Now she was divorced and the godmother to other marriages. Hugo seemed to prefer her to Sandra, and in a way so did Cassidy, for she possessed what he called a decent quiet, a pastoral repose to her broad, comfortable body. Sandra said divorce had broken her heart, that she wept a lot, and was given to outbursts of great anger, mainly against men, but Cassidy found no sign of this in her company.

"Look," said Heather. "Herons."

"I like herons," said Hugo. "Don't you, Daddy?"

"Very much," said Cassidy.

Heather smiled, and once more the sunlight made a gold downy line along her cheekbone.

"You're so *good* Aldo," she said. "Isn't he, Hug?"

"He's the best daddy in the world," Hugo agreed.

"You do so much for others. If *only* we could do something for you."

"I want to make people happy," said Cassidy. "That's all I care about."

From a call box within sight of the gibbons, he consulted the office switchboard. Nothing, they said. Nothing but business.

"You have the instructions?"

"Yes, Mister Aldo, we all have."

"It's the export drive," he explained to Heather emerging from the kiosk. "We're waiting for an urgent shipment."

"You work so hard," said Heather, whose smile shone straight as the sun.

And still waiting, went to Sherborne, where Old Hugo had bought him his polish and his learning.

Sat in the Abbey under the shell-torn flags of disbanded country regiments reading the names of great battles, Alma, Egypt, Sevastopol, and Plassey, and loving passionately the heritage he had never had.

And sitting thus, prayed.

Dear Lord this is Aldo Cassidy who last prayed to you under these same flags at the age of fifteen. I was then a schoolboy and not happy. The occasion was Remembrance Day; my cheeks, be it noted, ran wet with love as the Last Post played, and I specifically asked you for a quick, useful death against appalling odds. I should now like to revise my request. I don't want death any more; I want life, and only Thou, oh Lord, can provide it. So please don't let me wait too long, Amen.

And attended a Rugby match on the first fifteen field and cheered for his old school, thinking of Sandra and wondering whether he had sinned against her, fearing the answer yes. There, vaguely scanning the home team for the kind of boy he might have been, he encountered Mrs. Harabee, one of a small army of women who had tried to teach him music.

"Why it's Doubtful," cried Mrs. Harabee, a little brown lady with short hair and a beret. "Wearing a buttonhole! Doubtful, how on earth are you?"

Doubtful because he was a doubtful volunteer to music, and had remained so until she had despaired of him.

Doubtful because Old Hugo had made them an offer on the fees and scandalised the Bursar. The offer had comprised a second mortgage on a commercial hotel in Henley, but the Bursar was no friend of catering. Doubtful because . . .

"Hullo, Mrs. Harabee," said Cassidy. "How are you? *Heard about Flaherty, Mrs. Harabee?*

And it came back to him that she had also been his mother, and housed him in a red-brick bedroom on the Yeovil Road at a time when he was in mortal conflict with Old Hugo.

"How did it all work out for you?" she asked, as if they were meeting in Heaven.

"Not too bad Mrs. Harabee. I went into advertising first, then I invented things and formed a company."

"Well done," said Mrs. Harabee in the tone she used for applauding an easy phrase of music. "And what became of that foul father of yours?"

"He died," said Cassidy, feeling it was easier to kill Old Hugo than explain him. "He went to prison and died."

"Poor lamb," said Mrs. Harabee. "I always had a *very* soft spot for him."

They walked slowly down the lane, carried by the stream of tilting straw hats.

"You can come to tea if you want," said Mrs. Harabee.

But Cassidy knew he was too old for her.

"I've got to get back I'm afraid," he said. "We've got a big deal coming off with America. I have to be on the end of a phone."

Before they parted, she became quite strict.

"Now Doubtful have you got boys?"

"Yes, Mrs. Harabee. Two. Mark and Hugo."

"Have you put them down for Sherborne?"

"Not yet, Mrs. Harabee."

"Well you must."

"I will."

"Otherwise *however* can we go on? If the Old Boys aren't loyal, who will be? And after all, you can obviously afford it."

"I'll do it next week," said Cassidy.

"Do it *now*. Run up to the porter's lodge and do it now, before you forget."

"I will," Cassidy promised and watched her up the hill, a steady pace and a healthy stride.

Walking again as the evening came, he found the narrow streets behind the Digby, and smelt the woodsmoke and the damp embracing smell of English stone; caught from the windows of schoolhouses scraps of woodwind music from half-instructed mouths; remembered the pain of loving and having no one to love; and envied Mrs. Harabee that her love could be at once so single and so diffuse.

And searched the darkening faces for the policeman's daughter.

Bella? Nellie? Ella? He no longer knew. She was fifteen, Cassidy sixteen; and since then his tastes had never seriously progressed, neither beyond her age nor the experience she gave him. Her breasts were irrepressible, her hips plump as cottage bread, and her hair was long and blond. He had her on weekdays in the summer after cricket, in the remoter bunkers of Sherborne Golf Course, lying side by side, hands only. She had never allowed him to enter her. For all he knew she was virgin to this day, for she had a terror of pregnancy and the most exaggerated notion of the agility of semen.

"They *walk*," she assured him once, as they lay in their tiny dune, her green eyes wide with sincerity. "They find the way by smell and *walk* there."

Despite these restrictions, he had never possessed anyone so fully, nor wanted anyone so urgently. She caressed him as skilfully as he caressed himself; in return he touched her as he pleased, lingered for hours over the gifts of her flesh. Her full, creaseless body was at once adolescent and maternal; her moist ovens, strained through membranes of cheap silk, were the incubators of his life and lust; as to her aweful susceptibility to his own progenital seed, it served only to deepen their relationship. As she had borne him, so she could conceive by him: mother and daughter had assumed him equally.

And thought of Sandra again, and whether he had ever loved her that way, perhaps he had, perhaps he hadn't.

In the pub, the television made its own blue firelight and a small dog barked for bacon-flavoured crisps.

"Zero," said Angie on the telephone. "Not a word."

"Not a hope," he told Sandra, pretending to call from Reading, where he had pretended to go on a pretended errand of charity; pretence being his only means of earning praise, and privacy. "Not a hope," he repeated with conviction. "The National Playing Fields Association have bagged the only possible site."

And drank six whiskies, Talisker, recently his favourite.

And bought a half-bottle of a blended malt, the flat shape, to fit into his pocket.

11

Dear Mark, he wrote in bed that night, in an old hotel in Marlborough, in the make-believe pages of his drunken fantasy. So that you never have to wonder who your parents are, or how you came to life, I am going to give you a brief rundown of how it all happened, so that you can decide for yourself how much you owe the world, and how much the world owes you.

Mummy and Daddy met in Dublin at a dance. Daddy was wearing his first dinner jacket and Grandpa Cassidy was the headwaiter. . . .

He began again. Not Dublin: Oxford. Why the hell had he thought of Dublin? *Nothing Irish about us old son, the Cassidys are English to the core.* Oxford. Oxford because Sandra was studying domestic science in a dark house in Woodstock. Oxford, that was it, a May ball, five guineas a single ticket, Old Hugo was not even on the horizon.

Mummy was a haunted, spindly girl, but very pretty in a death-wish sort of way and she wore a Cinderella dress that sometimes looked silver and sometimes seemed to be covered in ash. . . .

Hating her parents, pressing her head against his puckered shirt front as they moved to their parents' music.

Daddy gave Mummy the benefit of his conversation to which Mummy listened with melancholy intensity and later, when Daddy left her in order to dance with someone jollier, she sat in a chair and declined all other invitations. When Daddy returned, Mummy rose to him with unsmiling obedience. Early in the morning, partly out of politeness, and partly out of a sense of occasion, and partly perhaps to challenge such evident integrity, Daddy took Mummy on a punt (which is a flat boat you push along with a stick) and explained in a succession of pleasantly apologetic sentences that he had fallen in love with her.

123

He chose a confessive style modelled on a very romantic French film star named Jean Gabin whom he had recently seen at the Scala: it was a style which leaned on a sense of loss rather than of gain. It was nothing she need worry about, he assured her, she should feel no guilt or obligation, he was a man after all and would find his own way of dealing with it. Before Daddy had quite finished, Mummy seized him in a refugee's embrace and said she loved him too, and so they lay in the punt exchanging kisses, watching the sun rise over Magdalen Chapel while they strained their ears to hear the choir singing from the tower. Because you know, every first of May the choir all stand on the top of the tower and sing a song, but all *Daddy* heard was the early lorries rumbling over the bridge and the laughter of upper-class undergraduates throwing bottles into the water.

A lorry changed gear; the ceiling rocked in the half-darkness. Watch that Heaven, Flaherty.

"I love you," Mummy said, closing her eyes and breathing the words inward like a drug.

"I love *you*," Daddy assured her. "I've never said that to anyone before," which is supposed, for some reason, to make it extra true. Putting his hand inside the Cinderella dress Daddy felt the frozen pips of Mummy's bosom and it was like touching an orphan somehow, touching himself, only a lady. Then he saw the light of eternity shining in her virgin eye and was *very* gratified to think that so much animal energy was exclusively available to himself.

Flaherty was drifting round the room chanting Old Testament slogans through glistening alcoholic lips. Opening his eyes wide, Cassidy successfully despatched him.

Throughout the term, so far as I remember, we met regularly. Mummy seemed to expect it and Daddy (naturally a very polite person) was of course quite ready, when

time allowed, to receive anybody's admiration, as we all
are. So we met on Sunday mornings at Something Lock
after Mummy had been to church, and on Wednesday
evenings at the Something Restaurant after Daddy had
been to the cinema. Sometimes Mummy brought one of
her lovely picnics made in the domestic science kitchens.
Daddy did not tell Mummy he went to the cinema because
he thought she might disapprove, so he told her instead
that he went to All Souls for tea with *Rowse*. Now A. L.
Rowse is a very grand historian and also something of a
popular name so naturally Daddy thought he would be a
good person to be protected by. Rowse had taken him up,
he explained, as a result of a few essays he had written,
and might very well be sponsoring him for a *Fellowship*,
which is something every undergraduate thinks he ought
to have.

"Aren't they all *bachelors* at All Souls?" Mummy asked.

"It's changing," said Daddy, because of course bachelors aren't married, and Mummy and Daddy had to be
married to have you and Hug, didn't they?

Now you may well wonder what Mummy and Daddy
talked about. Well, they talked about *their* Mummy
and Daddy. Grandpa Groat was in Africa (where he
still is) busy completing his time. The mere mention of
him made Mummy extremely angry. "He's so *stupid*," she
said stamping her foot on the towpath. "And Mummy's
stupid too," meaning Granny. Most of all she despised
their values. Grandpa Groat, she said, cared only for his
pension and Granny Groat cared only for her servants
and neither of them had ever stopped to wonder what life
was really all about. Mummy hoped they would stay in
Africa for ever, it would serve them right for going
there in the first place.

Not to be outdone, Daddy told Mummy about Grandpa
Cassidy, how all his life Daddy had camped in places
and never lived in them, fleeing before the wrath of
Grandpa's creditors; how his housemaster at Sherborne
had told him that Grandpa Cassidy was the devil, and how
Grandpa Cassidy had said very much the same about his
housemaster; and how Daddy had found it very hard to
know whom, if either, to believe.

"I mean *God* what a way to bring somebody up,"
Daddy protested.

"Specially you," said Mummy and it was understood between them that their own children would get a better chance, which is you and Hug. So you see, Mummy and Daddy were child martyrs to a grown-up world and that is what I will never let you be if I can ever prevent it, I promise. They wanted to be *better* and in a way they still do. The trouble is, they never discovered how, because you can't really spread much love around unless, in a funny way, you love yourself as well. Sorry to preach, but it's true.

So Mummy and Daddy watched each other very, very closely, each waiting for the other to revert to the follies of his parents, so in the end we did, both of us, because we're inheritors, like everyone else, and because sometimes the only way to punish our parents is to imitate them. But all that came later.

So anyway.

Well, one day, Granny Groat turned up with a big trunk, all the way from Darkest Somewhere, looking not at all like the little old lady in the Babar books, which is how she looks now; oh no. She arrived with that mute, declining beauty which Daddy has always mistaken for great intelligence, and immediately Daddy loved Granny Groat, loved her more than Mummy in fact because she wasn't cross, and appointed her a Life Mother, which was very, very unwise. Mummy knew it was unwise but Daddy wouldn't listen to her, because he wanted love all round him even if he couldn't have it close. And of course, Granny got very excited because she had never had a son, and she was *specially* pleased that Daddy was blond after all the black children she'd had to look at for so long.

"You're quite *sure* you want to marry her?" she asked him with a terribly intelligent giggle. "She's such a *funny* little thing."

"I love her," said Daddy, which when you're young is a sort of snobby thing to say, and makes you feel better, particularly when you're not sure you do.

"Get out, Flaherty."

Flaherty refused to move.

"*Get out!*" Cassidy sat up sharply. Someone was banging on the wall.

"Get out!" he yelled a third time, and the figure withdrew.

Mark; contrary to all you may have heard the wedding was not a success.

Mummy wanted the Church of Saint Somebody of Somewhere, beside the lock where she and Daddy had talked so much of love. She wanted no one for herself except a seedsman called Bacon who lived in Bagshot and had been her gardener when she was a little girl, and she wanted no one for Daddy but A. L. Rowse and just ordinary witnesses brought in from the fields. Finally we were married in Bournemouth where Granny Groat had taken a flat, in a moorish red-brick church bigger even than Sherborne Abbey, with a very old organist playing "Abide with Me." I'm afraid Mr. Bacon never came. Perhaps he couldn't leave his seeds, perhaps he was dead, we never knew.

Or perhaps, Cassidy reflected, gazing at the prints of deformed race horses, he never existed at all, save in the sad, imagined places of her childhood.

A. L. Rowse never came either. He was in America giving a course of lectures. He didn't send a present but Daddy (who had intercepted the invitation) explained they knew one another far too well for that kind of silly formality. The bridesmaid was your Auntie Snaps, Mummy's sister, fifteen and very premature in low red velvet, and Auntie Snaps sulked all through the ceremony. A few weeks later, back at boarding school, she gave her maidenhead to a labourer in the potting shed. *"You* do it," she told Mummy. "So why the hell shouldn't I?"

As a religious ceremony the service reminded Daddy of his Confirmation: an awesome contract with someone he did not know. And he could not help wishing, as the processive anthems drove him into the daylight, that he had not been quite so taken with Jean Gabin.

But Mark, tell me. Is this love? After all, *you're* innocent, *you* should know. You see, just possibly it's all there is; the best the world has got, and all the rest is waiting, like Daddy is waiting now.

Goodnight, Mrs. Harabee.
Goodnight, Flaherty.
Goodnight, Sandra.
Love, goodnight.

12

And incredibly, back in London, Cassidy waited still.

"You've got a simply smashing horoscope," said Miss Mawdray.

Breasts like doves, he thought, lusting after her in his idleness, little beaks pecking the angora. Legs of a boy, hips of a whore, hoares and hips; joke. God knows what she can wear up there. No white or black to mark the spot; just the burry brown fog of a touched-out photograph, a vaginal phantom yet to be recorded . . . Ha! See how she folds her thighs to embrace the unseen member!

"I got a new book," Angie explained, meaning magazine.

He was standing at the familiar window. His desk repelled him, a symbol of sedentary inertia. Miss Mawdray, having no such inhibitions, was balanced on her babychair.

"I could do with a bit of luck," Cassidy confessed.

She began reading him a long prophecy; it must have been half a page. He heard it at a distance, believing nothing. His birth group had been singled out, she said; special consideration for the Scales. Commerce would smile on him, she promised, friendships would flourish; have courage, she exhorted, go forward, advance, thrust, brandish. Do not allow unnecessary hindrances to impede you, impediments to hinder you, obstacles to obstruct you: a rare constellation would bless all initiatives.

"*All?*" Cassidy repeated, being jocular. "Well, well, I must try some new ones."

"And in the field of love," she read, keeping her head well down and following the line with her finger as her voice became slightly louder, "Venus and Aphrodite will jointly smile on your boldest venture."

"Fine," said Cassidy. "Just fine. Why don't they clean these curtains?" he asked, tugging at the net.

"They've just been done," said Angie with spirit. "You know very well they have. You were only complaining last week they'd been taken down."

Cassidy did not care for that kind of reply.

"Tell me," he said casually, his back still turned towards her, "what's happened to your engagement ring?"

He would not have asked, but for her retaliation. "Your engagement ring," he insisted, turning now and pointing to the extra quarter-inch of nakedness. "You haven't *lost* it, have you, Angie? That would be very bad."

"I'm just not wearing it, am I?" she said in a small voice, and though she must have known that he was still facing her, did not lift her head.

"I'm sorry," he said, "I didn't mean to pry."

Hangdog, he returned to the window. A scene, he thought glumly, we're going to have a scene. I've been an oaf again and now she's hurt. The last scene had involved Meale, he remembered; Angie had wanted Cassidy to provide an excuse for her not to accept an invitation from him and he had declined.

"You must get out of it for yourself," he had told her, Cassidy the champion of plain dealing. "If you don't like him, tell him. He'll only go on asking you if you don't." Well now he had made a second, equally unfortunate sally into her private life, and he was about to pay the price.

He waited.

"I wear it when I feel like it," said Angie at last, to his back. Her voice was still quiet, but it was already breaking with anger. "And if I don't feel like it I won't bloody bother, so sod it."

"I have apologised," the Chairman reminded her.

"I don't mind if you have or not. I'm not interested in apology am I? I've gone off him, that's all, and it's none of your business."

"I'm sure it's just a tiff," Cassidy assured her. "It'll blow over, you'll see."

"It *won't*," she insisted, furious. "I don't want it to blow over. He's rotten in bed and he's rotten out of it, so why *should* I marry him if I don't want to?"

Not quite certain whether to believe the evidence of his ears, Cassidy remained silent.

"They're too young," said Angie, smacking her book on her knee. "I get bloody sick of them. They all think they're marvellous and they're just *babies*. Fucking selfish, silly *babies*."

"Well," said Cassidy stalking the safety of his desk. "I don't know about *that*," and laughed, as if ignorance were a joke. "Angie, do you often swear like that?"

She rose in a single movement, taking his cup with one hand and tugging at the hem of her skirt with the other. "Not unless I'm goaded, do I?"

"How was the dentist?" he asked, hoping by small talk to restore a certain formality.

"Smashing," she said, with a sudden very tender smile. "I could have eaten him alive, honest."

Cassidy's dentist; part of a private health scheme for the staff. A man of forty-five; married.

"Good."

He made the next question even more casual: "Any messages at all . . . nothing out of the way?"

"A daft parson rang, that's all. Wanting free prams for orphans. I put a note on your desk. Irish."

"Irish? How do you know?"

"Because he spoke Irish, silly."

"He didn't leave a message?"

"No."

Warmer. "He didn't leave his number?"

"Look, he was daft, I told you! Lay off."

She gazed at him, her hand resting on the door handle, an angel of puzzled compassion.

"If you'd tell me what it is, Aldo," she said at last very quietly, "I'd know what to look for, wouldn't I?"

The resentment, the aggression had all gone. Only a childish supplication remained. "I'm dead safe, honest, Aldo. You can tell me *anything,* they wouldn't drag it out of me, no one would. Not if it's about you."

"It's personal," said Cassidy at last, his tongue clicking awkwardly on the dry roof of his mouth. "It's something very personal. Thanks."

"Oh," said Angie.

"Sorry," said Cassidy, and returned to his curtained window on an unresponsive world.

And still waiting, went to a crucial dinner at the unstately home of Dr. John and Somebody Elderman.

Mrs. Elderman was a sublimated graduate and the leader of the local dramatic set; while to her husband fell the important rôle of Cassidy's medical advisor. The Cassidys had not so much met the Eldermans as descended to them, gone back to them, as it were, when brighter social hopes had been extinguished. John Elderman was a small man physically, and though meticulously faithful to his general practice, was known to read widely on the subject of the mind. Some years back, he had written a paper called "Positive Divorce," and the tear-sheets were still generously displayed in every avant-garde room. Since then, the Eldermans had been much consulted in the Crescent, not only by the Cassidys, and they enjoyed a great reputation in the field of marriage guidance, and in all matters relating to love. Their principle, where Cassidy had met it, was to urge self-expression in the interests of self-discipline; no one, they insisted, was *obliged* to be unhappy; love was a gift, derived from flowers and rock.

The obscurity of this advice was deepened by the figure of Mrs. Elderman, a very big woman who wore gowns of brown hemp and ran a tangled garden on lines laid down by Rudolph Steiner. Her hair, which was mainly grey, similarly flourished. Separated rather than parted, it was bonded with flax on either side, like two enormous egg-timers made of steel wool. Loathing her, Cassidy had permanently forgotten her first name.

Even before they arrived there, the occasion had taken on for Cassidy a quality of dream-like frightfulness. He had come home late, by way of the Audley Arms, after a long and exceptionally tiresome meeting of his Export Ginger Group, and Sandra accused him of smelling of drink.

"How many did you have?"

"One. But it was meths."

"How *can* you be so cheap?"

"Have one yourself. Plenty in the broom cupboard."

"You wouldn't find it *in* you, would you, to tell me what on *earth* is making you so bad-tempered?"

"Spring," said Cassidy, scrubbing his teeth. From the main drawing room came a sudden burst of machine-gun fire. "What the *hell's* that?"

"What's *what?*"

"That hammering. Who's at the gates for Christ's sake?" He knew very well what it was.

"The workmen are putting up a moulding. An eighteenth-century *moulding* which Heather and I bought two *months* ago from a breaker's yard for ten shillings. I've told you about it fifty times; but still."

"Ten bob!" He used his Jewish rag-trade voice. "Ten bob for the moulding, fine. Ten bob I can afford. But Christ Almighty what about the *labour* already?"

"Do you mind speaking properly?"

"It's after five o'clock, those lads are getting about twenty guineas an hour!"

Sandra chose silence. He returned to his East End Jewish.

"So will somebody tell me what the hell's the point of an eighteenth-century moulding in a nineteenth-century house? Everyone knows this place is Victorian except us, ask a rabbi."

Still she chose silence.

"I mean *Christ*," Cassidy demanded of the bathroom mirror, in which, like a female sentinel before the doors of Downing Street, Sandra waited vertical and motionless.

"*Christ*," he repeated, in an Irish brogue he had been working on for several days. "I mean why the hell can't we live in the *twentieth* century for a change?"

"Because you're not to be trusted with it," she snapped, and Cassidy secretly awarded her set and match. "And there's no post," she added nastily, "if that's what you're bothered about."

Cassidy, studiously applying lather, offered no reply.

"Anyway, why isn't Hugo in bed?" he asked, knowing that answer also.

"He's been invited."

"What to?"

"The Eldermans'. *As* we have. *As* you know. If there's any point in going still," she added looking at her watch.

The Eldermans had squadrons of children and dined early so that their guests could have the benefit.

"*Bloody* silly. Dinner for a kid of seven! *Needlessly exposing him to danger*: that's what it is. A doctor, I ask you. A fully fledged paid-up medic, even if he does come from Gerrard's Cross. What if Hugo falls over? What if he stubs his toe? What if he gets kicked? Hugo hates those children, you know he does. So do I. Otiose little prigs," he said.

"You know what *I* think." Sandra's mother, hovering thinly at their bedroom doorway, in blue-tinted glasses and a dress of little-girl yellow, gave a titter of terrified goodwill. "I think mercy and truth are married together."

"Shut *up*, Mummy," said Sandra.

"*Come* on, darlings," her mother begged. "*Kiss*. I would at your age."

"*Mummy*," said Sandra.

"Darling, shouldn't you give something to the workmen?"

"He did," Sandra snapped. "He gave them five pounds. He's utterly *gross*."

They left in procession, five yards between each along the pavement, Cassidy carrying Hugo in his arms like a casualty of war, and Sandra's mother bringing up the rear, jingling precariously in her cowbell jewellery.

"At least he's a *doctor*, darling," she called enticingly to Cassidy over her daughter's head.

"Aldo *hates* doctors," Sandra retorted. "You know he does. Except specialists of course," she added nastily. "*Specialists* can do no wrong, can they? Specialists are absolutely perfect, even if they do charge fifty guineas for an X-ray."

"Why's Mummy cross?" Hugo asked from inside the blanket.

"Because Daddy's been drinking," Sandra snapped.

"She's not cross," said Cassidy. "It's just Granny getting on her nerves," and pressed the bell marked "House."

"Bet you've got the wrong evening," said Sandra.

"Greetings old man!" John Elderman cried. Perhaps to augment his height, he wore a chef's hat. From beneath it pink-fringed eyes of palest blue regarded Cassidy with innocent sagacity. He stood very straight, thin shoulders braced, but the effort did him little good.

"Sorry we're late," said Cassidy.

"Smashing buttonhole," said Elderman.

"He's been wearing them all week," said Sandra, as if she were giving him in charge.

She's been briefing them, thought Cassidy; and now they're going to observe me.

Heather Ast had already arrived. He could see her kneeling in the doorway, her agreeable rump lifted towards him while she played with the Eldermans' foul children.

"Hi, Heather!" he cried cheerfully.

"Oh hullo, Sandra," said Heather, ignoring him.

"Hi, Ast," said Cassidy, but found no audience.

He was in a menagerie, he noticed, of human apes. Posturing witless apes. He had not seen the Eldermans in quite that light before, but now he realised that they were not people at all but gibbons and their children were emerging gibbons, coming on fast. The Niesthals alone escaped his censure. They were an old, stately couple dressed in black and they ran musical evenings for friendly Gentiles in a very valuable house in St. John's Wood. Cassidy loved them because they were hopeless and kind. The Niesthals had come a little late because the old man did not close his Old Master gallery till seven; and they stood among the warring children like benefactors visiting a workhouse.

"Who is this one?" Mrs. Niesthal cried, bravely handling a junior Elderman. "Ah *naturally*, it is a Cassidy, see Friedl, you can see it from the *eyes*, it is a Cassidy."

"I say John old boy," said Cassidy.

"Yes, old man."

"Those Niesthals hate kids, you know."

"Never mind. Give 'em supper and shove 'em all upstairs."

Not Hugo you won't, butcher.

"Been refreshing ourselves I hear," said Heather nastily, out of the corner of her mouth. "Who's the button-hole in aid of, anyway?"

"Meeow," said Cassidy, rather more audibly than he intended; and two Elderman girls, picking up the note, repeated it very loud: *"Meeow, meeow."*

"Like a cat," Mrs. Niesthal explained to her husband, and they trooped into the dining room, stepping over several dogs which scavenged at the door.

Cassidy was feeling sick, and no one cared. He was sure he looked pale, and he knew he had a fever, but no one comforted him, no one lowered his voice in his proximity.

He had eaten boiled tongue, which reminded him of the Army, and he had drunk homemade wine which reminded him of nothing he had ever tasted in his life. Nettles, they made it of, apparently, foraged in Burnham Beeches and transported in their proudly distintegrating van.

"*God* it's alcoholic," one woman said. "I mean honestly John, I'm feeling *so* tipsy."

"Has it got cinnamon in it?" asked another—Mrs. Groat, in fact, for whom cinnamon was an objection, it loosened the stomach.

"No," said Cassidy, and won an embarrassed silence.

At the stove, John Elderman was adding Marc de Bourgogne to a pudding nobody wanted.

Cassidy was seated between two divorcées, a class of woman the Eldermans encouraged. To my left, Heather Ast, normally congenial to me, but tonight abhorrent, having been corrupted by the Abalone Women's Liberation Front. To my right, weighing in at about four stone one, an emaciated sea plant called Felicity, also a wine brewer, also divorced, also of the Unaligned Left, star of the Abalone Rep and famous in voluptuous rôles. The conversation however is being hogged by a Foreign Office couple; they have been brought by a child which speaks only Portuguese, it sits on one side of Hugo dressed in earrings and national costume. The wife is an improbable veteran of remote trouble spots, and very disenchanted. Who will teach Libby English? she moans. It was the price for going native; the English school in Angola was too reactionary.

"Oh, she will pick it up," said Mrs. Niesthal confidently. "Listen we also had that problem." The Niesthals laugh to one another, the rest of us are too progressive to admit that European Jews are not descended from Oliver Cromwell.

"It's such a joy," said Ast, admiring Elderman, "to find a man who can *really* cook."

"So many are just frauds," the Sea Plant agreed from his other side, waving in a slow current.

"We all are," said Cassidy.

"Frauds?" cried old Niesthal, making a joke of it. "Don't talk to me about frauds my God, I am buying them every day two dozen."

A friendly laugh went up, led by John Elderman.

"Friedl says *terrible* things," Mrs. Niesthal declared cheerfully.

"So does Heather," said Cassidy, regretting it too late.

The children had been put at the far end of the table and Hugo was reading the *Evening Standard*, his thumb wedged into his mouth like a pipe. Two Elderman girls, supine with food, clutched each other in a grimy embrace.

"Warsaw," John Elderman proposed through the steam of his concoction, referring to an earlier conversation about the Free East. "That's the place. Never seen medicine like it." He was wearing a short-sleeved shirt, and his arms were thin and silky like a girl's. "Drink deep," he exhorted, throwing back his head. "Drink deep. Be merry."

"Well," said Mrs. Groat, ever anxious to show that she was attending. "Well, not *too* deep," and giggled through the blue windows of her unnecessary spectacles.

"Well, *well*," said Cassidy, and Sandra shot him a glance of loathing. "Well, well, well, well, *well*."

The Elderman wife said she wished we could abolish private medicine. She was sitting not at the table but on the floor, half lying, a casualty of her husband's cooking, and as she spoke she pulled at her long, frizzy hair in frightful imitation of a mediaeval princess. She had recently taken up with *art nouveau* and wore a buckle of unpolished lead.

"Particularly specialists," she added, not looking at Cassidy. "I think it's so disgraceful that anyone can go in and *buy* specialist medical attention at the drop of a hat provided he's rich. It's so against the sense of it all. So *unorganic*. After all, if there *is* natural selection, it's not going to be done by money is it?"

Her face had reddened with the nettles.

"Quite right," said Sandra, and closed her mouth quickly, ready for the next round.

"Darling are you sure?" her mother asked with a frightened lowering of the jaw. "We could *never* have managed *without* in the Tropics."

"Oh *Mummy*," said Sandra in a rage.

"Sandra was born there," said Cassidy encouragingly. "Weren't you, Sandra? Why don't you tell them about it Grans, they'd like that. Tell them about the doctor who was plastered."

Hugo, turning a page, snorted into his fist.

"We were in *Nebar*," Mrs. Groat immediately began explaining to the Sea Plant. "It used to be the Gold Coast, then it was Liberia—is it Liberia, darling, I never remember these new names?—or is Liberia the *old* name?—well of course there *wasn't* any Liberia in our day!—" rather as if there wasn't penicillin either "—so it *had* to be the Gold Coast really, didn't it? We didn't have Liberia," she declared loudly with an arch smile to advertise the joke. "We had the Army instead."

"You see," Sandra hissed triumphantly to her mother, "*nobody* finds it funny. *Aldo,* shut up."

She was too late; Cassidy was already applauding. It was not a deliberate provocation. Rather, it was as if his two hands, bored with lying on the table, had decided to get up and do something of their own; not till afterwards, uncomfortably reliving the moment with Sandra, did Cassidy secretly recall a different pair of hands applauding Helen at the restaurant in Bath.

"They laugh when your father says it," her mother replied when the applause ended; and blushed.

"Coming up," said John Elderman, as a pillar of smoke shot from the overheated pan. "Who's number one?"

Ignoring him, his nameless wife rolled on her massive hip and, jamming a bottle into the mouth of an adjacent baby, raised the subject of South East Asia. Had they all had the news? she asked, naming a country Cassidy had never heard of. They had not. Well the Americans had invaded it, she said, the local government had requested intervention. They had marched in at five that morning, the Russians were threatening to retaliate.

"Up the Marines," said Cassidy, but not loud enough this time for anyone but Heather to hear.

"Hey you," Heather said softly, laying a cautionary hand on his knee. "Ease off, you'll frighten the game."

At the same moment Hugo asked his question. He had played no part in the proceedings till now, so his intervention had at least the advantage of novelty.

"Why can't you love snow?"

His thumb was still wedged in his mouth and his brows were drawn hard down over his grey unblinking eyes.

A concentrated silence preceded the volley:

"Because it melts!" Prunella Elderman shouted. "Because it's too cold, because it's all white and wet."

The other sisters joined in. A baby was screaming. A child was banging a spoon on the table, another was jumping on a chair. Seizing the carafe of nettles, Cassidy replenished his glass.

"Because it's not alive!" the velveted sisters screamed. "Because you can't eat it! Why then? Why, why, why?"

Hugo took his time, shifted his plaster leg, turned a page of his newspaper. "Because you can't marry it," he announced gravely.

In the general groan, Shamus made his appearance.

He could not have been further from Cassidy's mind. His thoughts, he afterwards recalled with clarity, had drifted momentarily to the distressing implications of Hugo's riddle: whether it betrayed a hidden preoccupation with domestic tension, whether the pains of a fractured leg had temporarily unhinged the tender child's reason. If he had anything else in mind at all, then it was Ast's hand: was it a restraining hand? Did she know it was still on his knee; had she left it there like a handbag? Was it an olive branch after her earlier, unprovoked irascibility? Seeking perhaps the comfort of a male ally in this moment of sexual uncertainty, Cassidy transferred his attention to John Elderman, mentally selecting as he did so a topic of mutual interest, a football match, John's fascinating old van; and was therefore surprised to find in his place Shamus, not standing but suspended in the steam stirring the evil-smelling pudding with Elderman's wooden spoon, his black eyes fixed upon Cassidy across the candlelight, his moist face glowing with impish complicity.

"Hey lover," he was saying. "Isn't it a bloody bore? Urban proles having compromisers' orgy."

Simultaneously or perhaps a fraction before, since psychic experience has no equivalent in time, he heard Shamus' names, Christian name and surname both, spoken out recklessly from his left side.

"*Such* a pity he died so young," Ast declared, her hand a trifle higher on his thigh. "After all, who else *can* one read who's *modern?*"

Then John Elderman gave him his pudding and he burnt his mouth.

In retrospect, of course, Cassidy was better able to understand what had happened. His senses, taken up by Hugo's riddle and Ast's understanding hand, had failed to remark that a second, independent conversation was going forward between the women to either side of him: that is to say between Ast and the Sea Plant. For some while, as he afterwards realised, they had been exchanging murmured intellectual commonplaces drawn from Sunday newspapers, no doubt upon the subject of the modern novel. Thus the abrupt, unheralded mention of Shamus' name, violently intruding upon an unprotected corner of his mind, had caused him in his confusion to imagine in the vivid frame of Elderman the features of his banished friend. It was also true that the four large whiskies at the Audley Arms —not to mention a recent visit to the lavatory where Bear had consumed a little something from a clandestine bottle —had lingered somewhat with the monotony of the evening.

Also he had drunk a lot of nettles.

But such insights came to him too late, for while his natural discretion implored him to be silent, he had already overcome his first experience of a ghost and was launched into a sprightly, if injudicious, argument about the great author.

"Dead?" he repeated as soon as he had emptied his glass. "Dead? He's not *dead*. He's just been kicked around so much he did a bunk. Can't blame him for *that,* can you? As a matter of fact I happen to know he's just about to turn in a new book—"

"I *hate* this pudding," Hugo loudly interjected but no one paid him any notice.

Ast's hand had reached, it seemed to Cassidy, a point at which no woman, however absent-minded, can unconsciously arrive. Abruptly, it was now withdrawn.

"—which by all accounts," he concluded confidently, "will knock all his other books into a cocked hat. *Moon* included."

How, so soon after the shock of Shamus' ghostly reappearance—or as now seemed possible, his reincarnation— Cassidy found the courage to speak up so boldly was a mystery he never solved, though he did wonder in his more playful moments whether Shamus belonged to a small élite known only to himself, of ghosts who had the gift of imparting confidence rather than alarm.

"He *died* in sixty-*one*," said Ast, articulating very clearly for the benefit of the deaf. Her wide breasts, roused with anger, had lifted against their seam of harvest twine.

"He's been in hiding," said Cassidy.

"How do *you* know?" Sandra demanded. "You've never read a novel in your life."

"It's got petrol in it," said Hugo and with a clatter pushed his plate into the middle of the table.

"Shut up," said Sandra.

"I *love* it," said Prunella Elderman and put her tongue out at the Anglo-Portuguese.

At this point, Cassidy was reminded of Heather Ast's husband, a reedy, bow-tied man who, she said, had woken up one morning and decided he was queer. He thought of him very specifically in pyjamas and a nightcap, sitting up with a jolt as the tea came in. "Heather," he says, "news for you. I'm a poof." This imaginative portrait set him giggling for some time so that Sandra was beside herself with rage.

"Just know," he said, at last recovering his composure. "Just keeping a finger on the literary pulse."

"*Ooh*," said Sandra, fists clenched.

"I want more pudding," said Prunella Elderman, undeterred.

"Then eat Hugo's," yelled Somebody Elderman from the safety of the floor.

"He *died* in *France*," Ast resumed, in the low tremulous voice of a woman martyred by patience, and laying her errant hand firmly on the scrubbed table, imprisoned it with the other.

"What did he die of then?" Cassidy asked with a distinctly patronising smile. "What's the diagnosis, eh John boy?"

"Of TB I assume," snapped Ast. "Isn't that what they all die of?"

"Meeow," said Cassidy, and the children at once took it up: "Meeow, meeow, meeow."

Ast's precarious calm was fast deserting her. Within its sprawling tent of blond hair, her face, emaciated by pointless intelligence, now suddenly darkened.

"You haven't the least *idea* what they go through have you? You're so damn rich you don't even realise what it means to die abroad, penniless . . . to be denied a decent burial by some idiotic Catholic priest . . . to *rot* in some shallow common grave . . ."

"No," Cassidy agreed cheerfully. "It's true I haven't made that experience. However," he continued, slipping into his smoothest boardroom tone, "I'm afraid you're wrong. My information is incontrovertible. It may be true that he was given out for dead. It is also possible that he deliberately inspired the rumour. The reason is simple" —he let them wait a moment. "He was driven to distraction by the publishing profession." Out of the corner of his eye he saw the once-coveted shape of Ast stir and then hold still. "Whom he describes as ghouls and Gerrard's Crossers, and anything else that comes into his head. They hounded him until he could hardly think straight, let alone write. He was their golden goose and as usual they tried to kill him. Escape was the only answer," helping himself to more nettles. "Thank God he made it, says I," he added, emptying his glass. "The Queen, God bless her."

Only the Niesthals joined the toast.

"The Queen," the old man muttered. They drank looking down, a private communion.

Allowing the focus of his eyes conveniently to mist, Cassidy saw Somebody Elderman's massive fingers close round her beads, which were brown and shrivelled like nuts, and her husband put down the Marc de Bourgogne. At the same moment, Sandra's mother began talking about the rain in Nebar, how it fell much more than people realised and cleansed nothing.

"Really the smells seem to thrive on it, I don't know why." The only place was the hills, but the Brigadier her husband had not cared for heights. "So I had to have her all alone," she said. "Just a nurse and this *dreadful* drunk doctor sent up by the Commissioner. He kept dogs I remember, there was moulting hair all over his sleeves, you wouldn't do that, would you, John? She was such a funny little thing," she added when no one spoke. "All red and angry. Hugo was just the same, weren't you Hug?"

"No," said Hugo.

Sandra had evidently decided it was time to put Hugo to bed. Taking him by the wrist she marched him to the door.

"Look after him," John Elderman advised, holding her in the enveloping embrace he vouchsafed to all afflicted women. "He seems to be under a spot of strain." He was talking about Cassidy not Hugo. "Give him one of your valium now and then, calm him down. Doesn't matter if he drinks."

"Sawbones," said Cassidy. "You think you're a great big butch specialist but you're just a rotten little leech. Sodder."

"Sleep it off, I should," said Elderman, smiling sportily. "Old man."

"Flaherty is God," said Cassidy in a valiant pre-trial gesture. "Flaherty rules the earth. A man is what he thinks he is."

And threw his buttonhole to Ast.

13

The nursery was also full of flowers: he slept among them often, banished there for cheek. Floppy blue flowers in different shades of pastel. Mark's bed was very narrow, no more than a mattress laid on the linoleum and draped in a soft woollen coverlet: monkish, he liked to think, conducive to sombre thoughts. Mark's toy chest was locked and that was where Cassidy kept his paperbacks, recipes for a secret culture. Some were on ancient Greece, some were on the German High Command; others were on skills he proposed one day to acquire, how to sail, how to cook for one, how to service his own car or conduct an ideal marriage. Safely contained within the bed's narrow walls, the coverlet pulled high, Cassidy selected Kahlil Gibran's *The Prophet* and turned to the passage on love.

"Daddy," said Hugo drowsily from his cot.

"Yes."

"Daddy."

"Yes, Hug."

"If Mummy goes away, do I go with you or her?"

It was a very practical enquiry.

"No one's going away."

From upstairs, they heard her telephone Auntie Snaps in Newcastle and offer to pay her fare to London.

That's right, he thought, *raise a posse.*

"Daddy."

"Yes."

"Be Shane."

Cassidy made his Wild West voice: "I'm the sheriff around these parts and these yere's *mah* deputies."

Nonsense. Sandra was saying. *He hasn't even heard of the man. He certainly hasn't read him. He couldn't anyway, he's far too lazy to read a book. . . . Nonsense, he's not under strain at all. His parasites run the office, I run the house, and every time he wants to run away he makes up some silly lie about his charities. He did it to annoy*

145

*Heather, and Beth and Mary and . . . Of course he loathes
women, that's not his fault, it's his upbringing, I realise
that, but still.*

"Daddy."

"Yes Hug."

"You *have* heard of him, haven't you?"

"Yes."

"Honest?"

"Honest."

"I knew you had. Goodnight Dad."

"Goodnight old fish."

"Dad."

"Yes Hug."

"Do Sturrock."

Western again: "Okay Sturrock, you low-down lyin'
Yankee, git off *mah* plantation."

"Bang," said Hugo.

"Bang," said Cassidy.

Another ping of the telephone.

John I'm most dreadfully sorry, said Sandra, *I mean I
really don't know what to say . . .* really . . .

Well, reality is also a problem. Not to you of course. To
me. The Eldermans. I fuck myself of the Eldermans. Who
lent them six thousand quid interest free to get rid of
their sitting tenants? Who lent them the chalet last year
for their foul kids to rip to pieces? Who—

Martial footsteps approaching.

"It's Mummy," Hugo explained, and getting up gathered
together his few necessaries.

Pogrom, thought Cassidy and dived under the bedclothes.

"Come along darling," said Sandra. "Your father's
drunk." And from the doorway, whence all her Parthian
shots were launched, "How on *earth* you have the *nerve*
to *pretend* you *care* about your *children* when all you do
is get *drunk* in front of them and *swear* and make *filthy-
imputations-against-people-they-respect . . .*" She dried up,
exhausted by emphasis.

"Come on," Cassidy urged, through the tartan blankets.
"Let's have a main verb. Let's have some bloody gram-
mar around the house, shall we? Set an example to the
children, shall we?"

Sandra sighed and drew the door nearer to her as a
shield.

"Now tell me I'm worse than my father," he suggested.

"If his leg doesn't mend," she said at last, "it will be your fault entirely."

"Night, Sturrock," said Hugo.

"Night, Shane," said Cassidy amiably.

"And in the morning," said Sandra, "I shall leave you."

Gradually the house dropped off. One by one the staircases creaked and fell silent. Her mother went to the lavatory. For a while he lay awake counting off the hours on Hugo's cuckoo clock, waiting in case she came to him. Once, still dozing, he fancied he heard again the rhythmic thudding of the fourposter and the long sharp cry of Helen's pleasure echoing down the fine curved staircase in the style of Adam. And once, struggling with the late effects of nettle wine, he discovered Shamus' strong arms locked rugger style round his aching ribs, and Helen, voice off, explaining the assault.

"You see Shamus *loves* people. It's the difference between paddling and swimming."

"When love beckons to you," wrote the Prophet, "follow him, Though his ways are hard and steep. And when his wings enfold you yield to him, Though the sword hidden among his pinions may wound you."

He fell asleep, dreaming of Hell, and Old Hugo walking over Cassidy's skull.

"Anyway," said Sandra in the morning, "I'm not going to Paris with you."

"Fine," said Cassidy.

"So you needn't think I am," said Sandra.

"I wasn't," said Cassidy.

"Don't worry," said Hugo. "You will won't you Mummy?"

Hugo is the blank slate, he thought; Hugo is me before I was written on.

He touched ninety on the motorway before the police caught up with him. For some reason they believed him when he said he had never been so fast before.

"It's my mother," he said. "She's dying."

They believed that too.

"She's at Bristol hospital," he said. "She's English born, but she's lived abroad all her life. She doesn't even speak English. She's very frightened."

"You don't own the road sir all the same," the older officer replied, embarrassed.

"What does she speak then?" the younger man asked.

"French. She's lived there all her life. She wanted to be here for the end."

"Well take it easy in future," the older one said, with a brave show of no emotion.

"I will," said Cassidy.

"What's that dial then?" the younger one asked. "The one with the orange light on it?"

"An ice-alert," said Cassidy and was about to show them how it worked when the sergeant intervened.

"Let him go, Syd," he said quietly.

"Of course. Sorry," said the constable and blushed.

He knew even before he reached the house that they had gone. The shirt was no longer hanging from the cable and the doves, hoping for food, fluttered restlessly on the portico. A tramp had left a chalk mark on the door, an arrow pointing downwards and two white crosses side by side. He pulled the iron bell and heard it clank in the Great Hall. He waited but no one came. Only the stables had word of them. A platoon of whisky bottles lay on the wet straw, shoulder to shoulder, set out by Helen's tidy hand. He picked one up. The neck was sticky with candle-wax; a film covered the mouth; at its centre, like a tiny bullet hole, a point of black carbon recalled the burnt-out flame.

His flowers were lying at the back door. "If there's no reply," he had told the girl in the green overall, "leave them on the doorstep." And there they lay, a fountain of wasted red wrapped in cellophane, big enough to commemorate a West Country infantry regiment, with the Moyses Stevens label from the lads who'd stayed behind. They must have been there a full fortnight, and the rain had kept them alive. Roses, he had told her, fine tight buds, three dozen of your very best—a dozen for each of us you see. Had written out the label with their scratchy, unwilling pen.

Loosening the card from its sodden envelope he read his own words:

To Shamus and Helen. For the fun of a lifetime, please come back. Cassidy.

Afterwards his telephone number in London. *Do please reverse the charges.*

There was a place he knew, a green hill far away in Kensal Rise, he had found it five years ago, waiting for news of Mark's operation. It lay between a graveyard and an infant school and was known as the Valhalla. No single impulse had pointed him the way, only a sense of emptiness, of blank, contactless availability, had with God's good help guided the driven father's footsteps. He had telephoned the hospital from Marble Arch: call again at seven, they would know at seven whether the operation was a success.

Walking he had found himself in a cemetery, crouching from stone to stone in a quest for buried Cassidys. And thus searching became conscious of a drift, even of a positive direction, in the movement of the crowd. Young men dressed in their Saturday uniforms, hitherto aimlessly posted in groups, glanced at their watches, formed ranks, and walked away. Not long afterwards a portly man in a mauve dinner jacket alighted from a taxi and hurried after them carrying what seemed to be a blunderbuss in a black leatherine box.

Then a miracle happened.

Barely had the mauve jacket vanished through the small wicker gate than a flock of young girls, flouncing and trembling on long uncertain legs, bright as tropical birds in their thin blouses and bell skirts, stockingless, knickerless perhaps, fell tittering from the open heaven and landed at his feet, brushing past him on the same mysterious path. Enthralled, Cassidy followed, his fantasy vaulting from one wild vision to another. What ritual, what ceremony was here observed? A hanging? A prophet? Or an orgy on the Teenage Scandinavian pattern? Time, place, even caution had deserted him. He sensed only the proximity of fulfillment drying his tongue and tantalising his soft loins. He was floating. A sexual vertigo conveyed him over the municipal tarmac. Trees, ponds, fences, mothers; in a single blur they skimmed the merest edges of his vision, guided him along the secret line.

Peritonitis was forgotten; Mark was cured.

He lived only ahead of him in the coloured squadron, in the lifting quarters and the plumed haunches, in the waft of baby powder that followed in their wake. Once he stumbled, once he heard a dog snap at him, once an old man yelled "Hey watch out" but by then he was inside, the three-shilling ticket lying like a wafer in his palm. Round him coloured stars were coursing the unwindowed church. From a raised sanctuary swaying priests pounded music he could almost hum.

He was dancing.

Dancing at arm's length with speechless girls. In small circles round their grounded handbags. Shuffling fairy rings in the French chalk. He never learned their names. Like nuns sworn to silence they took him, comforted him with the dispassion of a higher devotion, and relinquished him for other sufferers. A few, not many, rejected him on grounds of age; some abandoned him because he was clumsy or when a more favoured partner intervened. Still he did not mind: their rejection was a discipline, attaching him closer to their impenetrable community.

"Here," said a brunette. "What's that long face for then?"

"Sorry," said Cassidy, and smiled.

These were the girls he could love. The girls who passed him in buses and dressed shop windows, worked for him as secretaries, peered at him from pavements as he sat in taxis, these were his nurses, his figureheads, agelessly beautiful on a changing sea.

"You can take me home if you like," said a blonde, "if you give me a nice present."

But Cassidy declined. In the world they inhabited for him, such girls had no home but this.

He drove there now. Drove there straight from Haverdown, three and a half hours looking through a windshield. He drove there to cure himself, the same cure that had worked for Mark. He drove there without a break, without a meal, thinking of nothing because there was nothing left. He parked at a meter and walked past the last two hundred yards. Unknown, even to himself.

The Valhalla had gone. Not requisitioned. Not bought by university or a great department store. Bombed. Eradicated. Cleaned down on both brick sides by a demolition contractor, picked away like meat from the bone by their yellow wrecking machines, and not even a doorstep left for the roses.

14

The day of the Annual Informal Meeting dawned with all the ominous tension of a first night when half the costumes are still with British Rail. Once, these meetings had been Cassidy's treasured innovation, an entirely new concept in company Management, aimed at the improvement of relations between Shareholders and Directors. Once, as from his father's pulpit, the adroit executive had addressed his faithful elders: first quarterly, then six-monthly, cleansed their souls of doubt, and refreshed them with new faith. Other companies, he had argued, gave as little information as possible; Cassidy's would reverse the trend. But time, as so often, had institutionalised the revolution: now the meeting took place once a year, an unwieldy blend of Board and Annual General, and more trouble, in Cassidy's revised opinion, than the two of them together.

By two o'clock the first arrivals had been sighted in the area of the ground-floor boardroom and report of them was brought to Cassidy by a succession of Shakespearean newsbearers. The firm's Earl, a retired steel magnate flown from Scotland, had sat for half an hour in the waiting room before being recognised, and was now in the Informal Conference Room drinking water from the carafe. Meale (good for his polish, the mawkish pup) was despatched to converse with him informally. A retired trade unionist named Aldebout, retained to pacify shopside disputes, had been seen testing the tea in the canteen.

"I told him to have it on the house," Lemming said proudly. "Those buggers'll do anything for a cup of tea."

Two brown-coated ladies from Shepton Mallet had had their mini towed away by the police.

"They tore the front bumper off too," said Angie Mawdray, who had watched the manoeuvre from her window.

A stockroom clerk was ordered to collect it and pay the fine.

Behind the scenes a condition of barely controlled chaos reigned. Today was Friday. The Fair opened on Monday. The new cee-spring chassis, finally assembled, despite Lemming's attempts at sabotage, had gone ahead air-freight to Le Bourget but the French shipping clerk telephoned to say it had been rerouted to Orly. An hour later he rang again. The chassis had been confiscated by French customs on suspicion, the shipping clerk thought, of being an instrument of war.

"Then *bribe* them! *Bribe* them for Christ's sake!" Cassidy shouted into the telephone, his maternal French having quite deserted him. "B . . . r . . ." and to Angie who was standing by with a dictionary, "What the hell's the French for bribe?"

"*Bri-ber*," Angie suggested promptly.

"Corrupt them!" Cassidy yelled. "*Corruptez!*" but the clerk said they were corrupt already.

Soon afterward the line went dead. A desperate telephone call to Bloburg, the Paris agent, produced no result. It was the feast of Saint Antoine of All Cities; Monsieur Bloburg was observing the local custom. By three o'clock when the meeting opened there was still no further word from the crisis front. Elsewhere in the building a battle was being waged with the revised brochure. The first edition, hurried through the printers at the last minute after prolonged haggling between Export and Promotion, was out of register and had to be sent back. While the second edition was still anxiously awaited, Cassidy discovered to his fury that it contained no German.

"For pity's sake!" he shouted. "Do I have to remember everything myself?"

Who spoke German? Lemming had fought them in the war and remembered them only with black hatred. He refused to co-operate. Faulk, desperately willing, had no German, but would a little Italian help? A translation agency in Soho sent a lady with blue hair and no English who was at that moment closeted in the copy room while Angie Mawdray, loving the crisis, combed the Public Library for a German-English technical dictionary.

To no one's surprise therefore the proceedings began late. Fighting to introduce a sense of calm Cassidy opened with minor matters of routine. Mrs. Aldo Cassidy sent her apologies. Apologies had also been received from General Hearst-Maundy in Jamaica. They had all been sorry to learn of the untimely death of Mrs. Bannister, a longstanding and loyal member of the Board. Mrs. Allan, after seven years' service, had accepted a senior post with another firm; Cassidy moved the customary bonus of one month's pay for every complete year served. The motion was carried without comment. Only Lemming, who had achieved her dismissal after months of venomous intrigue, muttered, "Great loss to us all, very gallant little lady," and appeared to brush a tear away.

It was almost half past three, therefore, before Aldo Cassidy, son of the distinguished hotelier, the Reverend Hugo Cassidy M.P. and bar., was able to deliver his long-awaited Chairman's address on the subject of Exports. Speaking fluently and without notes, he sounded a battle cry that would have chilled Prince Rupert's heart.

"Ideals are like the stars," he told them—a favourite dictum of the great hotelier. "We cannot reach them but we profit by their presence. The Common Market—" almost ignoring the applause "—the Common Market—thank you!—the Common Market is a fact of life. We must either join it or beat it. Ladies and gentlemen, fellow shareholders old and new, Cassidy's are prepared to do both."

Having painted a somewhat paradoxical picture of a Europe crumbling under the impact of his firm's assault, but mysteriously held together by its fastenings, he came at last upon the specific matter of the Fair.

"Now I make no apology for taking a strong, a very strong selling force to Paris. We've got the guns, and we've got the troops as well!"

More cheers. Cassidy lowers his voice.

"Now we shall be spending your money and we shall be spending a lot of it. No one ever did good business with a dirty shirt. There will be two teams. I shall call them Team A and Team B. Team B, under the distinguished leadership of Mr. Faulk, whose brilliant promotional record will stand us in good stead—" loud applause "—will set sail to-night. It's a young team—" an unfriendly glance at Meale, who had recently taken to wearing pointed shoes, and humming in the corridors "—it's a tough team. It is there to sell. Man the tent, demonstrate the prototype, stimulate interest, yes. But above all, it will *sell*. And I hope that by the time the Fair opens officially on Monday one or two order books will not be quite as empty as they are at this minute. The point is this. Many of these foreign buyers have limited resources. They arrive with so much to spend, they go when they've spent it."

Lifting a folded sheet of blank paper he passed it across their enchanted vision.

"Furthermore we have done a little bit of spying. I have here a list of all the principal buyers attending the Fair, together with their addresses while they are in Paris. It seems to me, you see, that if these fellows haven't all that much to spend—" a nicely judged pause "—then the best thing they can do is spend it on Cassidy's, and *that* means before they spend it on someone else!"

As the laughter and applause gradually died, the Chairman's expression was seen to harden and his voice took on a more severe tone.

"Fellow stockholders, members of the Board, I leave you with these words." Slowly one hand rose, the fingers half uncurled as if in benediction. "A man is judged—as judged we shall all be, my friends—by what he looks for, not by what he finds. Let it never be said that the House of Cassidy has been deficient on the score of enterprise. We shall seek and we shall find. Thank you very much."

He sat down.

During the tea break the Earl as elder statesman took him aside. He was a decrepit, silvery man and he had lunched at the Connaught at Company expense.

"Listen to the advice of an old man," he said speaking very slowly through the fumes of a rare whisky. "I've seen it in steel, I've seen it in deer. Don't burn yourself out. Don't try to run the whole course before breakfast."

"I won't," Cassidy assured him, laying a steadying hand on his shoulder. "I really won't."

"What you do in your twenties you pay for in your thirties, what you do in your thirties you pay for in your forties . . ."

"Yes but look here—" they had reached the Directors' lavatory "—I've got all *you* people to worry about haven't I, sir?"

"You've not been drinking by any chance, have you?" the Earl enquired.

"Good God no!"

"You know," the Earl continued, his head propped conveniently against the cistern, "I've been watching you. You're the most terrible bloody liar. Eh, tell us," said the Earl, drawing closer and affecting to wash his hands. "You seem to be making a hell of a big profit. Do you need a dash more working capital by any chance? On the QT, you know. So's we don't have to bother the tax laddies, *you* know."

The Informal audience had thinned a little after tea, and something of Cassidy's verve had also left him. Skating over the detailed function of the B team (responsible for the *logistics of the second phase*) he for a while drifted a little glumly round problems of creating new agencies and opening spares depots.

"There is even a possibility," he said, "I speak of course of the long term here, let's have no misunderstanding about this—that Cassidy's will eventually—I refer to the distant future—arrange for local, even *regional* manufacture of their product under licence and on the basis of part profit-sharing."

This time, no one was inclined to applaud, even Informally.

"The A team incidentally will be separately accommodated in the centre of the city, where it can enjoy the advantages of mobility, separate communication, and the rest, and it will consist almost entirely—" he meant it as a joke, had even prepared it as a joke, practised the timing, shaped and reshaped the cadences "—of myself. I say *almost* because I am happy to tell you that my wife will be accompanying me."

Only the palest murmur greeted this Informal insight into family togetherness.

"Do you want to go on to any other business?" Lemming asked, quite loud. "I think they've had about enough."

From the corridor they heard a clatter of feet as someone ran for the Chairman's telephone.

"That'll be Paris," said Faulk rising.

"Please stay where you are Mr. Faulk, my secretary will call me if necessary."

Furious, but only inwardly, Cassidy picked up an agenda and glanced at the next item.

"Catering," he read aloud with an inward shiver of discomfort.

Old Hugo's pocket money. Tread gently, raise the tone to one of metallic nonchalance, look anywhere but at the Earl, who always objects to this uncomfortable entry in the ledger.

"Catering. In view of the satisfactory profit position I propose to make a retrospective one-time ex-gratia payment to—" here he took a small breath and glanced upwards as if the name had momentarily escaped him "—our valued catering consultant Mr. *Hugo* Cassidy whose wise and politic counsel has added so much cheer to the works canteen." Someone was knocking at the door. "May I take it that the payment is approved?"

"How much?" Aldebout asked.

The door opened and Angie Mawdray peeped into the room.

"One thousand pounds," Cassidy replied. "Any objection?"

"Absolutely none at all," said Clarence Faulk.

Out of the corner of his eye, he saw the Earl's white head lift, and his white eyebrows come together in a frown, and one white hand lift in tardy intervention.

"Mister Aldo, it's Paris," said Angie.

"I wonder if you will all excuse me for a moment," he asked smoothly. "I happen to know this *is* a matter which requires my personal attention."

A deferential pause.

"May I take it, ladies and gentlemen, that we can go on to the next item on the agenda? Mr. Lemming, you have that in the Informal Minutes? Mr. Faulk, perhaps you'll stand in until I come back? You might care to say a word about our Scottish promotion scheme. Mr. Meale, I may need you."

Lemming opened the door for them. "The Frogs have called it off," he hissed as Cassidy brushed past. "Pound to a penny they've called it off."

"It's a *Frenchman*," Angie Mawdray said triumphantly. "He sounds *terribly* excited."

"Did you find that technical dictionary?"

"No."

"Pity." Meale handed him the telephone. "Hullo?"

" 'Ullo, 'ullo, 'ullo!"

"*Hullo,*" Cassidy repeated raising his voice to carry across the Channel. "*Hullo.*"

" 'Ullo, 'ullo, 'ullo!"

"Hullo! Can you hear me? Meale, get hold of the exchange. Tell them to give us another line."

Meale lifted the second telephone.

"Cassidee?"

"*Oui?*"

"*Comment ça va?*"

"Listen, *écoutez, avez-vous le pram?*"

"*Oui, oui, oui, oui. Tous les prams.*"

"Where is it? *Où?*" And to Meale, excited now, "It's okay. He's got it!"

"Cassidee?"

"*Oui?*"

"*Comment ça va?*"

"Fine. Listen, *where-is-the-pram?*"

"*Ici* Shamus."

"Who?"

"Jesus lover, don't say you've killed us already."

Lemming had followed him upstairs and was standing in the doorway.

"Well?" he said, hoping for bad news.

Cassidy stared at Lemming and then at the telephone. He put his hand over the mouthpiece.

"I'm sorry," he said firmly. "Do you mind shutting up? I can't conduct two conversations at once. I'll be with you in a moment. Go and hold the fort. Make yourself useful."

Scowling, Lemming withdrew. Meale trooped after him.

"Shamus," he whispered, "where are you?"

There was a slight pause before the answer came, and he thought he heard a second voice in the background as if Shamus were conferring with someone close to him.

"In bed," he said at last. "A Ladbroke Grove bed."

"Is Helen with you?"

"No, lover, it's just Daddy this time. Come and join us."

More consultation in the background, followed by a strange cajoling as between dog and master: "Say hullo to Butch . . . go on . . . *say hullo* to Butch." And much louder: "Butch, say hullo to Elsie." A soft rustle as the receiver changed hands. A girl's shy giggle, thin as rayon.

"Hullo Butch," said Elsie.

"Hullo Elsie. Elsie . . . is he all right?"

"Of course I'm all right," said Shamus. "Come round."

"I'm in the middle of a meeting."

"So am I."

"A Board Meeting," said Cassidy. "It's supposed to be my big day. They're all waiting for me downstairs."

Shamus was unimpressed. "I've been trying to ring you all week," he objected. "Didn't anyone tell you? Hey and listen: who was that sexy bitch I spoke to?"

"My secretary," said Cassidy.

"Not her, the other one."

"My wife," said Cassidy offering prayers to God.

"Lot of woman there boy. Very naive. Fond of Russians too. Want to watch out for her."

"Shamus look, I was going to write to you . . . when can I see you?"

"Tonight."

"It's no good tonight. I'm leaving for Paris on Monday, there's a convention on. We've got frightful problems with printers and God knows—"

"For *where?*"

"Paris."

"You going to *Paristown?*"

"On Monday."

"To sell prams?"

"Yes."

"I'm coming with you. And bring the Bentley, we'll need the back seat."

15

The house was in darkness when he returned. It reminded him, as he groped his way upstairs, of the day Old Hugo's father had died and the aunts had put the house into mourning. They had never had a death before but they knew exactly how to dress, both themselves and the house, where to find black and how far to draw the curtains, where there was religion on the wireless and what to do with all the smiling magazines.

The bedroom door was locked.

"She's asleep I'm afraid," Mrs. Groat called from the kitchen. "Uh-ha."

A towel was laid out on the nursery bed and his toothbrush beside it. Hugo was asleep. He undressed slowly thinking she might come in, then decided to shave to annoy his mother-in-law. The irritation dated from the birth of Mark, whom Sandra had had at home. Sandra had said there would be no pains—she had read books proscribing them—but her confidence proved unfounded. Soon the house had been filled with her sharp screams as she stubbornly rejected Pentothal and her mother sobbed in the kitchen reliving her own fights like a boxer retired from the ring. "Oh *God* you men," she shouted at Cassidy as he boiled water for purposes he dared not contemplate. "God if only you knew . . ." Ridden by guilt but furious at what he considered to be an odious display of female self-indulgence Cassidy had exercised the one male prerogative left to him. He shaved.

For similar reasons the same impulse overtook him now. Unbuttoning his shirt he rattled the razor in hot water, clanked the brush on the glass shelf, then needlessly shaved his amazingly youthful face.

Sandra kept him waiting a long time.

"I know you're awake," she said. "I can tell from your breathing."

She was standing in the nursery door, silhouetted against the landing light, and he imagined her face locked in the tension of uncomprehending resentment. She must have been there a good while for he had heard her first sigh ten minutes ago.

"You are without nobility," she continued quietly in her Ophelia voice. "You are without any scrap of decency or moral fibre or human compassion. You haven't got one instinct that is remotely honourable. I know perfectly well you're lying again. Why don't you admit it?"

Cassidy grunted and shifted one arm in a restless slumber but his mind was working fast.

I'm lying. Yes. I've always lied to you and I always will, and however many times you catch me out I'll never tell you the truth because you don't know how to deal with it any more than I do. But this time, big joke, I'm lying because I'm beginning to discover the truth and the truth, my angel, is outside us.

He waited.

Silenzio.

Or take the academic approach shall we since you have no degree? If I am without the qualities you enumerate and for the sake of argument I will largely concede that I am, why should I have the nobility, decency, and moral fibre to admit it?

Silenzio.

"I suppose you're taking A. L. Rowse," she suggested nastily, "*instead* of me."

Pulling up the blankets Cassidy did his swan act, swaying his head in the muddied water of Something Lock.

"Who was that Russian who rang you?"

I don't know.

"Who was that Russian who rang you?"

Lenin.

"Aldo!"

A business contact. How the hell should I know?

"Actually," said Sandra sadly, "he sounded rather fun."

Actually, thought Cassidy, *he is.*

Go. Grow. Stay.

"You're a complete child. Which is exactly what homosexuals are. You can't take menstruation or babies or death or *anything*. You have absolutely *no* sense of reality. You want the whole world to be pretty and tidy and full of love for Aldo."

She became grim.

"Well the world isn't like that, and *that*, my boy, is something you've got to learn. But still. *Aldo?*"

Meeow.

"The world is a tough, bitter place," she continued using her father's tone, elbows and feet apart. "A *damned* tough and bitter place. Aldo, I *know* you're awake."

I believe in Flaherty, the Father, the Son, and the little Boy.

"I'm going to leave you Aldo, I've decided. I'm going to take the children to Shropshire. Mummy has found a house near Ludlow. It's simple but it will do us perfectly well if you're not going to be there. We all live much more frugally when you're not with us. As for the children they must have father substitutes. I shall look for them in Ludlow. Thisbe and Gillian will go to kennels till we have moved."

Thisbe and Gillian were the Afghans. Bitches of course.

"I'm very sorry for you," she continued. "You know nothing about love or life and least of all women. But still."

Under the blankets Cassidy vigorously concurred. *That's why I'm going to Paris, you see. That's why I'm not taking you. I'm going to look for what you always say you've got, so fuck it. But still.*

"John Elderman says you have taken a subconscious vow to avenge yourself on your mother. You hate her for sleeping with your father. For this reason you also hate *me*. But still."

Jesus, don't say you've been having it off with Old Hugo. Well, well, well, this is a dirty house.

"So I'm very sorry for you," she repeated. "It's not your fault, there's nothing you can do. I've tried to help you but I've failed."

That's it, he thought, mentally raising one hand. *Keep it there. You have totally failed. You have failed to read my mind, my expressions, and my considerable distress in your company. You think you've got a monopoly of the metaphysics in this house but I tell you mate you wouldn't recognise God if He punched you on the jaw.*

Annoyed, apparently, that he still had not spoken, let alone contradicted her, she became more specific.

"Your responses are *entirely* homosexual," she declared, returning to an earlier charge. "Both towards your father *and* towards your sons. You don't love them as relatives—"

Relatives to what? Why can't you say relations? Why do you end all sentences with but still? Quite soon young lady you will tax me too far and I shall be obliged to fall fast asleep.

"You don't love them as relatives you love them as *men.*"

But still, Cassidy thought, *you hang around don't you?*

"Meanwhile you lie to me about those stupid charities. *I* know you're lying, *Mummy* knows you're lying, *everyone* knows. They're just a *stupid* excuse. *Bristol!* Do you really think *Bristol* needs a playing field from *you?* They wouldn't look at it if you *gave* it to them. *Footbridge. Pavilion. Levelling. Tchah!*"

She returned to her room.

Blank, he repeated.

Blank, blank, blank, blank, blank. Brainwash myself. Cassidy washes blankest. No lies, no truths, only a condition, only survival, only faith. Flaherty we need you. "If I wasn't blank," he thought, shading his eyes from darkness with his cupped hands, "I would call you an inexorable bore. You block me. I could be a writer if it wasn't for you. As it is I'm stuck in bloody prams."

The tears were back, slipping through his fingers. He named them one by one: remorse, fury, impotence, the Holy Trinity. I baptise thee in the name of apathy. He'd a good mind to go and show them to Sandra, that was what she did after all, waited till she'd got a good head of steam, then bled it all over him drip drip and boo-hoo. "I hate your fucking tears," he would shout. "Look at *mine.*"

"Good night, Daddy," said Hugo.

At breakfast as usual after such scenes Sandra made herself extremely agreeable. She kissed him maternally, vouchsafed him glances of great complicity, kept her mother in bed, and gave him tea instead of coffee, which she normally considered low.

"About what John Elderman said," Cassidy ventured as she cuddled him from behind.

"Oh don't worry about that, I was just in a bad mood," she replied lightly and kissed his head.

"Did you have a good night otherwise?"

"Fine, did you?"

"Sorry about Paristown."

"Paristown," she repeated with a smile. "What a baby you are." Kisses again. "It's going to be a real fight for you isn't it?"

"Well maybe."

"Don't be silly, I know it is. You can't fool me you know." She kissed him again. "Women *like* fighters," she said.

But Cassidy had not yet finished with John Elderman.

"You see the truth is, Sandra, I don't have motives."

"I know, I know."

More kisses. Cassidy consolidated his position. "I mean not even subconscious ones. I mean I could set up all those arguments so that they read absolutely differently."

"Of course you could," she said. "It's just John showing off. And you're *much* brighter than John, as he perfectly well realises. But still."

"I get into a fix and I react. It's got nothing to *do* with being queer."

"Of course it hasn't. And it was sweet of you to lend all that money to him," she added generously. "It's just that *sometimes* I don't understand your motives. And of course I believe in your football fields. It's just I wish those foul people would say *yes* for once."

"But Sandra, they're so *corrupt*."

"I know, I know."

"It takes *years* to wear them down . . ."

Skilfully he set up his operational defences. I'll be out day and night . . . The Embassy's sending a car for me to the airport . . . After that anything can happen . . . Don't ring me, let *me* do it on the Company . . .

"So they *should* send a car," she said. "All their cars. Have a motorcade just for Aldo. Poop poop like Toad."

By the time he left, the charwomen were already arriving, some by taxi, some driven by their husbands. In the hall, dogs were barking, the telephone was ringing on several floors. The builders had already begun; the mason was making tea.

"I'll ring if it gets easier," he promised. "Then you take the next plane. Not the one-but-next, the next."

"Goodbye, Pailthorpe," she said. "Lover."

Turning out of her sight he glimpsed her mother standing behind her hovering like a senile nurse ready to catch her if she fell. Nearly he turned back. Nearly from a call box he rang her. Nearly he missed the plane. But Cassidy had been near to things all his life, and this time, come what may, he was going to touch them.

In Paristown.

Paris

16

Love affairs, Cassidy had always known, are timeless, and therefore elusive of sequence. They occur, if at all, beyond the branches of our customary trees, in certain half-lit clouds from which day creatures are excluded; they occur at moments when the soul, in some unfathomable way, is more sublime than the loveliest environment, and all that the eye perceives illustrates the inner world.

So it was with Paris.

Haverdown was a night, the Paris Fair (according to the Pramsellers Association, Cassidy was never able to obtain independent corroboration) lasted four days. Yet each commanded for Cassidy the same compelling rhythm: the same fumbling first encounter, the same blind walk from the predictable to the unimagined; an inward walk to the closed-off places of his heart; outward to the closed-off places of a city. Each hung at first upon an instinct of failure; each was crowned by the same triumphal climax; each instructed him, and left him more to learn.

They met, it was arranged, at number-two terminal, in the departure lounge. The Many-too-Many were everywhere but Shamus had found a place to himself, a corner reserved for bath chairs. It was some time before Cassidy discovered him and he was beginning to panic. Shamus sat crookedly in the steel frame, as if twisted by a terrible injury, and he was wearing dark glasses and a beret. His powerful shoulders were hunched forward inside the familiar black jacket and he carried nothing but an orange which he was quietly rolling from one hand to the other as if to bring the life back to his limbs. He spoke in a cracked whisper. It was Elsie, he said; Elsie had made demands. Also she drank formaldehyde, which dissolved the glottal stop and caused spasms of the vertebrae. It was the first time Cassidy had seen him by daylight.

"How's the book going?"

"What book?"

"The novel. You were bringing it to London. Did they like it?"

Shamus knew of no novel. He wanted coffee and he wanted to be pushed round the lounge so that he could see healthy people and hear little children laughing. Over coffee —the attendants were assiduous, cleaned the table, removed unwanted chairs—Cassidy enquired after Alastair the railwayman and other characters of that great evening, but Shamus was not informative. No, he and Helen had not returned to Chippenham; the taxi-driver had gone out of their lives. No, he could not remember when they had left Haverdown. The sodders had cut the water off so they had headed for the East End of London, two friends called Hall and Sal, Hall was a boxer, the bread of life.

"He hits me," he added, as if that were a recommendation. And that was all.

"Don't hold with the past, lover, never did. Past stinks."

With quivering hands he drew the warm cup closer to his chest. Only the mention of Flaherty brought a spark to his lifeless eyes. The correspondence was flourishing, he said; he had little doubt that Flaherty's claims were justified.

They ate the orange in silence, half each. On the aeroplane, to which Shamus was assisted by burly stewards, he slept with his beret pushed up against the window like a cushion, and at Orly there was a small embarrassment. Firstly about another bath chair—the French had brought one on the runway, but Shamus indignantly refused it— secondly about luggage. Cassidy had purchased a new pigskin grip to match his globe-trotting camelhair coat, and he was watching the baggage chute fretfully because he knew what the French were. Having successfully recovered it, he found Shamus already at the barrier, empty-handed.

"Where's yours?"

"We ate it," Shamus replied. A hostess, drawn by his compelling looks, scowled at him. "Bitch," he shouted at her, and she blushed and went away.

"Hey, steady on," said Cassidy, embarrassed.

"I *loathe* air hostesses," said Shamus, and meeowed.

A limousine assumed them and for a while both were silent, stunned by beauty. The city was bathed in perfect sunlight. It fired the river, shimmered on the pink streets, and turned the golden eagles into phoenixes of present joy. Shamus sat in his favourite place beside the driver waving very slowly to the crowds, and occasionally lifting his beret. A few people waved back and a pretty girl blew him a kiss, a thing which had never happened to Cassidy in his life. At the St. Jacques they were received with all the ostentatious tolerance which French hoteliers accord to homosexuals and the unmarried. The staff assumed at once that Shamus was in charge. Cassidy had taken a suite with twin beds to cover all eventualities and the manager had sent a bowl of fruit. *Pour Monsieur et Madame,* the card read. *Avec mes compliments les plus sincères.* Shamus ordered champagne on the telephone in French, calling it shampoo, and the telephonist laughed a great deal. *"Ah, c'est vous,"* she said, as if she had already heard about him. They drank the champagne warm because the ice had melted by the time it was delivered, and afterwards they walked down the rue de Rivoli where they bought Shamus a suit and three shirts and a pair of handsome lacquered shoes.

"How's the Bentley?"

"Fine."

"Bosscow in the pink?"

"Oh yes."

"Nipper?"

"Also yes."

"Leg?"

"Leg fine. On the mend."

And a toothbrush, Shamus reminded him, so they bought a toothbrush as well, because Shamus had left his at Elsie's in case her husband needed it when he came back from prison.

"How's Helen?" Cassidy asked.

"Fine, fine."

In a minuscule flower shop, buying two carnations, Shamus kissed the girl on the nape of the neck, a salute which she received with composure. He appeared to have a way of handling women which caused them no offence, like Sandra with dogs.

"Charm the lady buyers at the Fair," he explained, as she pinned the buttonholes in place. "Worth a fortune."

At six o'clock Bloburg, Cassidy's Paris agent, lumbered massively into the foyer, exuding mad compliments even before he was through the swing door, and Shamus withdrew to the bedroom to read about prams.

"Aldo by God you are two hundred years younger how do you manage it my dear fellow look at me I am dying already! Cassidy how are you, listen tomorrow I give you a fantastic dinner, a place only the French are knowing, the best place Cassidy, the cream!"

All Bloburg's hospitality was enjoyed tomorrow. He was a sad, noisy man who had lost everything in the war, children, houses, parents. On previous visits Cassidy had made much of him, even advising him on his luckless love life.

"Cassidy you are number one! All Paris is speaking of you listen I am telling you! You are an *artist* Cassidy! All Paris is fantastic for an *artist!*"

Paris is fantastic, artists are fantastic, Cassidy is fantastic; but not even Cassidy, who could take a great deal of flattery, any longer believed in sad Bloburg as his champion.

"Let's have a drink," he suggested.

"Cassidy you are so generous! All Paris is saying . . ."

He left late, having lingered in the hope of food, but Cassidy was hardened against him. He wanted to eat with Shamus and time was important to him.

Dining in the hotel, feeling their way with one another and not yet finding the right note, they drank to the book.

"Whose book?" said Shamus, lowering his glass.

"Your book. Your new one, ass. May it be a massive success."

"Hey lover."

"Yes."

"Great brochures. Punchy, confident, persuasive. I enjoyed every word."

"Thanks."

"Write them yourself?"

"Largely."

"Great talent there lover. Want to work on it."

"Thanks," said Cassidy again and returned to his lobster. They did it very well, he thought, in a garlic butter flavoured with rosemary.

"How long since you invented that braking system?" Shamus asked.

"Oh ten years . . . more, I suppose."

"Anything since?"

"Well the sales side, you know. Manufacture, marketing, exploitation. We've even started producing our own bodies. In a small way, you know."

"Sure, sure."

Catching sight of his own reflection in the mirror, Shamus paused to admire his new suit, lifted his glass and drank to himself, then lifted his glass again to acknowledge the toast.

"But no new earth-shattering invention?" he resumed, settling back into his chair. "Huh? Huh?"

"Not really."

"What about that new folding chassis?"

Cassidy gave a confessive laugh.

"I put my name on it but I'm afraid it was my design people who dreamed it up."

"Christ," said Shamus. "You've really got it made."

Cassidy mentioned Helen. Helen was fine, said Shamus. She was staying with her mother, princesses had to be locked in towers.

"Time she was deprived," he explained. "She was getting cheeky."

"Did she enjoy London? Being with Hall and . . ."

Being not quite into the language, he had wanted to say Hall and Saul, but saved himself in time.

"Sure, sure," said Shamus, and brushing Helen aside, embarked on a somewhat desultory enquiry into the dangers of foreign competition in the Pram Trade. Was a French pram sexier? A German pram more solid? How were the Russians coming on? While he was asking these questions, Shamus' attention strayed to a young girl in the corner of the room. She was twelve years old, no more. She sat alone under a chandelier and wore Sandra's silver dress from the May ball at Oxford. She had ordered something *flambé* which required fruit and a quantity of liqueurs. Two young waiters, under the eye of the *maître d'hôtel*, were ministering to her from a trolley.

"Christ never said anything about us, did he?" he remarked suddenly. "Not a word in the whole manifesto. All we're supposed to do is keep the score."

Taken by surprise, Cassidy faltered.

"Us?"

"Writers. Who do you think?"

He was still watching her but his expression was neither

friendly nor curious, and his voice, as he continued speaking, had a trace of the familiar Irish brogue.

"I mean the pramsellers, all right: they're for the high jump. Hard luck but you know where you stand. You've got it in this world so you can sing for it in the next."

The girl was selecting bottles: not this one, that one; pointing with her small gloved hand. She wore a black band round her neck, a single diamond glittered at the centre.

"The peacemakers are laughing: they're the children of God and no one could wish for better parents. But I'm *not* a fucking peacemaker, am I?"

"You certainly are not," said Cassidy heartily, not yet fully woken to Shamus' change of tone.

"I'm a collision man. A truth-teller, that's me."

"And an Old Testament man," Cassidy reminded him, "like Hall."

Had Shamus *really* boxed? Cassidy had boxed at Sherborne. He had made the mistake of taking a bath before the contest because he wished to please his housemaster, who had an elevated view of his religious potential. Though he had stood for quite a while being hit, he was obliged to lie down in the third round, and for years afterwards leather car seats made him sick.

"Piss off," said Shamus.

"What?"

"Piss off. Shut up about Hall."

"Sorry," said Cassidy, puzzled.

It was the girl who still commanded Shamus' entire attention. The *maître d'hôtel* poured a little lemonade into her wine glass. "Enough," her frail hand said, and the bottle was removed.

"And that little bitch is all right because she's a kid," Shamus continued, still upon the subject of the saved. "And kids get blanket protection. Quite right and proper too. I'm a fervent supporter of the breed myself though I happen to reckon the age limit could come down a bit. But what do the writers get? I tell you one thing: we're not meek, thank you, so we certainly don't inherit the earth. And we're not poor in spirit either, so we can't count on the Kingdom of Heaven, for instance."

His expression hesitated at the brink of anger. Taking Cassidy's hand, he stroked it devotedly, soothing himself against it.

"Easy lover, easy . . . don't get cross . . . easy . . ." Relaxing, he smiled. "You see, lover," he explained in a gentler voice, "there's just *not enough information,* that's my view. I put this to Flaherty only last week. Flaherty, what are you going to do about the writers? I said. Do they get it now, or later? You do see my point, don't you, lover? You're the boss man after all. You're paying."

"Well you do have your *freedom,*" Cassidy suggested cautiously.

Shamus rounded on him.

"Freedom from what, for fuck's sake? Freedom from all that lovely money? *That* freedom? Or was it by any chance the unbearable captivity of public recognition you were thinking of?"

Too late, Cassidy reached for his conference voice. "I suppose I was thinking more of freedom from boredom," he said easily, using a passing waiter to order brandy.

"Were you now?" said Shamus pleasantly, the Irish brogue in full flower. "You may be right about that. I will concede that freedom from boredom is a privilege I may well have overlooked. Because after all, I could sleep all day, that's true, and no bugger would raise a finger. Not everyone can say *that* now can they? I mean the warders wouldn't come and bang on the door or tell me to empty my bucket, I'd just hear the sounds of laughter that's all, and the fellows getting their exercise out in the fresh air with their girls maybe. Only trouble is, the nights are such a problem, don't you think?"

"Yes indeed," Cassidy agreed.

With child-like fascination Shamus watched him tip the waiter. It was a very large tip but Cassidy abroad believed in laying strong fences against disrespect.

"What'll you do in nineteen eighty?" Shamus asked, when the transaction was complete.

"I'm sorry?"

"World population's growing seventy million a year, lover. That's a hell of a lot of people to tip, isn't it? Even for you."

Their parting was equally enigmatic.

"You do feel *well?*" Cassidy asked doubtfully as he saw Shamus to the lobby.

"Don't worry lover, I'll be all right on the night."

"Bit too much of Elsie I expect."

"Who?"

"Elsie."

"Sure . . . Lover?"

"Yes?"

"You will let me have a go on those prams, won't you?" An odd defencelessness had replaced the earlier menace. "Only . . . well *you* know, it's what I came for. I feel I could *do* it you see. Sell. I reckon I could turn it into a real vocation. Hey lover."

"Yes."

"Thanks for the suit."

"That's all right."

"The lobster was great."

"I'm glad you liked it."

"Great bread too. Crisp outside, squidgy in the middle. There's so much of you I could *use*," Shamus remarked suddenly, putting his hands on Cassidy's shoulders. "Hey listen . . . " Cassidy listened. "We got to love each other, see. It's the great experiment, like blacks and whites and all that shit. But if I don't have you *all*, I don't get any of you, do I? You're such a big slimy fish. I can put my hands on you but I don't know where you end. . . . You're *awful*, honest. . . ."

Cassidy laughed awkwardly. "Perhaps it's just as well you *don't* know," he said, releasing himself in case Shamus was contemplating a public embrace. "I say you didn't bring a copy of the book, did you?"

Somewhere in the brown darkness of Shamus' eyes, a warning light went up, and stayed.

"What if I did?"

"It's just that I'd love to read it, that's all. If you've brought one. What stage is it *at* actually?" he added. Receiving no answer, he deemed a subsidiary question politic. "Will it be a film, like *Moon?* I'll bet that's worth a bit just by itself. Let alone the book sales. . . . Paperback, too, I suppose?" As he continued speaking, Shamus was already backing into the lift.

"You know," Shamus said as his feet ascended into the shaft, "if I was Flaherty I could work this thing alone."

It was midnight by the time Cassidy joined him. He had business in the Bristol Bar and another meeting with Blo-

burg, and at eleven o'clock a public relations girl called
to check handouts. Shamus was lying like a dead onion-
seller dressed in the black coat again, flat on his stomach
on the coverlet with his face in the beret. His new suit
was hung carefully in the wardrobe with an Exhibitor's
badge pinned to the lapel. The brochures were still strewn
beside him on the floor. A ruled pad was propped on
the chimney piece.

Honourable Sir, the message read, *Kindly to wake the
undersigned tomorrow morning punctual for the Fair your
obedient humble servant Shamus P. Scardanelli (Vendor).*
The postscript said, Please *lover.* Please. *Major commit-
ment. And lover forgive, please forgive. Vital.*

A lorry was parked outside the window and workmen were
unloading crates on the cobble stones, shouting jokes he
couldn't understand.

I should have bought him pyjamas too, thought Cassidy.
Why does he have to wrap himself in that coat?

He sleeps like Hugo but quieter, cheeks squashed against
his forearm in a pout.

Down in the street a woman was calling, a tart by the
sound of her and drunk. Is that what I want him to do:
pimp for me? *Forgive lover, forgive.* You're so full of
truth, Cassidy thought, looking at him again, what is
there to forgive?

"Dale?"

Shamus was muttering but Cassidy couldn't hear the
words. You're dreaming, he thought, turning to look at
him again, you're dreaming of Elsie and selling prams.
Why not dream of Helen?

Suddenly Shamus cried out, a short hard cry of *"No!"*
or *"Go!"* swinging his shoulders in angry rejection.

"Shamus," Cassidy said quietly and put out his hand to
touch him. "Shamus it's all right, it's me; Cassidy. I'm
here, Shamus."

No, he thought, as Shamus settled again, better to be
just the two of us. Dream of Helen another time.

"Dale you bugger."

"It's not Dale. It's Cassidy."

A long silence.

"Can I come to the Fair?"

"Yes, you can come."

"In my new suit?"

"In your new suit."

Minutes later Shamus woke again, abruptly.

"Where's my carnation?"

"I put it in the toothmug."

"It's for the lady buyers you see. At the Fair."

"I know. It'll slay them."

"Goodnight lover."

"Goodnight Shamus."

17

The day was dull for Cassidy, for Shamus balm. The pramseller rose without haste, his ears already full of the greedy, unproductive clichés of the trade; but the great writer was already dressed save for his feet; was pacing the floor with the alacrity of the young executive bent on increasing his figures. His lacquered shoes were back with the valet; dust had been identified in the welts. Cassidy had planned to leave late, but Shamus would have none of it. Great conquests were in the air, he insisted; Cassidy and Shamus must be in the field early, breathe heart into the troops.

They arrived in fine rain; the tents were sagging dismally on their masts, smelling of rugger and changing rooms.

"Bee-Line?" Shamus cried indignantly. *"Bee-Line?* Never heard of them."

"Our main competition," said Cassidy.

Two Beefeaters guarded the entrance; halberdiers were serving bitter beer in pewter tankards.

"You mean you camp with the enemy? Jesus lover, you got to burn them down! Rape their women, nippers to the stake!"

"Take it easy," said Cassidy. "Hullo Mr. Stiles."

"Oh *hullo* Mr. Cassidy. How's business? Doing anything, are you?"

"Not much; I hear it's pretty quiet."

"I think it's the same everywhere," said Stiles with satisfaction. "I don't think devaluation's bitten the way it ought, do you?"

"I'm sure it hasn't," said Cassidy.

"Creep," said Shamus, as they left. "Toady."

"You've got to keep on terms with them," Cassidy explained. "After all, it is us against the foreigners."

The Cassidy tent restored him to humour. Introduced as an important contact of the Chairman's, Shamus tested the chassis, rode in a pushchair, flirted with the girls, and talked about Saint Francis with Meale, who had recently become extremely sullen, and was expressing a desire to take Holy Orders. They all *own* him, Cassidy thought, mystified; they all own him. If *I* was the hanger-on they'd chuck me out in minutes. A large crowd had just entered the tent, mainly Scandinavians, women of a certain age. Over luncheon, befriending a Froken Svenson from Stavanger, Shamus sold her a hundred chassis at thirteen to the dozen. She should pay when she liked, he said, Cassidy's had the large approach to money.

"Get hold of Lemming," Cassidy said quietly to Meale. "Tell him to rescind the deal."

"How?" said Meale, aggressively.

"Meale what *is* the matter with you?"

"Nothing. I happen to admire him, that's all; I think he's truthful and fine."

"Lose the order, d'you understand? Bury it. She hasn't signed anything, nor have we. We've never given thirteen to the dozen in our lives and we're not starting now."

"I made it, lover!" Shamus cried as the limousine returned them to the city. "I made it! Jesus I can swim! See the way I gave her the oil?"

"You were terrific," Cassidy agreed. "You were absolutely great."

"Jesus, that whole place, I could *die* there; I tell you, there's no better compliment than that now is there? The tent, the music, the flags . . . Lover, listen, before it goes to my head, was there anything I did wrong?"

"Nothing."

"Not too much?"

"No."

"Not too familiar? The hand on the arm?"

"Just right."

By the time they reached the St. Jacques he was even capable of reproof.

"You know lover you shouldn't have let those Japs in. I mean they were just standing there photographing the exhibits. I mean look what they did to the car trade. You should throw the sodders out, honest. Put a notice up 'No Japs,' I would."

Lying in the bath, playing with the carnations, Shamus added his own bizarre appreciation of market trends: "Hey lover, what about Paisley now? I mean if that feller's going to murder all us procreating Catholics there won't *be* any bloody babies."

"Ask Flaherty."

"You know when you come to think of it, prams are a very worthy thing to be in. I mean prams are your *ploughshares,* aren't they, for tomorrow's world. I mean there's other buggers churning out swords by the million but you and me are absolutely in the non-belligerent camp, wouldn't you say so lover?"

"See you after the party," Cassidy said benevolently.

"Why can't I come?" he demanded sulkily. "I sold the prams not you."

"Principals only," said Cassidy. "Sorry."

"Meeow," said Shamus. "Those people loved me," he continued reflectively, "and I *loved* them. A perfect marriage. A great pointer for the future." He sang a few bars of an Irish melody. "Hey, lover, you never answered my question."

"What question?"

"I asked you once: any views on the meaning of love?"

"I must say, you pick your moments, don't you?" said Cassidy with a laugh.

With his toe, Shamus guided a carnation away from the jet of the tap. "Oh do not die," he recited, apparently to the flower, "For I shall hate all women so when thou art gone. Chippie chippie, lover."

"Chippie, chippie," said Cassidy.

His last sight of Shamus was of him sitting in the bath wearing the black beret and studying stock prices in the *Herald Tribune.* He must have used the whole bottle of Cassidy's bath essence; the water was a dark green and the carnations floated on it like lilies on a stagnant pond.

The British Minister (Economic) was one of those fastidious, small, very rich, unworldly men whom, in Cassidy's experience, the Foreign Office invariably appointed to deal with trade. He cringed at one end of a long room in the shelter of a powerful wife, beside a marble fireplace stuffed with red cellophane, and he received his guests one by one after a butler had thinned them out

at the door. Cassidy arrived early, second only to Mc-
Kechnie of Bee-Line, and the Minister shook their hands
very separately as if he would referee their fight.

"We know some Cassidys in Aldeburgh," the Minister's
wife said, having listened carefully to his voice and
found it phonically acceptable. "I don't expect they're any
relation are they?"

"Well we are a pretty big tribe," Cassidy admitted,
"but we do all seem to be related in some way."

"What does it *mean?*" the Minister complained.

"I'm told it's Norman," said Cassidy.

McKechnie, who had not been favoured with such inti-
macies, stood off glowering. He had brought a wife.
Cassidy had met her in the tent that morning, a freckled red-
headed lady in yellow and green, and she looked like all
the wives he had ever met since he had begun in prams.
"You stole our Meale," she had said to him, and she was
getting ready to say it again. She had put her hair up
and bared one shoulder. Her handbag had a long gold
chain to it, enough for at least one prisoner, and she
held her elbow wide in case she needed to jab anyone.

"How's the Fair going?" the Minister asked. "They're
having a *Fair,*" he said, for the benefit of his wife. "Out
near Orsay, where poor Jenny Malloy used to walk her
dog." It was more an objection than an explanation. Fairs,
his tone suggested, had replaced dogs, and the change was
not for the better.

"We've taken ten thousand quid in eight hours," Mrs.
McKechnie said straight at Cassidy. She came from near
Manchester and did not care for side. "We've not a grad-
uate on the books, have we Mac?"

"I thought they'd all arrive together," the Minister said
hopelessly. "In a charabanc or something. It is extraordinary. What about drink?"

"Two up," his wife warned. The butler announced Sanders and Meyer of Everton-Soundsleep.

"*Norman* did you say?" the Minister enquired. "Norman *French,* that kind of Norman?"

"Apparently," said Cassidy.

"You ought to tell them that. They'd like it. *We* get
by because she's half a Lamey, it's the only reason. They
loathe the rest of us like poison, always did. They loathe
us too, really, except she's half a Lamey."

A pack of junior diplomats entered through another door.

"Can we tempt you to a drink?" they asked of Mrs. McKechnie, picking by training on the plainest woman present. One held canapés on a government tray and another asked whether she would have time for pleasure.

"She's laying it on a bit about the ten thousand," McKechnie told Cassidy aside. "It's more like two."

"There's plenty of room for both of us," said Cassidy.

"She's loyal, mind."

"I'm sure she is. Where are you staying?"

"Imperial. Here, have you had the Japs in?"

"They came this morning."

"It's got to be stopped," said McKechnie, and to Sanders who had just joined them, "I was saying to young Cassidy here, we've got to do something about the Japs."

"Japs?" said Sanders, mystified. "What Japs?"

McKechnie looked at Cassidy and Cassidy looked at McKechnie and they both looked again at Sanders, this time with pity.

"I expect it's just the big firms they go for," said McKechnie.

"I'm sure it is," said Cassidy and moved away as if in answer to a call.

They were about twelve in the room, fourteen perhaps including their hosts, but reinforcements were arriving fast. Their topic was transport. Bland and Cowdry had shared a taxi; Crosse had walked and the tarts had nearly eaten him: "Lovely some of them were, just kids, nineteen or twenty, it's a disgrace." Martenson had almost decided not to come as a protest against the Ambassador whom he thought should have been at the Opening. As soon as he returned to Leeds, he said, he proposed to complain to his Member of Parliament.

"Bloody peacock I'll have his bloody balls off. We earn it, he spends it. Look at the size of this room THEN! *One man* from Commerce: that's all you need. *One man*. You could close the whole bloody Embassy apart from him."

It was while listening to this piece of intelligence that Cassidy heard the butler call an unfamiliar name. He did not catch it precisely but it sounded like Zola; it was certainly Conte *et* Contessa, and he turned to watch them enter. Afterwards he said he had had an instinct; only instinct, he argued afterwards, could explain why he had freed himself from Crosse and Cowdry and stepped back a full pace to get a clearer view of Shamus bowing courteously over his hostess' hand.

He was wearing his rue de Rivoli suit and a pale salmon shirt belonging to Cassidy, a coveted garment which he had been keeping in reserve for a special occasion. A dark-haired girl waited at his side, one hand lightly on his arm. She was serene and very beautiful and she stood directly beneath the light. From his point of vantage Cassidy noticed, with the acuteness of perception which accompanies sudden shock, the bold imprint of a love bite on her lower neck.

"You've not had *trouble* from him?" asked McKechnie, who had joined him again. "My wife says he's queer as two left shoes."

"Who?"

"Meale."

"I'm sure not," said Cassidy. "In fact I think if anything he's too much the other way."

"It's *frightfully* enterprising of you," the Minister's wife was moaning, "to keep your own man in Warsaw. What does he *do* all the time?"

"Oh we have quite a lot of trade with them actually," Cassidy confessed modestly. "You'd be surprised."

Never hold him back, Helen whispered. *Promise you never will.*

Shamus had charmed them all. Stately and subdued he moved graciously from group to group, now talking, now listening, now gently deferring to the girl as he offered her canapés and whisky. His gestures, to those who knew him, might have seemed a little slurred; his Polish accent, where Cassidy could hear it, occasionally yielded to a faint Irish intonation, but his magic had never been more compelling.

The Minister was particularly impressed.

"If only *more* of you would look east," he complained. "Who is she?"

"Great dignity," the Minister's lady agreed. "Make a *marvellous* diplomat's wife, even in Paris."

"She's stoned out of her mind," Shamus warned him *en vol* between two admiring wives. "If we don't get her out she'll fall flat on her arse."

"Give her to me," said Cassidy.

Receiving the full weight of her he walked straight out of the room.

"Here," he heard McKechnie say, "that's the fellow who kicked my stand. Bloody well kicked it and told young Stiles our canopies were crap. He's not foreign, he's Irish!"

"Tour d'Argent," said Shamus. They were standing on the pavement watching the girl's departing taxi. Shamus looked slightly dishevelled, as if he had been pushed by several people at once.

"Shamus are you *sure?*"

"Lover," said Shamus holding his forearm in an iron grip, "I've never been hungrier in my life."

"To the suit," said Shamus.

"To the suit," said Cassidy.

"God bless her and all who sail in her."

"Amen."

Once again the unpredictable had proved itself the rule. Cassidy had claimed his corner table with the gloomiest foreboding. He did not know how much Shamus had drunk but he knew it was a lot and he was seriously wondering whether he could handle him without Helen's help. He did not know whether anyone had played Fly in the Tour d'Argent before, but he had a pretty good idea what would happen if they tried. In the cab Shamus had taken one of his quick naps and Cassidy had been obliged to wake him under the eye of the commissionaire.

Now, against all expectation, they were in paradise: Old Hugo's paradise, with food and waiters, the fragrance of angels and of heavenly flowers.

Diamonds surrounded them: hung in giant clusters in the window panes, pricked the orange night sky, were

draped in the eyes of lovers and in the brown silk of
women's hair. Cassidy heard nothing but the sounds of
love and battle, the whispers of longing couples and the far
sharpening of a knife. Vertigo seized him, stronger than
Haverdown, stronger than Kensal Rise. Of all the places
he had ever been, this was the most exciting, the most in-
toxicating. Best of all was the company of Shamus himself. Something—the drink, the girl, his conquest of the
Embassy, the magic of the city—something had freed
Shamus, soothed and softened him and made him young.
He was alight and yet at peace, he was miraculously sober.

"Shamus."

"What is it lover?"

"*This*," said Cassidy.

Shamus' eyes were shadowed behind the candles, but
Cassidy could see he was smiling.

"Shamus, it was wonderful what you did. It was just
fantastic. They really believed in you . . . more than in
me. You could have told them anything, just anything
you wanted. You could run my whole business with your
left hand."

"Great. And you write my books." They drank to that
as well.

"I wish Helen was here," said Cassidy.

"Never mind lover, woods are full of them."

"What's it like being married to someone like Helen? To
someone you *really* love?"

"Guess," said Shamus, but Cassidy, who had an ear
for such things, sensed that he would be wiser not to.

Shamus talked.

Over linen, candles, chalices, and plate, he talked of
the world and its riches. He talked of love and of Helen,
and the search for happiness and the gift of life, and
Cassidy, like a favoured pupil, listened to every word
and remembered almost nothing but his smile and the beguiling softness of his voice. Helen is our virtue; we talk,
but Helen acts. Helen is our constant; we rotate but she
is still.

"I've never met a woman like her," Cassidy confessed.
"She could be . . . she could be . . ."

She *is*, Shamus corrected him. Helen has no potential;
Helen is fulfilled.

"Does she *mind* about . . . Elsie and people, Shamus?"

Not as long as they are called Elsie, said Shamus.

Of the obligation to live romantically and feel deeply. He talked of writing, and what a feeble task it was beside the vocation to experience.

"A book . . . Jesus. Such a *little* thing, just a handful of days. *Enoughs,* that's what a book is. Get pissed enough, get the guilts enough, get screwed enough, and suddenly . . . it's a natural. Honest, lover."

Creation was an act of moderation, but life: *life,* Shamus said, existed only in excess. Who wants *enough* for Christ's sake? Who wants the twilight when he can have the fucking sun?

"No one," said Cassidy loyally, and believed he spoke the truth.

He talked about inspiration, that much of it was genuine but useless, you left your soul out in all weathers, the birds shat on it, the rain washed it, but you had to leave it there all the same, there was no backing out, so fuck it. About equality, how there was none, and freedom, none either, it was crap, and the act of creation made it the biggest crap of all, whether God's or Shamus' creation. Because freedom meant the fulfilment of genius, and the existence of genius precluded equality. So the howl for freedom was New Testament crap, and the howl for equality was the howl of the Many-too-Many, Shamus fucked himself of them all. How he hated youth, it made an artist of every little pig who could afford a paintbrush; how he hated age, it retarded the genius of youth; how the world was in existence because Shamus witnessed it, it was certain to die without him.

And when Shamus had told him about life, he told him about Art as well. Not Vatican art, not history book art, nothing for School Certificate, attempt any two of the following questions.

Art as a destiny. As a calling and a lovely agony.

And out of the air, out of the undefined edges of Shamus' magical conversation, Cassidy discovered that Shamus was chosen.

Fatally, wonderfully chosen.

That he belonged to a body of men who never met; of the gifted early dead; and their embrace was already on him.

Whom waiters loved although they never tipped them.

That he was one of a Pack, a Few against the Many-too-Many, but each hunted alone and none had help in time of need except the comfort of knowing.

"Knowing *what*, Shamus?"

That you belonged, and nothing more.

That you were best, and could only elect yourself; that Flaherty was the only true and living God, because Flaherty was self-appointed, and Self-Appointed Man was divine, and limitless, and out of time, like love.

As to what it was exactly that joined Shamus to the others, that, as Cassidy's tutor would say, was concept rather than fact. The concept was to choose yourself very early, and to be precociously familiar with death: with premature death, romantic death, sudden and very destructive of the flesh. To live always testing the edges of your existence, the extreme outlines of your identity. To need water, not air; water defined you, there was a German poet always bathing in fountains; man is invisible until the cold waters of experience have shown him who he is, hence total immersion, violence, boxing with Hall, the Baptist church, and (somehow) Flaherty again.

Gradually, with the aid of a third bottle of wine and several names supplied by Shamus, Cassidy formed a picture of this wonderful band of brothers, this Few: a non-flying Battle of Britain squadron captained by Keats and supported by a long list of young men.

Not all of them were English.

Rather, a Free Europe Squadron, as it were, which included the pilots Novalis, Kleist, Byron, Pushkin, and Scott Fitzgerald. Their enemy was bourgeois society: the Gerrard's Crossers again, the fucking bishops in drag, the doctors, lawyers, and Jaguar drivers who thundered towards them in black, mechanical fleets; while Somewhere in England, waiting for the last Scramble, they penned fraught elegies and made up peace-loving verses in writing.

Such men by definition survived more in the promise than in the fulfilment; and commanded most respect by what they had left undone.

Also they took a lot, because it was not long before they themselves were taken.

"Who can write about life and run away from it at the same time?" Shamus wanted to know.

"No one," said Cassidy.

Of this squadron, Shamus was that night and for all the nights to come the one survivor. Cassidy believed that. He knew he would always believe it, because somehow that night and for ever Shamus had stolen into his childhood, and would stay there like a favourite place or a loved uncle. As to Cassidy himself, he was their squire, frying their bacon, carrying their helmets, and polishing their fur-lined boots; posting their last letters and giving their rings to their Helens, wiping their names off the blackboard when they didn't come back.

"You know Shamus," Cassidy said much later—they were rowing somewhere, one oar each—"I'll always be there when you need me."

He meant it. It was a promise, more real to him than marriage because it was an idea, and one that with Shamus' help he had found for himself, that night, in the Tour d'Argent in Paristown.

"Why are you crying?" Cassidy asked, as they left.

"For love," said Shamus. "You want to try it some time."

"Who's Dale?"

"Who?"

They had taken a limousine to the seventh district, Shamus had friends there.

"Dale. You talked about him in your sleep. You said he was a bugger."

"He is a bugger."

Shamus' head was very still against the window, but the lights from the street played over it like gold coins, rais-

ing him and pushing him back, so that his silhouette wore
the passive look of a man not able to control what the outside did to him.

"Then why don't you drop him down a hole?"

"Because he dropped me first, and they're the ones
you can't beat."

"Did he love you?"

"I suppose so."

"As much as . . ."

Reaching out, Shamus took Cassidy's hand in both of
his. "No lover, not like you," he assured him gently, turning his hand over and kissing the palm. "Not like you're
going to learn. You'll be the best. Number one. In the
first position. Honest."

An instinct made him say it. A moment of profoundest
empathy, of prophetic anxiety.

"Shamus . . . you're the greatest writer of our time. I
believe that. I'm very proud."

The face was turned away from him, very beautiful
and sudden against the night, against the running glitter
of the street.

"You've got me wrong lover," Shamus whispered, gently
putting away his hand. "I'm just a failed businessman."

Still in Paradise they went to Paris.

Not Cassidy's Paris of hissing vacuum doors and bad
American accents, but Shamus' Paris of hydrants and cob-
blestone streets and rotten vegetables and doors with no
name; a Paris which Cassidy had not dreamed of, not
aspired to even, since it answered appetites he did not
know he had, and showed him people he had not imagined; relaxed, gay people of unworldly wisdom who gravely shook Shamus by the hand and called him *maître*
and asked him about his work. They went to the Sulpice,
to a square full of bookshops, through a dark courtyard
buoyant with music, to a door that led straight to a lift,
and they emerged into a sea of chatter and laughing girls
and men with bare chests and beads.

"They love you, Shamus," Cassidy whispered to him,
as they drank the whisky and answered questions about

London. "Look at you," Cassidy kept saying. "You're *famous*."

"Yes," said Shamus, without bitterness. "They remember."

They went to an island, to a high grey house belonging to an American, and someone gave Shamus his own book to sign, *Moon*, a first edition, and he stood in a pulpit reading aloud from it, to sleeping couples breathing in the dark. Indians, white girls, murmured their applause. He read very quietly so that Cassidy, even had he wished, could not have heard the words, but he knew from the rhythm and the fall of them that they were the most beautiful words he had ever heard, more beautiful than Shakespeare or Kahlil Gibran or the German High Command; and he sat alone, eyes half closed, letting them go through him like the language of love, and his pride knew no bounds, pride of possession, pride of creation, pride of love.

"Shamus let's stay. Please let's stay."

"Negative."

"What about *her* then?"—for Shamus had found a girl and was gently turning her breast inside her dress.

"No good," said Shamus. "It's her house. *His* house," he corrected, indicating her husband.

The American gave them both another whisky. He was a big, kindly man, very pugnacious in his sympathy and a keen opponent of aggression.

"Get the fuck out of here," he advised them. "Have a drink and go." And to Cassidy: "I'll crucify him. He's a great guy but get him out."

"Of course," said Cassidy. "You've been very kind."

In a bright bar, drinking Chartreuse because Shamus said it had the highest killing power, shielding their eyes against the neons, they found their first whore.

"Shamus, why do you live so alone when they all want you so much?"

"Got to keep moving," Shamus said vaguely. "Can't stand still, lover, they'd get you right between the eyes. Twenty years since I wrote that book."

His gaze had drifted to the girl. A dark girl, pretty but austere; Angie Mawdray asking for a rise in salary. For a while he studied her in silence, then slowly raised his glass to her. She came to him without smiling. The barman did not even look up as they left.

18

Sitting on the curb, waiting for his master to return from the Crusade, the faithful squire watched the river and dreamed of perfect love. Of big beds made for himself and Shamus and the dark-eyed girl, of houseboats hung with lights and filled with naked bodies which never creased and never tired. White boats floating to a Hollywood Heaven of Interminable Dawn, rocking to the music of Frank Sinatra.

You see, Hug, for Shamus and the French it's different. They are lovers because they believe in love, not because they believe in people. Is that clever, Hug? They are lovers out of joy, not because they are afraid to be alone.

"I need money," Shamus said.

He was reeling a little and his face was very bright.

"How much?"

Shamus took a hundred francs.

"The passing of money," Cassidy advised him contentedly, "is a very sexual transaction."

"Piss off," said Shamus.

"Was that love?" Cassidy asked as they walked slowly away.

"Ours is for ever," said Shamus with his old smile, and put his arm round Cassidy's shoulder.

"Lover."

"Yes."

"Go soon. Paris stinks."

"Okay," said Cassidy laughing. "Wherever you like."

Fast now, and angry, a lot of drink inside them. The young squire exerting himself to keep abreast of his questing, errant master. His feet sting through his thin city shoes as the two men bound up the long stone stairway. Above them the white, incandescent dome offers its single breast to the starlit sky. Lanterns, windows lure them but the master is bent on one place, one place only, a green place, it has a green door. They turn a corner; the steps make them turn a corner, and suddenly there are no houses at all, no handrail even for the height-sick apprentice, only the deep blackness of a cave, and the lights of Paris scattered over it, the walls, the ceiling, and the floor, like the wealth of buried kings. But Shamus has no eye for magic, the past is his enemy, he has his own new Vatican ahead. He is half running, thrusting onward up the endless staircase, face wet where the street lamps catch it, driving himself from the shoulders, all the body following.

"Shamus where are we going?"

"Up."

One day, maybe we climb the Eiger; and there'll be a green light waiting on the peak. One more, Shamus said. One more whore and we get out of town.

It was early for that trade, or late. A dream-like silence hung in the green glow of the table lamps and the girls of Kensal Rise sat sleepily as if they had missed the last train home, listening to Sandra's chords played on an unseen piano. Shamus, loving terminals, has entered ahead of Cassidy, his arms raised to shoulder height as if he is about to take off his coat. The girls shift to receive him, a single herd moving to the cowman.

"*Monsieur ne veut pas?*" a middle-aged lady enquires politely, not unlike the Minister's wife, but with a greater show of interest. "*Vous voulez quelqu' chose à boire?*" Norman, thinks Cassidy, Norman French. This part may not be happening; this part, actually, *is* a dream.

"*Shamus!*"

The girls have gathered to him: to Shamus the impeccable Knight. His arms are high above his head, and suddenly it is happening, it is realised, the subject of innumerable dreams. Their hands steal over him, make him their prisoner; pry, invade his knightly shirt, wrestle with the essentially English arrangement of his French waistband; rob him, strip him as the music rises, throw his absurd male clothes to the floor, divide his cloak, it is a martyrdom. Some are ugly, some are naked, but a green light makes virgins of them all, disguises their shadowed places and give a children's eagerness to their movements.

Suddenly to the thud of Sandra's slow piano, Shamus has grasped the tallest girl, a broad-buttocked, black-haired enemy, mouthed and bearded, wide-thighed. And is down on her. Has fought her down, pulling her by the arms, has forced the same arms back to pinion her. Now she averts her hips to escape the sword but Shamus is fighting with his head, shark-like, using it as a hammer to quell her white flesh.

How dark he is against her breasts, her belly, even her infernal places! Now he flings her. Has her wallowing, crying, while she holds him obediently in the scissors of her thighs.

"Shamus!"

Cassidy's voice. Who touched the light? Foul, free kick to England! The light has dimmed on their wedged bodies. This is the clinch, the hold! Wait. She stirs. Groans, draws in her breath, the sword is home! Will she resist? She writhes; shifts her spread knees, but only to admit him further.

Silence and music, one above the other.

The audience has broken ranks, drawing nearer to observe the climax. The defeated one becomes articulate.

Listen! Aha! The whore is confessing her infamy! Conceding battle, begging forgiveness, praising the everlasting king! In vain. They give her no succour. No seconds to throw in the towel; no referee to count the strokes, suppress the screams, administer the morphine. One shout is left in her.

One long-drawn sigh.

Accompanied by a frown; a grid of sexual confusion, drawn in deep fine lines at the centre of the Gallic brow. My God. My French God. My Flaherty.

He is finished? He is not finished? It is safe to approach? A typical French confusion.

Excuse me madam, do you mind?

Lights please. Lights.

Just a minute please, do you mind?

"I'll go," says Cassidy, and stepping quickly forward, helps the drenched Crusader to his feet.

"Monsieur ne veut pas?" Madame enquires again, touching the squire's keen but unproven weapon through the strained worsted.

He has to have an audience, Helen explains. *When we were rich it was the maid. Now we are poor it is Cassidy.*

Five hundred francs, traveller's cheques are acceptable. Green for go.

"I need a church, lover," Shamus whispers to the night lights of the sleeping city. "Quick! I need Flaherty and I need him express."

At High Mass in the Sacré Coeur, among more candles than they had had at the Tour d'Argent, more even than at Sherborne Abbey, Shamus and Cassidy watched the devout gestures of pure boys while covertly passing back and forth the half bottle of whisky.

Dear God this is Aldo Cassidy who last prayed to you when Helen and Shamus were missing believed killed and I faced the crime of innocence for the rest of a long and boring life. Well, since then I must tell you that my prayers have been answered and that I owe you a substantial debt of gratitude. It will take me a considerable time, in fact, to evaluate the many experiences which the reunion promises to put in my way, and in due course we shall have to get together again with Old Hugo the well-known Member of Parliament and work out between us what is the nature of love, what is good and bad, and what is the relevance of it all to our Shared Design for Living. In the meantime, once again, an interim "Thank you" for lifting me quite a few rungs very quickly in the Ladder of Beings, and all safely outside Sandra's earshot.

"It's for the fabric," Cassidy explained. "For rebuilding the church. It's falling down."

"Jesus," said Shamus, staring at the mute mouth of the offertory box. "Jesus. There must be *someone* you don't pay."

It is not easy to leave Paris when you are drunk and tired and on foot; when you are lurching through columns of yellow-lit concrete, looking for a field; when no whore

knows the way and taxi drivers decline your custom.
First they tried to find the Fair: they would creep into the
marquee and sleep in prams. But the Fair had moved.
Twice they recognised the road that led to it; each time, it
led them false. So they decided to look instead for a river
that would guide them to the sea, but the river path ended
at a bridge, and beyond the bridge rose a forest of hideous
buildings blocking their escape. At a tram station they
found an empty tram, but Cassidy could not locate the
power and prayers did not avail them.

"Dance," Shamus proposed. "Maybe he likes dance
best."

In a cobbled alley two men of equal height, different only
in their colour, are dancing. One of them is Shamus; one
of them, as the ever-observant Cassidy correctly records,
is himself.

It is dawn, not evening, because no one is paying attention, no one is up, no one is there. Occasionally, from
Heaven, voices address them in a mother language, Flaherty presumably, or Mrs. Flaherty even, they are here
incognito, a week's trip to inspect the Franco-Irish faithful. But the text of God's message, as so often alas,
reaches them in garbled form, it would be rash to act on
it. Their movements are for an audience; complex but perfectly performed. A divine audience; one that will transport them from a city no longer congenial to Shamus.
They have completed *Swan Lake* and now they are playing Shadows, stalking one another's image along the moist
stucco of an uncomplaining wall, but Shamus finds this
number unrewarding, and having dealt the wall a quite unreasonable kick, bids Cassidy follow him in a dance of his
own invention. Cassidy, anxious to oblige, is trying to keep
time while sending many cordial greetings to his retired
musical instructors, including Mrs. Harabee of Sherborne
School Dorset.

Now Doubtful, think.

I am thinking Mrs. Harabee.

Well think harder Doubtful.

Yes, Mrs. Harabee.

Come on Pailthorpe, says Sandra, *you imitate people's
voices, well now imitate their songs, that's all.*

I can't.
Of course you can. I've heard you singing perfectly
well in church, but still.
But that was with other people, Sandra.
You mean you can't put up with me alone? I'm sorry.

Doubtful I shall report you to your housemaster.
"Yes Shamus."
"Well then fucking listen."

Shamus sings a line likening Helen's breasts to the twin
hills of Shamaree. Obediently Cassidy tries to repeat it.

"I can't," he says, breaking off. "It's all right for you,
you're artistic."

Touched by Cassidy's musical incompetence, Shamus the
darker one embraces him, kissing his cheeks and mouth,
twining his fingers in Cassidy's conventionally heterosexual
hairstyle. Cassidy has no particular feelings at the point of
oral impact, but is embarrassed by his own unshaven
state. About to apologise to Shamus, who appears to have
gone to sleep on his breast, the Oxford undergraduate is
abruptly summoned by bells. Not merely the peal, as Shamus later said, but the bells themselves, despatched in
place of thunderbolts by Flaherty's angry hand, hurtle
downwards over the rooftops and smash into the courtyard in multiplying chaos, inflicting sonic tortures normally reserved for the inhabitants of Sodom. In terror,
Shamus puts his hands over his ears and shouts:

"Stop it! Stop it! We repent. Pooves' penitence, Flaherty lay off! Christ, lover, you bloody fool, look what
you've *done!*"

"You started it," Cassidy objects, but the great writer
having already taken flight, his disciple follows.

They are running therefore, Shamus leading, his hands
still over his ears, weaving and ducking to avoid the
falling bells, his jacket billowing like a life belt.

"Don't look back, you fool, run! Christ why did you
take us to that church, you fucking idiot! Flaherty, you
live! Lover! Hell!"

Cassidy is down.

He falls probably full length, cracking his knee against the lid of a Parisian dustbin and distinctly feeling the knee-cap dislodge itself and roll away into the opposing scrum. Shamus drags him to his feet. The horse is looking round at them as they unwind the brake. Of some age this horse, its face is grey, black rings surround its eyes.

The bells have stopped.

"What did I tell you?" says Shamus contentedly. "South," he tells the horse. "*Sud*. We would have shunshine."

Pulling up the blanket, he turns to Cassidy and draws him down into the leather cushions of the *fiacre*.

"Come on lover, give us a kiss."

Salt sweat joins the loved ones' faces, Old Hugo's stubble recalls a lifetime's quest.

"Jesus I hate that city," Shamus declared. "Can't think why we ever went there."

"Nor can I," said Cassidy. "It's a heap."

"Is he a good kid?" Shamus asked.

"Super. They both are."

"Can't take them with you, lover, little buggers live on. Then they want what you want. The fucks, the laughs, the drinks, the bosscows . . ."

"It'll be better for them," said Cassidy.

"It wasn't better for us, though, was it, lover?"

No answer. Cassidy is asleep. No conversation. Shamus is also asleep. Only the horse has life in him, moving ever further south.

In fact, however, Cassidy was awake. Sentient, fast-thinking, acute. His body was stiff and aching but he dared not move because Hugo was sleeping in his arms, and only sleep would mend the injured child's kneecap.

It's a *coach* Hug, he is explaining in his mind; drawn by a super grey horse, the kind they have in Sainte-Angèle only in Sainte-Angèle it's a sledge.

A coach has wheels, Hug. Wooden, wobbly wheels, and the horse is the hunter they offered me at Haverdown, a thoroughbred of great docility, sent by God to take us away from a stinking city.

"Dad how much money have you got?" Hugo enquired drowsily. "How much in the whole world?"

"Depends how the market goes," said Cassidy. "Enough," he added, thinking: who wants enough?

Stretching—and simultaneously releasing the infant Shamus from his arms—Cassidy braced himself more comfortably against the seat and, rolling up his trouser leg, cautiously examined his injured knee. It was still in place and no mark was visible. Must be internal, he thought, accepting the bottle; the bleeding is internal, and poured a little whisky on the afflicted area.

"Is it all in prams?" Shamus asked, still on the matter of money.

"God, no. It's spread."

"I was rich once," said Shamus. They were going down the ride at Haverdown: an interminable avenue of tall trees. Not south but east: red sun lay at the end of it and the tarmac was swimming red.

"I was rich once," Shamus repeated, tossing the empty bottle into the road.

"Meeow," said Cassidy, quoting the master. "I fuck myself of self-pity."

"Well done," said Shamus with approval, and pushed him on to the road. But Cassidy was ready for the assault and landed neatly thanks to his army training.

"Lover."

"Yes."

"Is Monte Carlo a place?"

"For a night or so," said Cassidy, who had never been there.

"Great. We'll go to Monte Carlo."

And gave revised instructions to the horse.

"Terrified of everything in life except the perpetuation of it," Shamus read aloud. "How's that? I've written it down about you. I'm going to make it completely permanent."

Trust your wooden wheels. Tumbrils. Aristos on the way to execution. Miss Mawdray, get on to Park Wards at once, will you, tell them I want the wheels fixed?

Dozing again, Cassidy lay this time with the elder Hugo, his father, the night they took a train to Torquay to buy the Imperial Hotel. Old Hugo was not long back in those days, a month, two perhaps, still stopping in front of doors and waiting for Cassidy to open them. They had agreed on a reconnoitre, afterwards they would discuss the finance, possibly approach one of the big people, Charles Clore or the Aga Khan, it depended on whom they could trust. On the train, waiting for the dinner call, the old man began weeping. Cassidy, who had not heard this sound before, thought at first he was choking, for the sobs came in a high-pitched retch, like one of Sandra's bitches when she had swallowed a bone.

"Here," he said, offering him a handkerchief, "Have this," and returned to his newspaper.

Then it dawned on him that Old Hugo had no bone to chew, nothing to choke on but his shame, in fact; and lowering the newspaper stared at him, at the broken figure hunched to fit so small a space, and the massive shoulders shaking in loneliness, and the bald head mottled red.

To lift the newspaper?

To go to him?

"I'll get you a drink," he said, and fetched a miniature from the bar, running all the way and crashing the queue.

"You took your time," the old man said, dead straight, when Cassidy returned. He was reading his *Standard*, the greyhound page had caught his interest. "What's *that?*" Eyeing the miniature.

"Whisky."

"When you buy whisky," the old man said, turning the little bottle in his enormous, steady hand, "buy a decent brand, or nothing."

"Sorry," said Cassidy. "I forgot."

"Lover."

"Yes, Shamus."

An hour had passed, perhaps a day. The sun had disappeared, the road was dull and dark, and the trees were black against an empty sky.

"Look at me very closely. Are you looking?"

"Sure," said Cassidy, his eyes still closed against Old Hugo's shoulder.

"Deep into the innerest recesses of my irresistible eyes?"

"Deeper."

"While you look at this picture, lover, thousands of brain cells are dying of old age. Still looking?"

"Yes," said Cassidy, thinking: this conversation came earlier actually; this is what made me think of my father.

"Now. Now. Bang! Bang! See that? Thousands dead. Spread over the cerebral battlefield. Coughing out their tiny lives."

"Don't worry," said Cassidy consolingly. "You'll go on for ever."

Long embraces under the warm blankets.

"I wasn't talking about *me*," Shamus explained, kissing him. "I was talking about you. *My* cells get a lovely time. It's yours we're worried about. I'm writing that down too, if I remember it."

Partly, Cassidy thought, this is an inward journey. Earthbound Aldo Cassidy, *en route* to Monte Carlo, relives his life in the company of his nomadic familiar.

"Lover."

"Mmh."

"Never go back to Paristown, will we, lover?"

Shamus' voice has a note of anxiety. Not everything is play on this journey.

"Never."

"Promise?"

"Promise."

"Liar."

Cassidy, sobering, revisits the question. "Tell me Shamus, actually, why *don't* you want to go back to Paris?"

"Doesn't matter, does it? We're not going."

Partly however, as recorded, an outward journey; for when he woke again the police were keenly disputing the horse's possession.

They were near a private airfield, in a lay-by between two blue vans; a small biplane was circling to land. Everyone was talking; however, the coachman, who had arrived separately by bicycle, was talking loudest. He was an old, grey man in sailcloth trousers and a long overcoat from the war, and he was kicking the grey's front legs and cursing it for infidelity. The coachman, who shared the view of the police that Shamus was in no way to blame, would not take Cassidy's traveller's cheques so they went to a bank and the police kept guard while Cassidy signed his name ten times along the dotted line.

How did I ever cash a cheque at dawn?

"Shamus," said Cassidy, thinking of Bloburg and Meale and letters from Abalone Crescent, "isn't it time we went back?"

"Blow," said Shamus.

They blew. From the pile of twigs a thin smoke rose, but no flame. Their suits lay beside them on the shingle like dead friends; beyond them a dried-up river, just a shallow stream where they had bathed, and cracking clay imported from the moat at Haverdown. Beyond the river, the fields, beyond the fields a wood, a railway line, and a bank of Flemish sky that reached for ever.

"You'll *never* do it without paper," Cassidy objected. He was feeling cold and rather sober. "I could ring for a taxi if you'd let me dress."

A train passed over the viaduct. There were no passengers but the lights were lit in the carriages.

"I don't *want* a taxi."

"Why not?"

"Because I don't, so piss off. I don't want to go to Paris and I don't want a taxi." He blew again, shivering. "And if you try to dress I'll kill you."

"Then let me get some paper."

"No."

"Why not?"

"Shut up! *Sodder!* Shut up!"

"Meeow," said Cassidy.

The last bottle was empty so they put it on a stick and broke it with artillery fire, ten stones each, fired alternately. And that was when the boy appeared. Mark's age but younger in the face. He carried a fishing rod and a rucksack and he was sitting on a Dutch bicycle of which Cassidy owned the United Kingdom concession. First he compared their genitals, one blond one black but otherwise little to choose, then he picked up a stone and threw it hard and straight at the post where the bottle had stood.

Cassidy wrote out a shopping list and gave him twenty drenched francs.

"And mind how you cross the road," he warned him.

"You see my view is," said Cassidy cautiously, pulling the cork with his teeth—the boy, a resourceful child, had persuaded the shop to draw it halfway—"that if we called a *cab*—"

"Lover," Shamus interrupted.

"Yes."

Encouraged by several editions of the Paris press, the twigs were burning with conviction. Farther down the bank, the boy was casting for fish.

"Lover do you reckon this is a clash of egos?"

"No," said Cassidy.

"Ids?"

"No."

"Ego versus soul? Ibsen?"

"It's not a clash at all. I want to get back, *you* don't. I want a bath and a change and you're prepared to live like a troglodyte for the rest of your life—"

The stone hit him on the side of the head, the left side just behind the ear. He knew it was a stone all the way, saw it coming as he fell, saw the map on it, mainly of the Swiss Alps, the Angelhorn massif leading. The distance to the ground was much farther than he expected. He had time to throw the bottle to one side before he landed, and time to get his arm up before his head hit the shingle. Then Shamus was holding him, kissing him, pouring the wine between his teeth, forgive lover, forgive, weeping, choking like Old Hugo in the train, and the boy was pulling a small brown fish out of the water, a child's fish for a child's rod.

"What the hell did you do it for?" Cassidy asked.

Shamus was sitting apart from him in self-imposed purdah, the beret pulled over his eyes for remorse, his bare back cut in two by the grimy watermark of the depleted river. He said nothing.

"It's a bloody odd way to behave, I must say. Specially for a master of words."

The boy threw back the fish. Either he had not seen the incident, or he had seen many such incidents already, and blood did not alarm him.

"For Christ's sake stop hitting yourself with that stone," Cassidy continued irritably. "Just tell me why you did it, that's all. We did everything you wanted. Froze in the bloody river to feel our identities, ruined our new suits, caught pneumonia, and all of a sudden you stone me. *Why?*"

Silenzio. Very slightly the beret moves in rejection.

"All right, you told me: you don't want to go back to Paris. Fine. But even great lovers can't camp beside a dried-up river all their lives. Well *why* don't you want to go back? Don't you like the hotel? Are you fed up with cities all of a sudden?" A pause. "Is it something to do with Dale? With your book?"

This time the beret does not move at all, not in rejection, not in acceptance; the beret is as still as Sandra at the door, when she is cross with him for not being cosmic, for not providing her with the tragedy she was groomed for.

"Shamus for God's sake. One moment we are halfway to being pooves, the next you're trying to kill me. What the fuck's the matter with you?"

As if shaken by the wind, the bare back sways. Finally the penitent lifts the bottle, drinks.

"Here," said Cassidy, crouching beside him. "I'll have some of that." Putting out his hand he received not the wine, but the battered carnation from Shamus' buttonhole. Gently lifting the beret, Cassidy saw how the tears had collected on the rim.

"Forget it," he said softly. "It didn't hurt, I promise. I don't think you even did it. Look. Look, no lump, no throbbing, nothing. Feel, come on, put your hand there."

He lifted Shamus' muddy hand and put it against his head.

"You've *got* to love me, lover," Shamus whispered, as more tears came. "I need it, honest. That's nothing to what I'll do to you if you don't love me."

His hand was like a second Confirmation, light and full of feeling, trembling on Cassidy's scalp.

"All of you, you've got to give me *all* of you. *I* do. I've given you a blank cheque, lover. Real."

"I'm trying to understand," Cassidy promised. "I am trying. If only you'd tell me what it was."

"Fucking little bourgeois," said Shamus hopelessly. "You'll never make it. Jesus!" he cried suddenly. Relinquishing Cassidy's hand he bounded into the air. "My identity! It's ruined!"

He was pointing at a patch of scrub grass where his passport lay face downward. A dead butterfly, wings spread hopelessly for takeoff. The blue dye oozing over the grass.

"Bleeding to death," he whispered, lifting it with both hands. "Lover, get me an ambulance."

At the village post office, fully dressed, they bought a French envelope and sent their carnations to Helen. The gum tasted of peppermint and the carnations were no longer young.

And two gliders to bring them closer to Flaherty. And a kite for despatching prayers.

And a notebook because on the way back to Paris Shamus was going to start a new novel, on the theme of David and Jonathan. Also, he had lost the old one in the river, and did not hold with the past.

Roads to Paris, Cassidy wrote in his private Baedeker, in the florid prose which was yet another of Old Hugo's countless gifts, *are long and various, often doubling back upon themselves. Some are bordered by great hills from which kites and gliders may be flown and avocations made to Irish gods, some by factories filled with sad proles and the Many-too-Many mounted on brakeless bicycles; some again by inns where whores banished from the city provide great writers with mediocre glimpses of the infinite. But all these roads are slow roads, made for the dragging of feet; for Paris is no longer popular, it is menaced by the mystery of Dale.*

Lying in the barber's chair, covered in choirboy white, the weary chronicler fell asleep while being shaved, and dreamed of naked Helen standing on the beach at Dover, two dead carnations at her breasts while she launched small sailing ships in races round the world. When he woke the barber was cutting his hair.

"Shamus I don't *want* it cut!"

Shamus was sitting on the bench, writing in his notebook.

"It's good for you, lover. New life as a monk," he said vaguely, not looking up. "Necessary sacrifice."

"No!" said Cassidy, pushing the man away. God in Heaven, how to face Trumper's now? *"Non, non, non."*

Shamus continued writing.

"He wants it longer," he explained to the barber with whom he was on terms of closest friendship. *"Il le veut plus long."*

"Shamus what do you believe in?"

At the world's edge the red sun rose or sank behind the swollen grid lines of a factory. Lights lay on the fields, and the gliders were wet with dew. "What *is* the light at the end of the pier?"

"Once I believed in a whore," said Shamus, after long thought. "She worked Lord's cricket ground. I never knew anyone who loved the game better. She kept all the batting averages in her handbag."

"What else?"

He hated clergymen, he said. Hated them with the passion of a zealot.

"What else?"

He hated the past, he said, he hated convention, he hated the blind acceptance of restriction and the voluntary imprisonment of the soul.

"Isn't that all rather *negative?*" Cassidy said at last.

"I hate that too," Shamus assured him. "Essential to be positive."

They were on stolen bicycles, one side of Cassidy's head now much colder than the other. And *that*, said Shamus, was Cassidy's problem.

Meeow.

19

Who would be Shamus? Cassidy wondered, watching him write at the inn.

The city was not far away now; perhaps that was why he was writing; to arm himself against whatever threatened him in Paris. A pink glow waited at the end of the avenue, and the evening air hummed like a boiler. They sat at a table beside the road, under an umbrella advertising Coca-Cola, drinking Pernod to clear their heads. The taxi waited in a lay-by, the driver was reading pornography.

Who would live with his own recording angel, life after life recorded, distorted, straightened and rounded off? Who would be Shamus, daily chronicling his own reality? Always attacking life, never accepting it; always walking, never settling.

"Will it really be a novel?" he asked. "A full-length one, like the others?"

"Maybe."

"What about?"

"I told you. Friendship."

"Read it," said Cassidy.

"Piss off," said Shamus and read: *"Reality was what divided them, reality was what put them together. Jonathan, knowing it was there, ran away from it; but David was never sure, and went looking for it every day."*

"Is it a fairy tale?" Cassidy asked.

"Maybe."

"Which of us is David?"

"You, you stupid sod, because you're fair. *David was a great sceptic, for he loved the present world and all its riches. Jonathan defamed the world, and was therefore the prophet of a better one; but David was too thick to understand that, and Jonathan too proud to tell him. David's world was one in which the ideals of the herd were realised, because he was of the herd, the best of the Many-*

209

too-Many. Jonathan had naivety of the heart, but David had rococo of the soul. . . ."

"But what does it *mean*, Shamus?"

"It means you need a drink," said Shamus, "before I stone you again for being a heretic."

To iron a passport—it is a truism of which Cassidy had not till then been sufficiently aware—you need a whore, whores have the most sensitive fingers.

"They're the best ironers in the world," Shamus explained. "Famous for it. And when she's ironed the passport," he added, with the pride of a time and motion expert, "you can fuck her. It's time you lost your hymen."

So they went to the Gare du Nord, a terminal of great attraction, to find a pair of hands.

Their return to the city had not been, could not be perhaps, as triumphal as their flight from it. Cassidy had assumed they would go at once to the St. Jacques. He had even worked out a system for getting in without going through the hall—to cross the doorman's palm and slip in by way of the staff entrance, as becomes an hotelier's son—for their suits, though moderately dry, were shrunk and not at all debonair. Also he had fences to mend; the Fair was becoming an anxiety; how about his mail and the phone calls?

Shamus would have none of it. The city had already darkened him; his mood was sharper and less kind.

"I'm sick of the fucking St. Jacques. It's a rotten little death cell. It's full of fucking bishops, I know it is!"

"But Shamus you liked it before—"

"I hate it. Fuck you."

He's running away, thought Cassidy suddenly: I know that look, it's mine.

"What are you afraid of?" he was going to ask; but learning prudence, abstained. So they went to a place that Shamus knew, somewhere off the rue du Bac, a white courtyard house near an embassy; the street was lined with diplomatic cars. Inspired by the cars perhaps, Shamus insisted on signing their names as Burgess and Maclean.

"Shamus are you sure?"

Of course he was bloody sure; Cassidy could mind his bloody business or do the other thing, right?

Right.

Good hands are not plentiful at the Gare du Nord, even at commuting time on a sunlit evening. There are hands that hold luggage, hands that hold umbrellas, and tender hands that are linked to lovers and cannot, alas, be parted. Being already tired from their exertions, the two friends sat on a bench and, emptying their crumpled pockets, fed remnants of bread to French pigeons. Shamus, morose, barely spoke. Cassidy's head was aching painfully and his kneecap, till recently quiescent, had started to play him up again after the cycling.

"Good," said Shamus, when he told him.

To ward off the encroaching despondency, therefore, Cassidy began singing. Not so much singing: droning. A lyric of his own invention, rendered in a modulated French monotone, a very passable imitation of Maurice Chevalier.

Which was how they found Elise, the well-known anagram of Elsie.

> *Ze leedle birds of Paris*
> *Zey 'ave a lerv'ly time*
> *Zey 'ave a lerv'ly time,*
> *Until ze snow take all zeir*
> *bread a-way . . .*
> *Until ze snow take all zeir*
> *bread a-way. . . .*

Woken from his melancholy, Shamus stared at him wide-eyed. It was the first time Cassidy had done a voice for Shamus, and Chevalier was one of his best.

"Lover go *on*. That's great. In the first position, go on! Jesus that's great, that's human. Why didn't you tell me?"

"Well your voices are so much better."

"Balls! Go *on*, you sodder, sing!"

So Cassidy continued:

> *Zey wiggle zeir feathers . . .*
> *Zey wiggle zeir pretty tails . . .*

> *Zey hop, and* lerve, *and sing*
> *zeir leedle song . . .*
> *Until ze snow, ze gruel snow . . .*
> *Take* all *zeir bread away. . . .*

"More, lover! Jesus that's great! Hey listen everybody, listen to Cassidy!"

Leaping up, Shamus was about to summon a larger audience when they saw the girl, standing, smiling at them, wearing a smart fawn coat and a red shiny handbag like a Swiss conductor's purse on the small trains that mount the Angelhorn.

She was young and quite tall, hair cut short like a boy's; a trim, fair girl with fine skin that wrinkled into crazing when she smiled. Her toes and heels were together, and her legs, though these were not relevant to the restoration of Shamus' identity, were very straight but not at all thin, Angie Mawdray's legs in fact, revealed on the same generous scale.

"Ask to look at her hands," Shamus urged.

She was smiling at Cassidy, not Shamus; she seemed to think him more her kind of man.

"She's wearing gloves," Cassidy objected.

"Then tell her to take them off, you ape."

"Do you speak English?" Cassidy asked.

She shook her head.

"No," she said.

"For Christ's sake, lover, this is important!"

"*Vos mains,*" Cassidy said, "*nous voulons voir. . . .* Wouldn't you like to sit down?" he asked politely, offering her his seat.

Demurely, still smiling, she sat between them on the bench. Lifting her right hand, Cassidy gently removed the glove. It was of fine white nylon and it slipped off very easily like a stocking. The hand beneath it was soft and smooth and it curled naturally into Cassidy's.

"Now ask her whether she irons passports," said Shamus.

"I'm sure she does," said Cassidy.

"Then ask her what she charges. One passport, one fuck. Taxes, service, the lot."

"I'd rather just pay her, Shamus. Please." And to the

girl: *"Je m'appelle Burgess,"* he explained. *"Mon ami est l'écrivain Maclean."*

"Bonjour, Maclean," said Elise politely, while her hand fluttered in Cassidy's like a tiny bird. *"Et moi je m'appelle Elise."*

At the reception desk of the white hotel Cassidy borrowed an iron, a black smoothing iron of about 1870, Sandra had one in the kitchen and preferred it to the Morphy Richards. The receptionist was an Algerian boy, a very tired accomplice, but the sight of Elise appeared to give him hope.

"She'll need blotting paper," said Shamus. "Blotting paper to put between the pages."

His temporary elation had left him.

"Okay, okay," said Cassidy.

The corridors were very narrow and dark. Through the connecting wall, a baby grizzled continuously. Cassidy helped Elise with her coat and sat her in a chair with a glass of wine to make her feel at home, and soon they were exchanging commonplaces about the weather and the hotel. Elise lived with her family, she said; it was not always convenient but it was economic and one had company. Cassidy said he lived with his family too, his father was an hotelier, the guests were sometimes tiresome. Shamus, meanwhile, deaf to such formalities, had gone straight to the window and pulled the table into the centre of the room. Tipping the electric heater on its back, he laid the flatiron on top of it.

"Ah vous avez deux chambres!" said Elise, as Shamus emerged from the bedroom with a blanket. *"Ça c'est commode, alors!"*

It was an entire suite, Cassidy assured her, and leading the way showed her the full reach of the premises. The courtyard had a vine tree and a fountain; the bathroom was lined with old marble. Elise found it romantic, but feared it was expensive to heat.

"For fuck's sake!" Shamus shouted. "She's not buying the place is she? Tell her to come and iron my bloody passport."

"She's washing," said Cassidy. "Shamus *please*—"

"Washing to hell. She's disinfecting herself. Spraying flit on her fanny, that's what they all do. Put you through a bloody sheep dip if they get half a chance. Here, take sixpence and get the blotting paper."

"What's the hurry?" Cassidy demanded, now quite cross. "What difference does it make? The iron isn't even hot yet. Relax."

"Get the blotting paper!"

Suddenly cautious, Cassidy said, "She'll be all right with you alone won't she?"

"Of course she won't. What the hell are you talking about? Do you realise that in an average working day that angel of light eats about ten of us alive? She does not observe, she does not *expect* to observe, either the inhibitions or the priorities of the English middle class. For all she cares—" They heard the flush of the lavatory; Elise returned from the bedroom. "—you and I can truss her up like a turkey and play football with her as long as we get her back on the street in good time to find two more of us."

He thrust the passport into the girl's hand.

"But Shamus, I don't think she *is* one. I think she's just an ordinary girl."

Like Heather Ast, he wanted to say; Hugo would like her very much.

Carefully, Elise turned the pages. Her fingers were slim and competent, and found their way most cleverly into narrow places.

"Mais vous vous n'appelez pas Maclean," she remarked at last, comparing Shamus with the photograph.

"Maclean, c'est son nom de plume," said Cassidy quickly, still at the door.

"Get the blotting paper!"

The stationer was across the road and Cassidy ran all the way. When he came back, out of breath, Shamus and Elise were standing at opposite sides of the room not looking at one another. Her hair was disarranged and she seemed angry.

"All right," said Shamus, looking from one to the other of them. "Have your big relationship. Christopher Robin and Wendy touch wees, go beddie-byes. But when I come back I want her *out* and that passport ironed."

"Shamus—" Cassidy called, but the door had closed on him with a bang.

"*Il n'est pas gentil, votre ami,*" said Elise.

"He's worried," said Cassidy, and so am I. And in his best maternal French explained that Shamus was a great writer, perhaps the greatest of his time, that she was the first person in the whole world not to find him irresistible, that he had just finished his masterpiece and was naturally concerned with its reception. His anxiety in fact (Cassidy felt he could confide in her) related to a matter of business. To the film rights. The sale was made but yet to be confirmed; these deals had a way of falling through. She may have seen the film *Doctor Zhivago,* well Shamus wrote it; also *Goodbye, Mr. Chips.*

Elise listened very gravely to these explanations, but although she admired Maclean's work they did not satisfy her. Men with two names, she said, reopening his identity at the first page, were not to be trusted, and Maclean was not gentle.

"*Vous êtes aussi artiste, Burgess?*" she asked.

"*Un peu,*" said Cassidy. Hearing him she smiled with shy complicity.

"*Moi aussi,*" she murmured, with a little nod. "*Un peu artiste, mais pas ... entièrement.*"

She was a very quiet girl. He had known at once she had a decent quiet, but now in the gathering dusk she filled the room with stillness. She ironed slowly and with concentration, head cocked a little as if she were waiting for Shamus' return, and when a footfall sounded in the corridor she paused and looked in that direction. Sandra, when she ironed, put her feet wide apart and stuck out her elbow like her father the Brigadier, but Elise kept very upright, conscious only of her task.

"I thought we might go out to dinner," he said. "Just the two of us."

Her head lifted; he could not see her expression but he took it for one of doubt.

"We could go to the Tour d'Argent if you like."

She ironed another page.

"No, Burgess," she said quietly. "*Pas de Tour d'Argent.*"

"Oh but I can afford it. *Je suis riche, Elise . . . vraiment.* Whatever you like, the theatre if you prefer."

"*Vous n'avez pas de théâtre à Londres, Burgess?*"

"Yes. We do, of course. Lots. Only I don't seem to go very much."

Again, for a time, she made no answer. Footsteps ascended the stairs but they passed without a pause, lacking Shamus' sprightliness. Closing the passport, Elise set the iron on its edge and folded the blanket on the table, then moved slowly round the room, picking up the dirty glasses and emptying the ashtrays.

"*Tu veux vraiment sortir, Burgess?*" she asked from the sink.

"I want to make you happy," he said. "I'd like to give you a good time. I'm quite safe, honestly."

"*Bon,*" she said, and smiled distantly, as if his wish were no longer her concern. "*Bon, c'est comme vous voulez.*"

Dear Lover, he wrote, *You are a bad-tempered sodder. Elise is taking me to her pad. Back by ten thirty.*

And left the note beside the freshly ironed passport.

At the door, letting him help her into her coat, Elise kissed him. At first it was a child's kiss, Mark beneath the mistletoe. Then, like a tiny paintbrush, her tongue traced the line between her lips, moved upwards to his eyelids.

"We could go to Allard," he said, stepping ahead of her into the corridor. It was a place which Bloburg recommended.

"*Burgess . . .*" Her hand was on his arm.

"*Oui?*"

"*Je n'ai pas faim.*"

Cassidy laughed. "Oh, come on," he said. "You'll be hungry by the time we get there." And left another note at the desk, virtually a duplicate but ending "Love."

At Allard, he offered her a trip to London to learn the hotel trade in which, he said, his father was immensely influential. Elise was very grateful but declined: her mother, she said, forbade her to travel alone. After that they talked little. Elise ate faster than Cassidy, and when she had finished she asked for a cab, which Cassidy paid for in advance.

She would have loved to stay longer, she explained to him, but she had obligations to her family.

Somewhere, nevertheless, in a white house in Paris, in an attic lifted from the warm streets and set above a court-yard that echoed with the rifle shots of beaten carpets, in a city trembling with the energies of love, in a wide brass bed with a down comforter washed white by the moon, somewhere between dusk and dawn, in that hour which after great exertion comes before intense fatigue, alone at last in the inward world of his romantic dreams, Cassidy loved Elise.

She came to him through the window, in long strides of her sheer white legs; lit by the striped moonlight of the shutters, she stood at his bedhead whispering *Burgess*. Her body rose like a white candle out of her fallen clothes, her tiny nipples were pink stains in the wax. *Burgess are you there?* Yes Elise. *Burgess tu es tellement gentil: do you really want to marry me?* Yes Elise. *Why are you dressed, Burgess?* I was going to find you Elise. I was going to walk the streets until I found you, then take you to the Sacré Coeur, where influential priests are wait-ing to perform the ceremony. *That is a very sensible ar-rangement. But what shall we do about money?* I have secreted twenty thousand pounds at the Banque Fédérale in the Elysées. I achieved this illegally by making fic-titious payments for French components. *Burgess*, she breathed.

She undressed him with gravity, loosening first his tie and lifting it in a loop wide of his ears in order not to crush the silk. *Burgess, mon artiste, my inventor, my child, my husband, my provider, is anyone as rich as you?* No, said Cassidy. But best of all it has not affected my integ-rity. *That is true*, said Elise. *You have great naturalness.* Sometimes, undressing him, she had to pause and settle him for her pleasure, pressing his head against her breasts or lap, his cheek into the silky odourless hair between her long closed thighs, arranging him like loved sculpture in the moonlight, commending his dimensions to unseen fe-male friends, calling him kind and virile, gentle, brave, and virtuous. *Venez*, she whispered at last, turning to him the long plain of her back. *Follow my immaculate and pert behind, my twin watermelons which slyly conceal the crev-ice of forbidden love, the Secret Flower of the uninhibited Orient.* Elise, my person is protruding and erect. Will you cohabit with me? *It is my highest ambition, Burgess.* She led him from the centre, encircling his manhood with her long, domesticated fingers as they drifted back and forth over the Paris sky. *Tu aimes ça Burgess? Do I give you pleasure? Shall I do it also with my mouth? I feel what you feel Burgess. My responses are entirely homosexual.* Just the fingers thank you, Cassidy replied. The fingers will do very nicely. *Burgess, you are so pure.* Elise, who is this helping you? he asked after a moment. Do I detect *other* fingers at work as well as your own, Elise? Surely I hear Frank Sinatra singing and discern the fumes of woodsmoke in your hair? *No one,* she assured him. *They are my hands only, you are dreaming of another.* Saying this, she opened his legs and traced with her nail's edge the tiny seam that joined him front and back, once, twice, three times. *More Burgess?* A little please. That will do thank you. *And here a little attention?* Elise enquired, cradling his grateful globes, making the hair of them signal with sharp small fires, making the skin taut and loving. *Now I leave you,* she whispered, *your manhood agonisingly suspended in the darkness.* You wouldn't like to finish it off, would you, while you're here? Cassidy asked. *You know the rules,* Elise replied softly, melting into the moonlight. *See you at the Sacré Coeur.*

Don't be late, Cassidy called. Don't be late. Late. Late. "Shamus?"

How could he face such solitude out there? What was he doing, far into the night? Out with the Few? I'm not enough for him. He needs writers; people who read his books.

An imitation ormolu clock glistening in the moonlight permanently stuck at half past two. Outside the window the bearing of carpets, tapping to nothing in slow drips.

Shamus, come back.

If only to turn me outward again; to turn my hand to better loves than me.

Darling, the outward Cassidy wrote next day, at frightful length, punishing his erring hand. It was nine o'clock in the morning, Shamus had not returned. *Things have not so far gone particularly well, and if it's any consolation to you—which I doubt!—you are well clear of the wicked city and its temptations. The Embassy people, true to form, made a complete hash of our Stand—no telephones,*

*no separate Cassidy tent for entertainment, just all thrown
together like cattle—and although we landed one big order on the first day, trade has generally been very sticky.
I have a hunch that as you predicted the Vietnam war is
finally having its effect—there is simply less money around,
people are wary of what they buy and quite bad about
settling. Our one big order—three hundred chassis—went
to a very suspect lady (middle-aged) who took a thousand
strollers from Bee-Line last year and still hasn't paid
up. McKechnie had to recoup from the Exports Credit
Guarantee people, and they won't cover her any more.
(sorry!) However, it was Meale's first major triumph
and I could hardly refuse to accept the order for fear of
hurting his confidence, which is to say the least a delicate
plant.*

*Also, I have to confess that I am not much good on my
own, which I suppose you knew all along. On the other
hand, the alternatives to solitude are none too beguiling
either. I have avoided Lemming and co. like the plague
—the idea of "doing Paris" with the trade is almost physically repellant to me.*

*As to Bloburg he is being an absolute pest. I know you
feel strongly that one should show him particular consideration, but even tolerance has its limits. Having landed
me with an exhausting and frequently worthless programme of entertaining etc., he is constantly trying to
"fix me up" as he calls it with female friends of his. One
of these, a damsel called Elise, actually appeared at my
bedroom door late at night with a note from him. Never
fear—she was a very scarey lady indeed, with those very
brown unblinking eyes which your mother rightly dis-
trusts. I am convinced she was on drugs, and when I sent
her off she just drifted away down the corridor as if she
didn't give a damn. Very unflattering! So much then for
vice and infidelity, but since I had poor McKechnie with
me at the time—he and his wife are in very deep water
and the poor fellow was almost in tears—the incident
passed off more as a joke than anything else. I honestly
feel that people who reach that pass should break it
up and have done with it, don't you?*

*Last night, Meale disappeared in a huff after a ridiculous
dispute with Lemming at the hotel—something to do
with an iron, if you please, who should have it first.*

Anyway, he waltzed off and I suppose that when he comes back I shall have to step in and bang their heads together.

I talk because I have nothing to say, he thought, numbering the fourth page; she would love me better if I *had* slept with Elise. Is that—rereading his turgid prose—is that in fact what I *want* her to believe?

In the few spare moments left to me, I have tried to make contact with the French playing fields people, but not much joy. Yesterday I did succeed in going out to one of the suburbs and inspecting a potential site, of all things in a dried-up riverbed—you might look into that possibility in England—what does the Water Board do with its dried-up riverbeds? But mainly it was the hair-raising drive there and back which left an impression! We did about ninety all the way—no brakes and of course no seat belts.
Incidentally, I tried to ring you last night and again this morning and just got a burr, burr, burr. Where are you all the time? I do trust you are not compensating for my absence in any inadvisable way!! I was going to propose you came out here for a few days after the Fair has ended—say on the Monday or Tuesday—and then perhaps I could give you the attention you have so long deserved, restore my somewhat frayed nerves after this silly, maddening week, and get to know you again the way we used to. If you still know what I mean. Do you? Please give my special love to Hug. I have bought you both super presents. Can't wait to deliver them.

Pailthorpe

P.S. Incidentally: somebody stopped me in the street yesterday and asked me whether I was Guy Burgess: can you imagine? It must be my louche look. How's John E.?

Waiting again, this time with real anxiety.

Telephone Helen? Place enquiries with the Economic Minister? *It's Cassidy the Norman Frenchman, we met in quieter times, you remember, haha. Well actually, he's going under the name of Maclean, it's hard to explain why.*

And I'm Burgess yes. Well it's a joke you see, we have an identity problem.

Waiting, Cassidy mended his fences, an excuse for great activity.

20

Leaving the white hotel gratefully behind him (notes to Shamus posted with the boy, in the bedroom, drawing room, and fine rococo lavatory) the President, Managing Director, Chairman, and Most Active Principal of Cassidy's Overseas Couplings, a company recently added to The Stock Exchange Index and widely tipped as a good long shot for the investor looking for a flutter, straightens his tie, puts his world back into shape, and fastens it at every threatened seam. Pausing on his way to the Hotel St. Jacques, an establishment known to him from previous business trips to Paris, he buys with the last of his traveller's cheques a cheap but passable raincoat which disguises the questionable condition of his suit. At the desk, where his return is received without comment, he takes possession of certain business mails of no pressing importance and enquires most casually after his associate and roommate Monsieur (note the name) not Maclean but Shamus.

The intelligence is not enlightening.

Monsieur Shamus came in yesterday evening and collected his post. Yes there was much post. Naturally: Monsieur Shamus was a person of the highest distinction. Thereafter Monsieur Shamus went to his room and made a two-hour telephone call to London, the manager hoped the cost could be covered by a separate and perhaps an earlier payment, since he understood that Monsieur Cassidy was charged with settling the accounts of his superior. To this request, the cunning negotiator readily assented on the condition that he be shown the telephonist's ticket. The ticket gave a number in Temple Bar which the well-known secret service agent Burgess covertly noted on the back of the bill, but afterwards lost. Ascending in Flaherty's lift he made quickly for the love nest and continued his search for the absent writer.

It is here that the crime took place. The room is in disorder. Cassidy's clothes cupboard has been ransacked and the best things removed.

Feeling markedly less concerned for Shamus, Cassidy turns his attention to other clues. He had lain on his bed, no doubt to make the forty-pound telephone call. Three typewritten messages from the hotel telephonist yield identical information: a Monsieur Dale has telephoned, Shamus should ring him back. On the eiderdown, several postcards to Shamus, written and despatched by the addressee before he left London and signed variously Keats, Scardanelli, and Perseus, wish him a useful rest and congratulate him on his well-attested existence. These cards include lists of places he must visit, together with information on rivers, public fountains, and the shrines of great writers now dead. One such card cautioned him severely against venery; another, from Helen, reminded him to bring home a *terrine* and gave him the name of a shop distinguished by its fine foods.

Also on the scene of the kidnap: one volume (in German, mysteriously) of Schiller's *Uber Naive und Sentimentalische Dichtung;* one tract from Flaherty on the subject of modern heresies, citing in particular the Pope and Archbishop Ramsey; one paperback work entitled *Flying Saucers Are Hostile* ("With 16 pages of photographs and the independent laboratory analysis of UFO Residues"); and one booklet on Mystical Practices laid down by the Master Aethesius from the Planet Venus for the maintenance of health and well-being. Further: one volume of the poems of John Donne, much thumbed.

Further: one empty whisky bottle, Glen Grant 1953, by Berry Brothers and Rudd.

Temporarily putting aside his search for Shamus, Cassidy himself now made a number of telephone calls, largely of a business nature, one to an agency requesting flowers for Sandra, one to his bank requesting a further draft of funds. The business world, it appeared, had not after all disintegrated in his absence. Orders at the Fair were respectable but not dramatic; McKechnie's wife had gone home in a rage. By skilfully playing off Bloburg against Lemming, and Faulk against Meale, Cassidy gave the impression of being too busy with everyone to deal with everyone else. Shortly before lunch, having bathed, shaved, and eaten a large plate of eggs, he actually took a limousine to the Fair and patrolled his lines with an expression of grave preoccupation.

"It's vitally important," he told Meale. "More important than you can possibly guess at this stage."

Having despatched extravagant gifts to Hugo and Mark, he remembered a jocular promise made in South Audley Street just before his departure and transferred a consignment of flowers to Miss Mawdray—no *arrière-pensée*, the welfare of my staff is paramount—but deeming it nevertheless wise to pay cash in order to avoid incriminating slips of paper.

On the way, however, he also remembered his dispute with Heather Ast and, needing comfort, sent her flowers as well. It was not a moment to nurse old grudges.

He returned to the hotel in time for the afternoon mail.

Dear Aldo,

You asked me to write to you so I am doing so. I trust you are all right and I presume you do not wish me to join you as you originally suggested you might, but still. My real reason for writing is to tell you that last night Mummy and I were cleaning out the nursery and came upon a collection of pornography which I assume is yours. Please correct me if I'm wrong. You can imagine what Mummy said. I suppose it's no good my repeating to you yet again that I don't care what you do as long as you tell me. If I had known you liked pornography, which in some people is perfectly normal, I would have cleaned the nursery alone. If your soul is imprisoned by our marriage, go away. Though I must say, I'd like to see what you do with it when it isn't imprisoned. I have of course no objection to your keeping a mistress, if you are not already doing so. I would prefer not to know who it is, but if I do know it will make no difference. Mark's report enclosed.

Sandra

Conduct
Mark has shown a complacent, easy-going approach to

*life typical of the present British attitude of lazy fare
which is affecting the whole nation, particularly the
Unions. He picks and chooses his activities and leaves
them off halfway, he is resentful when chased, beaten, or
ticked off, he hates discipline.*

These communications drove him back into the streets
where for an hour he walked beside the Seine looking for
a good place to jump in. When he returned, Shamus was
lying on the bed, his face in the beret again, legs splayed,
as if he had never left the island.

"Your passport's on the dresser," Cassidy said.

Ironed by loving hands.

"One of these days," said Shamus to the black beret,
"I'll find a whore I like."

"Cassidy," said Shamus quietly, head once more buried
in the pillow.

"Yes."

"Go on about your mother."

"I wasn't talking about my mother."

"Well go on about her all the same, will you?"

The death cell had no ormolu clock, but time had stood
still for quite a while. They had had two drinks for certain—Shamus was on cognac and Perrier, he gave no
reason for the change—but this was the first attempt that
either of them had made to speak. Shamus was using his
Haverdown voice, not quite the Irish but a little bantering.
Tense, on an edge, and slipping to either side.

"She was a Frog. A tart, I think, knowing the old
man."

"About how she left you. That's the bit I like."

"She left me when I was small. Seven."

"You said five before."

"Five then."

"What effect did this have on you, Cassidy?"

"Well . . . it made me lonely I suppose . . . it sort of
. . . robbed me of my childhood."

"What does that mean?" Shamus enquired, sitting bolt
upright.

"What?" said Cassidy.

"What do you mean by being *robbed of childhood?*"

"Denied normal growth, I suppose," Cassidy faltered. "A sense of fun . . . I had no female reference, no one to make women . . . human."

"Normal *sexual* growth, in other words."

"Yes. It drove me in on myself. What's the matter with you?"

Placing the beret over his face, Shamus resumed his recumbent pose.

"We are not concerned with *me*, we are concerned with Cassidy. We are concerned with a man in whom the absence of maternal love has induced certain negative symptoms. I woud describe these symptoms of Cassidy's as follows. One, timidity, right?"

"Right."

"Two, guilt. Guilt arising from Cassidy's secret conviction that he drove his mother forth from the household. Possible?"

"Oh yes," said Cassidy, as ever willing, when the subject was himself, to see the force of any argument.

"Three, insecurity. The female sex, represented by Mummy, at a crucial moment rejected him. He has felt her rejection ever since, and in various disguises he has made futile attempts to regain her favour. By making money for instance, and engendering little babies. Correct?"

"I don't know," said Cassidy, very confused. "I'm not sure."

"His relations with women are accordingly apologetic, morbid, and frequently infantile. They are doomed. That is the substance, is it not, of your complaint? How was the whore?"

"Who?"

"Elise."

"Fine."

"You fucked her, did you?"

"Sure."

"She was satisfactory? She moved in mysterious ways for you? Or did you have her flog you with barbed wire?"

"Shamus, what is it? What's eating you?"

"Nothing is *eating* me. I am merely attempting a diagnosis."

Rolling on to his back he put the brandy bottle to his mouth and drank for a long time.

"That's all, lover," he said, Irish now; and gave a sudden, brilliant smile. "Just giving the devil a name, no offence. Surely to God we can't prescribe the treatment till we've diagnosed the symptoms now, can we?"

Cassidy wanted very much to ask about the two-hour telephone call to London, but he had learned by now that Shamus did not care to be questioned, so he wisely held his peace.

"You're my treatment," he said lightly. "Where shall we eat?"

After dinner, which passed largely in silence, Shamus returned to the theme of the Maternal Frog.

What did she look like, he enquired, striding purposefully at Cassidy's side through darkening streets, what were Cassidy's earliest memories of her, his last? What were her names, would he tell him; did Cassidy remember all her names?

Ella, said Cassidy.

"Did Ella have any distinguishing marks now, a walleye for instance," he required good-humouredly, but still using the Irish. "Did she have a walleye at all, the poor soul?"

They turned into a side alley.

"Not that I remember," said Cassidy laughing.

"Any mannerisms then? I'm trying to get a picture of her you see, after all Cassidy I am a writer of some stature, am I not? My subject is man, after all, in all his rich variety and complexity. I mean did she pick her nose or scratch her arse in bed?"

"She wore cashmere pullovers," Cassidy said. "She loved pink, I remember. Can we leave her alone now Shamus? I'm a bit fed up with her to be honest."

Shamus did not hear, apparently. They were walking faster, Shamus was quickening the pace, looking upwards at the street signs as he strode ahead.

"Shamus, where are we going?"

They crossed a main road, plunged into another maze of little alleys.

A light over the door said "Bar." They went in, Shamus leading.

Girls sat on a horseshoe bench, drinking and looking inward at the mirrors, studying their bodies, their reflected ghosts. A few pimps, a few customers, a slot machine for pills to stop you smoking.

"Paging Mrs. Cassidy," Shamus called, drawing Cassidy after him by the wrist. Shamus' hand was wet, but its grasp was as strong as ever. "Her small son is looking for her." At the bar, a few faces lifted. "Is *Mrs. Cassidy* here now?" He turned to Cassidy. "See her, Oedipus?" he asked.

"Please, Shamus—"

"Is she Chinese at all, is that a possibility?" indicating a lady of South East Asian extraction. "Not mainland, of course, just the fringe islands, you know."

"Shamus I want to go."

"Should have thought of that before, shouldn't you? I'm not a guest in your life, you know. I'm here to stay. I warned you, lover, don't say I didn't."

"For God's sake, Shamus, they'll murder us."

"No Chinese blood. A pure Caucasian lady. Okay I'll take your word for it. Now, will you stop that jiggering please and pay attention. Maybe you'd better have a drink?" he suggested, forcing Cassidy's hand against the wrist as he backed him into the bar.

Two tall and rather handsome elderly ladies offered refreshment to the afflicted. Cassidy wondered whether they were sisters.

"I don't want a drink."

"Er, two homosexual whiskies please miss, one with milk and sugar."

There were seats empty but Shamus preferred to stand.

"Tell us," Shamus continued still addressing the sisters, "has a wee grey-headed body come in at all, about five foot two and sixty-five years of age, somewhat fragile of build, Aryan, wears pink shirts, answers to the name of Ella?"

The sisters, shoulder to shoulder, were smiling broadly at them both. They collected miniatures, Cassidy noticed; there were several hundred on the mirrored shelves behind them; Old Hugo, himself an aficionado, would be enchanted.

"*Tu es hollandais?*" one asked of Cassidy.

"*Anglais,*" said Cassidy.

"*Ella!*" Shamus called, cupping his hand like a lost mariner. "*Ella!*"

"*Y'a pas d'Ella,*" a sister assured him.

With his free hand Cassidy paid for the drinks. They were ten francs each, he gave an extra ten, and when he had done so Shamus drew him close again, up and under.

"Don't you believe 'em," Shamus advised him in an undertone. "They've got her hidden upstairs." He drank. "*Mon ami s'appelle Rex,*" he announced proudly.

"*Il est* très *beau, Rex,*" the sisters assured him.

"*Il veut dormir avec sa mère.*"

"*Ah, bon,*" the sisters cried in pleasure. "*Elle est ici sa mère?*" And looked round the room for a likely candidate.

"She never ran a pub, did she, lover?" Shamus asked, close to his ear. "You know those two dykes remind me very much—"

"Shut up," said Cassidy. "Just shut up and get me out."

The double curtains which gave on to the street parted. Three men, as dark as Shamus but smaller, entered and sat down at a table. The girls round the bar did not move. The sisters were smiling more broadly than ever.

"You're a *lovely* pair," Shamus assured them, and having carefully finished his whisky, threw his glass on to the floor.

"Now I'll tell you what we'll do," Shamus murmured, drawing him yet further inward until their faces were actually touching. "We'll take it *very* easy indeed, all right? No rushing, no jumping, no dramatics."

"Couldn't we just pay them?" Cassidy whispered. "Honestly I don't mind. I'm sure they'd take cash instead."

"You see, I know damn well what they're up to. Those two dykes there: look at their faces. Know what they are? *Kidnappers.* What they have done is *transform*—by means of *plastic surgery* you understand—they have with diabolical cunning *transformed* our Ella into a person of totally different appearance."

"Shamus," Cassidy said, using the name as a prayer.

"It's all right don't worry, we'll outwit them. I made a terrible mistake when I came in here, *declaring our interest,* that's all. Now don't say a word, keep moving."

Bending Cassidy's wrist still further forward, using both hands to increase the pressure, he began walking the line of girls, brushing the bare backs of them one by one as he studied their white faces in the mirror.

"Drugged," Shamus explained, in the same conspiratorial murmur. "Look at that, drugged to the gills, every one."

He pulled back a head so that Cassidy could see her better: a German girl perhaps, strong teeth and blue eyes. Her lips parted in pain as Shamus held her hair.

"See?" he said, as if her silence only proved his point. "Listless. Stuffed, good as."

He released the head. It bent forward again, into the mirror.

"What we have therefore is a *sleeping beauty* problem."

A glass of something white, a cocktail probably, perhaps an advocaat, also a drink much favoured by Old Hugo at a certain period of his development, stood before her on the bar. Shamus drank it.

"Women," he declared in the tone of a Dublin academic, "women whose natural loves have been extinguished by strong potions. Never mind, we shall conquer yet. What mother on earth would fail to recognise the kiss of her own beloved son? Would not open her eyes and cry—" For his female impersonation he required a lot of volume:

"My Rex! My swain! My passion!"

Taking the girl's hand, he offered it to Cassidy and the girl came with it, trying to relieve the pressure.

"Here, take it," he invited. "Would not with her g-narl-ed fingers forage in the copious petticoats for a wee fondle of the familiar organ, eh Cassidy?"

Still holding her hand, he savagely swung her round on her stool. Two dull eyes, black-lidded, peered at them expressionlessly, first at Cassidy for help, then at Shamus for information.

"Tu veux?" she enquired.

"Now," Shamus urged. "Kiss her! Kiss her, call her mother! *Ella,* Aldo is *here!* Rex has come home to *Mrs. Oedipus.*"

Abruptly stooping, Shamus buried his head in her bare shoulder, black on white like an advertisement.

For a moment it seemed as if the girl would accept him. Forced forward, one hand lifted to touch him, she watched him curiously as he pastured on her flesh. Suddenly her body stiffened. Fighting loose from him she let out a sharp cry of pain, seized his hair, and with her other hand—the fingernails, Cassidy noticed, were chewed quite low—hit him, splitting his lip.

"It's worked!" Shamus cried. "We have *impact*, Cassidy! We have reaction!" Standing back, one finger to his bleeding lip, he proudly surveyed his assailant. "It's her! It's Ella! She wants *you* not me. Her Aldo! Go on, lover. Just a little peck, that's all."

The lights went out, three torches shone at them, and a man was talking politely in French.

"They want us to follow the torches," Cassidy explained.

The taxi was waiting at the curb. They helped Shamus in first and Cassidy followed. He gave them a hundred francs.

"For God's sake!" Shamus shouted. "Why didn't they hit us?"

That's a very nice place, thought Cassidy, that's the nicest place I've ever been to, and if I can remember how to find it I shall go back and apologise and offer those sisters the chalet.

"The *girl* hit you," he said, consolingly.

"Jesus, who cares about a woman?"

"Shamus, for pity's sake tell me what's the matter with you?"

"There's a place called Lipp's," said Shamus. "They'll hit me there all right, it's a writer's haven. Lipp's," he told the driver, his eye already on the radio.

"Shamus, *please.*"

"Shut up."

"It's to do with Dale. You rang him for hours, I saw the messages and everything."

"If I wanted," Shamus promised him in his most detached voice, holding Cassidy's handkerchief to his mouth, "I would kill you. You know that don't you, lover?"

"Lipp," Cassidy repeated to the driver hopelessly. *"Brasserie Lipp."*

"I keep you alive for one reason only: because you are a reader. You realise that, I trust. Being a prole, you are the commercial hinterland of my genius. Know what Luther said?"

"What did Luther say?" Cassidy asked wearily.

"He said, if I were Christ, and the world had done to me what it has done to Him, I'd kick the beastly thing to pieces!"

"But Shamus," Cassidy asked, gently, when Shamus had more or less settled again, "what *has* the world done to you?"

Shamus seemed about to say something serious. He stared at Cassidy, at the blood on the handkerchief, at the passing lights, opened his split mouth as if to speak, closed it again, and sighed. "Holy God," he said at last, "it's filled itself with halfbreeds like you."

They had eaten once already that evening, a fact which Shamus had apparently forgotten. Cassidy was in no mood to remind him. The son of an hotelier and innumerable mothers had learnt long ago that there was no better sedative than good plain food, served hot.

Dining at the Brasserie Lipp, Shamus was quiet and conciliatory.

He stroked Cassidy's arm, vouchsafed him small, erratic smiles, gave the waiter ten francs from Cassidy's wallet, and generally by word and deed showed signs of regaining his lighter, affectionate mood. Observing this, Cassidy deemed it wise to take command of the conversation until the good Burgundy and the soothing, old-world atmosphere of the restaurant had completed the process of recovery.

"A writer's haven eh?" he said. "Well I'm not surprised. It's just the place not to be recognised. Can you point any out?" he asked, with a suitably conspiratorial reverence. "Any in *your* bracket, are there Shamus?"

Shamus looked round. A heavy middle-aged couple, eating slowly and apparently without implements, returned his stare. A pretty girl, out with her boyfriend, blushed, and the boy turned and scowled at Shamus, who put his thumb to his nose.

"My *bracket*," he repeated. "No I don't think so. There's Sartre over in the corner—" Rising, he bowed gravely to a gnomic, mottled gentleman of about eighty-five. "—but I think we can reasonably say I outgun Jean Paul. Has Monsieur Homer come in yet?" he asked the waiter, with that effortless complicity which Cassidy now took for granted.

"*Monsieur . . . ?*"

"Homer. *Omer*. Old Greek with a long white beard, looks like Father Christmas. Poof."

"*Non, monsieur,*" the waiter regretted. "*Pas ce soir.*" A ghost of a smile, too fleeting for disrespect, enlivened his elderly features.

"Well, there you are," Shamus said pleasantly, with a resigned shake of the head. "Quiet night I'm afraid. Boys all at home."

"Shamus," said Cassidy, holding with difficulty to his policy of breezy small talk, "about my soul."

"I thought you'd had it out," said Shamus.

A burst of laughter issued suddenly from the kitchen.

"No truly. Listen lover. I really do think I'm redeemable, don't you? Now, I mean. Since I met you. I don't think it's a hopeless quest any more, looking for it, do you? I know I'm reluctant. I've got a lot of bad habits but, well you have shown me the way, haven't you?" Receiving no encouragement, he added, "After all, there must be *something* there."

Shamus was playing with the water jug, dipping his finger and watching the drops fall.

"Well don't you think so? Come on."

"I am the light," said Shamus. "I am the light and the way. Follow me and you will end *on your arse*," and reaching out, turned Cassidy's face upwards and sideways, adjusting it for closer examination.

"Shamus don't . . ." said Cassidy.

"You know what you radiate, don't you? The nasty allure of an undiscovered absolute. Every poor fool who picks you up thinks he's your first friend. What they don't realise is, you were born with your legs crossed. Penetration," he concluded, carelessly releasing him, "can never take place."

A merciful waiter brought them food.

"I've never told you," said Cassidy, helping Shamus to vegetables, filling his glass, and trying now by every means to win him back from his state of hostile melancholy. "I've always been a bit dotty about writers ever since I was at school. I used to write short stories in bed after lights. I even won prizes. Hey what about that?"—with a brave if somewhat synthetic effort at enthusiasm—"Why don't I make a stab at it? Give up the firm, give up Sandra, give up my money, waste away in a garret . . . be like Renoir."

"It wasn't Renoir. It was Gauguin."

"Perhaps I'd make it . . . starve the talent out of me . . ."

Shamus had gone back to the water jug, was trailing his finger back and forth over the surface the way they had played with the sticklebacks by the river. A little resentfully, Cassidy said—it was a point he had made to Sandra not long ago—"Well if I *am* so bloody empty, why do you bother with me anyway?"

"Tell me, lover," Shamus said, very seriously, lifting the jug an inch or two off the table. "Is that smile waterproof?"

Standing up, he began pouring the water slowly over Cassidy's head, starting with a slowish trickle directed at the crown, then gradually increasing the quantity as the mood took him. Cassidy sat very still, thinking clearly about absolutely nothing; for nothing is also a concept, being neither a place nor a person but a blank, a vacuum and a tremendous help in time of trouble. He did however record that the water was running over his neck and down his spine. He did also feel it spreading over his chest, his stomach, and into his groin. His ears were full of water too, but he knew that the conversation in the restaurant had stopped because he could hear Shamus' voice and no one else's and the brogue was very strong.

"Butch Cassidy, son of Dale, in that you do earnestly repent you of your oafish ways, and faithfully promise to follow always in the paths of truth, experience, and love, we hereby baptise you in the name of . . ."

He stopped pouring. Thinking the jug was empty, Cassidy lifted his head, but Shamus was still standing over him, and there was a good half pint to come.

"Go on Butch. Hit me with your handbag."

"Please don't pour any more," Cassidy said.

He was beginning to feel quite angry, but there seemed to be nothing he could do. The injunction, however, moved Shamus unaccountably to fury.

"For Christ's sake," he shouted, pouring the rest in one

long sustained movement. "Grow, you little weed, *grow!*"

The waiter was an old, kindly man, and he had the bill ready. Cassidy kept the money in his back pocket, and somehow the water had got in there too, and the notes were all stuck together. The waiter didn't mind because Cassidy gave him a lot of them.

A copper urn stood in the corner for walking sticks and umbrellas. Taking out a silver-handled cane, Shamus began piping on it, swaying from the hips like a snake charmer and emitting a low wailing noise through his nose. Everyone waited, but no snake emerged. Using the stick as a club, Shamus drove it in sudden fury against the heavy chasing.

"All right you sodder," he shouted into the urn. "Go on. Sulk. Jesus Christ, lover," he breathed as they got outside, "oh God, lover, forgive, forgive." Shaking his head, he took Cassidy's hand and held it against his tear-stained cheek. "Lover, oh lover, forgive!"

21

"Shamus, tell me! Please tell me. What the hell's the matter? What's happened to you? Who the hell is Dale?"

"He's the bloke who bombed Hiroshima," Shamus explained.

Shamus drunk.

Not high or tight or any other pretty word, but dirty, violent drunk. Sweating terribly, reeling and staggering as he held to Cassidy, refusing to go anywhere he knew but demanding always to move. Vomiting.

"Wander, Jew, wander," he kept saying. *"Wander."*

His arm, hooked round Cassidy's neck, is divided between destroying and embracing him. Twice they have gone down, toppled by his iron grip, and Cassidy's trouser is cut from the knee to the foot. We're all that's left of an army, the rest are dead. The night is dead too, and the dawn is limping after them. They are in a square again but not dancing any more, the dancing is over, no horses either, just an early bitch of Sandra's, long dead, eyeing them from a doorway.

Shamus is vomiting again punctuating his spasms with cries of anger.

"Fucking body," he shouts. "Do what you're bloody told! How the hell can I keep my promises if my body won't work? Tell it lover. Shamus has promises to keep. *Tell it to carry me!"*

"Come on body," Cassidy says, trying to hold its sinking weight, "Come on body, Shamus has promises to keep."

"For I have promises to keep . . ."

Shamus is trying to set the words to music. He sings

quite well in Cassidy's unmusical opinion, a very Shamus sort of singing, half talking, half humming, but with a lot of quality to the voice even when (as watchful Cassidy accurately surmises) he is out of tune.

"The night is lo-v-e-ly, dark and deep—*sing* you bugger, Dale—the night - is - lovely - dark and deep—sing!"

"I don't know the words, Shamus," Cassidy said, catching him again as he lurched forward. "I'm not Dale but I'd sing if I knew the words, I promise."

Shamus stopped dead.

"Who wouldn't?" he said at last. "Jesus, who wouldn't?" Putting both hands over Cassidy's face, he lifted it into his own. "It's singing when you *don't* know the bloody words that tears your guts out, lover."

"But you *do* know the words, Shamus."

"Oh no I don't. Oh no I bloody don't, Dale my lovely. You *think* I do. Why I love you: worshipping prole. What more can a man ask? The roar of the proles at the door, dizzy faces . . . cameras click. . . . It's all anyone wants. Queen, me, Flaherty, all of us."

Putting his whole weight on Cassidy's shoulders, Shamus forced him down on to the curb.

"Now give yourself a nice comfy rest Dale, old son," he said in Irish, "while your poor Uncle Shamus tells you the secret of the universe," and pulled the bottle of Scotch from Cassidy's inside pocket. After a couple of mouthfuls, he became quite sober but his arm was still locked round Cassidy's in case he tried to run away.

"I'm not Dale," said Cassidy again, patiently. "I'm your lover. Cassidy."

"Then I'll tell Cassidy instead. What do we have in common, you and me, Cassidy, in ourselves? Guess." He shouted very loud. "*Guess,* Cassidy! Before I turn you into Dale again, you crawling little funk!"

A window opened on the other side of the street.

"You American?" a man's voice enquired, in an American accent.

"Piss off," Shamus yelled, and back to Cassidy: "Well?"

"Well we *love* each other, if that's any help," Cassidy suggested, using one of their earlier dialogues as a working guide. "We've got *love* in common, Shamus."

"Balls," said Shamus, and brushed away a tear. "Sheer

bloody romantic bollocks, if you'll forgive me, which you will, as usual."

Two tarts were standing a few feet away from them. One of them carried a loaf of bread, and was eating mouthfuls off the end of it.

"The greedy one looks like your mother," said Shamus.

"I think we've done that one," Cassidy said wearily.

"Êtes vous la mère de mon ami?" Shamus enquired.

The tarts scowled and went away, tired of the prolonged joke.

"Well perhaps that's it. Perhaps we *are* queer," said Cassidy, still working on the false assumption that he would do best to rely on Shamus' themes, and offer them as his own.

"Zero," said Shamus. "Did I ever once venture just the smallest finger up your skirts? Not the tiniest little digit, did I?"

"No," said Cassidy, as Shamus hauled him abruptly to his feet. He was more tired than he had ever been in his life. "No, you didn't."

"Then will you listen to me please? And will you *stop* putting forward low-grade arguments, *please?"*

Cassidy had little option, for Shamus was holding him in a cruel embrace, and their faces were pressed together, rough cheek on rough cheek.

"And will you please give me your very fullest attention, Dale? What we have in common is the most dreadful, hopeless, fucking awful pessimism. Right?"

"Okay, I'll buy that."

"And the other thing we have in common is the most dreadful, awful, hopeless, fucking awful . . . mediocrity."

Real fear seized Cassidy; real unreasoning alarm.

"No Shamus, that's not true, that's absolutely not true. You're *special* Shamus, we all know that—"

"You do, do you, lover?"

The grip tightened.

"I *know.* Helen knows. We *all* know. . . ." Cassidy was going now, really frightened; holding on and desperate to survive. The Bentley was sinking in the river; Abalone Crescent was falling to its knees. "Christ you idiot you only have to walk into a room, tell a story, give them your rat's-eyes, and they *know,* we *all* know, that it's *you,* Shamus; your world. You're our chronicler, Shamus, our magus. You've got all we want, the truth, the dream, the guts. Okay you're impossible. But you're the best! You make it real for us, we *know* how good you are."

"You do?"

It was Cassidy's left arm Shamus had taken now; he had driven the upper part into the shoulder socket, and the pain was like the water at Lipp's, spreading and creeping and screaming all at once.

"Shamus you'll break it in a minute," Cassidy warned.

"You really believe that crap I tell you? Listen, I am the lousiest fucking conjuror in the business and you fall for every fucking trick. Nietzsche. Schiller. Flaherty. I never read those fucking people in my life. They're scraps. Tit-bits. Fag-ends. I pick them out of the gutter for breakfast and you poor fuckers think they're a bloody feast. *I am a bum.* You want to throw me out, pramseller: that's what you want to do. I don't work, I don't write, I don't exist! It's the fucking audience that's doing the magic, not me. *I am a fraud.* Got it? A con man. A fucking clapped-out conjuror with an audience of one."

"No!" Cassidy shouted. *"NO! NO! NO!"*

"You think I'm your friend." Shamus had found a place to lie down, so Cassidy was obliged to lie beside him, partly to hear the words and partly not to lose his arm. "Well I don't *want* a fucking friend. I don't even know how to deal with a friend. I want a fucking archaeologist, that's what I want. I'm *Troy*, not a fucking bank clerk. There are nine dead cities buried in me and each one is more rotten than the next fucker. And what do you do? You stand there like a bloody tourist and bleat, '*No! No! Shamus no.*' Yes, Cassidy. *Yes*, Shamus is a *bum.* There's a nasty smell around here. Know what it is? Failure!"

"Shamus," said Cassidy quietly. "I would swap all my fortune for your talent . . . for your life, and for your marriage . . ."

"All right," Shamus whispered, letting him loose as the tears came. "All right, lover. If I'm so bloody marvellous, why did you turn down my novel?"

Cassidy's world swung, and held still.

"It's okay, lover," Shamus whispered, seizing his arm

again and twisting it more tightly, "I'm your friend, remember."

Cassidy looked into the troubled eyes, so full of suddenness and chaos, looked at the whole iron, wild face of him, taut at the cheeks, careless at the mouth, and he wondered almost with detachment how one body could hold so much, and hold together. There seemed, as Shamus crawled slowly to his feet, still arm in arm with Cassidy, to be something cosmic in his self-destruction; as if, knowing that the creative genius of mankind was also the cause of its ruin, he had determined to make that truth personal, to take it for his own.

"He turned down the last one too," said Shamus, grinning through his tears. And releasing Cassidy's arm, fell back full length on to the cobbled street.

22

Aldo Cassidy, lately of Sherborne School and an undistinguished Oxford college, the preserver and lover of life, sometime Lieutenant Cassidy, national service subaltern in an inconspicuous English regiment of foot, secret negotiator of the world's unconquerable agonies, clandestine owner of foreign bank accounts, drew in that moment on resources of positive action which he had written off for dead.

Seizing his lover Shamus roughly by the collar of his black coat—now known to him mysteriously as the death-coat—he dragged him to a bench. He thrust the wet, hot head between the parted male knees and held the wet unshaven face while the discarded writer again vomited on to the Paris cobblestones. He loosened the discarded writer's necktie as a precaution against suffocation, and having crouched beside him, one knee on the bench in order to force down his head a second time, entered a telephone box across the square and found the right change and the right number to summon a taxi. The telephone connection being out of order, he returned to Shamus, lifted him bodily to his feet—the dejected writer's vitality, if not his actual life, lay at his feet like the milky map of his unnative Ireland—and guided him towards a fountain which however turned out to have run dry. In the course of making this short journey, he discovered Shamus to be unconscious and quickly diagnosed an excessive heart rate and suspected alcoholic poisoning. With the aid of a passing policeman, to whom he gave at once a hundred new francs—£8.62 at the currently prevailing devalued rate, but certainly deductible from his generously viewed expense account—the Managing Director and Founder of Cassidy's Universal Fastenings finally obtained transport in the form of a green police patrol car armed with a blue light which revolved, apparently, inside the car as well as on the roof. Recumbent in the rear compartment, which was divided from the driver by a jeweller's screen of black steel, Shamus was again sick and Cassidy succeeded, during the brief spell of subsequent articulation, in obtaining from him the name of the white hotel where, as the resourceful Second Lieutenant Cassidy resourcefully remembered, two missing British diplomats had neither paid for, nor relinquished, their reserve accommodation.

To the driver and his companion, who had prudently remained in the front of the car, but were not inclined to criticise Shamus too hastily, Cassidy gave a further hundred-franc note and apologised profusely for the condition of the rear seat. His friend, he said, had been drinking in order to overcome a great personal loss. In the field of love no doubt? they enquired, examining the handsome profile. Yes, Cassidy the preserver slyly conceded, one could say it was in the field of love. *Eh bien,* Cassidy should look after his friend, supervise his recovery; with such men as this, the path was steep and slow. Cassidy promised to do his best.

The Algerian boy, keeping watch over the reception desk through the open doorway of a windowless downstairs bedroom, where he was recovering from a night of sexual exertion with a colleague he did not introduce, received a further one hundred francs for putting on his pyjamas, unlocking the front door, handing over a key, and switching on the lift, an antiquated backless box of rosewood in which Shamus attempted without success to vomit yet again. In the drawing room of their suite the small table had been replaced in its proper position in front of the window, but traces of Elise's inexpensive scent still lingered in the threadbare pile of *ancien régime* upholstery. Here Shamus, having now rejoined the ranks of the walking wounded, insisted on going alone to the bathroom, where Cassidy the preserver soon afterwards found him asleep on the floor. With a last heroic effort, Cassidy the passable rugger forward removed his sodden clothing, sponged down the naked body of his heterosexual friend, and lifted, actually *bore* him to the double bed, where he was soon well enough to sit up and request a drink of whisky.

"Lover," Shamus said brightly, clapping his hands, "what a *clever* boy. You done it all alone!"

A few hours, a few lives later the same preserver of life applied himself painstakingly to the urgent task of restoring to the bedraggled, naked figure in the bed the ideals, dimensions, and glory of his fallen familiar.

By then, the world had turned for Cassidy several times. He woke first to hear the howling of a gale and the hotel cracking like a ship and he imagined the wet pavements heaving in the torrent and the mother whores clinging to the lampposts for their lives. The storm, of Shakespearean timeliness in view of the extreme turbulence of Cassidy's immortal soul, also woke Shamus, whom Cassidy discovered at the window, leaning outwards and down, over three floors to the courtyard below. Without fuss, Cassidy went to him and gently put his arm round the powerful back.

"I dropped my fag," said Shamus.

Sixty feet below, a red ember burned miraculously in the dancing rain.

"That's all we are," Shamus said. "Bloody little glows in a great big dark."

Having by dint of his latent mechanical skill succeeded in locking the antiquated brass latch, which by means of rods and hooks uncomfortably joined the fat window frames, Cassidy returned Shamus to the bed and climbed in after him.

He did not however sleep.

The storm ended as suddenly as it had begun, it was replaced by a Sunday quietness reminiscent of the house in Abalone Crescent on the rare occasions when the builders were not on site.

Straddled across the pramseller's naked limbs, the writer was finally asleep.

Peace, thought Cassidy; Sandra has gone upstairs.

"Great night," said Shamus, not looking at him.

"Great."

The double bed. Eggs and coffee brought by the Algerian, sunlight on the eiderdown.

"Convivial, enlightening, broadening. Lover, give me a job."

"No."

"Listen, I sold those prams didn't I? I'll write you lovely brochures, lover, promise."

"No."

"Look, I drafted one the other night, want to hear it?"

"No."

"I'll be your number one. Carry your bags, answer your phone . . . I'm better than that tight-arsed secretary of yours any day. Change my name, go straight . . ."

"Get on with your eggs," said Cassidy.

While Shamus dozed, Cassidy made several telephone calls to his public world. Occasionally, hearing him mention a figure—five, tens of thousands, free on board, back it with a loan—Shamus groaned or covered his face with his hands. Sometimes he wept. And in the afternoon, still in bed, a subdued, rested, and definitely ordinary Shamus gave his own elusive version of the hellhound Dale.

How Dale was a spy, posing as one of the Few but actually a sworn supporter of the Many-too-Many. How under cover of darkness he accepted bribes from bishops and Jaguar owners, and was loyal to his frustrated wife. How *Moon* had made money, but the others hadn't; how the hardback advances had dwindled and the paperback advances ceased; and he talked quite knowledgeably of options and copyrights and things that Cassidy, being versed in Patent Law, at least marginally understood. How Dale wanted the centre pages rewritten, and would then seriously consider a second submission. And how Shamus must hurry back and shoot him, he would borrow a gun from Hall, there was not a day to lose.

"Alternatively," said Cassidy lightly, "you might rewrite the middle."

Long silence.

"I'll shoot you too," said Shamus.

"Of course I haven't read the middle. But if everything you write is perfect, that's a different matter."

Sulking, Shamus rolled to the other side of the bed. Later, however, dressing to go out, he was sufficiently revived to give Cassidy some useful instructions on the conduct of his private life.

"That bosscow."

"Yes, Shamus."

"You know, lover, you've got that lady wrong. That's a very steady and meaningful figure in your life. You want to get her back in the team."

"I'll try."

Don't try, said Mrs. Harabee: do it.

"Be *faithful*, lover. You're such a shit. Be *truthful*."

"Okay."

"Lot of woman there, boy."

"Sure."

"And don't read. Reading is out."

"No problem."

"And keep right away from Dostoevsky. That man was a criminal."

"A maniac."

"I need constants, lover. None of this shifting sand. How can I write if all the proles are growing long hair?"

"No way," said Cassidy.

"Listen lover, you've got to stay frustrated. The whole order is in the balance. Promise."

"Do you feel better now?" Cassidy asked as they left.

"Piss off," said Shamus. "I don't need *your* sympathy."

Walking down the rue de Rivoli, buying a second set of clothing, *terrines* for Helen, a handbag for Sandra, Shamus also counselled him on the tactic of wooing bosscows into a generous frame of mind.

"Tell her you're broke," he urged. "Cheer her up. Christopher Robin in Carey Street, all I've got left is you."

"All right," said Cassidy.

"Flood's come, fleet's all washed away, no mink, no diamonds, no Breughels—"

"No cornices," Cassidy put in. "No eighteenth-century fireplaces . . ."

"There is *nothing* that rejuvenates a lady faster, titillates her, stimulates her, jacks her up . . . better than catastrophe. Jesus, lover, I should know."

"And you'll have a go at the middle pages, won't you?" said Cassidy. "And you'll go a *tiny* bit easier?"

"Never," said Shamus.

For their last dinner, Cassidy chose Allard again. Eating there with Elise he had noticed a duck being enjoyed at a neighbouring table and he was anxious to give it a try.

Shamus' cure was complete.

"Now the first thing you've got to do, lover, is screw Angie Mawdray, right? Face to face, frenzy all the way."

"Right," said Cassidy.

"Then there's this other bird you fancy."

"Ast."

"Correct. Phase two. Proposition Ast."

"Right."

"But don't *ask*. Take. All this looking for an ideal cow. Don't do it. There's a bit of her in all of them and not much in any of them. You have to collect it wide and put it together for yourself."

"All right."

"As for your beastly wife . . ."

"Yes?"

"I hate her, lover."

"I know you do, Shamus."

"And she hates you, so why the bloody hell don't you drop her down a hole?"

"I know. I will, I will."

"Well do it. Don't just finger it, do it."

"I will, I promise."

"You know what you forgot?" said Cassidy in bed at the St. Jacques.

"What?"

"We were going to build a cairn to Flaherty. We never did."

"Do it another time," said Shamus.

"That's right," said Cassidy.

"Goodnight, lover."

"Goodnight," said Cassidy.

"Maybe I'll do those middle pages instead."

"Great," said Cassidy.

"I love you," said Shamus as they fell asleep. "I love you. And one day, I'll give you back your faith, the way you gave me mine."

Smiling in the darkness, Cassidy touched his hand.

"Poof," said Shamus. "Vandal. Bourgeois."

And made train noises, pooff, pooff, pooff, until he fell asleep.

Sandra with the sun on her looked very pretty and she smiled to see him back.

"Hullo bosscow."

"Poor love. You look worn out."

"It's all those fast Parisian women," Cassidy said with a lean smile, breathing the smells of home.

"How was the Fair?"

"Actually rather good. We took quite a few orders, considering." A char's husband emerged from the kitchen and took his suitcase. "Mind you," he added shrewdly, pursing his lips and lowering his eyes, "the revaluation of the Deutschmark helped a good deal. Those Germans are knocking the bottom out of their own market."

"Silly things," said Sandra, leading him towards the drawing room. The disputed cornice was in place. Gilded, it looked rather handsome.

"They'll begin the other wall as soon as the plaster's dry," she said.

"Fine."

They've changed her over, he thought, like they do with babies when their blood's wrong; they've just kept the outside of her and changed everything else.

"Sorry about that letter," said Sandra.

"That's okay," said Cassidy, numb-headed.

"*Look! Look! Look!*"

One "*look*" for every flight of stairs. Hugo's leg was out of plaster.

London

23

An unusual silence fills the house and no birds sing.

The piano is locked. The key, well out of Hugo's reach, shares a picture hook with an unknown Florentine master whose value old Niesthal has guaranteed, he does business only with friends. In the hall, the carved eighteenth-century fireplace, completed in all but the pointing, is draped in Haverdown dust sheets, a monument never to be unveiled. The unfinished section of the cornice reaches this far only; the plasterers have been sent away. On the street side, windows are closed to noisome traffic, and curtains partly drawn in mourning. In the Crescent, neighbours have been cautioned. Even the cleaning women, customarily an important element of Sandra's social life, are tamed. They Hoover like conspiratorial bees behind closed doors and tea is taken quietly; their many children have been placed elsewhere. The Austrian cook has instructions not to weep, on pain of dismissal; whether Hugo insults her or not.

As to Mrs. Groat, she addresses her departed world in a fraught whisper which passes in bands of high energy to every corner of the house. At midday her alarm clock sounds, in forty years she has not mastered it. The signal sends her galloping six full flights. Once, mistaking the occasion, she boils water, and Sandra reproves her with discreet fury. Light is also rationed. A watchful gloom illuminates the corridors, which smell of broth as well as paint. Hugo plays in the basement, pop music is proscribed. Only John Elderman is welcome. He comes twice daily on a private basis, regardless of socialism or expense.

At the antique wrought iron gate (Sotheby's again, a snip at four hundred pounds) the press waits deferentially.

"Please keep very quiet," Sandra sends out to them with dignity. "A bulletin will be issued as soon as there is anything to say."

Aldo Cassidy, alone in high fever in the sick wing of his costly London house, is dying.

A virus, said Sandra; a special virus which assailed the overworked.

A *French* virus, said Mrs. Groat, she had had it in the Tropics, Bunny Sleego's brother died of it in an hour. It was the chrysanthemums, she said; she had never held with having chrysanths in the house, the pollen could be fatal. Additionally, she blamed the London water, which the Brigadier also disapproved of.

"Though he's not here to drink it, of course. *We're* the ones who've got to drink it," she complained. "We" were the female race, discarded when we lost our looks. "*He's* out there drinking *pure* water, no wonder he's healthy, but still." In support of this theory, she crept into Cassidy's ward while Sandra was shopping and poured commercial bleach down the waste pipe of the basin.

"Don't tell Wiggie, will you darling?" she begged (Wiggie was a patronymic for her daughter) and having kissed him nervously with her pursy mouth, walked the bitches on Primrose Hill to keep them quiet and healthy.

"He's freaked out," said Snaps admiringly, younger sister to Sandra, but sexually much her senior.

Down from Newcastle, she had moved into a spare floor, where she played provocative records late into the night. Being a full girl and jolly, she brought occasional cheer to Cassidy's fading spirit. "Darling you are *all right* aren't you?" her mother would ask her in a terrified whisper behind half-opened doors, meaning "Are you pregnant?" or equally, "Are you not pregnant?" For though Mrs. Groat had no particular opinion on which her younger daughter should be, the two conditions were closely associated in her mind. In recent years Snaps had had several pregnancies; either she rang Cassidy and borrowed a hundred pounds or she went to an unmarried mothers' clinic she liked down in Bournemouth while Sandra mounted a nationwide search for the father. These attempts were seldom fruitful; when they were, the culprit too often proved unworthy of the search.

"Been on a thrash have you?" Snaps asked him, more

directly, sitting on his bed reading a comic. "Fancy little Aldo painting Paris red, didn't know you had it in you. You'll be taking a swing at me next."

"No I won't," said Cassidy, who for some years had wondered, off and on, whether such a thing would be incestuous.

Cancer, said the charladies; wherever would they go next? And poor Mrs. Cassidy, how would she ever cope, a big house all on her own?

Runny tummy, said Hugo. Daddy's got runny tummy so he can't go to work.

"I *like* it when you have runny tummy, Dad."

"So do I," said Cassidy.

They played a lot of dominos, Hugo winning.

"He's faking," said Cassidy's father, telephoning from the penthouse, needing money badly. "He's been faking all his life, *course* he has. Ask him about his spasms in Cheltenham then. Ask him about his hernia in Aberdeen! That boy's never had a genuine affliction in his life, he's as phoney as a seven-pound note—"

"You should know," said Sandra and slammed down the receiver.

In confidence, John Elderman diagnosed a mild breakdown.

He had seen it coming, he whispered, but was helpless to prevent it; and pumped up rubber tubes round Cassidy's upper arm.

"Call it psychosomatic, call it what you will, it's one of those times when the old mind puts the body to bed, and the old body just *has* to do what the old mind tells it. Eh?"

"I suppose you're right," Cassidy conceded with a weakly smile.

"Any *history* at all, old man?" asked the physician, reading "normal" for the third day running.

"A bit," Cassidy confessed, hinting at stresses overcome, brainstorms peculiar to the brilliant.

Tactfully John Elderman abstained from further question.

"Well," he remarked instead, "you've Sandra to look after you, that's one good thing, old man. *She* knows her Aldo, doesn't she?"

"Poor Pailthorpe," Sandra sighed, holding his hand on her lap and regarding her adult child with timeless love. "Poor, silly Pailthorpe, what *have* you been up to? *You* don't have to chase money like that: *we'll* get by."

It was the balance of payments, Cassidy explained; he had wanted so desperately to help the export drive. Not for Cassidy's. For the nation.

"I wanted to get Britain off the ground," he said.

"*Dear* one," said Sandra, kissing him again, lightly in order not to excite him. "You're *such* a striver. And I'm such a drag."

For an hour or more she sat with him, studying his effigy in the gloom. Her stillness was very comforting, and Cassidy loved her in return.

The malady had taken him by surprise. Had stalked him in the night and overwhelmed him with the dawn. First a nightmare, then daylit visions had assailed him; hallucinations, dialogues between the many characters of his mind. Their theme was retribution. He was striding through London over grassy, secluded squares, drawing weightless children by the hand; he was floating down the rue de Rivoli in the Bentley, driving it from the top deck; he was charging through noisy female streets, and suddenly—it could be anywhere—he would be confronted by an alp near Sainte-Angèle, the Angelhorn. No Entry, No Diversion, and No Exit. An alp of twisting jagged spires, Wilde's upturned sow; of giddy paths and incalculable embarrassments, where whores, hoteliers, tax inspectors, police officials, and coachmen leered and gesticulated from steaming caverns or hugged each other beside diminished riverbeds. Sometimes, nervously approaching its lower slopes and feeling already the onslaught of his vertigo, he saw himself opening a copy of the *Daily Express* and reading aloud from its erudite pages: *Is Pram Maker Fourth Man? Anarchist Writer also connected? Algerian porter tells of night orgy in thunderstorm; honeymoon couple claim: we heard them through wall. Writer's wife utterly innocent. Chapman Pincher Exclusive.*

Also, of his own bankruptcy, on inner pages lit in brothel green: *Are Cassidy's burnt out? Have Fastenings Come Unstuck? M.P.'s Son answers Official Receiver: "I spent it on tipping. My crime was generosity."*

"Comfort!" the wretched sinner cried miserably to the whores. "Look what has become of me!" But before he could rid himself of his cassock (a monkish sinner, this Cassidy) they ran off white-buttocked into the avalanche gullies where Shamus, already armed and disencumbered, was waiting to enjoy them.

Such a vision was not entirely of Cassidy's own invention. Its prototype hung in the ever-lit chambers of his childhood, in the days when God was still pleased to have Old Hugo feed the mind, in the kitchen of his first mother, where she sighed and ironed surplices of her husband's own design: an alp named Hades drawn by pious artists, printed in polychrome by an early process, and framed in inflammable timber. At its foot were depicted all the horrors which small boys long to commit: theft and arson; gaming and veiled lechery. On the fearful peak, black angels burned the same offenders.

He was recalled from this torment by Ast thanking him for flowers. Sitting on his bed, close, to emphasise her gratitude. Ast in ripe harvest yellow, loose fitting at the looser places.

"Did you mean it?" she asked softly. "What you wrote?"

Sandra was out buying pigs' trotters, their gravy would give him nourishment.

"With all my love," Heather recited. *"And all my sorrow.* Aldo, you *couldn't* have made that up. Sent from *Paris* too, with all those distractions."

She too held his hand; but folded, worked into the higher cushions of her thighs; at the point, on her own person, which she had reached at dinner at the Eldermans', on his. Having first closed the door against extraneous disturbance.

"You were so *right* to rebuke me," she whispered. "And I was so *pompous* wasn't I?"

Hard upon these early visions came their physical counterparts: outbreaks of sudden sweating accompanied by erratic beatings of the heart, inflammation of the ears and throat, and a hot dryness of the eyes; written calculations by Sandra to turn Fahrenheit to Centigrade.

"He's a *hundred and four*," she told John Elderman on the second visit. "He's *miles* sub," she assured him on the third. Thereafter they discussed his condition over nightly dinners in the basement, for John Elderman liked to come at seven when the rest of the world was healed.

For a while, still hovering on the brink of death, and loudly protesting his innocence of the many crimes of which, in his other mind, he constantly accused himself, Cassidy decided that Shamus was a myth. "He never existed," he told himself, and pulling the blankets to his nose, pretended he was in a sledge.

Appalled by the memories of outlandish heresies in the Sacré Coeur, he availed himself of Sandra's extensive library on the lives of holy men, and resolved, during luxurious hours in the lavatory, to follow their example.

"I've matured," he told her. "I'd like to consider going into the Church again, it's sort of fitting into place."

And later: "Let's get out of the rat race for a while, go somewhere we can think."

Sandra suggested Oxford; they had been happy there. "Or we might try Scotland. The dogs would adore it."

"Scotland would be fine," said Cassidy. Using the bedside telephone he made bookings at Gleneagles. But only in his imagination, for Scotland had no appeal for him; it lacked the company he craved.

In answer to the patient's summons, Angie Mawdray also called. She brought the mail and twelve small roses in a white tissue.

"They're for you," she said in a low voice. "To make up for the ones you sent me from Paris."

Rummaging in her Greek bag, she drew out a handwritten letter from the country which he hid under the bedclothes. She did not look at him during this transaction, and her expression discouraged conversation.

"They're from Faulk," Cassidy told Sandra, to explain the young buds. "From all of them really, but Faulk chose them."

"People really *care* about you," Sandra said generously, sniffing their elusive scent. "People really *love* you, don't they."

"Well," said Cassidy.

"We *all* do," Sandra insisted.

And settling, resumed her vigil of unblinking adoration.

For his convalescence, Cassidy wore a blue cashmere dressing gown which Sandra bought him specially from Harrods: sickness was an emergency, money could be spent on it. At first he lunched in bed and came down for an hour only, to play with Hugo.

"That's not proper billiards," said Hugo contemptuously, and reported him to Sandra for illegal practices.

"Now you listen to me, young Hugo," said Sandra with serene indulgence. "If your Daddy wants to play billiards with a candle, then that's his way of playing billiards."

"It's the *best* way too, isn't it Dad?" said Hugo proudly.

"It's called Moth," Cassidy explained. "We used to play it in the Army as a way of passing the time."

Next morning, surveying the cloth, Sandra was extremely cross.

"How on earth am I supposed to get the wax off?"

"She's baity with you for getting up," Hugo explained. "She likes you better in bed."

"Nonsense," said Cassidy.

Continuing his cautious return to normal life, the invalid went to great lengths to spare himself collision. To telephone Helen in the country, for instance, he used his credit card to avoid distressing entries on the bill; to speak with Miss Mawdray at South Audley Street he selected moments when Sandra was out shopping. Despite these precautions, he was exposed to some hard bargaining.

"But *Cassidy*," Helen insisted, not flesh yet, but an excellent telephone personality; also an angel. "You can't possibly afford it!"

"For God's sake, Helen, what's money for?"

"But Cassidy, *think* what it's going to cost you."

"Helen, look. What would *you* do if *you* were me, and loved him *my* way? Right?"

"Cassidy," said Helen, beaten down.

For the same reasons Messrs. Grimble and Outhwaite of Mount Street W. had firm instructions not to ring him at the residence. Deal only with Miss Mawdray, he told them; Miss Mawdray knows exactly what is needed.

Nonetheless, it was Cassidy who had to keep them at the wheel.

"Water," he insisted to old Grimble, speaking under the blankets. The house, though solid, had strange acoustical tricks; chimneys in particular were dangerous ducts of sound from floor to floor. "It *must* be near water. All right, use sub agents; yes of course I'll pay double commission. Good heavens it's a Company flat isn't it? Pay whatever you have to and bill Lemming for it. I mean really it's *too bad.*"

Such conversations reminded him that he was not wholly mended, for they moved him to intemperate reactions which he afterwards regretted. Sometimes, collapsing against the heaped pillows, his heart stammering with anger, his complexion red with heat, he wept to himself in the mirror. Not a sane man left in town, he told himself. And worse: they're all against me.

"The one in Chiswick's not bad," said Angie wearily, calling on him after a long day's hunting. "If you don't mind Chiswick. It's got a fabulous *gloom* and it looks right on to the river."

"Is it noisy?"

"Depends, doesn't it. Depends what you call noisy."

"Look: could you work there? Creative work I mean ... something you had to be inspired for?"

It was Angie's third day out, and her temper was running short.

"How should I know? I can't count the decibels, can I? Tell her to go and listen for herself, I should."

Sulking, she lit a cigarette from a thin box of ten.

She? Cassidy repeated to himself; what a ridiculous, disgraceful notion! Good God, she thinks I'm ...

"It's not a *she*," he said very firmly. "It's a *he*. A writer if you must know. A married writer who needs support at a critical time in his career. Not just moral support but practical support. He's suffered a professional reverse which could seriously affect the course of—what the devil are you laughing at?"

It was not a laugh but a smile; a sudden, very pretty smile; to watch it was to smile himself.

"I'm just happy that's all. I know I'm silly; I can't help it, can I? I thought you were setting up a designing bitch, didn't I? Redhead in a leopardskin . . . dry martinis . . ."

Such was her merriment, and her pleasure, that she was obliged to take her bedridden employer's hand to steady herself; and to borrow his handkerchief from under the pillow to dry her eyes. And to return it to its proper place under the pillow again. And to take her leave of him affectionately, as became the informality of their situation. With a kiss, in fact, a neat, dry, soft, and very loving kiss, such as daughters bestow on fathers at their coming out.

"I like that lady," said Hugo, meaning Angie, who was still lingering wistfully at the gate, as if reluctant to leave. "She gives me hugs *all* the time. . . . Dad?"

"Yes Hugo."

"Do you think she's nicer than Heather?"

"Maybe."

"Nicer than Snaps?"

"Maybe."

"Nicer than Mummy?"

"Of course not," said Cassidy.

"That's what *I* think," said Hugo loyally.

Next morning early, a loud hammering filled the house in Abalone Crescent. From the hall and drawing room, unclassical male singing issued, often with improvised librettos. To the wailing of electric drills the workmen had returned.

24

Externally, Helen had not changed.

To the outward eye at least she was the same: the Anna Karenina boots were a shade more scuffed, the long brown coat a trifle more threadbare, but to Cassidy these signs of poverty only enhanced her virtue. She came down the platform first, carrying a paper parcel in both her hands as if it were a present for him, and she had that same gravity, that same essential seriousness of manner, which for Cassidy was a prerequisite of mothers and sisters alike. Her hair was also unchanged, and that was particularly fortunate since variations unnerved Cassidy; he frankly considered them fraudulent.

True, she was several feet shorter than his expectation, and the new lights at Euston Station robbed her of that angelic luminosity which candles and firelight impart. True her figure, which he remembered as fluid and noble beneath the uncomplicated Haverdown housecoat, had a certain mundanity about it when set among the Many-too-Many with whom she had been obliged to travel. But in her voice, in her embrace as she kissed him across the parcel, in her nervous laugh as she glanced behind her, he discerned at once a new intensity.

"He's been absolutely pining for you," she said.

"Look at *you*," said Shamus in his poofy voice, pulling her aside, much as he had done at Haverdown. "Fancy wearing *eelskin* at this time of year."

"Jesus," said Cassidy boldly. "Didn't know *you* were coming."

In Cassidy's glimpse of him before the long embrace, he thought it was the collar of the deathcoat. Though he remembered also thinking, as the strong arms pulled him in, that the deathcoat had no collar, or none you could turn so high. Then he thought it was a bird, an Alpine chough, pitch black, swooping to peck out his eyes. Then the barricade of tiny pins pricked and broke before him, and he thought: *this is Jonathan because he's dark, he's grown a beard to be like God.*

"He's decided he's got a weak chin," said Helen, waiting for them to finish.

"Fancy it, lover?"

"It's terrific. Marvellous. How does Helen like it?"

They made the short journey by cab. The Bentley was too high-hat, Cassidy had decided; but take a plain ordinary London taxi which would not embarrass them.

Inevitably, after Cassidy's high excitement at their coming, not to speak of the countless small preparations of an administrative and domestic character—would the curtains be ready in time, had Fortnum's mistaken the address?—inevitably, that first day was something of an anticlimax. Cassidy knew that Helen, after their many clandestine telephone calls in Shamus' interest, had much to say to him; he knew also that his first duty was to Shamus, who was the reason and the driving force of their reunion.

But Shamus placed heavy burdens on their forbearance.

Having sat Helen on the jump seat so that he and Cassidy could hold hands in comfort, Shamus first showed Cassidy how to stroke his beard: he should do it this way, downwards, never against the nap. Next, he undertook a physical examination of Cassidy, searching his arms and legs for any sign of damage, smoothing his hair, and studying the palms of his hands. And finally satisfied, he resumed his admiration of Cassidy's suit, which was of Harris tweed, not eelskin, a grey houndstooth chosen for semi-formal occasions. Was it French? Was it waterproof?

"How's work?" Cassidy asked, hoping to start a diversion.

"Never tried it," said Shamus.

"He's doing wonderfully," Helen said. "*All* the news is just marvellous, isn't it, Shamus? Honestly Cassidy, he's been working marvellously since he came back, haven't you Shamus? Four, five hours a day. More sometimes, it's been just fantastic."

Her eyes said more: we owe it to you, you have made a new man of him.

"I'm delighted," said Cassidy, while Shamus, licking a corner of his handkerchief, wiped a smut from Cassidy's cheek.

The best news of all, Helen confided, was that Dale had come down from London and that he and Shamus had had a fantastic relationship for the whole of one day.

"Great," said Cassidy with a smile, gently warding off more intimate embraces.

"Not jealous, lover?" Shamus enquired anxiously. "Not put out? Honest, lover? Honest?"

"I think I'll survive," said Cassidy, with another knowing glance at Helen.

"Actually," said Helen, "Dale isn't Dale at all, is he Shamus? He's Michaelovitsch, he's a Jew, *all* the good publishers are Jews, aren't they, Shamus? Well of course they *would* be really, they've got the most fantastic taste, in art and literature, in everything, Shamus always says so."

"That's *perfectly* true," Cassidy agreed, thinking of the Niesthals and recalling something Sandra had recently said. "That's perfectly true," he repeated, grateful to have a topic of conversation on which he could shine. "It's because historically the Jews weren't allowed to own land. Virtually throughout the *whole* of Europe, *right* through the Middle Ages. The Dutch were marvellous to them but then the Dutch are marvellous people anyway, look at the way they resisted the Germans. So of course, what happens? The Jews had to specialise in *international* things. Like diamonds and pictures and music and whatever they could move when they were persecuted."

"Lover," said Shamus.

"Yes?"

"Fuck off."

"Please go on about Dale," said Cassidy to Helen, trying not to laugh. "When's he actually *publishing*? That's the point. When do we start looking in the best-seller lists?"

Helen was prevented from replying by a sudden unearthly shriek which filled the cab and caused both herself and Cassidy to start violently. Shamus was working a laugh machine. It was a small cylinder made of Japanese paper, with steel ribs inside. Every time he turned it over it gave a dry cackle which, carefully controlled, slowed to a choking, tubercular cough.

"He calls it Keats," said Helen, in a tone which suggested to Cassidy that even maternal angels do not have unlimited patience.

"It's fantastic," said Cassidy, recovering from his alarm. "Mirthless and right. Carry on," he called to the driver. "It's okay, we were just laughing." He closed the partition window. "We'll be there soon," he said, with a reassuring smile at Helen.

She's tired from the journey, he thought. Shamus has probably been playing her up.

No one mentioned Paris.

It was a place on its own over a warehouse, with an outside steel staircase to the red front door. A nautical place, right on the river, with a view of two power stations and a playground to one side. Cassidy had taken it furnished for a great deal of money, and changed the furniture because it was too ordinary. There were flowers in the kitchen and more beside the bed, and there was a crate of Scotch in the broom cupboard. Talisker '54 from Berry Brothers and Rudd. There was a ship's wheel on the wall and rope for a bannister, but mainly it was the light you noticed, the upside-down light, that came off the river and lit the ceiling not the floor.

Demonstrating each tasteful feature—the new Colston washing-up machine, the coyly stowed deep-freeze in its random Iroko boarding, the draft extractors, the warm-air heating system, the Scandinavian stainless steel cutlery, not to mention the all-brass window fastenings of his own design—Cassidy felt the pride of a father who is giving the young couple a fair start in life. This is what Old Hugo would have done for me and Sandra, he thought, if he'd not been Tied Up With a Deal. Well, let's hope they show themselves worthy of it.

"Cassidy, *look,* there's even brown sugar for coffee. And serviettes, Shamus. Look, *Irish* linen. Oh my *God,* oh no, oh no . . ."

"Something wrong?" Cassidy asked.

"He's had our initials put on them," said Helen, almost crying for the sheer joy of her discovery.

He left the bedroom till last. The bedroom was his very particular pride. Green, he had wanted. Blue, Angie Mawdray had urged. Wasn't blue rather *cold*? Cassidy countered, quoting Sandra. In Harrods they found the answer: floppy blue flowers on the palest green background, the very same print which for years had given him such pleasure in Hugo's nursery at Abalone Crescent.

"Let's put it on the ceiling as well," Angie urged, with a woman's sympathy for Helen. "So they've got something to look at when they're lying on their backs."

To match, they had selected a Casa Pupo coverlet, the biggest available size to cover the biggest available bed. And sheets with a fabulous blue print, and fabulous pillowcases in the same way-out pattern. And white curtains bordered with a green-blue braid. And a fabulous white drugget to set it all off.

"Cassidy," Helen breathed, "it's the biggest bed we've ever had." And blushed, as became her modesty.

"Bathroom through there," said Cassidy, more to Shamus this time, in a very practical voice, as if bathrooms were men's work.

"Big enough for three," said Shamus, still looking at the bed.

They stood at the long window, watching the barges, Helen one side of him, Shamus the other.

"It's the loveliest place I've ever seen," said Helen. "It's the loveliest place we've ever had, or ever will have."

"I rather like *views*," said Cassidy, playing it right down to make it easy for them. "That's what first drew me to it actually."

"And the water," said Helen, understanding.

A long string of barges slid by, slow and out of step, overtaking one another as they passed the window, falling back into lines as they disappeared.

"Anyway," said Cassidy, "should be all right for a while."

"We don't want *all right*, do we, lover," Shamus quietly reminded him. It was some time since he had spoken. "Never did, never will. We want the sun, not the fucking twilight."

"Well there's plenty of sun *here*," said Helen brightly, with another confiding glance at Cassidy. "I adore picture windows. They're *so* modern."

"And free," said Cassidy.

"Exactly," said Helen.

"It needs movement," said Shamus.

Thinking he meant the river still, that he had entered their conversation with an aesthetic objection, Cassidy put his head on one side and said:

"Oh ... *Do* you ... ?"

"The three of us," said Shamus. "Or we'll just go into the mud."

Turning to Cassidy, he embraced him.

"Dear lover," he said softly, "that's a lovely, innocent thing you did. Bless you. Love you. Forgive."

Over Shamus' shoulder, he saw Helen shrug. *One of his moods,* her smile said. *It'll blow over.* Drawing close, she kissed him too, where he stood, held in her husband's arms.

After shampoo, which Cassidy had put ready in the High Speed Gas refrigerator, he tactfully made his excuses and left them to unpack. With the same nice tact, Helen left the two lovers to say goodbye. Shamus came down the steps with him.

"You don't know where I can buy a football, do you?" he asked, looking at the playground.

It was a dark, sullen kind of day, the grass very green and a lot of pink behind the power station as if the brickwork had stained the sky. A group of black children was playing hopscotch.

"You could try the Army and Navy," said Cassidy, a little disappointed to think he had forgotten something. "Shamus, there's nothing wrong is there? Nothing *bad* ..."

"Moral judgment?"

"Good Lord no—" said Cassidy hastily, knowing the rules.

Again Shamus was silent.

"God took six days, lover," he said, smiling at last. "Not even Butch can do it in a morning."

"And you really got stuck into those centre pages?" Cassidy asked, wishing to end it on an upward note.

"All for you. I'm a very obedient lover these days. No booze, no whores. Enoughs all the way. Ask Helen."

"She told me," said Cassidy, injudiciously.

"Bye, lover. Great pad. Bless you. Hey, how's the boss-cow? I thought I'd ring her up some time."

Cassidy barely flinched:

"Away I'm afraid. Gone to shack up with Mum for a while."

Helen from the balcony watched them hug, a princess in her new tower, the broad moat of the river at her back. His last sight of Shamus was of him standing with the children in the queue for hopscotch, waiting to take his turn.

At home meanwhile, contrary to Cassidy's little piece of artistic licence, all was happiness and activity. Cassidy's stock was much improved; his illness had done him good, they said; John Elderman was a genius. Aldo eats well, Aldo's eye is brighter, he has a sense of purpose: the word was passed from one female mouth to another, with allowances for domestic status. The cleaning women clubbed together and bought him a backrest for the Bentley; the dogs recognised him, Hugo drew him hooray cards and illuminated them with soluble crayon. Heather Ast came almost daily, witnessing Aldo's recovery while discussing with Sandra the resuscitation of human wrecks.

"We should open a place in the country," they said, loving the summer weather. "A place where they can all dry out."

This brightening of Cassidy's domestic sky was not without its cause; for Cassidy had finally recognised his true vocation, and Sandra in particular was delighted with it. Playing fields were a dead loss, she said; one could waste whole years and get nowhere; local Councils were corrupt beyond belief.

"It's just what you need," she said. "To give you an interest."

The ideal solution, she said; the natural compromise between Church and Trade:

"I can't think *why* you didn't hit on it earlier, but still."

"It came to me while I was ill," Cassidy confessed. "I had that awful feeling I'd wasted so much of my life. I lay there, I thought *who are you?—why are you?—what will they say of you when you're dead?* I just didn't want to worry you until I was sure," he added.

"Darling," said Sandra, a little ashamed all the same, as she later admitted to Heather, that she had not been more alive to her husband's inner turmoil.

For Cassidy had decided to enter politics.

As a precaution, however, she consulted John Elderman. They went together as if their problem were bridal. Would it be too much of a strain for him? Would it get him down the way Paris had? Much travel was involved, lonely nights in dismal northern hostelries. Was John absolutely sure that Cassidy's physique could take it? After some demur, John Elderman gave the green light.

"But watch that old ticker," he warned. "The smallest tweak and you call me in. No hiding it away, right?"

"He'll hide it if he gets a chance," said Sandra, knowing her Aldo.

"Then you watch *him*," said John Elderman.

Hallowed now by a profound sense of sacrifice, they set to work in earnest. The first thing was to settle on a Party. Though Sandra's mind was absolutely made up, Cassidy, with his harsher experience of the world, his fabled understanding of the fleshly weaknesses of men in trade, had yet to reach a firm decision. Sandra thought it vital she should not influence him in *any* way, therefore (as she later told him) she witnessed in silence the dialogue between his conscience and his purse.

"I just can't get over being Socialist and rich," he said. "It doesn't seem to add up."

"You're not *that* rich," Sandra consoled him.

"Well I am really. If the market keeps up."

"Then give it away," she snapped, "if *that's* your problem."

But Cassidy felt that giving it away was too easy.

"I'm sorry, Sandra, it's just not the answer. I can't run away like that. I've got to stand for what I *am*," he told her over dinner, on the eve of Helen and Shamus' arrival. "Not for what I ought to be. Politics reflect *reality*."

"You used to say we were judged by what we looked for."

"Not in politics," said Cassidy.

"Then why not the Liberals? There are *masses* of rich Liberals, look at the Niesthals."

"But the Liberals never get in," Cassidy objected.

Better to be a free Independent than a tied Liberal, he said.

"You mean you'll only back winners?" Sandra demanded, as ever the custodian of her husband's probity.

"It's not *that*. It's just . . . well the Liberals speak with too many voices. I want a Party that knows its mind."

"Well as far as *I'm* concerned," said Sandra, "the Conservatives are absolutely *out*."

Conservatives hated the poor, she said, they had absolutely *no* sympathy for the underdog, Conservatives were *stupid*, her father had been one, and if Cassidy went anywhere *near* the Conservatives she would leave him *at once*.

"I'm absolutely damned if I'll be a Tory M.P.'s wife," she said. "Except in a country area. It's different in the country, more traditional."

Soothing her, Cassidy explained his plan of campaign. He did this very judiciously, admitting her bit by bit to a complex and delicate secret. Did she *promise* not to tell anyone?

She did.

Was she *sure*?

She was.

He didn't mind her telling Heather and the Eldermans and the cleaning women because they would all find out anyway; yes, and the Niesthals if they asked but not unless.

She understood.

Well, he had cleared the decks entirely at the office. It was the silly season, the Trade had pretty well packed up after the Paris Fair, a lot of the staff were on holiday. So anyway, Cassidy had been in touch with the Unions—

"The *Unions*," Sandra echoed, much excited. "You mean you're going to join the—"

"The Unions," Cassidy repeated patiently, brushing aside his virtue. "Now *will* you let me finish?"

Sandra would; she had not meant to interrupt.

Very well, there had been discussions. Did she remember that Wednesday he had to go to Middlesbrough and Beth Elderman said she had seen him in Harrods?

Sandra remembered it clearly.

Well, that was one of the discussions.

Sandra was contrite.

As a result of these discussions, which had ranged over several weeks, the Unions had now invited him to make a thorough examination of the whole organisation of the Labour Movement from the businessman's angle.

"Oh my *God*," Sandra breathed. "But that's *dynamite!*"

In effect (though this was highly confidential) a Business Efficiency Analysis. At the end of his researches he would put in a Paper, and if he still liked them and they still liked him, well, maybe a safe Union seat could be found . . .

"They might even publish it," Sandra said, still very excited as they undressed for bed. "Then you'd be a *writer* too. The Cassidy Report. . . . When do you start?"

"The first leg's tomorrow," said Cassidy, showing his full hand at last.

"And you're not to compromise," Sandra warned him. "Don't go saying things just to please them. Those Unions are an absolute pest."

"I'll try," said Cassidy.

"Good luck, Dad," said Hugo.

"I mean it," said Sandra.

"Politics my arse," said Old Hugo at the penthouse, receiving his secret fortnightly visit and his fortnightly cheque. "Politics my Aunt Fanny Adam. You haven't got the guts for it, take my word. You need the guts of a *lion* to be in politics today, a *lion*, Blue!"

A Mrs. Bluebridge was in residence, Old Hugo's female advisor and a longstanding mother from Cassidy's childhood. She had put a typewriter on the drawing room table—her own way of establishing respectability—and her sponge-bag in a separate bathroom, Cassidy had seen it when he went in to brush his hair. "Who's Bluebridge?" he used to ask. "Is she your wife? Your sister? Your secretary?" Once, to set a trap, he had spoken French to her, but though surprised she had not responded guiltily.

"Well I do *think*, Aldo . . ." Bluebridge began, and

drifted away into the problem of understanding the needs of young people in the world today.

A faint Scottish accent distinguished her from other members of her team. Her mouth was at the very centre of her painted lips, a frayed black line that parted and joined like a poor seam under pressure. He owes her money, Cassidy thought; he's giving her love instead. Soon she would come to him, they always did. Call at South Audley Street on a Monday morning having mulled it over all weekend, sit in the deep leather chair beside Angie Mawdray's coffee cup, twisting her fingers round old envelopes full of broken promises. *Now I don't want to say anything against your father, Aldo. Your father's a lovely man in very many ways . . .*

The young were still her concern. Having shown him her reasoning, she proceeded to announce her conclusion:

"It's sex, sex, sex, all the way, that's all they think of, truly Aldo. Politics or young girls, it's the same thing. I've seen it all my life, I have too."

"It's a carve-up," Old Hugo cried, in very high spirits, pointing to the distant outlines of Westminster. "It's a carve-up of vice, greed, and influence, that's all politics is, mark my words. You listen to Blue, Aldo; that woman has seen the world."

"Now Aldo's seen the world too, Hugo, he's not a babe any more. Well don't you agree now, Aldo, deep down?" the seam enquired.

Letting him out, she squeezed his hand and wished him luck.

"I'm so glad you're going Conservative," she whispered. "But don't do it on your dad's back, will you dear, it never lasts."

"Was *he* Conservative then?" Cassidy asked, meaning Old Hugo, and still smiling to have pleased them so exceptionally.

"Ssh," said Blue, smelling of oatcake.

At the office in South Audley Street, too, all was sunny, all was content. Meale, taking three weeks' holiday at once, had withdrawn to a monastery in Leeds; Lemming was on the Scilly Isles; Faulk had rented a cottage in Selsey and was living in much-publicised happiness with a Metropol-

itan policeman. Of his *cercle,* only Miss Mawdray had nobly stayed behind to attend the Chairman's needs. Most of
her time was spent on shopping. If she was not ordering
bound works on revolution, sanitation, and the Common
Market (either for despatch to Abalone Crescent or to
adorn the gateleg table in the waiting room) she was
engaged in the many small tasks which went towards the
welfare of her master's *protégés.* She arranged for library
facilities at Harrods and daily newspapers from a local
newsagent; for credit at a theatre ticket agency, charges
to be remitted to the Company. All this on Cassidy's in-
struction, all with great aplomb. She sent round stationery
from Henningham and Hollis, and arranged for typists to
be on call at an agency in Pimlico.

Having persuaded Helen (outside Shamus' hearing) to
accept a small allowance to tide them over till the new
book, Cassidy also decided she should have a credit card,
and after some difficulty and much animal persistence
Angie Mawdray succeeded in sponsoring her enrolment
with one of the major companies.

"Jesus," she said with a giggle, "she'll ruin you, I
would."

Angie's morale had never been higher. Hitherto, she had
objected to misleading Sandra on small matters of fact,
such as whether he was in London or Manchester, whether
he was still in Paris. Now, her scruple was gone, and
though Cassidy did not confide in her about his Trade
Union project, she knew enough, and guessed enough, to
protect his interests when the need arose. As to her appearance, it spoke of purest happiness. Her breasts, often
unsupported, remained sharp despite the summer heat; her
summer skirts, never long, had shrunk to a festive brevity,
and her movements seemed calculated to solicit, rather
than inhibit, his gaze.

Once, to reward her efforts, he took her to the cinema, and she held his hand in mute submission, watching
Cassidy rather than the screen, her little face flickering on
and off as the beam switched above them like wartime
searchlights.

As to his relationship with Helen and Shamus, Angie
Mawdray was neither shocked nor curious.

"If you like them, it's good enough for me," she said.

"And he's a smashing writer, truly. As good as Henry Miller, whatever the beastly critics say."

Within days of their arrival, she had learnt to recognise their voices on the telephone and put them through without enquiry. Once, using his Russian accent, Shamus asked her to go to bed with him. He was the Reverend Rasputin, he said, and tired to death of princesses.

"He would too," said Cassidy with a laugh, "if he got half a chance."

"What's so funny about that?" said Angie, stung.

But mainly he said he was Flaherty, an Irish fanatic in search of moderation.

25

Up Hall's Shamus called it.

They went there for Impact, it was better even than
water. They went there for Abstinence, it was Shamus'
new mood; to keep fit, and preserve himself to a fine
Old Testament age. They went there by bus riding at the
front on the top deck, after six, when the eastbound buses
were mainly empty. To a black-bricked warehouse behind
Cable Street, with ropes swinging from the girders, and
an old trampoline stretched above the concrete floor, and
a rope boxing ring rigged under arc lights, the canvas
blotched with blood. Cassidy wore squash kit with a little
blue laurel on the left breast, but Shamus insisted on the
deathcoat, he refused to dress for Impact. Hall wore white
ducks as broad at the cuff as they were at the waist, and
a cotton singlet with creases ironed across the shoulders.
Hall was a small, round, toothless man with quick brown
eyes and darting fists and a complexion made in squares
like an old brown eiderdown. To Cassidy, he had a lot of
the naval chaplain about him, the same shipshape philoso-
phy and a pious way of drinking, the same way of shaking
hands while he looked for God behind you.

He called Shamus Lovely.

Not my lovely, or lovely one, but plain lovely as if it
were a noun. *Le beau,* thought Cassidy, hearing it for the
first time; the Regency tradition. Before Impact they
watched the sparring of Hall's White Hopes, and played
on the trampoline and rode the anchored bicycle. After
Impact they went up to Sal's place, which was Hall's name
for where he lived. Sal was Hall's bird, Hall's body; he
loved her better than life. She was nineteen and simple, by
profession a tart, but now in retirement owing to Hall's
insistence.

For this reason, Hall seldom allowed her out, but
banged her up to keep her safe.

"Bangs her up?" asked Cassidy.

Bang up was prison talk, Shamus explained proudly; Hall had been in stir. *Bang up* meant lock the cell door at night.

That's why Hall's a parson, Cassidy thought, reminded of Old Hugo; he's learnt the piety of granite walls.

For Impact, Shamus fought with Hall, when the gym was empty of all but Cassidy and a man called Ming, a blood-wiper and stone deaf.

Hall would only oblige when the gym was empty; that was his rule, that was his pride, Hall's sense of what was proper in a well-run gym, for Shamus had no art at all, and would not learn it.

"Wait," Hall would say firmly, bolting the doors. "Wait, Lovely, I'm telling you," and then duck quickly under the ropes and into the ring before Shamus could get at him.

Shamus in attack relied solely on the charge. He charged in sudden onslaughts, shouting and flailing his arms under the deathcoat: "Fucker, sodder, prole!" And if he reached his adversary, embraced him, squeezing his ribs and biting him until Hall was obliged to beat him off. Sometimes, affecting a Japanese style, he tried to kick him, then Hall took his foot and threw him on his back.

"Take it easy, Lovely, take it easy, I don't want to hurt you now," Hall would say, quite misunderstanding the purpose of the engagement.

Very rarely, provoked beyond endurance, Hall smacked him on the cheek, most frequently a backhanded blow, to deflect him from the charge. Then Shamus would stand off, very pale, frowning and smiling together, feeling the pain and rubbing his cheek with his black sleeve.

"Jesus," he would say. "Wow. Hey, go and do it to Cassidy. Cassidy, feel, it's fantastic!"

"I can imagine," Cassidy would say, laughing. "Thanks very much, Hall, all the same."

"He'd be a grand fighter," Hall declared, back at Sal's place, as they drank the Talisker out of Cassidy's brief-case. "It's his footwork, that's the trouble, it spreads him out, don't it Lovely? You're a murderous bugger though, aren't you?"

"I think he's nice," said Sal, who was very prim for her age and seldom said much else.

Hall enjoyed his whisky neat, from a tall glass so full it looked like still pale beer.

"That's how *we* should drink it," Shamus explained as they returned to Helen. "If it wasn't for me being dedicated."

"I must say," Sandra told John Elderman. Heather was present and passed it on to Cassidy. "I must say he's keeping very fit. He's lost four pounds in a week."

"It's all that Trade Union food," said John Elderman, who knew his lower classes.

"He's been taking exercise too," said Sandra, with (Heather reported) a most unusual smile.

Observing, Helen called it.

It was her own idea; she advanced it one morning while Cassidy sat on the end of the blue bed finishing up their toast from a Michael Truscott plate. He had dropped in early on his way to South Audley Street. It was the holiday season, and the business world was almost at a standstill.

The cups were also Truscott: stoneware of great delicacy, he had thought the plain form would appeal to her.

"Honestly, Shamus," she said. "He's just never lived, have you, Cassidy? He's been in London all his life and he doesn't know anything about it at all. Honestly, you ask him where anything is, or when it was built, or honestly . . . *anything,* and I'll bet he doesn't know the answer. Cassidy, have you ever been to the Tate? Listen to this, Shamus. Well, Cassidy?"

So that afternoon while Shamus toiled, they went to the Tate, stopping on the way to buy Helen some sensible shoes. Finding the Tate closed they had tea at Fortnum's instead, and afterwards Helen insisted on visiting the Baby Carriage Department to inspect one of Cassidy's prams. The salesman was extremely respectful and, without knowing that Cassidy was of his audience, praised the excellence of his inventions. Also he assumed Helen and Cassidy were married and that Helen was pregnant, and this led to much secret laughter between them, and squeezes of the hand and confiding glances. Then Helen said actually it *might* be twins, there was quite a record of twins in the family, particularly on *her* side.

"My father's a twin, *and* my grandfather and my great-grandfather. . . ."

And Cassidy put in, "It led to awful trouble with the title, didn't it darling?"

So the salesman showed them a Cassidy Two-in-Hand carriage with a Cassidy Banburn canopy over the top and Helen wheeled it very solemnly up and down the carpet until she got the giggles and had to be removed.

At the zoo Helen made straight for the vultures, studying them gravely and without apparent fear. Hugo's gibbons gave her particular pleasure, causing her to laugh out loud. No, Cassidy quietly corrected her, they were not making love in the air, that was the baby holding on underneath, it was the way they carried their young, almost like kangaroos.

"Nonsense, Cassidy, don't be so prim, of *course* they're—"

"No," said Cassidy, firmly, "they're not."

In the night animals' house they watched badgers preparing a set and bats cleaning their ears and small rodents burrowing against the glass. No, said Cassidy in answer to the same question, they were just using each other's backs for steps. In the dark corridor, watched by a crowd of bleary children, Helen was moved to kiss Cassidy in gratitude for all the wonderful things he had done for Shamus; and she promised Cassidy that she loved him, in her way as faithfully as Shamus, and that he would always have a home with them however bleak the other parts of his life.

And when finally, by way of several pubs, they reached the Water Closet (Shamus' name for the flat) and found him still working, still in the beret, crouched at the river window, they told him everything they had observed, and all the fun they had had; everything in fact except the kiss, because the kiss was private and, like the actions of certain animals, liable to facile misconstruction.

"Great," said Shamus quietly, when he had heard it all. "Great," and having taken each of them in an affectionate embrace, returned to his desk.

A few days later the two men went down to Hall's for Impact and Shamus succeeded in landing Hall a painful blow on the eye. For retaliation, Hall punched him in the stomach, hard, just under the rib cage, on what boxers call the mark, and Shamus became white and sick and even more quiet than before.

With Shamus wholly given to work, abstinence, and contemplation, it was inevitable that Helen and Cassidy should spend much time observing on their own. Now in his deathcoat, now stark naked before the window, the beret pulled like a cage low on his dark brow, he would sit for hours on end, head bowed, driving his pen across the paper. Not even for *Moon,* said Helen, had he shown such zeal, such application:

"And he has *you* to thank for it. *Dear* Cassidy."

"Is it *all* rewrite?" Cassidy asked, lunching with her at Boulestin. "It looked like a whole new novel to me."

Helen said no, she was sure it was the rewrite. He had promised Cassidy he would do it, he had made the same promise to Dale: Shamus never, never forgot a promise.

"He always pays what he owes. I've never met anyone with a greater sense of honour."

She said this without drama, as a statement concerning someone they both loved; and Cassidy knew it was true, a fact beyond pretending.

London was her city.

Shamus was Paris. The Celt, the nomad, the dreamer, the practitioner: all were met in the unfathomable artistic genius of Paris. But Helen was London, and Cassidy loved her for it. She loved its worthiness, its dingy pomp and ordinary grime. And though they both subscribed to Shamus' dictum that the past was not worth discussing, Cassidy by now had learnt enough of her to know that London was where most of her life had been spent.

She led him.

She led him along wharves, past Dutch warehouses painted with impossible professions: cane importers, whalers, grinders of fine curry. She led him down dangerous Dickensian alleys, gaslit and haunted by bollards, where for twenty seconds they thrilled to a sense of being young and well-dressed and desirable to evildoers. She showed him City churches with postage-stamp edges; took him into synagogues and mosques, held his hand at the place where poets were buried in Westminster Abbey. She showed him empty markets where brown dogs ate Brussels sprouts by lamplight, and Mussolini's statue in the Imperial War Museum. She took him to the Anchor and stood him on a wooden platform and made him gaze at the sunlit outline of St. Paul's across the water; and she asked him to become Lord Mayor all in furs and chains so that she could visit him and eat roast beef by candlelight. And Cassidy knew he had never seen any of these places before, not one of them; not even the Tower of London or Piccadilly Circus, until Helen had shown them to him.

For conversation they had Shamus: their star, their parent, their lover, and their ward. How they loved him more than themselves; he was their bond. How his talent was their responsibility, their gift to the world. That to damage him in any way would be to violate a trust.

Shamus, meanwhile, had cut his beard square at the end in order to look like a rabbi.

"Solid for the Old Testament," he explained, still writing.

While at Abalone Crescent, Sandra was extremely impressed by Cassidy's portrait of dockside conditions.

"When will they realise it's the *quality* of life that matters, not the amount that people earn?" she demanded.

"Jesus," said Snaps. "Hear you."

"Still, darling, money is *nice*," countered Mrs. Groat, who had recently put her arm in a sling on the grounds that it hurt when she had it straight.

"Nonsense," said Sandra. "Money's just token. It's happiness that matters, isn't it, Aldo?"

To compensate for his prolonged absences Sandra had wisely acquired a new interest.

"What are the dockers doing about birth control?" she wanted to know. Were there advisory centres for wives? If not, she and Heather would open one *at once*. Or—a sensible thought—should they postpone their decision until Cassidy had his Seat?

"I think," said Cassidy shrewdly, after some thought, "that you might do best to wait and see where we end up."

The change in Shamus, when it came, was at first barely distinguishable from the strains of an arduous routine, and only loosely related to external events. Hall had much to do with it; yet the part he played was probably, in the end, analogous rather than contributory.

For several weeks now, Helen and Cassidy and Shamus had lived a life of quite unusual happiness. As Shamus added page after page to the neat piles of paper before him so, it seemed to Cassidy, did his own contentment rise in an ever-ascending swell of perfect companionship. Cassidy came most often after lunch, when Helen had put behind her the majority of her domestic duties. Sometimes she was still washing up—the machine, for all its simplicity, had defeated her—and in that case Cassidy would dry the glasses for her while they planned their afternoon's entertainment. Often they would consult Shamus: did he think it would rain? What did he feel about a trip to Hampton Court? Should they take the Bentley or get a car from Harrods? And when they came back, they would sit at the table hand in hand and tell him, over a frugal Talisker or a bottle of shampoo, of all their many adventures and impressions.

Occasionally, in return, Shamus read to them from his manuscript, and although Cassidy on such occasions deliberately induced in himself a kind of inner vertigo which left him only a broad impression of genius, he readily agreed it was better than Tolstoy, better even than *Moon*, and that Dale was the luckiest publisher alive.

Occasionally, Shamus said nothing at all, but rocked back and forth in his chair, letting Keats shriek for him at the funny places.

And sometimes, if Cassidy had not actually spent the night there, he would call in the morning, early enough to share their breakfast in the blue flower bedroom and in the freshness of the hour discuss with them the world's problems, or better still their own. It was a time of exceptional frankness in all matters affecting their collective relationship. The love life of Helen and Shamus, for instance, was an open book between them. Though Paris was never spoken of—indeed Cassidy sometimes wondered whether they had ever been there—Helen had made it clear that she knew Shamus in *that* mood also, and that Cassidy was not concealing from her anything that could hurt her pride. Nor was it at all unusual for Shamus or Helen to make a reference to a recent sexual encounter, often with humorous overtones.

"Christ," she said to Cassidy once as they rose from a prolonged luncheon at the Silver Grill, "he's practically broken my back," and confided to him that they had been reading the *Kamasutra* and following one of its more ambitious recommendations. From other chance remarks let slip in the ordinary line of conversation, Cassidy learned that for the same purpose they were given to using telephone booths and other public amenities; and that their most treasured achievement had taken place on a parked Lambretta in an alley behind Buckingham Palace. While in the more general way, he could not help noticing (since he quite often slept in the adjoining bedroom) that his friends enjoyed at least a daily exchange of views, and not infrequently two or three.

The first sign of a flaw in this idyllic relationship came with their visit to Greenwich. As one perfect summer's day followed another it was very natural that Helen and Cassidy should wander farther afield in search of pleasure and information. At first, they contented themselves with the larger London parks, where they flew kites and gliders and floated yachts on ponds. But the parks were full of the Many-too-Many and rutting proles in pink underclothes, and they agreed that Shamus would prefer them to find their own place, even if it took longer to get there. Therefore they took the Bentley to Greenwich, and while they were there they found themselves looking at the yacht in which Sir Francis Chichester had sailed singlehanded round the world. It was not in water, but concrete; embalmed there for ever, within a few feet of the embankment.

For some while neither spoke.

Cassidy in fact was not at all sure what his reaction should be. That the boat had superb lines, God look at those proportions? That it seemed an awful waste to put a perfectly good boat out of service, was public money involved? Or he wished they could sail away in it, just the three of them, possibly to an island?

"It's the saddest thing I've ever seen," said Helen, suddenly.

"Me too," said Cassidy.

"To think it was once *free* . . . a living, wild thing . . ."

Cassidy at once took up her argument. It was indeed a most tragic and affecting sight, he would write to the Greater London Council the moment he got back to the office.

Thrilled by the similarity of their separate responses they hurried home to share their feelings with Shamus.

"Let's all go down there one night," Cassidy suggested. "With picks, and set it free!"

"Oh do let's," said Helen.

"Jesus Christ," said Shamus and went to the lavatory, ostensibly to be sick.

Later he apologised. An unworthy thought he said, forgive, lover, forgive. He had had visions of Christopher Robin, all wrong, all wrong.

But when Cassidy, leaving for home, made his way down the steel steps, he was met by a shower of water that could only have come from the bedroom window; and he remembered Lipp's restaurant in Paris, his baptism and Shamus' pain.

The cloud, it seemed, had passed, until one day—a week later, perhaps two—Hall's gym closed. Cassidy and Shamus went down on a Monday and found the iron door locked against them and no lights burning in the air-raid-glass window.

"Gone to a fight," said Shamus, so they played football instead.

They went down again on the Thursday and the door was still locked, now with a crowbar and a curiously official-looking padlock with sealing wax over the hook.

"Gone on holiday," said Cassidy, thinking of Angie

Mawdray, who had left for Greece the day before with a ticket bought by the Company. So they went for a run round Battersea Park and played on the seesaw.

The third time they went, there was a notice saying "Closed," so they rang the bell at Sal's place until she answered it. Hall was in stir, she said, very frightened, he had clobbered an American bosun for being fresh, he was doing three months at the Scrubs. She had a bruised eye and one hand bandaged and she shut the door on them as soon as she had told them the news. But there was a smell of cigar in the parlour and the sound of a radio upstairs, so they reckoned the American bosun had not suffered irreparable harm.

This news had a curious effect on Shamus. At first, he was incensed and, like the unreformed Shamus of old, made elaborate plans to effect his friend's escape: to kidnap the American Ambassador, for instance, or sequester the bosun's ship. He assembled an armoury of secret weapons: wire nooses, files, and pieces of bicycle chain attached to wooden handles. His plan was a mass break-out involving all inmates.

This aggressive mood was followed by one of deep melancholy and disappointment. Why had Hall allowed himself to be captured? Shamus would commit a crime in order to be joined with him. Prison was the only place for writers, and he fell back on the familiar examples of Dostoevsky and Voltaire.

But as the weeks passed and Hall was still not released, Shamus gradually ceased to talk about him. He seemed instead to enter a dream world of his own from which the excited accounts of his wife's exploits with Cassidy no longer woke him. But he did not turn away from Hall; to the contrary, he drew closer, developing, in some way which Cassidy could not fully understand, an inner partnership with him, a secret union, as it were; to languish with him waiting for a certain day.

Condemned still for hours at a time to the imprisonment of his novel, he even acquired, to Cassidy's skilled eye, a prison pallor and certain prison mannerisms, a slough of the feet and shoulders, a furtive greed at table, and the habits of listless servility when addressed and of following them round the room with shut-off, unwatching eyes. In conversation, when he could be drawn, he was inclined to volunteer incongruous references to atonement, hubris, and the social contract, loyalty to one's private precepts. And on one unfortunate occasion, he let slip a most damaging comparison between the sublime Helen and Hall's bird Sal.

It happened late at night.

On Cassidy's suggestion they had been to the cinema—Shamus also liked the live theatre, but he was inclined to shout at the actors—and they had seen a Western starring Paul Newman, whose features Helen had recently compared with Cassidy's. Returning by way of a couple of pubs, they had linked arms as was their custom, Helen in the middle, when Shamus suddenly interrupted Cassidy's spirited rendering of the film's key scene with a cry of:

"Hey, look there's Sal!"

Following the direction of his gaze, they looked across the road at a middle-aged woman standing alone on a street corner, under a lantern, in the classic posture of a prewar tart. Irritated by their interest, she scowled at them, turned, and toppled a few ridiculous steps along the pavement.

"Nonsense," said Helen. "She's far too old."

"You're not though, are you? You've got a few years in you, haven't you?"

For a moment no one spoke. To look for Sal they had drawn to a halt, and were standing, still linked, outside what was probably Chelsea Hospital. The windows were lighted and uncurtained. A complex of pale shadows ran outwards from their feet. Cassidy felt Helen's arm stiffen inside his own, and her bare hand turned cold.

"What the hell's that supposed to mean?" she demanded.

"Jesus," Shamus muttered. "Jesus."

Breaking away from them he hurried into a side street and returned to the flat late and very pale.

"Forgive, lover, forgive," he whispered, and having kissed Cassidy goodnight, put his arm round Helen and guided her gently, reverently to the bedroom.

On the next day the incident at football occurred.

It was for both of them conclusive. Shamus was over-worked; abstinence had gone too far.

In the absence of Impact, football had become their main recreation. They played it twice a week: on Tuesdays and Fridays. It was a fixture, always at four. On the stroke of the clock, Cassidy would roll his trousers to the knee, toss his jacket on to the blue bed, kiss Helen goodbye, and run off across the road to the playground to reserve the goal. A few moments later, dressed in the inevitable deathcoat, Shamus would descend the iron steps and after a few preliminary exercises on the swings take up his position either as striker or goalie according to his mood. A rigid points system was applied, and Shamus kept all manner of records in a drawer of his desk, including diagrams of intricate manoeuvres he had performed. He even spoke of publishing a book on method football; he would talk to Dale about it, the sodder. Generally he was better in attack than in defence. His kicking had a wild, undisciplined brilliance to it which frequently lofted the ball far over the railings, and once into the river, for which he claimed a prize, an afternoon exchange of views with Helen. As a goalie he tended to rely on nerve tactics, which included shrill Japanese war whoops and many exotic obscenities on the subject of Cassidy's bourgeois nature.

On the day in question, it was Shamus' turn to attack. Taking the ball quite close to the goal mouth, he dug a mound, set the ball on it, then stalked slowly backwards preparatory to a self-awarded free kick. Since the ball was no more than five yards from him, and the line of Shamus' run appeared to direct it at his head, Cassidy decided on a defensive charge, which he executed without difficulty, clearing the ball to the other side of the ground, where it was intercepted by an old man and kicked back. The next thing Cassidy knew was that Shamus had hit him on the nose, very hard, and that a stream of warm blood was running over his mouth and that his eyes were watering profusely.

"But it's the *game*," Cassidy protested, dabbing his face with his handkerchief. "That's the way it's played for God's sake!"

"You buy your own fucking ball!" Shamus shouted at

him, furious. "And keep your fucking hands off mine. Sodder."

"Here's to no rules," said Helen, back in the Water Closet, quietly observing them over her Talisker.

"Here's to *my* rules," said Shamus, not at all mollified.

"Well I wish you'd tell me what they are," said Cassidy, still smarting.

"It's the book," Helen assured him, as he left. "It's right on the brink. He always gets like this at the end."

"I think you're absolutely *wonderful*," said Sandra, her eyes bright with excitement as she staunched the wound that same night. "You haven't hurt him *badly* have you?"

"If I have, I have," Cassidy retorted irritably. "If they want their politics rough, that's what they must expect."

Next day Helen and Shamus disappeared.

26

Waiting again.

Visiting Birmingham to discuss the Common Market with the local Liberal Party, Cassidy took Angie Mawdray, ripened by Greek suns, to dinner in Soho.

"You know what I demand of a woman?" he asked her. "A pact to live fully."

"Gosh," said Angie. "How?"

"Never to apologise, never to regret. To drink whatever life provides"—they had had a lot of retsina, Angie's favourite. "To take whatever is offered, never counting the cost."

"Why don't you?" she asked softly.

"I want to *share*," he told Heather Ast at Quaglino's the following night, a Tuesday, returning from Birmingham by way of Hull. "To cherish, to be cherished? *Yes,*" he conceded. "But never to . . . live on my second stomach like a cow. A couple of glimpses of the infinite, that's all I ask. Then I'll die happy. You know what the Italians say: one day as a lion is worth a lifetime as a mouse."

"Poor Sandra," said Ast quietly. "She'd never understand."

"It's *virtue,*" Cassidy insisted. "The only virtue, the only freedom, the only life. To make *wanting* the justification. For everything."

"Oh Aldo," said Ast, wistfully touching his hand. "It's such a journey, such a *lonely* journey."

"The ordinary hours are not enough," Cassidy declared to Sandra on Wednesday, driving back from a late dinner through empty streets. "I'm sick of enough. I'm sick of making *convention* an excuse for being bored."

"You mean you're bored with *me*," said Sandra.

"Christ *of course* I don't!"

"Don't swear," she said.

"I'm sure he didn't mean it, darling," said her mother from the back. "All men do it."

"What's eating you then, all of a sudden?" Snaps murmured as, ladies first, she went upstairs to bed. "You're like a bloody bitch in heat."

"We're back," said Helen, calling him at work. "Did you miss us?"

"Certainly not," said Cassidy. "I have unlimited substitutes."

"Liar," said Helen and kissed him down the telephone.

Hall was out: that was the occasion. Not sprung, as Shamus would have had it, not swapped for the American Ambassador, but out, honourably liberated with the full co-operation of the Wormwood Scrubs authorities, after remission of sentence for good conduct. His release had coincided almost to the day with the return of Shamus and Helen: valid causes both for celebration.

But surely not at the Savoy?

At the Bag o'Nails, yes. At the Victoria Palace, at one of the drag pubs which Helen liked, across the river in Battersea or Clapham. But not—in Cassidy's book at least —never for such a purpose, his beloved Savoy.

Was it Helen's idea? Cassidy doubted it.

Helen, for all her fearless virtue, had a considerable sense of decorum.

Shamus then? Was it Shamus' idea?

The finger pointed strongly in his direction. Much enlivened by his journey to the country—a tiny *lapse,* Helen said vaguely, he was cracking a bit under the book, best not refer to it—he had come back full of suggestions as to how they should celebrate. His first was a dockside firework display, the biggest London had ever seen, bigger than that of the Great Exhibition; all Cassidy's money should be devoted to it. But Cassidy claimed to remember having seen oil tankers at Egg Wharf, so that plan was dropped in favour of a *dancing.* Not an ordinary *dancing,* but a great ballet, written by Shamus to celebrate the virtues of passionate crime. Everyone would have a part, they would take the Albert Hall and forbid entry to Gerrard's Crossers.

To this plan, Helen had the sternest objections. He should finish the centre pages, she said, before he even *thought* of writing anything else. Moreover, he knew no choreography. If Shamus wanted to dance, why didn't they go somewhere where dancing was already available. . . . ? And from there somehow, they agreed on the Savoy.

Therefore it was most likely, but not proven, that Shamus had started the movement, and that Cassidy and Helen, as so often, joined it once it had begun.

The matter settled, it was at once their principal, indeed their only, concern. Whatever reservations Cassidy and Helen might secretly have shared were at once set aside in favour of the excitement of preparation. They planned for it, they lived for it. While naive Shamus put on his beret and settled, naked again, before the open window, the sentimental Supporters' Club took up residence in the kitchen and wrote out menus and place cards.

"Oh Cassidy, what *will* it be like? I'll bet it's absolutely *peachy*. Cassidy, can we have caviar? Say we can? Oh *Cassidy*."

News from Shamus' agent gave them fresh cause to celebrate: he had been offered a lucrative if inglorious contract to visit Lowestoft for three weeks to write a documentary on trawlermen for the Central Office of Information. The Office would pay his expenses and a fee of two hundred pounds. Helen was delighted: sea air was just what Shamus needed.

"And you *will* come and visit us, won't you Cassidy?"

"Of course."

They would leave on the morning following the party, settle in over the weekend; Shamus would start work on the Monday. Shamus called it his *Codpiece* and left the arrangements to Helen.

"But won't it interfere with his novel?" Cassidy asked, very puzzled.

Helen was oddly indifferent.

"Not madly," she said. "Anyway I want to go, and for once he can damn well do something for me."

Which left them with the vital question of what Helen would wear.

"Oh God, I'll borrow something of Mummy's, what does it *matter?*"

"Helen."

"Cassidy, *please* . . ."

So one afternoon, while Shamus was still working, they went back to Fortnum's where, in a sense, they had begun. The choice was absurd, for she gave style to everything she put on.

"Well *you* decide, Cassidy, you're buying it."

"The white one," Cassidy said promptly, "with the low back."

"But Cassidy, it costs a—"

"*Please,*" said Cassidy impatiently.

"That was the one *I* liked," said Helen.

From Piccadilly they went to the Savoy and selected a table for five and ordered a special cake with "Welcome Home Hall" in icing, a fruitcake because Helen said fruitcake would keep, they could take home what they didn't eat. Sitting in the cab again Helen became suddenly very solemn.

"Shamus must never know," she said. "Never in his whole life. Promise, Cassidy?"

"Know what?"

"About this afternoon. About the dress. About all we did, the fun we had, the laughter, and your kindness. Promise."

"But God," he protested, "this is *us,* this is friendship, it could be *you* two, or Shamus and me, or . . ."

"All the same," said Helen; and Cassidy, bowing to her superior knowledge, promised.

"But how will you explain the dress?"

Helen laughed. "God, you don't think he counts things do you?"

"Of course not," Cassidy said, ashamed by his own vulgarity.

27

Suddenly it was Friday, and they were driving in the Bentley to the river entrance.

The night was as warm as Paris; lighted candles waited on the table; the river bank was hung with white jewels palely mirrored in the stiff black water.

"Look Shamus," Cassidy breathed in his ear. "Remember?"

"Meeow," said Shamus.

Nothing in the fulfilment, it is said, matches the excitement of anticipation; yet as Cassidy took his place on Helen's left, in the most effective position, as it happened, to admire the flowers he had sent her that morning, and the scent he had given her the day before, to study with fraternal reverence the long fall of her white neck and the discreet swell of her white breasts; to admire with but a turn of the head the sudden, handsome profile of his beloved Shamus, he was filled again with that unearthly joy, that elusive ecstasy, short-lived though it would always be, which had become since Haverdown the purpose, and the occasional prize, of all his striving. This is the moment, he thought; now it is all here, under one spell, this is what was missing in Paris.

Sal seemed to have come unwillingly. She kept very close to Hall and trembled while she ate. Her choice was pale green, and a silver ring on her little finger. Addressed by any but Hall she seized the ring and turned it for a charm, but it brought her little luck.

"Come on Sal. Aren't you going to drink to Hall?" Cassidy asked in a jocular voice, coping well with the folk backstairs.

Shrugging, she drank to her man; but did not lift her eyes.

But Hall adored her. He sat beside her with a showman's pride, holding his knife and fork like the handlebars of the training cycle, smiling whenever he looked at her. Th. dinner jacket made no difference to him. Hall was a boxer; he had been a boxer in prison, now he was a boxer in a dinner jacket; only a tiny twinkle in each hooded eye suggested that he was temporarily off duty.

"Doing all right, Hall?"

From one clenched fist, a jointless thumb jerked into the air.

"All right, Lovely," said Hall, and winked.

As to Shamus, the evening had not come a moment too soon. The stresses of tomorrow's departure, of interrupting, if only for a few weeks, his rewrite of the novel, had once more taken a heavy toll of his humour. His manner, though benevolent, was drawn and preoccupied; Hall's release, now it had taken place, was of no further interest to him. Catching Cassidy's eye, he stared at him blankly before lifting his glass.

"Great party, lover," he murmured, with a sudden, loving smile. "Kiss kiss. Bless you lover."

"Bless you," said Cassidy.

He could not help wishing all the same that Shamus had worn a dinner jacket. He had even taken him aside the previous day and offered to buy him one, but Shamus had declined.

"Got to wear the uniform lover," he insisted. "Can't let down the regiment."

Uniform was the deathcoat and a lavishly confected bow tie of found material, a belt, perhaps, from an old black dress of Helen's. He wore it in silence, musket reversed.

To Helen and Cassidy, therefore, fell the burden of conversation; they assumed it nobly. Helen, passing olives and smiling at the ever-attentive waiters, talked brilliantly about the theatre.

"I mean how can it live? How many people *understand* Pinter; how *many?*"

"I don't," said Cassidy boldly. "I go in, I sit down, I wait for the curtain, and all I'm thinking is: God, am I up to this?"

"If only they could be more *explicit,*" Helen lamented

—all this to bring in Hall and Sal. "I mean *Shakespeare* reached the masses, why can't *they*? And after all, let's face it, all of us belong to the masses when it comes to art. I mean for something to be any good, it *has* to have universality. So why can't they, well, *be* universal?"

"Take *Moon*," said Cassidy. "*Moon* was universal."

Failing by these subtle excursions to bring in either Shamus or their guests of honour, Helen wisely changed the subject.

"Tell us about your *greatest* fight," she said to Hall, over the smoked salmon. "The one you would like most to be remembered by."

"Well," said Hall, "I don't know."

"Getting Sal's knickers off," Shamus suggested. And to the wine waiter, whose attentions for some time had been annoying him, "Just bring us a bottle each and piss off."

"To Hall and Sal," said Helen quickly, lifting her champagne glass.

"To Hall and Sal," they said.

"Shamus, drink to Sal."

Obediently Shamus emptied his glass. The band was playing something fast to warm the evening up.

"Is he all right?" Cassidy asked, out of Hall's hearing.

"Dale rang," said Helen.

"Oh Christ. Not about the rewrite?"

"It's still not vulgar enough."

"I hate that man," said Cassidy. "I really hate him."

"Dear Cassidy. You're so loyal."

"What about *you* for God's sake?"

Shamus and Sal were dancing. Sal danced very upright, the way people dance on ships, away from him, watching the other people as if to copy them. Shamus' ballroom style, by contrast, was essentially his own. Having gained the centre of the floor, he set to work consolidating his position by means of a series of wide, wolf-like gyrations, while Sal waited patiently for his return.

"He's got this territorial thing," Helen explained. "He longs for land. He bought a field once, down in Dorset. We used to go and walk over it when he was feeling bad."

"What happened to it?"

"I don't know." The question seemed to puzzle her, for

she frowned and looked away. "Still there I suppose."
Cassidy waited, knowing there was more. "It had a cottage on it. We were going to convert it. That's all."

"Helen."

"Yes."

"Will you *use* the chalet? Go there, as my guests? Will
you let me do that?"

Her smile was so weary.

"Listen," he continued, "I'll *lend* him the travel money,
he can pay it back from *Codpiece* when he gets his
cheque . . ."

"It's all *owed*," she said. "It's all spent."

"Helen *please*. It would do you so much good. You'll
just *love* the mountains."

The music had stopped but Sal and Shamus were embracing under the spotlight. Sal neither resisted nor cooperated. Shamus was kissing the nape of her neck, a
prolonged, explicit kiss which captured the attention of
the band and reminded Cassidy of the search for Mrs.
Oedipus.

"Sal likes a dance," said Hall as they finally returned.

There was no telling, from Hall's expression, whether he
was pleased or not; his face had been folded that way for
years and prison had not made it more responsive.

"So do I," said Cassidy.

The music started again. At once, Helen led him back
to the dance floor.

"Shouldn't I dance with Sal?" he asked.

"She's Hall's," said Helen, not looking at him; and
Cassidy with a small shiver remembered the American
bosun.

"Shamus seems much chirpier anyway," he said, but
for once Helen did not respond to his optimistic tone.

Dancing with Shamus' wife, he danced much better
than he had danced with Shamus in Paris, and suffered
less criticism. He had held her like this at Haverdown
when she had run to him in the woodsmoke; held him
without music; and he remembered how her breasts had
nestled on his shirt front, and how he had felt the nakedness of her through her housecoat.

"You never *really* told me about Paris, did you?" Helen
said. "Why not?"

"I thought I'd leave that to Shamus."

Helen smiled a little sadly. "I knew you'd say that," she

said. "You've *really* learnt the rules, haven't you Cassidy?"

She drew him closer in a mature, sisterly embrace.

"*Lover,*" she said. "That's what he calls you. Let's ring lover. You're so reliable. Such a rock."

Cautiously he made a turn. Cassidy had never danced so well. He knew himself to be a bad dancer; it had not required the admonitions of the angels of Kensal Rise to tell him so; he knew he was tone-deaf and he knew he was heavy on his feet; secretly he also believed that he suffered from a rare pelvic deformation which rendered even the most elementary steps virtually impossible; yet Helen, to his astonishment, gave him the assurance of an expert. He backed, he advanced, he turned, and she neither winced nor cried out, but followed him with a skilled obedience which left him astonished by his own dexterity.

"How can we ever thank you?" she wondered. "*Dear* Cassidy."

"You're the loveliest person in the room," said Cassidy, having made cursory comparisons.

"You know what I wish?" said Helen. "Guess."

Cassidy tried, but failed.

"That we could make you *really* happy. You're so lonely. We look at you sometimes and . . . we know there are things we can never reach. It's just muscle," she said, touching his cheek. "That's all there is that's holding up this smile. . . . Cassidy?"

"Yes."

"How is it with the bosscow?"

"Grey," Cassidy conceded, in a tone which held back more than he was willing to own to.

"That's the worst," said Helen. "Greyness. That's what Shamus has been fighting all his life."

"You too," Cassidy reminded her.

"Have I?" She smiled as if her own condition were more of a memory than a present fact. "Shamus says you're frightened of her."

"Balls," said Cassidy sharply.

"That's what I told him. Cassidy, did Shamus . . ." They made another turn, this time under Helen's guidance, but she guided so gently so unobtrusively, so unlike Sandra, that Cassidy did not mind a bit. "Did Shamus," she began again, "have a *lot* of girls in Paris?"

"God, *Helen* . . ."

Again she smiled, pleased no doubt to encounter the firm borders of the two men's friendship. "Dear Cassidy," she repeated, holding him far away but keeping her gloved hands on the thickest part of his arms. "You needn't answer. I just hope they made him happy, that's all." She returned to him, laying her cheek against his shirt front. "Isn't Hall super?" she asked, dreamily, and looked past him towards the table.

"Super," Cassidy agreed.

But Hall was nowhere to be seen. Shamus was sitting alone among the bottles. He was leaning right back in Cassidy's chair, smoking a cigar, and the black beret was pulled down over his eyes, embracing his ears and nose, so that he must have been in total darkness. His feet were on the table and the cigar smoke poured out of him as if he were on fire.

"I think we'd better go back," said Cassidy.

"Hi," said Cassidy.

"Who is it?" said Shamus.

"It's your lover," said Helen, coaxingly.

"Come in," said Shamus, lifting the beret. "Nice dance?"

"Great. Where have they gone?"

"Pee-break," said Shamus vaguely.

"*You* dance with her," said Cassidy.

"Thanks," said Shamus. "Thanks very much." And lowered the beret again.

They waited for some time to see whether he would come out, but he didn't, so they danced again just to be convivial.

"It's a very long pee," said Cassidy doubtfully, wondering whether he ought to go and look for them. "You don't think they've . . ."

"They've what?"

"Well it is a *bit* of a strain for them. . . ."

"Nonsense," said Helen, "they're adoring every moment," and squeezed his hand. "And even if they aren't . . ."

Something quite hard had entered her face. In Sandra it would have been anger, but Helen was above anger. In

Sandra it would have been determination, a sudden wish to assert herself against an oppressive, though apathetic, world; but Helen, he knew, was at peace with the world.

He was about to investigate this unexpected change of mood—an outburst, almost, in relation to the bright contentment which had preceded it—when the music stopped in the middle of the tune and they heard Shamus screaming.

Looking round for him, Cassidy found himself standing beside the Niesthals. The old lady was hung in black, a mantilla perhaps. She held her husband's arm and they both craned their heads to see where the noise came from; and they wore, both of them, the sad, expert expression of people who had heard a lot of screaming in their time.

"Look," said Mrs. Niesthal, noticing Cassidy. "It is Aldo who has the musical wife."

"Hullo," said Cassidy.

"My God that poor fellow," said the old man, meaning Shamus.

He was standing on a table at the far end of the room, not their own table but someone else's; his jacket was flung aside. He was wearing a piece of red cloth over his short-sleeved tennis shirt, a cummerbund slung shoulder to waist like a military bandolier, and he was doing a sword dance among the knives and forks, not missing them.

"Oh Jesus," said Helen, frightened.

The tablecloth was screwed round one foot and he looked as though he would fall any minute. His face was scarlet and he was clapping his hands over his head. By the time Cassidy reached him, several waiters were converging and neither Hall nor Sal had reappeared.

"Shamus!" Cassidy called, upwards from the table's edge. "Hey, lover!"

Shamus stopped dancing. His eyes had that hopeless wildness that Cassidy remembered from Lipp's.

"Let *me* have a go," Cassidy said.

"What's that?" said Shamus.

Now everyone was watching Cassidy, and somehow they knew that Cassidy held the key. Even the waiters were looking at him with respect.

"I want to do a sword dance," Cassidy said.

"You can't do a fucking sword dance," Shamus replied, shaking his head. "You'll fall off the fucking table."

"I want to try."

With a sudden lovely smile, Shamus leaned forward and flung his arms round Cassidy's neck.

"Then try. Oh Jesus, try. Beg you, lover, beg you."

"You don't have to beg," said Cassidy, heaving him gently off the table. Someone came forward, old Niesthal, familiar with catastrophe; someone else was passing the deathcoat to Helen.

"Get your things together," Cassidy whispered to Helen. "We'll meet you at the door."

Once again, he was aware of Shamus' great physical strength. Half carrying him, half embracing, he led him to the lobby.

"I want a whore," said Shamus.

"Good idea," said Cassidy. And to Helen, "Take his head."

The pale assistant manager helped them to the lift. The fourteenth floor, he said; a chance vacancy. Cassidy knew him well and had once offered him the chalet. He was a tender, patient man who had learnt that certain of the rich are very humble in their needs.

"Would you like a doctor?" he asked, unlocking a door.

"He doesn't believe in them," Helen whispered, reminding him.

"No thank you," Cassidy replied. "I don't either," he added, thinking of John Elderman and not knowing why.

"You lying bugger," Shamus whispered. "You never will do that dance."

The suite was on the river side; the bowl of fruit included peaches and black grapes, but there was no card for *Monsieur et Madame;* there were telephones in the bathroom. He would not be put to bed so they laid him on the sofa, undressing him together, Shamus their common child. In the bedroom, Cassidy found an eiderdown and put it over the shaking body. Emptying out the fruit, he set the bowl on the floor in case Shamus wanted to be sick. Helen crouched in a chair watching him.

"I'm cold," she said.

So he found a blanket for her as well and put it over her shoulders. She had hunched herself together as if she had a stomach pain. From the bathroom he fetched a damp towel and wiped down Shamus' face, then held his hand.

"Where's Helen?"

"Here."

"Christ," he whispered. "Oh Christ."

The telephone rang; it was Niesthal. He had found a doctor, a damn good friend, an old fellow no longer in practice, completely discreet, look here, should they come up?

"It's very kind," said Cassidy. "But he's all right now." *I'm in Bristol,* he thought of saying, but he hadn't the nerve. Ring him in the morning, give him lunch perhaps.

"Can you get me a drink?" said Helen, still not moving.

Cassidy ordered two Scotches, yes, large ones thank you. For some reason he thought it prudent to include Shamus and rang back. Make it three.

"Have you got five shillings?" he asked Helen.

"No."

He gave the waiter a pound and saw him out.

"Water?"

"No."

"Ice?"

"No."

They sipped the whisky watching Shamus. He lay just as they had put him, one bare arm across the saffron coverlet, head turned out to them, eyes closed.

"He's asleep," said Cassidy.

Helen said nothing, just drank her whisky in small sips, nodding into the glass like a bird. She was very groomed still; more ready to go out, one would have thought, than to come home.

Cassidy switched off the overhead light. With the darkness came silence. Shamus lay so still, so young to die; only his chest moved, keeping pace with his short, fast breathing.

"He was like this in Paris, wasn't he?" said Helen.

"Sometimes."

"No wonder he loves you," she observed dully. "It used to be fun. Making hell, he called it. Not raising it, *making* it. You *make* heaven. You make hell. Make them in the same place sometimes. At the same time. As long as you make *something*. Just for a moment I wished he'd not make anything for a while. I must be getting middle-aged."

"If he didn't make hell he wouldn't make books," said Cassidy loyally.

"Other people manage," said Helen.

"Yes but look at what they write."

"You don't *know* what they write, Cassidy. You don't read, nor do I. For all you and I know there are *hundreds* of writers all with wives and two veg, churning out super books on lemon juice. For all *we* know."

"Come on," said Cassidy gently. "You don't think that really."

From the river a solitary barge sounded its horn.

"Well," said Helen, "he's got his blasted water again," and they both laughed in relief.

"Why?" she said suddenly.

"Why what?"

"Why did it hoot? It's not foggy. Why does one barge hoot at half past eleven on a fine summer night?"

"I don't know," said Cassidy.

Taking her drink with her she walked to the window and gazed out, her naked shoulders sheer and black against the London night.

"Can't even see it. Christ." She continued gazing. "Air's no good. Air's too soft for him, you know that don't you? Not enough impact."

"Like the New Testament," said Cassidy.

"Exactly like the New Testament. Masochistic, guilt-ridden, and . . ."

"And ghostwritten," said Cassidy, completing Shamus' dictum for her.

"There's a hero of his who went round bathing in fountains. Has he told you about him?"

"Can't remember," said Cassidy.

"A German poet. Spink or Krump or somebody. *The impact confirms the shape*, that's what he said, or Shamus did, I don't know who. Do you think he makes those people up?"

"It doesn't really matter, does it. He told me once he made *me* up."

"It hooted again," said Helen accusingly.

"Perhaps it was an owl," Cassidy suggested.

"Or a nightingale," said Helen, ready as ever with an erudite reference.

"Krump," said Cassidy, calling her back from reverie. "You were talking about Krump."

"*The impact confirms the shape.* That's why we have to collide all the time. To confirm our shape. To *feel* our outer edges." She drank. "Trouble with *that* is, if you have too much impact, you lose your shape altogether. Bash it to bits. Till there's nothing left to confirm."

"That won't happen to him," said Cassidy sternly. "Not while we're around."

"No," Helen agreed, after long reflection. "No. It mustn't must it? I wish you could sing. I'd like to do that with you. Sing with lover."

"Well I can't," said Cassidy.

Like a swimmer she lifted her arms to shoulder level, first forward, then sideways, then raised herself on her toes, as if preparing to dive out of the window.

"Funny to think of them dancing down there," she said. "To sleep while other people dance. That's not the way we used to be, me and Shamus."

Without warning, her voice changed. "Cassidy, why am I miserable?"

"Reaction," Cassidy suggested. "Shock."

"Because I'm *bloody* miserable. I'm a miserable, maudlin, middle-aged cow."

She puffed, then sniffed her breath, testing it for alcohol.

"Miserable, maudlin, middle-aged, and pissed," she confirmed. "*God* what a fool!"

"Helen—"

She was speaking too loud, loud enough to wake him in fact.

"Here I am sitting in the peachy Savoy Hotel in a peachy white dress and what am I doing?"

"Helen," Cassidy admonished, but too late; she was already taking off her shoes.

"All because my *bloody* husband blows a gasket. Dance with me."

"Helen please, we'll wake him up—"

Her arms were already round him, seeking his hand, guiding his shoulder. Lightly, tentatively, their eyes still on the prone figure of their sleeping prophet, the two disciples followed the far drumbeat of the band. The carpet was very deep and made no sound.

"Oh Cassidy," she murmured, "what a *fool* I nearly was."

Her cheek was against his, her hair was in his eyes, and all down the length of him her body swayed and trembled like his own.

"After all," she remarked, "it's what *he* would want if he was awake."

Somehow, it was not at all clear how—a common will conveyed them, neither lover steered—somehow they were in the bedroom. The connecting door was probably open: Cassidy had his eyes closed, he could not tell; and waking, as it were, and finding the angel Helen in his arms and the ominously large bed behind her (robbed of its saffron eiderdown) he saw that her eyes also were closed. Fate, therefore, must be held responsible: there was no human author.

"Wafted," Helen announced. "Is that you Cassidy?" And to confirm the identification, held her hand over his face like a muzzle.

"Bark," she said.

"I can't," said Cassidy.

Settling more comfortably into his arms, she affectionately possessed herself of his ears and fondled them between her forefinger and thumb.

"*Dear* Cassidy. How soft your fur is. Kiss me."

"No," said Cassidy.

"Seduce me."

"No," said Cassidy. "Absolutely not," and closed his eyes again.

The kiss seemed to approach from a long way off. It began far up river among the black steel forests of East India Dock, tipped the taut spanned bridges of the Embankment, skimmed the tide's smooth surface as it glowed ever larger, brighter, and more bold; until, part heat, part liquid, part light, it scaled the fourteen rigid storeys of the Savoy and found its final resting place in the inflamed interiors of Aldo Cassidy and his best friend's wife.

"Cassidy," Helen said severely, "unhand me," and putting him aside, addressed herself to the domestic task of making the bed respectable while Cassidy went to the bathroom in case he had caught her lipstick.

"I do wish I was a whore," she remarked, slapping the pillows into shape. "I'd be a damn sight better at it than Sal, I'll bet. Why *can't* I be a whore? I *like* this hotel, Cassidy. I like the food, I like the drink, and I like the people. *Very* much. I've got a *super* body too. Sturdy, workman-like, resilient. So why can't I?"

"Because you love him," said Cassidy.

"Doesn't stop *him*, does it? He fucks around. *He* seduces people, *he* goes screwing all over Europe. So why can't I?"

"I'll go and see how he is," said Cassidy. "Then perhaps we can go home."

He was in the bedroom again, but strictly in transit, making for the drawing room and safety, when Helen to his alarm suddenly sprang into the air and landed on all fours on the bed.

"Fuck him," she declared in exasperation, pulling her hair down over her eyes. "I Helen *fuck* myself of Shamus. Fuck, fuck, *fuck*. He's a reactionary, don't you realise? A drooling old Victorian fuddy-duddy. One law for him, another for us. Hogswallop. Shamus has *conned* us, Cassidy. Shamus has pulled off the biggest bloody load of hokum since . . . whoever pulled off the last load of hokum. Shamus *hates* convention. That's the message. But we mustn't. Oh no. *We've* got to love it. I'm hungry," she added, straightening her hair. "He ruined our dinner too. *Our* dinner, Cassidy, and he just stepped on it."

"Shamus," Cassidy breathed urgently, on his knees before the body. "Wake up. Please wake up." And shook him, out of her hearing, quite hard.

"The scales," Helen announced from the bedroom, "have fallen from my eyes. A revolution of one, that's me. His freedom for my freedom and fuck the consequences."

"*Shamus,*" Cassidy insisted. "For Christ's sake. We need you."

But Shamus refused to wake. He was lying on his stomach, dead to the world. The coverlet had fallen to the floor and his naked back was slippery with sweat.

"Cassidy," Helen called. "Is it true? Do wicked ladies *really* have it off with waiters in hotels? Just lie prone when their Horlicks arrives, exposing their irresistible charms through diaphanous nightshirts?"

"Give me a towel," said Cassidy. "And shut up. *Lover, listen, we've got to go.*"

A damp towel flopped at his feet.

"Listen, I did things for you . . . all sorts of things. I dragged you out of the gutter didn't I? Stripped you, bought you suits, fed you, cleared up your sick . . . I believe in you. I really do. More than anyone in the world. Well, I try, anyway. Shamus, you *owe* me . . . wake up!"

"Bold," said Helen, still in the bedroom. "That's what you were tonight. Bold, bloody, and resolute. *Doughty* Cassidy. You had *grip*. I admire grip in a man. *Good* evening," she continued into the telephone. "This is suite fourteen thirty-eight. Is there *any* chance of getting a little something to eat, a snack of some sort? Two fillet steaks, a bottle of . . ." It ran on, enough to hold out for a week.

"Don't order for me," Cassidy called. "I don't want anything. *Shamus.*" Turning him over, he laid the cold towel over his face, pressing it quite roughly against his brow, his cheeks.

"You haven't any *crackers,* have you?" Helen was enquiring. "Not to eat, to pull . . ."

He heard the shuffle of her dress as she settled more comfortably on the bed.

"Are you brown, Cassidy? I always think of you as golden. Just a neat white bottom and the rest all gold." More rustles from the bed. "I'm in a sledge," she explained. "Wrapped in bearskins. *Swish, swish.* With Siberian wolves all round." A wolf howl: "Ow-oo-oo. That's a good life out there, Cassidy."

"Yes," said Cassidy, who treasured a similar fantasy.

"*You'd* protect me, wouldn't you, Cassidy? One look at you and a wolf would . . ." She lost the thread. "*Wolf-*

wood," she repeated. "Sounds like a railway station. Cassidy, which would you rather be: raped by Cossacks or torn to pieces by wolves?"

"Neither," said Cassidy.

"Me too," Helen agreed amiably. "You know gorillas rape. I wouldn't like that. Cassidy."

"Yes."

"Have you got a hairy chest? Hair's virile isn't it?"

"Supposed to be."

"You know quite little boys get erections. Even babies, it's amazing. Cassidy."

"Yes."

"I feel very *naive*. Do you?" Silence. "Or just sentimental?"

"Hullo lover," said Shamus, opening his eyes.

Seizing him by the shoulders, Cassidy set to work, patting his cheeks, sitting him upright, trying to remember what boxers' seconds did to get their champions back into the ring.

"Shamus listen, listen to me. Shamus, she's planning murder, take her away, you've *got* to . . ."

"Where's Hall?" said Shamus.

"He disappeared. Hey, let's go and find him, how about that? Go down to Cable Street, how about that? Get pissed, have a fight or two, really hit the moon for once, why not? Cable Street! That's a real place down there, not like this, all hygienic and clean—"

"Why didn't he hit me?"

"Why should he? He loves you. He's your friend, like me. You don't hit friends, you hit enemies."

"She told him," Shamus related, with sudden clarity of recall. "Sat there and told him straight out. 'Hall, Shamus has offered me five quid to have it off with him and I want to go home.' He just looked at me. Why did he do that, lover? Christ he could have killed me with one hand. Look what he did to that bosun, that fellow was maimed for life. What's wrong with me? I mean a *boxer!* If a boxer won't hit me, who the fuck will?"

Receiving no answer, but seeing perhaps Cassidy's face, fresh and nicely polished by the soap, he swung his fist at it and missed.

"Jesus!" he shouted. "Won't *anybody* hit me?" And fell back, square on to the pillow, where he closed his eyes in pain.

"Cassidy," Helen called.

"Yes."

"Didn't you hear me?"

"I don't know. No."

"I've stopped being a whore now."

"Good."

Shamus frowned. "That sounded like Helen," he said.

"It was. She's having a bath."

Listening, Cassidy heard the rustle of clear water running on the moon and casual dance music issuing from a space-born radio, school of Frank Sinatra.

"Well what the fuck is Helen doing in Paristown?" Shamus demanded testily.

"It's not Paris. It's London."

Which is the trouble really, Cassidy reflected. In Paris it would all have been tolerable, somehow. In London, I'm afraid it's not; not really.

The sound of water stopped.

"Cassidy," Helen called again.

"Yes."

"Just Cassidy," she said, with the deep content of someone lying naked in a warm bath. "It's just a pretty name, that's all. Cassidy. I like saying it, you see. Because it's a pretty name."

"Fine," said Cassidy.

"Lot of woman there, boy," said Shamus, and rolling over, fell asleep.

"Cassidy," Helen was saying. "Cassidy. Cassidy. Cassidy?"

At Sherborne, Shamus, we called it bullying.

We may not have had a very high opinion of *ourselves*—that would have been hubris and not at all to be encouraged—but we did, I think, respect one another. The nicer of us did anyway. That, it seems to me, Shamus, is the definition of a reasonable man. He doesn't mind what you do to him, but he minds what you do to other people. Sorry I'm not being clearer, but I'll get there slowly, I'm a bit of a plodder in some ways; not a flyer like you, I'm afraid, Shamus.

Sit down, will you?

There are a few things I have to explain to you, seeing you are new here and not quite our class. A *bully* is someone who picks on those who are weaker than himself. Not physically weaker necessarily; spiritually too. Emotionally also, perhaps. A *bully* performs acts of brutality against those who cannot retaliate. Our code does not like bullies. The regimental flags in the Abbey, for instance, were not scarred by unfair battles, our forebears did not march on undefended cities for their conquests. Well they may have done, but not often. Well, they wouldn't *now*.

So I'm afraid, Shamus, we do not approve. Sal may be a slut. Conceded. But Hall was your friend. He loved you and he loved Sal, and that's why he didn't hit you.

Perhaps he even loved Helen too, in a pure way.

"Cassidy," said Helen. She was trying different pronunciations. *"Cassidee,"* she said, in unconscious imitation of Elise. "Cassidy," she growled in a deep, Sinatra drawl. *"You are a* MOLE, *you live in a* HOLE. How's the patient?"

"Bearing up," said Cassidy.

"Will he live?"

"Maybe."

Hall you see, Shamus, was here in double trust. You've read *Macbeth,* haven't you. A prescribed work for O-Level English? Hall was your kinsman and your subject, or whatever it says. You appointed him to the Few, even if he wasn't really a playing member; even if the Few are by nature self-appointed. You gave him his wings and then you shot him down. Which makes you rather low and small, don't you think?

That is why you deserve to be beaten, I'm afraid; that is why, in a minute, you will be asked to lower your handsome black head into the third washbasin from the left, hold the taps firmly, and offer a passive target to myself and my under-prefects. Do you understand? Is there anything you would like to say in mitigation?

Because actually, at this precise moment in time I am very anxious to hate you.

Yes lover, said Shamus, but not aloud. Of course I've got something to say. Bags in fact. Ready? Pen poised?

Shamus, the great guru, speaks:

Never regret, never apologise. That's the upper classes.

Let's be Old Testament, lover; Old Testament's for the upper classes, New Testament's for compromisers.

To live without heed to the consequences; to give everything for today and not a damn for tomorrow: that's the upper classes.

One day as a lion is worth a lifetime as a mouse: that's the upper classes.

Never regret, never apologise.

Got to find a new innocence, lover, old one's worn out.

Those who love the world take it; those who are afraid make rules.

All relationships have to be pursued to their end. That's where the Blue Flower grows.

Immoralism, lover, is a necessary precondition for the creation of new values. . . . When I fucks, I revolts. . . . When I sleeps, I acquiesces.

Don't hold with motives, lover, never did. Act first, find the reason afterwards, that's my advice.

Acts are truth, lover. Garbage, the rest is. Horseshit.

And finally, lover, you're the biggest fucking liar in the business, you treat your wife with pig-like indifference, and you're in no position to beat anybody, see my portrait of you after Haverdown. Good morning.

"I'm not *brown*," said Helen from the bathroom. "I'm *white*."

"I know," said Cassidy, still at Shamus' side. "I saw you at Haverdown. I always wondered how you heated the water."

"Kettles," Helen explained. "We got the bath ready, but by the time we'd made love it was cold again. So we had to heat it up. That's why the fire was still going when you arrived."

"I see."

"There's an explanation for everything if you look for it."

Seizing his hand, Cassidy put his lips close to Shamus' ear.

"*Shamus.* Lover, wake up!"

Shamus you are a terrible shit but you are our priest and if you're not careful you'll marry us.

Shamus, I love you and you love me, I can see it in you even when you're hating me, you long for me. Alive or dead, Shamus, naked or in your deathcoat, screwing in the green brothel or carrying candles in the Sacré Coeur, you are our genius, our father, our creator. Therefore, if you love me, wake up and release me from this improbable situation.

"Shamus. Wake up!"

I am not like you, Shamus, I am not emotional, I am not drastic. I am an hotelier's son. I'm not anything more than that. I am rational and I like things as they are as long as they favour my situation. I'm a lover not of people but of compromise and orthodoxy. You might very well call me the archetypal victim of Fly. I'm a Jaguar driver, a Gerrard's Crosser, a doctor, and quite frequently a bishop in drag. I hold very much with the past, and if I knew where I came from I would return there like a shot. Also, you are right, I am a mother-fucker.

Now Shamus, having proved all that to me, proved it quite conclusively, will you kindly wake up and get me out of this!

"Cassidy? *Ici parle* Helen. *Bonjour.*"

"*Bonjour,*" said Cassidy politely.

He shouldn't have poured water over me at Lipp's.

He shouldn't have hit me at football.

He shouldn't have propositioned Sal just because he needed a collision.

"Forgive lover. Forgive. Please forgive."

Without opening his eyes, Shamus drew Cassidy's hand into the bed and held it against his hot cheek.

"There's nothing to forgive," Cassidy whispered. "It's fine. Listen, how about some more formaldehyde?"

Rising, he was about to switch on the overhead light when Shamus spoke again, in quite a strong voice.

"Lots, lover. Lots to forgive."

"What, then?"

"Lent the Bentley to Hall. He was pissed, you see. Anyway, couldn't have him going home in a cab, could I? Got to travel in style. Not angry, lover?"

"Why should I be?"

"Not hit me?"

"Go to sleep," said Cassidy.

"Je m'appelle Hélène," Helen announced still from the bathroom. She had recently started French lessons at an academy in Chester Street.

"Hélène est mon nom. Hurrah *pour Hélène. Hélène est beau. Belle.* Fuck. Beau-belles, bow-bells, bow-bells, bow-bells!"

He sat in the dark. He had put out the lamp by the sofa so that the only light came from the bedroom and, indirectly, through the open bathroom door.

"Cassidy, I know you're listening."

Lucky I bought the place then, really. Now that I've got to live in it. The basic essentials of life, Old Hugo said. Food drink and now this. Lucky the market was looking the other way.

"Did you have lots of girls in Paris?" Helen asked, over the gentle splashing of water.

"No."

"Not even one or two?"

"No."

"Why not?"

"I don't know."

"I would if I were a man. I'd have all of us, bang bang bang. We're so *beautiful.* I wouldn't ask, I wouldn't apologise, I wouldn't care. To the victor the spoils. Fuck!" —she must have banged against something. "Why do they put the door handle on the door?"

"Carelessness," said Cassidy.

"I mean take Sal. Moronic. Totally. So why *not* be a whore? It's fun, it's profitable. I mean it's nice to do *one* thing well, don't you think? Cassidy."

She was getting out, one leg, two legs; he could hear the rubbing of the towel.

"Yes."

"What do you want most in the world?" she asked.

You maybe, thought Cassidy; maybe not.

"You," he said.

There was a knock at the door. The floor waiter wheeled in the trolley. A middle-aged man of great courtesy.

"In here, sir?" he asked, ignoring the figure on the sofa. "Or next door?"

"In here, if you would."

He set it parallel to Shamus, a hospital trolley waiting for the surgeon. Signing the bill Cassidy gave him a five-pound note.

"That's all right. That covers everything else we may need. For tips I mean."

The waiter seemed unhappy.

"I have *got* change, sir."

"All right, well give me three pounds." Transaction. "They still dancing down there?"

"Oh yes, sir."

"What time do you get off?"

"Seven o'clock, sir. I'm the night waiter, sir."

"Tough on your wife then," said Cassidy.

"She gets used to it, sir."

"Any kids?"

"One daughter, sir."

"What's she doing?"

"She's up at Oxford."

"That's fine. That's great. I was there myself. Which College?"

"At Somerville, sir. She's reading zoology."

For a moment Cassidy was on the brink of asking him to stay; to sit down with him at a long ritual dinner, to share the wine with him and eat the steak, and gossip with him about their different families and the intricacies of the hotel trade. He wanted to tell him about Hugo's leg and Mark's music, and hear his views on cantilevered extensions. He wanted to ask him about *Old* Hugo and Blue; whether he'd heard rumours, was Old Hugo still a name?

"Shall I draw the cork, sir? Or will you be doing it yourself?"

"You haven't got a toothbrush, have you, Cassidy?" Helen

called from the bathroom. "You'd think they'd provide them, wouldn't you, for people like us?"

"Just leave the corkscrew here," said Cassidy, and once more opened the door for him.

"The head porter will have a toothbrush, sir; I can send you one up if you wish."

"It's all right," said Cassidy. "Don't bother."

World population's going up seventy million lover. Lot of people to tip, lover; lot of people to tip.

"Is yours tough?" asked Helen.

"No it's fine. How's yours?"

"Fine."

They sat on opposite sides of the bed, eating steak, Helen in a bath towel and Cassidy in his dinner jacket. The towel was very long, pale green, with a rich woolly nap. She had combed out her hair. It lay in smooth auburn tresses down her bare white back. She looked very childish without her make-up; her skin had that luminous innocence which in certain women comes with the experience of recent nakedness. She smelt of soap, a nutty masculine soap, the kind that Sandra liked to put in his Christmas stocking; and she sat just as she had sat at Haverdown, on the Chesterfield in the morning twilight.

"By *want*," she said, "do you mean *love?*"

"I don't know," said Cassidy. "It was your question, not mine."

"What are the *symptoms?*" Helen pursued, being helpful. "Apart from lust which, while we know it's lovely, doesn't really last the whole drink through, does it?"

Cassidy poured more wine.

"Is that claret?" she asked. "Or Burgundy?"

"Burgundy. You can tell by the shape. Square shoulders are claret, rounded are Burgundy. You're all I want. You're witty and beautiful and understanding . . . and you like men best."

"You mean we have that in common?" Helen enquired.

He wished very much that he had Shamus there to say it all again. Helen is our virtue; that part he remembered, that part he believed: Helen will go where her heart is, she knows no other truth. Helen is our territory; Helen is . . . Also there was a formula. Shamus had drawn it for him on the wallpaper, at a drinking in Pimlico the same night he told him about the Steppenwolf, who from the spaces of his wolfish solitude loved the security of the little bourgeois life. The formula had a fraction; why could he not remember it, Aldo Cassidy the inventor of gadgets, fastenings, and couplings? *Cassidy divided by Shamus equals Helen*. Or was it the other way round? *Helen over Cassidy equals Shamus*. Try again. *Cassidy over Helen . . .*

Somewhere in Shamus' law of human dynamics, his love for her was inevitable. But where?

"Cassidy, you still love Shamus too, don't you? I'm only trying to *diagnose* you see. Not prescribe."

"Yes. I love him, too."

"You haven't ratted?"

"No."

"Which means," she remarked contentedly, "we *both* love him. That's *excellent*. We *must* get marks for that. You see, Cassidy, I've never had a lover apart from Shamus. Nor have you, have you?"

"No."

"So I think a certain *amount* of forethought is advisable. Is that coffee?"

He poured it for her, adding cream but no sugar. He poured the cream Sandra's way, spoon upside down over the surface to prevent it from penetrating too far.

"Do you think a fair test would be: what we would give up?" Helen suggested. "Would I give up Shamus, for instance? Would you give up the bosscow and the two veg? You see, Cassidy, we are talking about ruin as well as love."

Cassidy was suddenly, if cautiously, conscious of a deep protective urge. A child might as well have talked about the world economy just then, as Helen about ruin; for she imposed a peace on him that was like a rest of arms after a long war. He perceived in her a potential honesty of companionship which till now, in all his isolated wandering, in all his attempts to live for himself, had seemed impossible. The laughter he had shared with Shamus was not gone; but in Helen he could possess it, trust it, rid it of its violence. She was smiling at him, and he knew he was smiling in return. Looking at her he knew also that it was the past that was a ruin, not the future: and he saw the empty autumn cities, the tarred warehouses, the bare road before the hood of his car, and he knew them only as the places where he had searched in vain for Helen.

"I love you," said Cassidy.

"Excellent," said Helen briskly. "I feel exactly the same."

The trolley squeaked as she pushed it. Fastening the towel more securely round her, she guided the tricky wheels skillfully through the open doorway to the drawing room.

Sitting alone on the bed, waiting for her return, Cassidy was victim to many conflicting moods. Mainly, however, they ran in the direction of terror.

First, Old Hugo addressed his Divine Employer.

Good morning Lord, he said cheerfully from the pine pulpit somewhere in England, his enormous hands folded in athletic piety. *How are you? This is Hugo Cassidy and his flock reporting from the Zion Tabernacle of East Grinstead, Sussex, offering up the prayers of our hearts this lovely Friday midnight. Look down in your goodness on young Aldo here will You, Lord? He is very much confused between sin and virtue just at the moment. My view, for what it is worth, Lord, is that he has put his hand into a snake's nest, but only* Thou, *oh Lord, in Thy wisdom can give a final ruling on this one; and so be it.*

There was still time. If he played his cards right, stalled a little, pleaded a small illness perhaps, such as a headache or a gastric disorder, he might very well get out of this yet. Some tricky talk perhaps to begin with—well he was good at that—some friendly kissing and making up and then get dressed, shake hands, and laugh about it later as a silly mistake they both nearly made.

Never regret, never explain, never apologise. . . .

Would she return? A sudden hope gave him solace. She's bolted. She looked at him, got the guilts, and decided to run . . .

In a towel?

Logic is my enemy, thought Cassidy; I should never have taken a degree.

He heard the door close softly and the latch slide; he heard her go back to the bathroom and he knew she was hanging up the towel because she was tidy. Suddenly, seized by panic, he imagined the total failure. He saw another Cassidy twisting, humping, recoiling, wrestling with his unrisen manhood; he heard Shamus' laughter ringing through the wall, and Helen's, Sandra's muffled grunt of irritation at his inadequacy.

The big decisions are taken for us; I have no part in this. I swim, I cannot affect the stream.

The bathroom light had gone out; Helen had put out the bathroom light. He saw the pale rectangle die on the wall before him. Economy; Jesus, does she think I pay the electricity here? I didn't really buy the place, you know.

Er, Sandra, Helen, whatever your name is, there's something you ought to know, I'm afraid: I have absolutely no expertise. If you think I can do anything for you that Shamus can't do, well (as Sandra would say) I can't finish the sentence. I don't know how you're made: that's the truth of it; none of you. I have absolutely no picture of how you're made or what gives you satisfaction. May I be absolutely specific here?

She was in bed. Cassidy had not moved, had not looked; he was preparing a speech for the Annual General Meeting:

"Now many of you have come here with the highest expectations. I know that. Many years ago I myself had similar expectations of the same act. There are certain things however that you should know, and to save you unnecessary time and trouble I will be very frank. As a

lover, your Chairman is a *non-starter*. Sorry but there it is.
His sexual encounters with his wife have always been essentially of the formal kind, confined to what is known
within the trade as the English missionary position. Many
of them, so to speak, never got off the drawing board.
Your Chairman is aware that there is a distance to descend
and a point at which to enter. And also, that any attempt
above or below that point gives rise to discomfort and
criticism. Practice has done nothing to enrich his knowledge; indeed you should know that after fifteen years of
sporadic congress your Chairman can still cause Mrs. Cassidy quite unreasonable pain by entering a wrong channel,
so that she has been known, not infrequently, to cry out in
indignation, rearrange herself with unfriendly care; and
thereafter to make no sound, but to accept your Chairman's gaucherie as the lot of every woman married into
the trade."

Break. The intimate tone.

"Now I am perfectly conscious of these deficiencies. In
my time I have read books, studied photographs, doodled
on telephone pads, attended, during national service, army
lectures; I have even, in rare moments of mutual frankness with Mrs. Cassidy, delved surreptitiously with my
fingers among the perplexing folds. Yet the terrain per-
sistently eludes me. In my imagination, it has the whorls
and curlicues of a fingerprint: no two examples, the brochure reads, are ever wholly identical. I am perfectly
conscious, here, of a cross fire of psychological interpreta-
tions—Dr. John Elderman, our medical consultant, will
happily give you a handbook on the subject—and I have
fought hard *over the years,* together with your other Directors, for a clearer orientation. In vain. Now you may
very well feel that a *younger* man, less—I believe the
fashionable word is inhibited is it not, Mr. Meale?—less
inhibited might serve you better. If so, well, let me assure
you that you will have the *fullest* and the most *whole-
hearted* co-operation of the entire Board, and no bad
feelings shall be allowed to interfere with a *healthy,* a
satisfactory . . ."

Still standing before an attentive if absent audience—a
rug's width, in fact, from the edge of the double bed—he
felt her gaze on him, and heard the silence of her contemplation.

"You're not very good at it, are you, Cassidy?" said Helen quietly.

"No."

"Well we're just going to have to put a lot of work in, aren't we?"

"Yes, I suppose we are."

"You can't do it in a dinner jacket," she said.

He undressed.

"Now what you do next is: you kiss me."

He kissed her, leaning across her, so that their lips met at a right angle.

"I'm afraid you'll have to get nearer," she said. And as if it were an inspiration: "Hey, how about getting into bed with me?"

He got into the bed.

"It's called foreplay," she explained. "Then there's consummation—" rather in the tone with which she had ordered dinner "—and then there's afterglow."

Swedish.

Just a Swedish episode. She probably doesn't even realise she's naked, a lot of people don't make anything of nudity at all these days, hardly know whether they're dressed or not. That was one of the things he liked about the films at the Cinephone, actually; you could look at them in their *wild state*. Might drop in there tomorrow, actually; see what they had running. Actually.

Tentatively, still listening for sounds from next door, he made the first reconnaissance. Her skin, he noticed, had a curiously flaccid texture, a cloying liquidity to the touch which he suddenly found unappealing. Her breasts particularly, which in repose largely assumed the requisite shape—and clothed were most distinguished—yielded too easily to his hand, betraying the hard bone underneath. Also, she was too white, with a whiteness that was not luminous so much as vegetable, moreover a vegetable grown underground, and entirely contrary to his appetites. Momentarily revolted by a body so shadowless and obscenely, whitely naked, he moved away from her and busied himself with the bedside light while he tried to think of something to say.

"You're not putting it *out*, are you?" Helen asked

crisply in the same tone which had earlier reminded him of Sandra.

"Of course not."

It's her purity, he told himself; this is what you feel when you sleep with a total woman.

"You're *thinking* aren't you?" Helen said sympathetically.

"Yes."

"What about?"

"Love, life . . . *us*, I suppose," Cassidy replied cautiously and lowered his head on to the pillow with a half-concealed sigh. "Shamus," he added, in a despairing appeal to her conscience.

"Would you feel better if you hated him?" she asked.

"Well it would be more Old Testament, wouldn't it?"

"That's what *he* thinks. What do you think?"

"Well . . . no."

"You haven't got the *guilts* have you, Cassidy? Because he's your lover and my husband?"

Cassidy might not understand everything, but he did know that between Shamus and Helen moral scruple was not a plea which would be accepted in evidence.

"Of course not."

"Then what is it? Touch me."

"I did."

"Touch me again."

"I am touching you."

"Only my hand."

"I love you, Helen," Cassidy said, allowing his tone to give the impression that this was only one side of an inward argument.

"But you don't want me," Helen suggested. "You've changed your mind. I must say you've picked a bloody good time."

Cassidy smiled. "God if only you knew," he said, with a poor shot at world-weariness.

"Is it *really* so difficult to take?" Helen asked. "After all the lessons we've had?"

Receiving no answer, she evidently decided to renounce the initiative and they lay in silence again for quite a long time, while Cassidy took advice from those closest to him.

"Dad."

"Yes, Hug?"

"You know, *Dad*."

"What do I know, Hug?"

"I like this lady."

"Good."

"She's not as nice as Heather, though, is she?"

"It's just that you know Heather better. And Heather knows us better too."

"Heather's not so *pushy*. Dad."

"Yes Hug."

"I like Angie better too. *Dad*."

"Yes Hug."

"Has Angie Mawdray seen your pennier?"

"Certainly not. Why on *earth* should she have seen it?"

"Mummy has."

"Mummy's different."

"Has Snaps?"

"No."

"Mummy's *lovely*," said Hugo. "Goodnight."

"Goodnight Hug."

"A lot of people do it," said Sandra, standing at the door in the darkness and sighing to wake him up. "And it's *perfectly* natural. Just because you don't enjoy it, it doesn't mean everyone else doesn't, but still."

"I know."

"Well get on with it."

"It's just that I'm impotent."

"Nonsense, you're lazy and you eat too much. It's all those *ridiculous* Conservative dinners. No wonder you're bloated. Socialists don't *have* dinners. They have tea and sandwiches."

"I think I'm queer too."

"Absolute nonsense. When we were young we did it just as well as other people and we thoroughly enjoyed it. It's just that I'm a bore. Sorry, but there's nothing I can do about *that*."

"Sandra, I love you."

Long silence.

"I love you too," she said. "But still."

Any fool can give, lover. It's what we take from life that matters.

"Shall I go and look at him?" Cassidy suggested.

"To get his blessing?"

"I'm sure he's awake."

"My God," said Helen, sitting bolt upright, her anger thoroughly aroused. "What a disgusting idea. He'd kill you if he found out, don't you realise. He'll be *far* worse than Hall ever was to that poor American."

"Yes, I suppose he would," Cassidy conceded.

"If he knew that you and I were in here, *naked*, *lovers* . . ." Her indignation found no further expression. "Christ!" she ended, and lay back with a thump.

"But we're not lovers, are we?" Cassidy asked cautiously. "Not yet." Meaning: penetration has not been effected, Counsel could still put up a pretty good case; she forced me into it.

"Do you think he cares what we *do?* It's what we *feel* that matters." She turned to him almost desperately. "And we *do* feel, don't we, Cassidy? Don't we? Cassidy, I've gone the bank. What the *hell* are you putting into this?"

"Everything," he said, having briefly passed in review all the things that had made him happy: Hugo, Mark, the Bentley, the Night Animals House, and Sandra in a good temper. "All I ever loved."

And suddenly was kissing her, taking her; was her master, conjured into her and over her; and Helen, his nimble, fluttering dying Helen, a brilliant conjunction of all his dreams. Her touch took nothing; she steered and danced, lay passive, rode above him; but still she only gave, and all the while she seemed to follow him, studying him for yes and no, testing the limits of his permission, creating in him, of her obedience, a growing obligation to love her in return.

"Natural break," she whispered, and lay beside him, her eyes on his.

"Bold lover," said Helen.

"I want to laugh," said Cassidy.

"I'll have to put it to the Board," she whispered, the passion trembling in her smile.

"I love you," said Cassidy.

"Get on with your work," said Helen.

Elise and Mrs. Bluebridge floated hand in hand, intoning sweet phrases from Old Hugo's good book; respectful waiters clapped to him in rhythmic unison; sinners and strivers, toiling up God's hill, turned to watch him with approval. The chorus multiplied. *Oui, Burgess, oui. Ça te fait plaisir? Beaucoup de plaisir, Elise.* In Kensal Rise the green lights switched excitedly while the band played a Sherborne song: *Vivat rex Edwardus Sextus. Vivat!* The girls looked on, no longer dancing, studying respectfully the master's effortless technique. Now mothers with prams appeared among the crowd, waving, thanking, owing him their babies.

"Sandra!" he cried in welcome.

She had brought her meths drinkers: in crocodile, dressed for church, clean-shaven.

"You chaps!" he called to them, arresting the movement, "look here, now, you'd enjoy this; take you out of yourselves!"

"It would teach them a lesson," Sandra agreed and sighed the way she sighed when he put his dirty clothes in the wrong basket.

Grow you little weed, grow.

Oh Christ, I *am* growing. Believe me lover, I have grown, I am growing, you have taught me *anger*, you have *kindled* me, fired me deep down; the fire spreads from the root; a running, faster fire, water won't help now, my lover, I'm up there with the best of you, drenched and still bathing; better than the best of you; cooking in your place, your cave, your oven; wake if you want. For pity's sake, lover, how can you sleep when murder is being done?

She was telling him: "Cassidy, you're the best, oh Christ, oh Cassidy, oh love!"

Lights were breaking in his eyes; at his back, the movement was small and agonised. She was calling to God and to Cassidy, to Shamus and her father. Her legs were laid wide like a Buddha's, she moved in a slow trance, patting him from side to side with her crooked knees. Captain, art thou sleeping there below? I'd like to be with you now, Shamus, actually; she's joined her own dark people, she's out there with the deep feelers. Actually, Shamus, I want you back.

It was achieved. A stretching of the back, two cats upon an ironing board. It was achieved. Hey ho and fuck it: a grateful end to waiting, a settling of chairs and mirrors in the moonlight, a clearing, an evacuation of the spirit as she let him die in her, keeping her body still to drink. He stayed there, being polite, waiting for the passage of years and the boy to climb out of the water. Thinking about the Bentley and had he heard it crash? Thinking about Shamus and was he watching from the door? Thinking about being Christ caught between two thieves; about being a thief and caught between two Christs; about being a child sleeping with his parents, and a parent sleeping with his children; about needing three, and about Angie Mawdray's signs of the zodiac: "Seven and three," she said. "They're the magic numbers." About Biafran children screaming on the piano and the new lifeboat in the almost finished hall, on the right as you go in, on the Sheraton satinwood dee-shaped table with the dropped leaf six hundred guineas. A paper lifeboat, issued by the Association, with a small slit for putting in the pennies; Sandra had discovered a new affection for the drowning.

Why can't we be one person? he wondered. Why do we have to be so many, mixed together in a single womb?

Released from her, performing the thoughtful father's duty of holding her hand because she was crying, Cassidy addressed the Board for the last time during his office as President.

"Consider the arithmetic, gentlemen, of this unusual situation. (Miss Mawdray, a little more coffee for Mr. Meale perhaps, he appears a trifle tired.) You have all read Nietzsche of course; those who have not will no doubt recall the German poet Somebody. Such men, gentlemen, have devised remarkable explanations for our human behaviour. They arrange us like stars in a horoscope. Well look at us. An example may be found in the perfect arrangement of our three parallel bodies. This is how, in our mystical assumption, we shall ultimately find our places in the firmament. In line, with our feet pointing east. Here, no longer in his dinner jacket, lying in his own hotel, is a bourgeois who gave his life in search of a dream. I will call him, tonight, on the customary Michelin rating, a two-star lover; good, but not quite worth a journey. To my left, separated from me by his wife and a mercifully insulated wall, lies an artist broken on the wheel of his genius: a galaxy of a man, but not organised.

"And between us, lover, between us, lies the truth. Naked, and a little exhausted, crying like a child."

Leaving her to sleep, he unlocked the door and crept back into the drawing room. The coverlet had fallen to the floor. He lay even more naked than Helen, even more childish, more young. Were his eyes open or closed? There was not enough light to tell. Bending over him, Cassidy put his ear as close as he dared to the bare chest and heard the restless unequal thumping of his heart.

Lay the blanket over him, but only to the neck. Sit in the chair and stare at him, Jonathan, my friend. Get the towel and wipe him clean.

Who wrote that? My book or his?

Sleep.

Outside the window, one star burned, but neither Elise nor any other fantasy was there to welcome him. From Kensal Rise to Abalone Crescent, from South Audley Street to the river where it passes Pimlico, there was no one who was not thinking of the dawn.

Dear Cassidy.

The envelope was covered in green stamps depicting palm trees and monkeys. It was postmarked several months ago. He must have put it in his pocket and forgotten to open it. The script like Sandra's was infantile but adamant.

Dear Cassidy, he read, while dressing in the bathroom. *Your monthly cheque to hand with Thanks. My daughter tells me you have elected to become a politico,*

*and that you are dabbling in lefty politics including
Communism and brawling in the docks. Don't. Your
duty is to be* attentive *and chivalrous to your wife and
children at all times,* not *go hobnobbing with pansy
Marxists from Balliol and treat your mother in law as a
damned cretin. I am in constant touch with Mrs. Groat
on this Matter and expect to hear of a general improvement bearing in mind she's as blind as a bat.*

It ended quaintly *P. Groat Brigadier (retd)* and
warned Cassidy in a P.S. to look after his tennis racquet:
*And Make Damn sure the press is tight P.G. (Brig.
Rtd).*

The Bentley stood in the bay where he had parked it. No,
the doorman said, jovially handing him the keys, of course
no one had taken it; not without Mr. Cassidy's consent, of
course not.

London

28

A spell of cold weather, bringing rain and unseasonable winds, coincided with Cassidy's descent into Hades. At home over the weekend he barely spoke; though he was tender to his child and noticeably protective of his wife, his outward manner remained aloof, preoccupied.

"There's trouble about the Paper," he told Sandra. "The Unions are in an ugly mood."

Concerned, she saw him to the car.

"If there's anything I can do to help, let me know. Sometimes a woman's touch is what they need."

"I will," said Cassidy, and embraced her fondly, if distractedly.

Alone in his Bentley, the louche criminal prowled the London streets, shunning the main thoroughfares and the gaze of inquisitive policemen. He drove distractedly, regarding with loathing his deceiver's eyes in the driving mirror, red-rimmed, shadowed with debauchery. Aldo Cassidy, fifty thousand pounds reward, crime innocence. I'd have drawn it better, he thought, I'd have made me more contemptible.

"You'll ring us soon, won't you?" Helen had said on the doorstep, looking into him and beyond. "Cassidy."

"Can't be soon enough, lover," Shamus whispered, shuffling ahead of them up the steel stairs. "Come and play football."

"I will."

"How about now?"

"I've got to put in time with the bosscow."

"I'll bet those bad-tempered ladies are *great* in bed," said Shamus, unlocking the kitchen door. "Helen smirks too much. Too happy. Hey Helen, maybe we ought to get miserable for a bit."

"Goodbye Cassidy," said Helen, smiling.

"Good luck with *Codpiece*," said Cassidy.

"We'll write," said Helen.

Shamus swung on her fast. "Will you? Can you do that? Maybe you could do *Codpiece* too."

"I meant letters," said Helen. "Not scripts."

Changing into his suit, Cassidy left his dinner jacket for Helen to press.

An airport drew him, possibly Heathrow. Parked in a lay-by, the loathsome sinner watched large jets take off to safety in the mist. If only he had his passport. Telephone the office, Mawdray can bring it in a taxi. For a while, coasting past petrol stations and motels, he searched for a secluded kiosk, then gave up. I'd never get away with it, they'd intercept the call, catch me at the barrier. *West End adulterer makes Airport Dash.*

Windsor, where the flag of Saint George dangled wetly over the historic stone. The obscene goat passed in unremarked shame, gazing at shoppers, coveting their dullness. Tradition; what had Cassidy ever had of tradition? Where was Cromwell Cassidy now, that valiant Puritan campaigner? In the Savoy Hotel, thank you, ten pounds extra for the staff and send the bill to the Company, sleeping with his best friend's wife.

Why did no lightning strike him? This lorry, hurtling over the narrow bridge: why did its articulated trailer not slam his preening hood, shatter the glass of his unnatural immunity? Perhaps he should kill someone; that would be an answer. A lonely cyclist, for instance, setting out for honest labour in the fields, mounting this very crest at the end of a long day's toil, his simple mind upon hearth and children?

Settling more comfortably into his seat, Cassidy allowed his ready imagination to complete the castastrophe: the granite church, the meagre grave, the tragic group unheeding of the rain. The widow pauses at the

iron gate. Cassidy, haggard and unshaven, lays a hand upon her arm.

Send the children to Harrow, he begs her. *I have some
influence with the headmaster. I would like to care for
them as my own.*

She does not weep but only shakes her head.

Give me back my Harry, she whispers. *That's all I want.*

My trouble is, I drive too carefully.

In Aylesbury, a pretty market town not normally fre-
quented by adulterers, the repulsive voluptuary bought his
wife a crocodile handbag and composed, over coffee in a
roadside hostelry, a letter of withdrawal to his former
friend Shamus, the well-known prophet.

> *You gave me the means to love and I have grossly
> abused your gift, turning it into a weapon of betrayal
> against yourself. No words can describe my agony; as
> high as you raised me, thus far have I fallen. I enclose a
> cheque for five thousand pounds in full settlement of
> all claims. Please keep my dinner jacket and any other
> small possessions which may be hanging around the
> flat. A banker's order takes care of the rent.*
>
> > *Your one-time friend*
> > *and eternal admirer*
> > *A. Cassidy*

To this letter, on reflection, he added a precautionary
postscript:

> *I should have told you long ago that I am subject to
> epileptic fits. These are of a very rare form. Once in
> their grip, I am powerless to resist and lose all re-
> sponsibility for my actions. If you don't believe me,
> please feel free to consult Dr. John Elderman of Aba-
> lone Crescent, whom I have instructed to pass to you
> whatever further information you may need. None but
> he and Sandra, hitherto, have been party to my secret
> grief. I beg you, whatever happens, to treat this in-
> formation in strictest confidence.*

Having sealed the letter, stamped it, and put it in his
pocket he ordered a fresh plate of hot scones and ate them

in grey despair. Now you know all, he thought; do with me what you will.

Leaving the café, he consigned the letter to a public litter basket. Forget, he told himself. Put nothing in writing.

It never happened.

They never existed, he told himself. I made them up. Come now, be honest, could I really have got away with it so long?

Driving to Labour Party Headquarters, he enquired at the desk how he should offer himself for adoption as a candidate. The girl did not know but promised to find out.

"It was *Labour* you wanted, wasn't it?" she asked rather doubtfully, looking past him through the window at the newly sprayed Bentley.

"Please," said Cassidy, and left his card.

It never happened. Forget.

So you see, Shamus is dead.
  Helen is dead.
  They never existed.
  I dreamed them.
  To nothing.

And yet, out of the pit of his agony, out of the misery of guilt, remorse, deceit, and regret, the little weed, as Shamus would have it—also grew. For his agony was tempered by a quite urgent will to live—the gift of certain unnamed friends whose influence upon him had by no means lost its sting.

Returning next day from an all-night debate at the dockers' headquarters, he fulfilled an engagement at the Elderman dinner table and won the respect of all who heard him. Well, he said, the Report was highly confidential; he did not honestly feel he could say much about

it. Yes, it would be called the Cassidy Report. *The scope?*
It covered pretty well everything from the reception pro-
cedure at Party Headquarters to the provision of recreation
facilities in Cable Street warehouses. *Terms of reference?*
Very much as quoted in the press (a nice touch—no one
confessed to having missed the notice) with a few additions he had insisted upon for his own protection.

In bed, armed with a virility brought on by extreme
anxiety—and stimulated perhaps by certain inexplicit
memories of events which had not occurred—he astonished his wife with a succession of sexual feats.

"And get rid of your mother," he told her. "I'm sick of
having her around."

"I will," said Sandra.

"I want you to myself," he said.

"It's all that matters," Sandra agreed. *"Dear* Pailthorpe."

Grew, burgeoned, and even, mysteriously, flourished.

And felt, among many other conflicting emotions—such
as panic, for instance, such as hatred of the scarlet whore
Helen, such as a profound sympathy with the extreme
right of the Conservative Party, which protects men of
property from the vicious assaults of penurious writers
and their unprincipled wives—felt that special superiority
only found among those who live eye to eye with destiny:
alpinists, the mortally ill, and the many heroes of the war
he'd missed. The weed was of the brotherhood at last; the
élite. He understood why Helen and Shamus talked so
much about mortality. Death is the property of those
who live; they should study it with every hour.

Also the weed slept less; ate less; worked better and
more briskly.

And finding, in the passage of that fortnight, that he had
neither contracted leprosy, nor been arrested by the police, nor had served on him those ever-threatening notices
from the Inland Revenue or the Board of Trade; and
having heard nothing from either Helen or Shamus, and
made no move to reach them on his own account; and
having therefore presumed them at first missing and later
killed, he decided it was safe, in a quiet way, to explore a
little further his new exciting policy of taking.

"You know . . ," Sandra began gratefully one night.

"What do I know?"

"Even if it were all a lie, the whole thing . . . the Paper, the Party, the safe seat . . . I'd still love you. I'd still admire you. Whatever the truth was."

But Cassidy was asleep, he could tell by his breathing.

"The truth is *you*," she whispered. "Not what you say. *You*."

29

Time out; borrowed Time; a past unlived, too long imagined, belatedly made real; a cashing-in before the final settlement; an ascent of the emotional scale; a claiming of his rightful dues; a renewed search for the Blue Flower: who cares? Cassidy stripped, stood in the fountain, and felt the edges of his existence.

"You know what I wish, Aldo?"

"What do you wish?"

"I wish all the stars were people and all the people were stars."

"What good would that do?"

"Because then our faces would be lit up with smiles all the time. We'd twinkle at each other and never be miserable any more."

"I'm not miserable," said Cassidy stoutly. "I'm happy."

"And all the people we don't like would be masses of miles away, wouldn't they, because they'd be in the sky instead of the stars."

"We've got all night," said Cassidy. "I'm not tired or anything. I'm just happy."

"I love you so much," said Angie. "I wish you'd grin."

"Make me," said Cassidy.

"I can't. I'm not clever enough." She kissed him with placid, expert sensuality. "I never will be."

He grinned. "How's that?"

"That's good," she said. "That's very good for a beginner."

Tasting of snail garlic from the Epicure, watched by a white dog called Lettice, they lay in naked mutuality on the thin, bony bed of her attic flat in Kensington, next to the stars. Lettice was born under the sign of the bowman, she said, and Bowman was the sexiest sign out.

337

"It means cock," she explained. "Julie told me. Everything's phallic really, isn't it?"

"I suppose it is," said Cassidy.

A Che Guevara poster hung on the wall beside a tapestry woven by Cretan primitives.

"Lettice loves you too," said Angie.

"And I like him."

"Her," said Angie. "Silly."

Yesterday he knew nothing about her; today everything.

She believed in the Spirit and wore rows of mystic beads against her bare and extremely beautiful bosom. She believed in God and, like Shamus, hated the fucking clergy more than any other living thing; she was a vegetarian but thought snails were all right because they couldn't feel and anyway the birds ate them; she had loved Cassidy from the day she joined the firm. She loved him as she loved no one in the world; Meale was a stupid bugger. She had identified the actual stars which determined Cassidy's fortune, and gazed at them for nights on end. She had broad, hard thighs and her fleece grew downwards very neatly from the upper line, she called it her beard and liked him to keep his hand there, she couldn't get enough. Her right breast was erogenous, she disapproved of abortion. She adored children and hated her fucking father. As a rule, Cassidy disliked swearing in women and had been hoping, at a suitable moment, to check it in Helen. But there was a hardy familiarity to Angie's obscenities, a sublime indifference to their connotations, which somehow disinfected them of sensation.

She was twenty-three. She adored Castro but her greatest single regret was that she had not fucked Che Guevara before he died; it was for this reason she had him nearest to her bed. Greece was fabulous, and one day when she had made lots of money she was going to go back and live there and have lots of babies: "All by myself, Aldo, little brown ones that play bare on the sand."

He knew also that naked she was very beautiful and neither shy nor afraid; and it amazed him beyond words or comprehension that she had lived so long fully dressed within his reach, and that he had not put out his hand to unzip her.

"Listening?"

"Yes," said Cassidy. "Don't let go."

"Pisces, right? That's Latin. Two fishes, joined by the

astrological umbilical cord, one swimming upstream and the other swimming downstream."

"Like us," Cassidy suggested humbly.

"Not *us; me,* silly. I've got a dual personality. That's what dual personality means: two whole different people inside one head. I'm not one fish, I'm *two,* that's the whole point, silly." She continued reading. "Decisive events await you this week. Your greatest desire will come within your reach. Do not flinch. Seize the opportunity but only before the ninth or after the fifteenth, Christ what's the date?"

I love you, he thought. I love the way your ears point through your long brown hair; I love the sheerness of you, the spring and ease of your young body, I want to marry you and share the Greek beach with your babies.

"The thirteenth," he said looking at the date window of his gold watch.

"I don't care," said Angie resolutely. "They're not always right so sod them."

She lay flat on her back, pensively studying Che Guevara.

"I don't care, I don't care, *I don't fucking care,*" she repeated fiercely, staring the great revolutionary in the eye. "It's a cloud. One day the wind will come along and puff it away and I *still* won't care. Do you do it a lot, Aldo? Do you fuck lots of girls?"

"It's just the way I'm made," said Cassidy and gave a traveller's sigh, hinting at the lonely road and the wandering, and the rare moments of consolation.

"Come off it, Garbo," said Angie.

Naked, she made him cocoa, a foulmouthed goddess clattering plates in the tiny galley; a child, backlit by the orange glow from the window, preparing a dorm feast. And afterwards, she promised him, they'd do it again. She loved him, he could do it whenever he liked. Her breasts moved with her, not a tremor; her long waist had the authority of a statue. She straddled him, knees spread, making a sand castle. Bending forward, she kissed him over and over while she stirred him slowly into the thick basin of her hips.

"He was *such* a sod, my Dad," she said afterwards, still in awe, her round cheek pressed gratefully against his shoulder, her hand still lightly holding him. "But *your* kids *really* love you don't they, Aldo?"

"I love *you,*" said Cassidy, not finding it, for once, at all difficult to say.

Ast, an older lady a good three years Cassidy's senior but not yet wholly infirm, lived nearer to the ground but in greater affluence. In bed she was very large, about twice her dressed weight he reckoned, thinking vaguely of Cassius Clay; and when she leant on her side to talk to him her heavy elbow staked him to the mattress.

The walls of Ast's room were hung with unframed canvasses by painters yet to rise; her windows faced a museum, and her interest in Cassidy, after the first round, was essentially of the historical kind.

"When did you *know?*" she asked, in a voice which suggested that love could be proved by research. "*Frankly,* Aldo. When did you have the first *inkling?*"

Frankly, Cassidy thought, never.

"Was it," she suggested, prompting his memory, "that night at the Niesthals', at the harpsichord concert? You looked at me. Twice. You probably don't even remember."

"Of course I do," said Cassidy politely.

"October. That gorgeous October." She sighed. "God, one says such corny things when one's in love. I thought you were just a boring . . . lecherous . . . merchant." Cassidy shared her amusement at this ridiculous misconception. "How wrong. How utterly wrong I was." A long, meaningless silence. "You *love* music, don't you, Aldo?"

"Music is my favourite thing," said Cassidy.

"I could tell. Aldo, why don't you take *Sandra* to concerts? She's so frightfully anxious to *understand* the spirit. You've got to help her, you know. She's nothing without you. Nothing." The significance of her words suddenly appalled her. "Oh God what have I said! Forgive me, say you forgive me."

"It's quite all right," Cassidy assured her.

"*God* what have I said?"—She rolled on to him—"Aldo, please, don't cut me off, please. *I forgive you.* Say *I forgive you.*"

"I forgive you," said Cassidy.

Peace returned.

"And then you went for me at the Eldermans'. I could hardly believe it. No one had spoken to me like that for months. You were so fluent . . . so *sure.* I felt like a child. Just a little girl." She laughed at the pleasurable memory. "All we stupid women could do was look insulted while you lectured us. My mouth went dry and my heart was going inside and I thought: he's right. He *cares* about the artist. *Publishers,"* she snorted. "What do *they* know?"

"Nothing," said Cassidy, thinking of Dale.

"As to those flowers . . . well, I just never had so many flowers in my life. Cassidy?"

"Yes."

"What *prompted* you to send them?"

"Paris," Cassidy said, nimbly. "I suddenly . . . missed you. I looked everywhere . . . but you weren't there."

He must have bolted overnight, Cassidy thought, peeking surreptitiously at the uncollected pieces, the clotheshorse for his suits, the leather reading chair for rejecting manuscripts. What a master. How did he do it? Write or ring? Or did he, the Hercules, *tell* her?

They lay still, side by side, and between them a little chasm about ten thousand miles across.

White dust sheets covered the bedroom floor in one corner, and a strong smell of linseed oil lingered in the blankets. Lying on their backs, Mr. and Mrs. Aldo Cassidy admired the newly painted ceiling.

"It will be really lovely when it's finished," Cassidy said. "Like a palace or something."

"You ought to *watch* him," said Sandra, referring to Mr. Monk the mason. "He's so steady. So loyal and decent. He was in the sappers in the war."

"The sappers were a fine bunch," Cassidy remarked shrewdly, their expert on military affairs.

"He thinks he remembers Daddy. He's not sure but he thinks so. He was on bridges for a while, in Bolton. Back in thirty-nine."

"I forget which lot was stationed at Bolton," Cassidy said, as if he had been wondering. They had recently seen *Patton,* and Cassidy was still enjoying a certain reflected prestige.

"He keeps his men in order too," said Sandra approvingly. "One of them has been making eyes at Snaps."

"I'm not having that," said Cassidy sharply.

"Shush," said Sandra with a conspiratorial frown, looking upwards at the ceiling.

"Well honestly I mean the way she tarts around—"

"Aldo!"—quieting him with little kisses—*"Grizzly* Pailthorpe . . . *Aldo* . . . it's only her age. *She'll* get over it . . .

anyway, she's got a new boyfriend, a visualizer called Mel."

They both giggled.

"Oh *Christ*," said Cassidy. "Do we *have* to have visualizers?" More kisses. "How's Grans taking it?"

"Who cares?"

They lay still, listening to the slow copulative beat of Snaps' music.

"He's not up there is he?" Cassidy demanded on a sudden impulse.

"Of course he isn't," she said, restraining him.

He lay back once more, placated, the custodian still of a certain standard of virtue.

A few days later, to celebrate Cassidy's good news, he and his wife dined at the White Tower. Angie made the booking, two for eight.

They liked duck best.

They ate it crisp with a heavy Burgundy Cassidy had learnt to remember, and for a short time under the influences of meat and wine they remade the illusion of their love. First, like old friends reunited, they exchanged intelligence from their separate worlds. Sandra said Mark had asked for a new violin: the music master had written that he did not shine at the instrument but it was certainly too small. This discussion, though homely, was privately confusing to Cassidy, for he had recently once more lost his sense of time. Mark had been home last weekend, but whether from school or from some other activity Cassidy could not precisely say.

"Let's run to one more size," he proposed and Sandra smiled her assent.

"Maybe it'll encourage him," she said, fresh from the experience of the piano. "Any instrument's a drag to start with."

"It would be super if the two of you could play together," Cassidy said. "Hugo too," he added and there passed through his mind a pleasing vision of a drawing room, all the holes filled in, and Sandra sitting at a much smaller piano while her young Haydns fiddled and piped for Father.

"I'm sure I could learn to like music," he said.

"You just need to hear more. No one's *really* tone-deaf, John said so."

Next on the Chairman's informal agenda, the long-projected extension to the house. The present phase of reconstruction being almost over, it was time to consider where they should go next. An extension was the natural solution, particularly if Heather was really going to live with them permanently. Cassidy favoured a cantilevered design that left the garden unspoilt. Sandra said there would be too much shade.

"What's the point of beds," she pointed out, "if the sun never gets to them?"

Alternatively, they could revise their original plan for the conversion of the basement.

"What about a sauna?" Cassidy suggested.

It was not a welcome inspiration. Saunas were a rich man's toy, Sandra said sternly, saunas replaced abstinence and physical exercise. They agreed to consider the cantilevered extension.

"Of course we could put a swimming pool under it," Sandra said reflectively, "if we had more children."

"Children have to be foreseen," said Cassidy quickly, playing upon Sandra's recent excursions into family planning. A small lull followed this objection.

A serious matter now, the parents confer. Mark's last report: should they take it seriously, should he be punished? This was dangerous ground. Sandra believed in punishment as she believed in hell; Cassidy until recently had been sceptical of both.

"I don't *quite* see what he's done wrong," Cassidy began cautiously.

"He's shirking," Sandra retorted, and closed her mouth firmly.

But tonight was togetherness night and Cassidy would not be drawn.

"Let's give him one more term to settle in," he suggested lightly, and by way of distraction brought her up to date with the news from South Audley Street.

"I've decided to put a bomb under them."

"High time."

"Ever since Paris they've been completely out of hand.

There's no dedication, no . . . how can I say it? No sense of mission or . . . loyalty. God knows, they're on a profit-sharing basis: why don't they work, and share? That's all I ask: devotion."

"You could sack that tarty receptionist while you're about it too," said Sandra, helping herself from the bowl of *crudités*.

"Do you *mind?*" Cassidy said sharply.

"Sorry."

Smiling roguishly, she put down her carrot and touched his hand to feel the anger.

The sunny side. Despite the threat of apathy, he felt that the export drive was worthwhile, and indeed was making strides. Paris, contrary to his initial fears, had paid handsome dividends. Moreover it was an excellent way of opening the minds of his staff; moreover the national economy needed every penny.

"They should spend less on arms," Sandra interjected.

Suspecting that they had had this discussion before, and alarmed by the prospect of another debate on the British defence posture, Cassidy returned hastily to the more encompassable problems of man-management.

Faulk was becoming outrageous, always threatening to resign or cut his wrists, a real *drama queen*.

"You must *not* discriminate against homosexuals," Sandra said.

"I don't."

"It's perfectly natural."

"I know."

Meale was also a headache. Moody, brilliant, impossible; what *was* to be done with him?

"Oh *Meale*," said Sandra in a jocular voice. "There's a hardy annual if *ever* I met one!"

"He's only been with us nine months," Cassidy replied, not meaning to contradict her but lured in some way by the metaphor.

"Ha, ha," said Sandra, furious, and drank some wine, staining her mouth.

"But you're dead right: he really *is* a hardy annual, however long he's been with us. I've never known anyone so temperamental. D'you know he spent his leave in a *monastery?*"

Still scowling, Sandra took a mouthful of duck.

"You don't object to his being *religious* do you?"

"Not if it makes him happy. But it doesn't. He's come back worse than when he left."

"Probably that secretary of yours been leading him a dance. Love takes people that way, you know."

"Nonsense," said Cassidy, tersely, and returned to the more tranquil field of politics.

Harold Wilson had impressed him, he said. The burdens of recent office had aged him certainly, as they age us all; but they had not blunted his intellect. In sum, Cassidy thought him an intelligent man, sincere and well informed, even if he was a bit Gerrard's Cross. The Chancellor, on the other hand, was a type Cassidy found very hard to deal with: tremendously agreeable, and gives absolutely nothing away, which was no doubt a sound way of dealing with p.q.'s (he meant parliamentary questions), but not so well suited to off-the-record, non-attributable, round-table get-togethers.

"Then you must break him down," said Sandra.

"I know. The trouble is he's so—"

"He can't just *lie*."

"He doesn't quite do that, it's just he comes up with these bland answers you somehow can't get round."

And then mysteriously, over the *baklava*, she left him.

He ran on, giving of his best, but she slipped further and further away from him. A shadowed silence descended on her from within, causing her features suddenly to age, and sadden, her eyes to find an object to her left, and her cuffed hands to join like troubled friends before a common dread.

He played for laughs; he did his voices; he populated the political stage with a carnival of exotic personalities. Old So-and-So was a kind of Carnaby Street Hemingway, acting tough and attending his wife's deliveries, but deep down he was just a puff-ball, Cassidy had fixed him in ten minutes. Someone else was always stealing the tea out of the canteen; the secretaries walked in fear of So-and-So, he was a pincher and pounced on them from doorways. He tried to play on her concern; very few really knew how grave was our economic situation. What was the Government to *tell* us? There came a moment when by telling the truth you made the truth more real and more terrible: "I mean God, we all know *that* problem."

"Yes," said Sandra, still in her own dark place, "we do."

"And what about the people farther away?" she asked, still distracted. "Up north, or wherever you went? How were they? Also fools and knaves?"

"Oh, the Trade Union barons. Well they're *really* tough. They were a real eye-opener, believe me. I mean if you like realism, those are the boys who know what it's all about."

"I'm glad somebody does," said Sandra, still looking away from him.

Only promises remained to him.

"Look," he said. "Now it's done, finished—"

"What is?"

"The Report. The Paper. It's off my hands. I told you. That's why we're here."

"I know. I do know. You told me."

"I thought we'd take a holiday. Up sticks and away. Dump the boys with John and Beth—" for once he remembered her name "—and *go*. Wherever you like. While we're still young." To himself, he sounded like television. How did he sound to her? He could not tell.

"Just you and me," he said.

And brought her back.

Not all the way perhaps but far enough. Slowly, not all at once, the shadows withdrew from her face and a puckish, rather gallant smile took possession of her homeless features. A laugh escaped her, mocking none but herself, and she took his hand, touched it rather, sliding the tips of two very pretty fingers up and down the back.

"We could take a castle in Spain," she suggested. And

then, to his considerable concern, for he was not in any mood that night to deal with weighty matters: "You're God really, aren't you, Aldo? After all, if we don't believe in you, what *do* we believe in?"

"Listen. First we'll have a party. As soon as they've finished the drawing room. Then we'll go. Next day. Take off. Now when's the drawing room promised for?"

Details now, details gave reality. Whom they would ask: just people they liked, no one official, least of all Trade and Politics. Maybe a few of Heather's friends to brighten it up. John and Beth of course, maybe a separate room for the kids. . . . Yes, said Sandra, it would be fun to have a children's party going at the same time.

Now, about the holiday. Problem one: *Where?* All right, if she'd gone off Tito how about the Bahamas, he would even stand the cost of a trip to Bermuda.

Very cautiously, Sandra counted off her unbreakable engagements; and broke them one by one.

There was something else on Cassidy's mind: they should *do* more together.

"Perhaps that's one of the things we might think about on holiday."

As a matter of fact he had been talking to Lacon and Ollier about it, his theatre ticket people, only yesterday.

"I thought you were in Leeds yesterday," said Sandra, almost as if she were thinking about something else.

On the phone. He was actually talking to them about travel, then they got on to the question of theatre, was there *anything* worth seeing in the West End these days?

"What I was going to say was—"

"Sorry," said Sandra.

"What for?"

"Doubting you."

Checked, Cassidy glanced at her to make sure she was serious, but there was neither irony nor any other kind of insurrection in her face: only that same inward sadness, returning like a grown child to the empty houses of her youth.

"What I was going to say was: why not go to the theatre once a week *automatically* just to get a show under one's belt so to speak? At least we'd have something to talk about."

They agreed on Wednesdays.

"And I want to go to church again."

"For my sake?"

"Well, yours and the children's. Even if they reject it later, it's right for them to have it now."

"Yes," said Sandra, very thoughtful again. "It will always be part of their lives, whether they reject it or not. After all—" he thought she had finished but she had not "—after all, if you live long enough with a dream, it *is* real isn't it?"

Desperately he searched his imagination for stronger remedies. He had heard from old Niesthal that there was a marvellous sale at Christie's next week, no dealers would be there because of the holidays. Why not go?

"Apparently there's some fabulous eighteenth-century glass. You've always wanted old glass."

"Have I?"

He talked about the chalet in Sainte-Angèle; perhaps they should drop in there on their way to Bermuda to make sure it was still in one piece; how the children had adored it last winter but he did wonder all the same whether Christmas wasn't better spent at home.

"It's up to you," she said. "We'll spend it wherever you say."

He was going to offer further thoughts on Switzerland; he had a lot ready. He was going to suggest they retired there, that it was a good place to die, the eternity of the mountains gave a kind of solace; he was going to draw her on an academic point: did mountains exist more in *time* than in *space,* did something massive by definition become something of great longevity? But instead she spoke to him on her own initiative, drawing on thoughts deep down.

"Aldo."

"Yes."

"You know I love you, don't you?"

"Yes, of course."

"I *mean* it," she repeated, with a frown. "I actually really love you. It's a whole condition of mind. It doesn't allow for . . ."

Not being an articulate girl, she found no end to her sentence, so she got up and went to the ladies' room. Cassidy paid the bill and called a cab. The same night they made love. For her own reasons Sandra was very slow. Finally, somewhere in the darkness, she called out; but whether from pain or joy he could no longer tell.

In the morning, she was crying again and he dared not ask her why.

30

"She's here," said Angie Mawdray in a sepulchral voice, perhaps the next day; perhaps autumn, since time had lost much of its reliability.

Several possibilities occurred to Cassidy; only the certainties were excluded. Heather Ast, for instance, popping in to say hullo on the way to have her hair done; Bluebridge wanting money, the obligatory scene; Mrs. Groat, Snaps, to discuss a new pregnancy. Heather Ast again, on a point of detail relating to Sandra's welfare.

"*Who* is here?" he asked, with a tolerant smile.

Angie's face, normally a treasure chest of appealing smiles and twinkling eyes, was ashen.

"You never told me she was a Beauty," she whispered.

The receptionist, a friend of Lemming, was also impressed, for she winked at Cassidy as he passed her on his way to the waiting room and Cassidy made a mental note to dismiss her very soon indeed. There had been, he remembered, an incident at last year's annual cricket match for which she had yet to pay—a matter of a locked changing room and an absent batsman—and that wink made retribution certain.

The waiting room door was ajar. She was sitting in the deepest chair, a recliner of black hide, leaning right back with her knees not quite together. Her eyes were closed and she was smiling.

"Grunt like a pig," she commanded.

Cassidy grunted.

"A lazy, non-telephoning, non-writing, head-in-the-mud pig."

He grunted again.

"That's authentic," she conceded and then she opened

351

her eyes and they kissed and went to tea at Fortnum's because she was ravenous after her walk.

She's here.

She's walked, he recorded, as the memories came rushing back, the fun, the laughter, the bodies tied. Tripped the country miles from cod-country to South Audley Street on her very much deteriorated Anna Karenina boots. Hitchhiked, a gorgeous lorry driver called Mason. Mason had stopped for her to pick the blue flowers, bought her tea, wrapped her blue flowers in the *Evening Standard*—she was carrying them still, on her lap, they would go beside the bed tonight—Mason had invited her to have it off with him.

"But I didn't, Cassidy, promise, just a kiss and a *thank you, Mason, I'm not that sort of girl.*"

"Very laudable," said Cassidy. "Exemplary in fact," and ordered her eggs, a second helping.

"Dear lover, are you in the pink? Can I kiss you, or will they call the lilly? That's what Mason called them, Cassidy: *lilly*. For police. Did you know? Cassidy, I love you *enormously*, that's my first vital piece of news. A blanket investment, Cassidy, not even my *toes* sticking out, Cassidy. Lock, stock, and body. Cassidy, you really *do*? Love me, I mean?"

"Really."

"God what a relief. I told Mason, I said Mason, if he stand me up you will *have* to go to bed with me, whether you like it or not it's a territorial imperative; is that the right expression? Like Schiller. To restore my pride."

She leaned forward, full of important information.

"Cassidy, you have opened me up. Is that rude? I was a toady till I met you. A lackey. A bourgeois housebeast. You have turned me into a *suffragette*, no fooling. Cassidy, *say* you love me."

"I love you."

"He loves me," Helen assured the waitress. "Him, and my husband, and a man called Mason, a lorry driver."

"Gosh," said the waitress and they all laughed.

"Cassidy, you are a *swine* not to ring me. Shamus was *very* put out. *Where's lover? Why won't lover ring?* It went on night and day until I got absolutely fed up with it. 'He's *my* lover not yours,' I told him—"

"Helen you didn't—"

"And I looked *everywhere* for the Bentley. I told Mason: Mason, if we see Cassidy's Bentley, you've got to make an emergency halt because me and Cassidy are lovers and . . . Cassidy, kiss me, you are a *total* pig."

"You could have rung *me*," Cassidy reminded her, having temporarily satisfied her needs.

"Cassidy, I did. I rang you the *whole weekend* and you just listened to it burr, burr and did absolutely nothing. Just sat there gawping at your carpet slippers."

"At the weekend?" Cassidy repeated, as iron bars gathered round his chest.

"Yes but I got the bosscow every time, so I rang off. At least I suppose it was the bosscow, she was *terribly* grey." She pulled a bovine face. "If you tell me who you *are* I *might* tell you where mah husband is," she said, in an uncomfortably good imitation of Sandra.

"I thought you were going to ring the office," said Cassidy. "I thought we agreed."

"But Cassidy it was the *weekend*."

"How's Shamus?" he asked, watching her eat the smoked salmon.

"He's absolutely *super* and I love him and *Codpiece* went like a song. I tell you, Cassidy, that fellow's on a real winning streak. Well we both are, aren't we? And *all* thanks to you."

What had happened to her? What had freed her? Did *I* do this?

"Those fishermen are *fabulous*, Cassidy, you should smell them." She ventured what Cassidy assumed was a Lowestoft accent. " *'Ya mine for the neet,'* that's what one of them said to me. I had to explain to him, Cassidy. I'm booked, I said. I've got a rich lover who invented the disc brake, and he guards me like a *lemur*. Do you like being described as a *lemur*, Cassidy?" Without a breath she returned to her other interest. "He's even been *paid,* that's how well *Codpiece* went. No rewrite, no Dale, no nothing. In fact—" indicating a little guiltily her new coat "—I'm wearing the fee. Don't worry, Cassidy"—leaning urgently forward—"I'm *nude* underneath, promise."

"Helen. Hey listen: you're completely out of control. What's come over you? You're not tight are you?"

"It's called *love*," Helen said, a little sharply. "And it's non-alcoholic."

A model moved slowly round them, a skeletal, moody girl of no attraction.

"I'm better than her anyway."

"Much," Cassidy agreed.

"He talks about you *masses*," she went on. "And he misses you *terribly*. He keeps saying, 'Is he all right? Shouldn't you ring him?' To *me*! And how he must keep faith with you because he loves you, and you gave him his, and the circle must never be broken." She lowered her voice. "And he's *terribly* ashamed about what happened at the Savoy, Cassidy."

"Oh well, I don't think he should be really."

"He's right back to self-denial. No booze, no bed, nothing. . . . Oh Cassidy he *so* missed you. He just wanted to hear you *speak*, Cassidy. He wanted to hear your *voice* and the slimy way you put sentences together when you're being boardroom." She looked round in case they were overheard. "He's imagined it, Cassidy. The whole thing, isn't he clever? Just as if he'd made us up. Cassidy, those flowers are *blue*."

"I take the point," said Cassidy, and went to the telephone.

The Minister of Labour, he told Sandra. A most mysterious summons from the Private Office; he wondered whether this might be what they were waiting for; he had heard there was a seat going begging in one of the East Anglican constituencies.

"An all-night session I expect," said Sandra.

"It looks like it," he conceded. "We're meeting in Lowestoft. I'm leaving in a couple of minutes."

"What did you mean?" he asked Helen, as they sauntered along the Embankment. "*Imagined* the whole thing? What *whole thing* exactly?"

"You and me as lovers, and himself as my husband. It's the theme of his new book, and it's *fabulous* Cassidy, honestly it is, *miles* better than the last one, you ought to read it. It's so *violent*, Cassidy. Honestly."

"That's marvellous," said Cassidy heartily. "By the way, what happened to the rewrite?"

"Oh, on the shelf marked *fragment*. You're to include it in his posthumous writings. He says you'll survive him by *decades*. Which you will, won't you Cassidy, because you're so dodgy. Dale's *livid*."

"I'll bet he is."

"It's as good as written. He's made a complete sketch, whole chunks finished. All he has to do is put them together. I mean I could *almost* do it for him, but you know what he is. . . . A quick dash to Switzerland, record the fleeting vision, back to England in triumph. That's the plan. Oh we'll want that chalet of yours by the way, Shamus says mountains will be *just* right for it. I'm to get the key off you."

"You are?"

"Well honestly, Cassidy, he doesn't suppose I'm walking all the way to London and not seeing lover does he?"

"What's *in* the book?" Cassidy asked. *Content* had never bothered him before; had been a hindrance in fact to the pure, celestial enjoyment of Shamus' unread works; but now, for reasons too close to him yet to be defined— Helen's excitement perhaps, the imminence of certain death—he detected signs, and wished them clearly shown.

She lowered her voice again.

"Cassidy, there's the most *fabulous* murder at the end, all in Dublin. Shamus buys a gun and goes mad and all *sorts* of things, it's really *super*. . . ." She giggled, noticing his expression. "It's all *right*," she assured him. "You kill *Shamus*, don't worry. Cassidy, I'm *happy*, are you?"

"Of course I am," said Cassidy.

"How's the bosscow?"

"Fine."

"No Thoughts?"

"Who?"

"The bosscow."

"No. No of course not."

"I want *everyone* to be happy, Cassidy. Shamus, bosscow, the veg, *all* of them. I want them to share our love and . . ."

Cassidy was suddenly laughing.

"Jesus," he said, "that *will* be the day."

Entering her embrace however—they were at the centre of the pavement, not far from Cleopatra's Needle—he was pleased to see no one he recognised, not even the Niesthals.

"Then *after* you've killed him," Helen resumed, in the taxi, holding his arm in both her hands, "you're sent to an Irish prison for life and you write a great novel thousands of pages long. *His* novel. What are Irish prisons like, Cassidy?"

"Beery I should think."

"And *very* insecure. Still, *you'll* be able to take me round one won't you? Dublin main gaol, that's his ambition for you. I'm going to do *all* his research, I've promised, and it's got to be completely authentic. He's written me the most super dedication, Cassidy. To both of us, actually."

"Marvellous."

"It's only *imagined*, Cassidy," she said, kissing him lavishly. "I haven't breathed a syllable about what *really* happened, promise. Cassidy, it was *you*, wasn't it, it wasn't a waiter? I couldn't remember whether we did it in the dark or not."

"We left the light on," said Cassidy.

"And it was me underneath?"

"Undoubtedly."

"You see *shooting him* is the only way you can survive, that's how he's worked you out. You've *got* to shoot him, for your sovereignty. He's the original, and you're the imitation, that's how he argues; so if you shoot him, you'll become an original in your own right, it's *extremely* classical. Then your genius will be liberated, but locked up in the prison so you can't piss it away, and all that lovely discipline you have will be further enhanced by—"

"I haven't *got* any genius. I'm a buffoon. I've got big hands and big feet and—"

"Don't worry, Shamus is giving you some of his. After all whoever sleeps with me *has* to be a genius, doesn't he? In Shamus' book at least. I mean it can't just be sordid and middle-class or there's no art. Hey Cassidy, I wrote you a letter."

Opening her handbag she gave it to him, and waited

while he read it. The envelope said: *To lover*. The page inside was lined, torn from one of Shamus' pads.

> *You have given me more in one night than anyone else in a lifetime.*
>
> *Helen*

"I thought it had rhythm," she explained, watching him as he read it. "I worked on it a lot. I wanted to check it with Shamus actually but then I thought better not. After all, I'm not his creature, am I?"

"Good God no," Cassidy cried, laughing. "Rather the other way round I would have thought."

"Cassidy. Don't knock him."

"I wasn't."

"Well don't. He's your friend."

"Helen—"

"We've got to protect him for all we're worth. Because if he ever does find out it will destroy him. Totally."

The football ground was empty; the children had gone. It was a quiet day for the river too, a holiday perhaps, or a day of prayer.

Nothing had changed, but the place belonged already to the past. His dinner jacket hung in the spare room still. A light powder, either human or mineral, greyed the shoulders. The kitchen smelt of vegetable; she had forgotten to empty the rubbish. The picture window was clouded with brown grime. The desk was just as the great writer had left it, except for the yellowed paper, curled by the sunlight, and the dust thick enough to draw in. Keats lay on the blotter. The beret hung on the corner of the chair.

They embraced, kissing; kissing in the dull daylight, lips then tongues; Cassidy caressing her, mainly on the back, tracing her spine to its end and wondering whether she would mind if he continued. Lipstick tastes different in the daylight, he thought: warm and tacky.

"Cassidy," she whispered. "Oh Cassidy."

She took his fingers and kissed them and put them on her breast and glanced first at the bedroom door and then at Cassidy again, then sighed.

"Cassidy," she said.

They had left it unmade, the sheets pulled back to air,

the pillows heaped in the centre as if for one person. The Casa Pupo coverlet lay on the floor, tossed aside in a hurry, and the curtains were partly drawn on the side where the neighbours overlooked. In the poor light the blue was very dark, more black or grey than blue, and the flowered wallpaper had a dishevelled, autumnal look which had never been a problem with the nursery at Abalone Crescent. Stepping over the coverlet, Cassidy went to the window and drew the curtains.

"I should have sent someone to clear up," he said. "It was stupid of me."

Making love to her, Cassidy smelt the familiar smell of Shamus' sweat, and heard the clip of carpets being beaten in the courtyard of the white hotel.

Afterwards they drank Talisker in the drawing room and Helen began shivering for no reason, like Sandra sometimes when he talked to her about politics.

"You haven't got *another* love nest have you?" she asked.

Over lunch at Boulestin, their spirits fully restored, they had a marvellous plan. They would use only sleazy boarding houses, like real illicit lovers.

The Adastras Hotel in the neighborhood of Paddington Station, Cassidy wrote in his secret Baedeker, *may be compared with a certain white hotel in Paris yet to be located by your chroniclers. It has the same elderly, unpretentious grace and many fine old plants long nurtured by the management. Terminus freaks will find a haven here; the bedrooms abut directly on to the shunting sheds, and afford an all-night, no-holds-barred spectacle of a little-known aspect of the British Transport system. The hotel is particularly favoured by illicit lovers: its fine, damp-consumed cornices dating from the nineteenth century, its marbled fire grates stuffed with yellow newspaper, not to speak of its outrageously impertinent waiters, who look to the unattached clientèle for the gratification of their sexual needs, all provide a background of desolate incongruity exceptionally conducive to high performance.*

"Shamus cramped me. He made me such a *prig. Observing.* Who the hell wants to observe? He's not a schoolmaster, and I'm not his pupil. It's over, all that stuff, and he's got to realise it. Fie."

"Fie."

"Pshaw."

"Pshaw."

"Meeow."

"Meeow."

"You're a bear, Cassidy. A big, wuffly bear. Cassidy, I want to be raped."

A *Pailthorpe* bear, thought Cassidy.

Cheeribye, the porter had said, seeing them to their room, mind you get your money's worth.

Do stations never sleep? he wondered. Clang-clang, clang. You must dance but I must sleep.

Got to be a lion tonight lover; mouse-time again soon.

"Cassidy."

"Yes."

"I love you."

"I love you."

"Really?"

"Really."

"I could make you the happiest man on earth."

"I am already."

"More, Cassidy."

"I *can't*. That was the full menu. *Honestly*."

"Nonsense. Put your mind to it and you can do anything. You are suffering from a thoroughly unrealised potential."

An announcer was calling the night sleeper to Penzance. Departs at midnight, Cassidy thought; a little after; his eyelids were very heavy. Bright bands of railway light lay on the papered ceiling.

"Promise?" Helen asked.

"Promise."

"For ever and ever and ever and ever?"

"And ever."

"I promise?"

"I promise."

There was no blood available so they had Talisker instead.

"What else is in that book?"

"I told you. You write the great novel in prison."

"But how does he find out?"

"Find out what?"

"That they're lovers, you and me."

"He read me that bit," Helen said gravely. "It was very spectral."

"What does that mean?"

"It was never really *dramatised*. It just happened."

"How?"

"In the book, he's called Balog. Shamus is. *Gradually Balog came to suspect what he already knew. That his virtue had gone into his friend and his friend had taken Sandra for his lover.*"

Discovering in himself physical resources he had long given up for spent, Cassidy sat up abruptly in bed.

"*Sandra?*" he repeated.

"He rather *likes* the name. He thinks it suits me."

"But that's absolutely *disgusting*. I mean everyone will . . ." He checked himself. Better to talk to Shamus directly on the matter. It's really too much. I mean, I take the man to Paris, dress him, pay his rent, and the next thing he does is lampoon my wife, make a public show of her. "Anyway," he said, in a nasty, academic tone, "how can you suspect something you already know?"

There was a long silence. "If there's one thing Shamus *does* understand," said Helen firmly, "it's the structure of the novel."

"Well it's ridiculous, that's my view. Comparing *you* with Sandra. It's insulting."

"It's art," said Helen, and turning her back lay a long way from him.

"You don't think you should ring Lowestoft do you?" Cassidy suggested. "In case he's back?"

"What would we do if he was?" Helen asked tartly. "Invite him up to join us? Cassidy, you're not *afraid* of him are you?"

"I'm worried about him if you must know. I happen to love him."

"We both do."

Gently she began kissing him. "Grinch," she whispered. "Grizzlebear, hellbeef."

Oxford, the announcer said. Your last chance to get aboard.

But by then she had decided he was in need of the ultimate comfort.

The day dawned very slowly, an internal dawn of yellow mist that gradually brightened under the sooty domes of the station roof. At first, watching through the window, Cassidy took it for the steam of locomotives. Then he remembered that locomotives had no steam any more, and he realised it was fog, a thick, venomous fog. Helen was asleep, cut off from him by the inner peace that comes with faith. No frown, no cry, no anguished whisper against the hellhound Dale: a deep repose, virtue is rewarded.

Helen *is* our virtue; Helen is eternal.

Helen can sleep.

Rising late, they spent the day visiting their favourite places but the gibbons took no pleasure in the fog, and the bust of Mussolini had been removed for cleaning.

"Probably stolen by Fascists from Gerrard's Cross."

"Probably," Cassidy agreed.

They did not go to Greenwich.

In the afternoon they saw a French film which they agreed was fabulous, and when it was over they went back to the Adastras for another exchange of views.

Afterwards, in the intimacy of shared repose, she told him with little prompting how she and Shamus had parted.

"I mean it was so easy, *Christ*. I just said, I think I'll go to town and do some shopping and see how Sal is, and tidy the flat and check on Dale and see lover, and he said fine, off you go. I mean *he* does it, why shouldn't I? Anyway he was perfectly happy. I said I'd ring him, and he said don't bother, how long would I need? I said a week and he said fine. Well that was all right, wasn't it?"

"Fine," said Cassidy. "Of course it was. Absolutely fine. Have you ever done it before?"

"Done what?" Helen asked sharply.

"Gone shopping. To London. To see Sal and people. On your own."

She thought for a long time before speaking.

"Cassidy, you have to try to understand. There is one edition of me, and one only. It belongs to you. Part of me belongs to Shamus, it's true. But not your part. Have you any questions?"

"No."

To please him however she put through a call to Lowestoft, but there was no reply.

Sandra, on the other hand, answered the telephone at once.

"They've offered me Lowestoft," he told her.

"Oh."

"Aren't you pleased?"

"Naturally. Very."

"How are the invitations going?"

For the party; the celebration. Whatever we're celebrating.

A hundred sent out, twenty so far replied, said Sandra: "We hope very much you'll be able to come."

"Thanks," said Cassidy, making a joke of it. "So do I."

31

During this exacting period of Cassidy's life—the next
morning perhaps, the morning after—there occurred one
of those small incidents which had little bearing upon the
central destiny of the great lover but nevertheless illus-
trated with unpleasant force the sense of approaching
reckoning which was overtaking him. Arriving at the office at about midday on one of his rare visits from the
greater stage on which he had elected to perform—an unbreakable engagement, he had told Helen, a political thing
and rather high level—he was met once more by the inso-
lent gaze of the receptionist and a mauve envelope addressed to him in Angie Mawdray's handwriting.

He found her in bed, in a state of high fever, Lettice
on her lap and Che Guevara on the wall.

"*How* do you know?" he insisted, holding her hand.

"I just feel it, that's all."

"But feel *what*, Angie?"

"I can feel it growing in my tummy. It's like wanting
to go to the lav. I can feel its heart beating if I lie still
enough."

"Listen Angie, love, have you seen a doctor?"

"I won't do that," she said.

"For a check, that's all."

"Feeling is knowledge. You said that. If you feel something it's true. My horoscope says it too. All about giving
my heart to a stranger. Well if I have a baby I *do* give it a
heart don't I, so sod it."

"Look," said Cassidy, urgent now. "Have you been
sick?"

"No."

"Have you . . ." he tried to remember their euphemism.
"Has the Chinaman been?"

"I don't know."

"Of course you know!"

"Sometimes he hardly comes at all." She giggled, pulling his hand down under the bedclothes. "He just knocks and goes away. Aldo, is she *really* your mistress? Truly, Aldo?"

"Don't be daft," said Cassidy.

"Higher up," she whispered. "There, that's it . . . *now* . . . only I love you, Aldo, and I don't want you fucking other ladies."

"I know," said Cassidy. "I never will."

"I don't mind you fucking your wife if you've got to, but not Beauties like that one, it's not fair."

"Angie, believe me."

After much argument he persuaded her—a day later? two days?—to let him send a sample of her water to a place in Portsmouth that advertised on the back of Sandra's *New Statesman*. She wouldn't send much—about a miniature, no more—and she wouldn't tell him how she had got it in there. He enclosed a seven and sixpenny postal order and a stamped envelope addressed to himself at the works. The envelope never came back. Perhaps they hadn't sent enough, or perhaps—an appalling vision—the bottle had broken in the post. For a time, a part of him worried about little else; scanned the office mail for his own handwriting the moment it came in, rummaged in the package room on the pretext of having lost his watch. Gradually the danger seemed to recede.

"They only tell you if it's positive," he explained to her, and they came to agree that she probably wasn't pregnant after all.

But now and then, unawares, he surprised himself, during his moments of great passion elsewhere, by visions of Angie's pathetic offering slowly darkening on the shelf of some back-street laboratory or, still with its lemon and barley label, bobbing out to sea past the Duke of Edinburgh's yacht.

32

"Look thy last on all things lovely," Helen announced, "every hour."

"Why? What's happened?"

They were shopping in Bond Street; Helen needed gloves.

"Shamus rang."

"Rang? Rang where? How did he reach you?"

A friend, she said vaguely; he had rung the friend's house and she had happened to be there.

"Just like that?"

"Cassidy," she said wearily, "I am *not* a Russian spy."

"Where is he?"

"In Marseilles. Collecting material. He's going on to Sainte-Angèle. I'm to meet him there at the weekend."

"But you said he was in Lowestoft!"

"He got a lift."

"To Marseilles? Don't be ridiculous!"

Irritated by this interjection, Helen devoted her interest to a shop window.

"Sorry," said Cassidy. "What else?"

"He's decided to set the book in Africa instead of Ireland. He thought of getting a boat and going straight there. He changed his mind. He'll take the chalet instead."

Inside the shop a girl attendant measured her incomparable hand.

"Did he talk about me?"

"Sent you his love," she said, laying the glove against her palm.

"How did he sound?"

"Collected. Sober, I'd say."

Cautiously, she slid her fingers into the black mouth.

"Well that's great. He's probably writing hard. What else?"

"He said please buy him a dressing gown, a black one

with red piping round the collar. So we can do that now, can't we?"

"We'll take them," Cassidy told the girl and gave her his credit card.

In the street again, she added very little. No, he didn't usually go abroad without telling her; but then he wasn't a very usual person was he? No, he hadn't said anything which suggested he was suspicious; he was most insistent she should enjoy herself in London; but the week was up and she should come to him.

"Rather as if that was my ration of you. There's a place called Alderton's, do you mind? In Jermyn Street. You haven't reconsidered your investment, have you, Cassidy?" she asked in the cab.

"What in?"

"Me!"

"Of course not. Why?"

"I would very much like you to hug me. That's why."

At Alderton's, both very quiet, they selected a dressing gown and Cassidy consented to try it on.

"May he?" asked Helen. "He's *exactly* my husband's size."

They went together up a winding steel staircase. The cubicle was along one wall, behind a curtain, in what seemed to be someone's drawing room. A faded portrait of Edward VII hung beside a fox's brush. Taking him gently in her arms, she stood against him, head down, the way he remembered her at Haverdown, at the Savoy, the way he had danced with Sandra at Oxford long ago. Her body felt suddenly very weak through the mohair of the dressing gown, and her passion was no longer his enemy. She took his hands and folded them against her breast, and finally she kissed him, lips closed, for a long time. They heard the salesman's footsteps coming up the iron staircase, and Cassidy thought of prison again, nothing to say except we've still got five minutes.

"Did I give it you, Cassidy?" she asked at the airport.

"What?"

"Faith."

"You gave me love," said Cassidy.

"But did you believe in it?" she asked, crying in his

arms. "Stop patting me, I'm not a dog. *Tell me.*" She held him away. "Tell me: did you believe in it? What do I say to him if he asks?"

"I did. I did believe. I still do."

The air hostess helped her to the departure gate. She used both hands, right arm across Helen's back to help her go along and left arm short to keep her vertical. Reaching the barrier, Helen neither waved nor looked back; just joined the crowd again, and let them take her.

The party had a disjointed quietness. As if the Queen had died, thought Cassidy; part of a national dismay. On the top floor behind closed doors Snaps, in churlish non-attire, was playing sultry gramophone records to selected friends. She appeared seldom, and then only to fetch more champagne and return peevishly to her unseen entertainments. In the kitchens Sandra and Heather Ast, too busy to be present, prepared hot canapés which found no distribution; while the children, for whom costly musical instruments had been set out in the basement, made no sound whatever.

"Leave them to *themselves,*" Ast urged him with a sanity only given to the childless. "They'll be all right, you'll see."

The Eldermans had stayed away. Large parties were against their principles, they discouraged an intimate exchange.

Such guests as had arrived were stuck at the centre floors like the victims of a faulty elevator, sheepishly waiting to go up or down.

"You've given them too much drink too soon," Sandra hissed at him, storming past with a Jonathan Cafe salver piled high with *vol-au-vents.* "As *usual.* They're *drunk, look* at them."

Over her shoulder, Heather transmitted an emphatic smile.

"It's all *gorgeous,*" she assured him when Sandra had gone, and tipped his elbow with her fingers. "Gorgeous," she repeated.

Several of Heather's friends had arrived; mostly men and mostly in publishing; they were distinguished by the brightness of their clothes and they had taken over the nursery, where they were admiring Hugo's paintings. Heather, in flying visits, explained the background. Yes, Hugo was amazing for his age; well so was Mark actually, they were on a par. She was looking forward enormously to having them to herself while Sandra and Aldo were on holiday. While she spoke, her solicitor sidled over to him, the one who had managed her divorce. His name improbably was Pitt, and Oxford had made him great.

"You're so lucky," he said, "having Heather."

The largest group, however, surrounded Mrs. Groat, who was quite drunk on bitter lemon. The familiar patches of red had appeared low down on her cheeks, and her eyes were swimming wildly inside their blue lenses. She was leaning back, flapper-style, on a low Regency chair, her hands linked round one raised knee, and she was talking to the new cornice, with which she was already on coquettish terms. A black walking stick rested against her chair and her foot was bandaged against cramp. Her theme was the goatishness of all men, and the offences which they had committed against her mysteriously hardy virtue. Worst of all was Colly, a childhood friend with whom she had recently passed a weekend:

"So anyway Colly had this Hillman Minx, why he bought a Hillman I shall *never* know but of course your father had a Hillman and Colly always *wanted* to live up to him, of course." Her dialogue was addressed to her daughters, though neither was present to hear it. "Not that your father was much to live up to, not like that, but still. So anyway, we were having a perfectly ordinary nice weekend at Faulkland Saint Mary, not marvellous but what can you expect, it was a place his mother took him to when he was a child or something, only a pub with rooms of course, but still. So Colly was being perfectly reasonable, dull but quite *nice,* and we'd had *quite* a nice dinner, not Claridges but still, and my dear I was in my room writing to Snaps when in Colly waltzes, asking whether I'm warm enough and grinning all over his face. Me in well just a wrap. Ready for bed. But *Colly* of course, wearing our *mulberry* dressing gown, my dear, right down to our feet, looking *just* like your father or Noel Coward or someone but more ashamed of it. 'What *do* you mean *warm* enough,' I said. 'It's midsummer and absolutely stifling.' He knows I loathe the heat. And so my dear, he just stands there, hovering and puffing. 'Well, *warm* enough,' he says. '*You* know,' and my dear he *points* to it through his dressing gown, like a beastly soldier or a tramp or something. '*Warm* enough,' he says. 'Warm enough. Down below.' And my dear, he was *quite* drunk, I could tell by the way he leered although I can't see a thing but still. I wouldn't have minded if he'd been able to carry it off, that's a different thing altogether, I *quite* agree with the younger generation there, I'm sure. Not with everything, but I do there."

The improbable frankness of this narrative drew no one out; only Storm, Cassidy's accountant, was moved to comment.

"What a *marvellous* woman," he whispered. "She's like Dietrich, better."

"Yes," said Cassidy.

"Cassidy my dear fellow, how is your poor friend?"

It was old Niesthal. His wife, in lovely black, was nodding brightly over his shoulder. His long, kindly face was wrinkled with concern.

"Now my dear," Mrs. Groat was saying, noticing Sandra's approach. "I was merely telling them about Colly, I'm not flowing white raiment whatever they may think, I'm flesh and blood my dear, it's only fair, I have my own life to lead, it's time you knew. Darling these aren't very *hot*, or is it the stairs? Still I never did hold with hot plates did I? Colly proposed to me, so there. He wanted me to leave your father and run away with him." She was appealing to the company. "But of course I couldn't, could I? Not with Snaps and Sandra to look after."

"That poor fellow, Cassidy, we were so *worried*, so *very* worried."

His wife added her concern. "He was like the face of a wild man." She turned to Sandra, accepting a *vol-au-vent*. "Dancing on the table," she told her, evoking pity with her eyes. "Shouting, screaming like he was being *murdered* and the waiters not knowing how to take him. And so *brave* your husband, just like a policeman—"

"Phone," said Ast.

"Thanks," said Cassidy.

"Jesus lover," said Shamus, with no accent except his own bewitching voice. "You don't half put a strain on friendship."

Next door, the children had begun to play the drums.

Sainte-Angèle

33

The enshrinement of a part of Aldo Cassidy's identity—not to speak of a part of his fortune, illicitly yielding a tax-free four per cent from Kantonal gilt-edged—in the remote but fashionable Swiss village of Sainte-Angèle was a matter upon which, in less turbulent times, he would freely have dilated. "It's my bit of aloneness," he liked to say with a world-weary smile. "My *special* place." And would paint a stirring picture of the Chairman and Managing Director—was he also still President? he forgot—of Cassidy, anyway, clad in rough alpine tweeds trekking from valley to valley, conferring with shepherds, whispering with guides in the bazaars, as he penetrated ever deeper into the interior of uncharted Europe on his lonely quest for seclusion from the hurly-burly of big business. "It's where I keep my books," he would add, leaving with his questioners a vision of scattered cow huts and one rough-built chalet where Cassidy, the scholar *manqué*, caught up on his Greek philosophers.

To Helen, stretched beside him in the luxurious comfort of the Adastras Hotel, he had emphasised the cultural and historic appeal of his chosen section of the Alps. The beauty of Sainte-Angèle was *fabled*, he said, quoting a brochure he had recently read in praise of his investment. Not a poet, not a member of the Few but had experienced profound movements of the artistic spirit upon contemplating its incomparable peaks, its dizzy waterfalls, its noble if rude domestic architecture. Byron, Tennyson, Carlisle, and Goethe, to name but a handful, all had paused here in breathless awe to sing their praises of the apocalyptic cliffs and the uncompromising sheerness of the valley walls: Shamus would be no exception.

"But is it *dangerous*, Cassidy?"

"Not if you know your way around. You have to get your mountain legs, mind."

"Well, shouldn't we go bicycling first or something? To prepare?"

As to the evils of modernity, he assured her, they had barely encroached upon the place. Balanced upon the upper basements of the great Angelhorn massif, Sainte-Angèle could only be reached by a single-track railway. There was no road. Jaguars, even Bentleys, must be left at the lower station.

"In a way, it's symbolic. You leave your troubles in the valley. Once you're up there, you're on your own. The world doesn't matter any more."

"And you're leading it all to *us*," Helen breathed, reminding him that he must put off the Eldermans or they would clash. "But I mean what do we do about . . . food and things? I suppose we just manage on cheese."

"Frau Anni will look after you," Cassidy replied cheerfully, omitting to mention, in his evocation of a faithful foreign retainer, the dozen food shops which served the fifty hotels and countless tourists who for the four winter months crammed the fairy-lit streets in search of rare souvenirs not available in the cities.

In a less romantic moment—eating alone, for instance, or driving on a secret errand—Cassidy would admit to more specific reasons for his affinity with the place. He would recall how old Outhwaite of Mount Street W. had happened to mention, the very day after Cassidy had made a big killing on the Stock Exchange, that he and Grimble were handling a Swiss property for a non-residential client; a snip at twenty-five thousand, mortgage available; how Cassidy had within minutes phoned his bankers and closed on premium dollars at eighteen per cent, which in the following week had risen to forty. Warming to the narrative, he would relive his arrival in the village to inspect his purchase; the long toil up the snowy hill, the magic moment when he first saw his own house raised against the Angelhorn, the rake of its gables perfectly answered in the angles of the peak behind it; and how, sitting on the balcony and gazing upwards at the great points and saddles of the Alps, he had recognised for the first time that a certain foreignness gave him comfort; and found himself wondering whether, after all, there had not always been a foreign corner to his heart, and whether his mother had not been Swiss. The mountains of Sainte-Angèle were appalling even on a perfect afternoon; they were also a shield, placing nature between himself and his fellow man, and reminding him of the larger relationships of his heart.

His conversations of the next day with local professional men, bank managers, lawyers and the rest, opened his eyes to another extraordinary feature of the mountain life. The Swiss *revered* commercial success! They admired it; saw it as the asset of a gentleman; stranger still, they not only held wealth to be forgiveable, but desirable, moral even. Its acquisition in their unclouded eye was a social duty towards an undercapitalised world. For the Swiss, Cassidy rich was positively more admirable than Cassidy poor, a view which in his own English circle found little acceptance and much derision.

Intrigued, he decided to remain for the weekend on the pretext of a local complication. He engaged rooms at the Angèle-Kulm, the chalet not yet being ready for his occupancy. And thus, alone, made other startling discoveries. That his father owned no hotels in Sainte-Angèle, and had no penthouse aerie overlooking the curling rink. That there were no meths drinkers in Sainte-Angèle to trouble a rich man's heart, that the chalet drawing room had no space for a grand piano. That in Sainte-Angèle, as long as a man paid his bills and tipped the delivery boys, his struggle for position was over before it was joined; that thereafter he would be known, saluted, and welcomed as a person in the tradition of the English tourist, as a patron of the Alps, collecting Bartlett prints and recalling the Empire connection.

Therefore Cassidy did not let the house, as he had intended—a small tax-free income on the Continent can do a man no harm—but left it empty. By the Tuesday of his departure he was causing diligent carpenters to fit sweet-smelling pine cupboards in the bedrooms; had bought furniture from Berne and linen from Interlaken; engaged a housekeeper and fastened nameplates to the doors, this room Mark's, this room Hugo's. And every winter from that day on, and every spring when Sandra allowed it, he had taken his family there, and walked his children in the evening pageant down the high street, and bought them fur boots and *fondue*. Sandra had not gone willingly at first; Switzerland was a millionaires' playground, the women had no vote. But gradually, on its neutral soil, they had formed a treaty of temporary co-existence. In Sainte-Angèle, he noticed, where she had him largely to herself, the world's agonies became markedly less pressing for Sandra; moreover the cold made her face pretty, she could see it in the mirror.

Lastly—though it took Cassidy a year or two to discover this—Sainte-Angèle was English. Was administered by an English government-in-exile, with an English cabinet recruited largely from the area of Gerrard's Cross, a government that was both legislative and executive, and met daily at a reserved table in the most popular bar, calling itself a Club, and moaning about the discourtesy of the natives and the rising value of the franc. In spirit, it was a military government, colonial, imperial, self-appointed. Its veterans wore campaign medals and decorations for valour; its young the uniform pullovers of English regiments. These people took decisions of immense import. True, the governed were not even always aware of the existence of their governors; true, the good Swiss continued to go about their lives in the sweet illusion that they ran their own community, and that the English were merely tourists like any others, except a little louder and less affluent. But in terms of history it was written for all who cared to see: the skill and power which once had bound all India, Africa, and North America into a single Empire had found a final enclave on this small and beautiful alpine ledge. The village of Sainte-Angèle was the last proof-rock of the English administrative greatness, of the super-race of clerks and merchants. They came here every year to own and to mispronounce it; and little by little they had added Cassidy to their ranks. Not all at once, and never noisily. Cassidy's desire for quiet, his un-English deference towards the local inhabitants, his stated wish to avoid controversy, all dictated that his function be subdued; and so it was. On their printed lists of office-bearers, in their announcements of annual honours and awards, his name either did not appear or was hedged about by qualifying adjectives: *co-opted, ex-officio, honorary.* At senate evenings on Tuesday, Council evenings on Wednesday, Praesidium conferences on Thursday, Get-Togethers on Saturday, at English Church on Sunday, his influence passed largely unacknowledged. Only when a great matter was

in hand—the recruitment of a new member, the raising of
advertisement rates in the Club magazine, or the purchase of a new piece of furniture for the gracefully disintegrating clubroom—would a small nocturnal troop of
cabinet ministers and their retinue, muffled against the
cold, wend its way up the narrow path for punch and wisdom at the Cassidy chalet.

"He's so awfully generous," they said, "and *such* a
good committee man." Many were ladies. "He's so *rich*,"
they said and spoke of quite large contributions made in
francs.

In the tearooms and afternoon dance-bars, in the little
groups that huddled round the English notice-board at the
end of the day's skiing, his prowess as an alpinist was
deferentially admired. A Renaissance man, they said; an
all-rounder of the alpine sports; he had climbed the Mat-
terhorn in winter; he had won the *quatre pistes* at Val-
d'Isère, he had held the bobsleigh record at St. Moritz, he
had taken part in night ski-jumping in a dinner jacket and
beaten all the Swiss; he had done the *haute route* with
A. L. Rowse. These feats were not recorded, and Cassidy
himself was too humble to own to them. But from year to
year, humility or no, he had become a small monument to
their collective greatness. And if he had not climbed the
pedestal of his own accord, neither had he so far found
reason to dismount.

Such, till now, the nature of Cassidy's foreign haven. A
mountain fastness, preserving at high altitude and low tem-
perature many of the harmless visions which comprised his
aspiring English soul; an extra life, not unlike its English
fellow, but rendered innocent by the vastness of the scenery which contained it. Yet on that cold, blank morning
of a nameless, sunless month, crouched in the rear compartment of the tiny train, Cassidy found neither pleasure
nor comfort in the prospect of revisiting his mountain self.

Outside, the scenery was white and listless. What was not
white was black, or chalked by cloud and squalls of gritty
snow which glanced the leaking window he faced. The fog
had drained the mountains of their colour; and something
had drained Cassidy also, paled him, attacked the last op-

timism which till now had always somehow vanquished in his features. He rose because he was lifted, but his body was without motion, sketched in complementary greys against the high white desert of the sky and hills. Sometimes, as if obeying an unheard command, he intoned a note of music; and catching himself, lowered his eyes and frowned. He wore gloves; his railway ticket was stowed in the left palm, recalling a habit he had learned from a mother while travelling on trolley buses in coastal towns. He had shaved early, probably near Berne, and to himself he smelt of the many-too-many other people who used the same night sleeper from Ostend.

34

Where had he been, for how long, when?

These questions had concerned him off and on throughout the journey. They were not an obsession but much remained to disentangle, and Cassidy had a nasty feeling, particularly just before food, that he might already be dead. On the white screen of the window as it carried him indifferently upwards, a formless array of visions played before his largely uncritical eye. These pictures were his mind; his memory no longer served him, it had joined his fears. I am outside my own experience, he thought; I watch it through this window. A carriage whose name is Cassidy, peopled by empty seats. Outside me lies the desert, my destiny.

Watch. Ha!

He sits up sharply. Who is this? Mark's headmaster, carrying a number-four iron, army waterproofs over his frightful suit, a Russian fur hat clapped over his hollow face, lollops through the frosty mists. The raindrops run off him as if he were a military monument, circling his zealot's eyes and washing lighter lines over the bronze campaigner's skin. You taught me too, cried Cassidy, and you were not one day younger even in those days!

"Marazion's a tough crowd. Always were. Pity your boy's not playing."

"He is," said Cassidy, used to these confusions. "I'm Cassidy, Mark's boy," he explained, meaning father but getting it wrong.

Snow here, rain there. Battle rain, rolling across the football field in directionless, icy clouds, enveloping, not falling. Only the nearest players are visible, reeling and groping in the gas attack. A 1916 whistle blows; put on your gas masks, the Boche are coming over the top; hands on shoulders, boys, and follow me.

379

"Think, Saviours, *think!"* the Headmaster bellowed. "Look at that fool Meadows. Meadows you're a fool, a cretin, d'you hear? An imbecile. *You're* not Meadows are you?" the Headmaster asked.

"No," said Cassidy. "I'm Cassidy. Mark's father."

A fat child in a mud-soaked shirt hacked wildly at a sodden football.

"Sorry sir," he whispers, dying for the colonel, and rolls over, shot through the heart.

"Use it!" the Headmaster yelled in a quite unsimulated frenzy. "Oh my giddy aunts, my gracious Lord, don't *kick* it, use it, *keep* it! Oh my God, my God, oh *God."*

From somewhere the gas alarm sounded again and a thin burst of applause pattered wetly to nothing.

"Was it a goal?" Cassidy asked, craning his neck to show enthusiasm, as a trickle of rain slid across his collarbone. "It's very hard to see."

For some time an agonised exhalation was the only answer.

"I do tell them," the Headmaster whispers, turning to him wide-eyed with the pain of defeat. "They don't understand but I do tell them. Can't win without God. Goalie, referee, twelfth man, He's all of them. They don't understand of course. But one day they will, I'm sure. Don't you think so?"

"I believed you," Cassidy assured him. "You used to say the same to me and *I* believed you. Look, I'm Cassidy, Mark's father, I wonder whether I could talk to you for a minute about my son."

But the Headmaster is howling again, hopelessly, for God's support, as out of the fog the baleful clapping of cold, wet hands issues once more.

"Who *did* that? Who kicked it straight at their forward line? Who *was* it?"

"Cassidy," says someone.

"It's only because he's smaller than the others," says Cassidy. "He'll kick it the right way when he's bigger, I'm sure. Look, I'm going away for a bit, I wondered if I could take him out to tea."

"Keep at it *hard!* Attack, Saviours, attack! Buffoons! Oh you *stupid* little apes."

Once more the cavernous eyes turned to Cassidy, scanning him vainly for traces of divinity.

"Send him to Bryanston," he advised at last. "First class for broken homes, first class."

Turning his high thin back, the Headmaster loped forlornly into the fog.

And we Cassidys, it is a maxim of our broken home, we *always* travel first class. Beyond the window, a clump of Haverdown conifers struck suddenly out of the mist; at their foot stood a dismal pagoda painted dark brown and dusted with old snow.

"Unterwald," he read aloud.

And watched himself, seated in the locker room, smoking to defeat the smell; watching the ageing, vivid face of an eleven-year-old boy at the end of a long day's fight.

Mark.

A continental little boy, this Cassidy, confiding and easily moved; fond of touching people while he spoke to them; Mark, my lover.

"If I was a goalkeeper," Mark murmured, numbly untying his boots, "I could wear gloves."

"You did jolly well," said Cassidy, helping him.

Seeing him again after so long, Cassidy was reminded how small he was, how slender his wrists. The other boys looked on with contempt, trying to catch the traitor's actual words.

"I *loathe* football. Why do I have to play it if I loathe it? Why can't I do something gentle?"

"I loathed it too," said Cassidy to encourage him. "Always, I promise. At every school I went to."

"Then why make *me* do it?"

Following his naked son to the shower room, Cassidy thought: Only the smell is warm. The fetid, sour smell of football vests and Dorset mud, and battle dresses drying in tomorrow's sun. Mark was much thinner than the other children and his genitals were less developed: cold and shrivelled, a very jaded sex. The boys crammed in together, shorn prisoners, the whole team under one disgraceful jet.

"Mummy says she hasn't given me enough love," said Mark, over tea in the Spinning Wheel.

"That's something silly Heather said to her," said Cassidy.

The boy ate in silence.

"I'm going to Switzerland," said Cassidy.

"With Heather?"

"Alone."

"Why?"

"I thought I'd try and write a book," said Cassidy at random.

"How long will you be?"

"Few weeks."

"I don't miss Mummy. I miss you."

"You miss us both," said Cassidy.

"What's it about?" Mark asked suddenly, as if he knew already, had a hunch.

"What?"

"The book."

"It's a novel."

"Is that a story?"

"Yes."

"Tell it me."

"You can read it when you grow up."

The tea shop sold homemade sweets, fudge and chocolates with varied centres. Cassidy gave him ten shillings to make his own purchases.

"That's *miles* too much," said Mark hopelessly and gave him five back.

The boy waited at the gatepost, a slender, balancing creature, hugging himself in his grey pullover as he watched the warm Bentley glide towards him down the drive. Cassidy lowered the electric window and Mark kissed him, his small lips full upon his father's, crumby from tea, and cold from the wait in the evening air.

"I'm just not suited for this kind of education," Mark explained. "I'm not tough and I don't improve by being bullied."

"I wasn't suited to it either."

"Then take me away. It's pointless."

Mark has only a quantum of courage, he thought; I am using it up for him, spending it before he is old enough to spend it for himself.

"Here, have this," he said, and gave him his gold pencil,

sixty guineas from Asprey's, a private indulgence from another life.

"What'll *you* write with?"

"Oh a pen or something," said Cassidy, and left him, still at the gate, working the lead in and out, fair head bowed in concentration.

Sometimes it was too much for me to bear, that face, Cassidy thought, gazing back on a dead life; it was too hung in grief, too yellowed by pain and by the effort of understanding. Therefore I gave him things to turn his face away from me: gold or money, or something miniature to make him stoop.

Or perhaps, thought Cassidy consolingly, wiping the tears from the window, perhaps it wasn't Mark at all.

Perhaps—since objectivity at times of crisis is still the Managing Director's greatest single asset—perhaps this child was Aldo, back at Sherborne, the day Old Hugo called to see me on his way to Torquay; the day he ran the Great Bike Race for all comers, a nice quid for the winner and a nice ten bob note for second place.

To this moderately cohesive, moderately earthbound vision of his leavetaking, as he continued to climb the mountain, Cassidy proceeded to add others more fragmentary and less capable of verification; and in the course of this put to himself questions of a quite metaphysical nature.

Had Christmas passed, for instance? Sometimes a shadow crossed the sterile white window, closing downwards from the left corner like a drop of blood upon his field of view, and he smelt the winter evenings drawing in, and glimpsed the spectral outline of a dusk-lit pine tree frosted on its windward side, the way they grew at Christmas in the wide bow-windows of the Crescent. At Mittelwald, still pondering this question, he was not surprised to observe the face of Granny Groat appear before him, drawn and sleepless, and took it as further proof that the feast was past: for only Christmas could strain her so severely. Her head was not framed centrally—she had got it wrong in some way—and she was waiting stubbornly on the wrong side of the track, so that he felt her presence behind him and had to turn to make the recognition. Her wide, witless eyes, doubled and vulnerable, washed blue by her tinted spectacles, were bright and frightened, but the dabs of fur at her collar and the rouge at her cheeks announced quite clearly that she was on her way to church. Also, she wore a paper hat; a festive yellow creation, mannishly grotesque.

Also, she carried a Christmas cracker in her twitching hand.

Ah but for what ceremony? A funeral?

Is she wearing black for instance? The Chinese are known to loose off firecrackers for the dead.

The train lurched forward, Groat was gone.

Well, it was not so improbable; he might very well be dead; others were. Such an explanation had been in the air for several days and very many nights. A lot of people are dead and it's *perfectly* natural, but still. Nor had he far to look for the cause of death. Suppose Old Hugo's green hand grenade, contrary to Cassidy's impression at the time, had after all exploded and removed him to another life?

To *this* life, in fact?

And that instead of merely travelling to Sainte-Angèle, he was ascending to heaven; and the railway guards were angels, hence the village name?

Momentarily stirred to optimism by this small hope of non-existence, Cassidy closed his heated eyes and with each hand lightly touched the other, determining its outlines. A don experiments upon his own body, the Haldane tradition, I'll get a knighthood yet. Then in an upward movement to the face—akin to washing, such gestures are made often by men in motion—with both hands together glumly located his nose and ample eyebrows, tip of tongue and youthful forelock; confirming, if confirmation were still needed, that though his spirit might be climbing, it was still attached to its terrestrial frame.

And that Old Hugo's hand grenade, for all his loud assurances, had been, like the rest of his father's armoury, a dud.

This incident involving War Department explosives was not, for security reasons, shown upon the white screen, but conveyed to Cassidy by the intimate smell of wet clover as he lay in the field somewhere in England, face downward, tampering wretchedly with the pin. Also it may have been—but *only* may have been—a dream; this much your Chairman will concede. Mr. Lemming, you may add that to the Minutes.

To reconstruct: this grenade is a gift, no father can do more. This grenade, Old Hugo has assured him, freeing it of its oily rags and bringing it to the lightest window in the penthouse, this poorly painted grenade, dull green but chipping even under wraps, is not only a gift, a truly wonderful gift, it is one of the finest grenades ever manufactured.

"They don't *make* a grenade like that today. You can scour London, I'm telling you, Aldo: a grenade like that is totally unfindable, isn't it, Blue?"

The grenade is also the climactic of a father's many endowments to his son:

"I've given you the *final* freedom, d'you hear? Look at that then: life and death, you owe them *all* to me. That's the most fantastic sacrifice any father can make, and I'm making it, right, Blue?"

But here is the nub, here is the curse of the Cassidys, they succeed in all but the consummation: the pin has rusted into its housing, the weakly boy cannot loosen it.

"*Pull.* Jesus Christ All Ruddy Mighty, Blue, after all I've done for him, after all the fantastic sacrifices I made for him, look at *that! He can't even pull the stupid pin!*"

"But he's not a *lion*, dear, is he though, not like *you*," Bluebridge whickers, handing him the flask. "*Go* on Aldo dear," she begs, calling to him *sotto voce* where he lies. "Try, Aldo, for your Daddy's sake, *please. Try.*"

"I am trying," Cassidy retorts churlishly, but still there is no apocalypse.

Thoroughly disenchanted, the family drives home in a temper, conversation zero till they reach the penthouse.

For a while to his great relief he thought of nothing. The train paused at certain intermediate stations, names were shouted and ignored. These stations offered no passengers, and received none in return. They were stages, formalities of religious progress as the little train continued its pilgrimage up the white hill.

Reaching a plateau, the engine relaxed its exertions and a sense of ease replaced the frenzied clatter. I am in the Bentley, Cassidy thought; I am in Superpram.

It is the Bentley which has subdued the clanging couplings and damped the eager vibrations of the cushion springs under the thin velveteen; the Bentley's English calm which has muffled the hysteria of the foreign guards.

I am inviolate.

Barely had he formulated this pleasing notion however than his sense of security was shattered by the entry of *little* Hugo (grandson of the great hotelier) who, undaunted by costly fastenings of his father's manufacture, had forced open the door and settled himself in the passenger seat. Lifting the child free, Cassidy carried him back to the house.

Hugo white, not crying, clutching a Pan Am flightbag filled with the few things he would need: a gramophone record, a new string for his toboggan.

Hugo very hot under the arms as they embraced once more on the doorstep.

Hugo white, and still not crying.

"Come along Hug," says Mrs. Groat. "Mummy wants you." At the fifth floor, Sandra's own now, John Elderman's silhouette; valium for a broken heart.

Heather Ast is hammering at the carriage window.

"I won't hear you," Cassidy assures her through the electrically closed glass of the Bentley. "I just won't. I never want to see you again, Heather. It's as bad as that."

The glass is too thick, she hears nothing.

You'll be a Groat in ten years, Heather; you'll all be Groats. Dust to dust, groat to groat, it's a woman's destiny, she has no other.

Mercifully, he has entered a tunnel, the change distracts him. At its end, five minutes away, lies Oberwald, the up-

per forest. After Oberwald comes Sainte-Angèle of the
Peaks; there is no halt between them.

With the tunnel, a moment's dark before the lights go
up. Wooden palings, painted cheap yellow by the overhead
bulbs, crowd the once-white window, flick past in a be-
wildering curve, like the splinted fingers of a smashed hand
waved across his passive face. The sounds are magnified in
this long cave. History, geology, not to speak of countless
set-texts from mediaeval faculties at Oxford, all deepen
and intensify the underground experience. Minotaurs, her-
mits, martyrs, miners, incarcerated since the first construc-
tions, howl and clank their chains, for this is under ground,
where old men scratch for knowledge, gold, and death.
Once, a few years ago, looking through the same window
at the same dull timbers, Cassidy found himself staring
into the black, patient eyes of a chamois crammed against
the tunnel wall. Reaching the village he at once made
representations to the station master in the interest of the
local wild life. There was nothing to be done, the official
said, when he had listened very carefully to the good man's
case, the chamois had been dead for several days.

These yellow lights are dull; they make me sleepy.

How long since he had slept?

Was there a record of how many nights? Mr. Lemming,
you might consult the Minutes.

Or was it *one* night doled out among different beds
and floors? The screaming now—be forensic—where did
the screaming fit in as she held my foot, Sandra my longstanding wife, to keep me in the bedroom? Held it against
her head, lying full length on the tasteful curly Wilton,
wetting Christ's ankle with her tears? Was that *one* incident of an eventful night, or a *whole* night by itself? Put
another way, in Sandra's Women's Army voice: *Who
broke the clock?* That grandfather clock. *Who broke it?*
Four hundred quid's worth of sixteenth-century inlay toppled from its hall stand? *Own up! It's perfectly natural to
break a clock I simply want to know who did it. I'll
count five, if no culprit volunteers I shall not finish the
sentence.*

One . . .

The first suspect (class has *much* to do with crime) is Snaps' libidinous visualizer, preaching free love over the bannisters in his corduroy claret suit. The resentful fellow gave the clock a push, it was his way of closing the generation gap.

But wait, Snaps has fled her lair, taking her visualizer with her. Hied herself to Bournemouth, pregnancy the cause, she likes to have them by the sea, water being ever preferable to air.

Two ...

Who else? Quick, who else?

Granny Groat, putative mother-in-law, sometime mother of the accused, floundering through dark corridors to save the electricity: *she* did it ...

Not guilty, alas. Decisive gestures are not her style, not even by mistake.

Three. I'm warning you ...

Very well: *you* did it! Sandra herself, wet-bibbed from crying, no strength left to sleep; Sandra, in her last exhaustion, lurched into the clock, toppled it, before she fell herself?

Not guilty. She would own up.

Four ...

Help! I accuse old Hugo, satanist, worker of spells, possessor of an evil eye! Staring out of the penthouse window, sipping a nice touch of brandy and ginger, the old wizard deliberately carved the air with a familiar gesture of his hand and set up waves of disturbance which found their way to Abalone Crescent and so destroyed the instrument of time!

"Father I need a bed."

"Then go home, it's waiting for you, isn't it?"

"Father, put me to bed. Please."

"Go home! You'll be a delinquent if you don't remarry that bitch, get out, get out, get out!"

The tunnel continued; to dance but not to sleep.

"Angie I need a bed."

Angie Mawdray, standing at her own front door, was dressed in a light bedwrap which did not conceal one side of her body.

"It's no good, Aldo," she said. "Honest."

"But Angie I only want to sleep."

"Then go to a hotel, Aldo, you can't come here, you know you can't, not *now*."

"But Angie."

"I'm *married*," she reminded him, rather sternly. *"You* remember, Aldo, you organised the whip-round."

"Of course," said Cassidy. "Of course I did, I'm sorry. Good evening Meale, how's it going?"

From under Che Guevara's uncompromising stare, the pallid face of Meale nodded respectfully to his master. He would have stood up no doubt, but his nakedness was against him.

"Good evening, Mister Aldo, step in, sir, do. Sorry about the mess."

"Come in the afternoons," Angie whispered. "I'm only working mornings, aren't I, *silly?*"

Went to Kurt's? Or stayed at Angie's after all? Certainly he felt a limpness round the loins, a sense of *after* rather than *before*. Did he then after all enjoy the very skilled embraces of Miss Mawdray the well-known top secretary, while Meale's apologetic eye turned sensibly away for the visit of the Chairman?

"You've been very good to us Mister Aldo, we don't know how to thank you, I'm sure."

"Think nothing of it," says the old boulevardier, nicely lodged among the dewy folds. *"You young people need a start in life."*

A howl from the engine. Daylight soon? Not in Kurt's grey, uncomfortable rooms; even the windows are smoked against the sun.

"Kurt, I need a bed."

Kurt had no one in his apartment, not Angie Mawdray, not Lemming, not Snaps, not Blue, not Faulk, not even Meale. He wore a grey Swiss dressing gown of best Swiss silk, and when Cassidy was tucked unsafely in the ever-prepared spare room he came to see him with a long white cup of Swiss Ovomaltine.

"No, Kurt."

"But Cassidy my dear fellow you *know* you are one of us. Listen. *One,* you prefer the company of men, correct?"

"Correct, but—"

"*Two* your physical encounters with women have been totally without satisfaction. Cassidy, look here I mean my God I can *tell*, I can see it in your eyes, anyone can. *Three*—"

"Kurt honestly, I would if I wanted, I promise. I'm not ashamed any more. I wanted to at school but that's just because there weren't any girls about. That's the truth. I've got too much sense of humour, Kurt. I think of you lying there with nothing on, holding it, and I get the giggles. I mean *what for* . . . do you see what I'm getting at?"

"Goodnight Cassidy."

"Goodnight, Kurt. And thanks."

"And look here, one day we climb the Eiger, right?"

"Right."

Dozing, he quite hoped Kurt would come back: exhaustion erodes the moral will as well as the sense of humour. But Kurt didn't. So Cassidy listened to the traffic instead, and wondered: does he sleep, or dream of me?

Daylight, and another warning scream from the small, incorruptible engine. The train has stuck. The doors hiss and fall open. The porter is calling Sainte-Angèle.

He called it in the *patois*, it could have been Michel Angelo or England. He called it loud, above the three-toned clanging of the mountain bell; he carolled it for Christmas past or coming, in a voice of male dominance which echoed over the empty station. He called it straight at Cassidy through the smeared white window of his first-class carriage; and if you want to go farther you must change. He called it as if it were Cassidy's own name, his last walk and his last stopping place. The porter was a bearded man and wore a badge of office on his smock. His eyes were masked by heavy black brows, and by the black shadow of his black peaked cap. Answering the summons, Cassidy got up at once, stepped blithely on to the empty platform, his overnight bag swinging in his strong hand.

"Tomorrow," said the porter consolingly, "we get *plenty* snow."

"Ah but tomorrow doesn't often come, does it?" Cassidy replied, never at a loss to cap a pleasantry.

The weather which greeted Cassidy at Sainte-Angèle was like a meteorological extension of the confusion which had recently taken possession of his mind. The best of holiday resorts has its uncongenial seasons, and not even Sainte-Angèle, famed though she may be for her dependable and temperate character, is exempt from nature's immutable laws. In winter, as a rule, her snowclad village street is a jubilant carnival of bobble-hats, horse-sledges, and brilliant shop windows, where Europe's affluent swains rub shoulders with the girls of Kensal Rise, and many insincere contracts of love are closed in the surrounding forests. In summer, their less pecunious teachers and elders stride vigorously into the flower-laden slopes and refresh themselves beside Goethe's ebullient streams, while children in traditional costume chant age-old songs in praise of chastity and cattle. Spring is a sudden and lovely time, with impatient flowers bursting through the late snow; while autumn as the first snows fall brings back forgotten hours of breathless, church-like quiet between the bustle of two hectic seasons.

But there are days, as every alpine visitor must know, when this pleasing pattern is without apparent reason violently shattered; when the seasons suddenly tire of their place in the natural cycle and, using all the weapons of their armoury, do violent battle until they have reached exhaustion. In place of winter's magic the village is assailed by querulous rains and morose, unheated nights, when thunder alternates with hybrid sleet and neither stars nor sun can pierce the swirling cloud banks. Worse, a *foehn* may come, the sick south wind that strikes the mountains like a plague, rotting giant slabs of snow and poisoning the temper of both the villagers and their guests. And when at last it takes itself away, the brown patches on the hillsides are laid out like the dead, the sky is white and empty, and the birds have gone. This *foehn* is the mountains' curse; nowhere is safe from it.

The first symptoms are external: a sourceless dripping of water, a mysterious departure of air and colour. With this depletion of the atmosphere comes a gradual draining of human energy, a sense of moral listlessness, like a constipation of the mental faculties, which spreads gradually over the whole psychic body until it has blocked all outlets. At such times, waiting for the storm, a man may smoke a cigar halfway down the village street and the trace of it will be there tomorrow, the smoke and the smell lingering in the dead air at the very place where he stood. Sometimes there is no storm at all. The lull ends and the cold returns. Or a hurricane strikes: a black, raging *Walpurgisnacht* with winds of sixty, seventy miles an hour. The high street is strewn with broken sticks, the tarmac is showing through the snow, and you would think a river has slid by in the darkness on its way from the peaks to the valley.

It was the *foehn* which ruled now.

The sight reminded Cassidy of a wet day at Lord's cricket ground. The village's two porters stood together like umpires, clutching their smocks to their middles and agreeing it was impossible. Above him, but very close, the superb twin peaks of the Angelhorn hung like dirty laundry from the grey sky. The snow was mostly gone. The clock said ten-fifteen, but it might have been stuck for years. Making his way towards the restaurant he thought: *This is how we die, alone and cold and out of breath, suspended between white places.*

"Hullo lover," said Shamus quietly. "Looking for someone are we?"

"Hullo," said Cassidy.

35

Haverdown woodsmoke lingered in the damp air, antlers loomed along the brown walls. A group of dark-faced labourers sat drinking beer. Away from them, at their own sad place, the waitresses read German magazines, secretly panting from the *foehn* like patients in a doctor's waiting room.

He was sitting near the bar, in an alcove, at a big round table all to himself, under the crossed guns of the Sainte-Angèle shooting club. A silk flag, stitched by the ladies of the community, proclaimed the village loyalty to William Tell. The alcove had a Flemish darkness, homely and confiding; the pewter glinted comfortably, like well-earned coin. He was drinking *café crème* and he had lost weight. A streak of white light from the window ran down the death-coat like a recent shock. He wore no hat and no beard; his face looked bared, and vulnerable, and very pale. Cassidy moved in beside him, holding his overnight bag in his arms like Hugo's beach crocodile, then shunting it down the polished bench, then dumping it on the floor between them with a sloppy thud.

Sitting down, he saw the gun.

It lay on Shamus' lap, a sleek pet, the barrel towards Cassidy. It was essentially a military weapon, and probably an officers' issue from the First World War. Only a full-grown officer could have worn it, however, because the barrel was about twelve inches long. Or it might have been a target pistol from the days when you steadied your weapon on your left forearm, and the range sergeant yelled "Well shot sir" when you hit a man-sized target. A lanyard was fastened to the butt. From the free end dangled a pink powder-puff.

In the kitchen, the wireless was broadcasting a Swiss time signal, a very war-like noise.

Cassidy ordered coffee, *café crème*, like the gentleman's. The waiter remembered him well. Mr. Cassidy who tips. He brought a gingham tablecloth and spread it with affection. He laid out cutlery and Maggi sauce and toothpicks in a silver box. And the children, the waiter enquired, they were well?

Fine.

They were not, for instance, suffering from the English habit of wearing short trousers?

Not noticeably, Cassidy said.

And they were hunting, hunting the foxes and the chamois?

At present, said Cassidy, they were at school.

Ah, said the waiter, pursing his lips, *Eton:* he had heard that standards had fallen.

"She's waiting," said Shamus.

They set off up the hill.

Pulling with all his strength, Cassidy found that the tape was cutting his shoulder. If he had not been wearing his camelhair coat, in fact, it would have broken the skin. The tape was of nylon, six foot of it and bright red, he held it with both hands, one at the chest and one at the waist, making a harness of it as he strained forward. Twice he had asked Shamus to walk, but received no useful answer beyond an impatient wave of the gun barrel, and now Shamus was sitting upright with Cassidy's overnight bag across his knee, throwing out the things he didn't like. The silver hairbrush had already gone, sliding like a puck backwards down the icy path, bobbing and spinning over the half-frozen eddies of snow and ice. He had thought he was fit: squash at the Lansdowne, tennis at Queen's, not to mention the stairs at Abalone Crescent. But his flannel shirt was drenched by the time they left the railway line, and his heart, unaccustomed to the change of altitude, was already thumping sickly. Fitness is relative, he told himself. After all, he's at least my weight.

Even taken downwards, the path was unsuitable for tobogganing.

From the chalet, it wound at first through scattered woods where snow barely covered the boulders, and jagged tree trunks awaited the careless navigator. Crossing an avalanche gully, it descended by way of two steep bends to a poorly fenced ramp which, being much in use by pedestrians, was strewn with grit which tore at the runners and slewed them off course. If other, hardier children ignored these hazards, Cassidy's did not, for it was one of his recurring nightmares that they would have an accident here, that Hugo would skid under a train, Mark would crush his head against a signal post, and he had entirely proscribed the route on pain of punishment. Uphill, though no doubt safer, the path was even less attractive.

Shamus had chosen Mark's toboggan, probably because of the crazy daisies which were glued to its plastic base. It was a good toboggan of its kind, a prototype sent up by a Swiss correspondent for possible exploitation on the English market. At first the design had told in its favour. But soon the broad keel was dragging heavily in the slush, and Cassidy was obliged to lean far forward into the hill in order to get enough purchase. His leather-soled London shoes slipped with every step; occasionally hauling at the tapes, he slid backwards into the bow of the toboggan, grazing his frozen heels against the plastic point; and when this happened Shamus would urge him forward with a distracted oath. The night case had gone. There was nothing in it, apparently, which Shamus thought worth keeping, so he had thrown it overboard to improve the unsprung weight, and now he was aiming the gun distractedly at whatever offered itself; a bird on the roof of a hotel, a passing pedestrian, a dog.

"My dear Mr. Cassidy, how *are* you?"

Introductions; sherry on Sunday, come round after church. Shamus bows and waves the gun; shrieks of merriment. A Mrs. Horegrove or Haregrave, a senior senator of the Club.

"What a *dangerous*-looking burden!"

"It's Hugo's," Cassidy explained, panting through his smiles. "We took it to be mended. You know what he's like about guns."

"My dear, *whatever* would Sandra say?"

About Shamus or the gun? Cassidy wanted to ask, for her eyes were moving from one to the other with mounting surprise.

"Go away," Shamus screamed at her, suddenly losing patience, and picking up a convenient stick, threw it hard at her feet. "Prole. Get out or I'll shoot you."

The lady withdrew.

A heap of horse manure obstructed their progress. Cassidy took the left side, favouring the verge.

"Pull, you bugger," Shamus ordered, still angry. "Mush, mush, *pull.*"

In the forest, the going was easier. The trodden snow, sheltered by the trees, had neither melted nor frozen; sometimes, for short distances, they even went downhill, so that Cassidy had to run ahead in order to remain covered by the gun. At such moments, Shamus became nervous and issued conflicting orders: lift your hands, put them down, keep left, keep right, and Cassidy obeyed them all, thinking of nothing, not even the hole in his back. The trees parted, giving a view of the brown valley and the banks of mist that rose like oil smoke from its narrow floor. They saw the Angelhorn in a fragment of perfect blue, its fresh snow glittering in the high sunlight.

And stopped.

"Hey, you," said Shamus quietly.

"Yes?"

"Give us a kiss."

His hands still above his head, Cassidy walked back to the toboggan, stooped, and kissed Shamus on the cheek.

"More," said Shamus. And at last: "It's all *right,* lover, it's all *right,*" he whispered, pushing away the tears. "Shamus fix it. Promise. We're big enough, lover. We can make it."

"Of course we can," said Cassidy.

"Make history," said Shamus. "Be a great first, lover. We'll beat the whole fucking system."

"Will you walk now?" Cassidy asked, after more breathless hugs. "I'm a bit tired actually."

Shamus shook his head. "Lover, I got to toughen you up, this is a very vigorous course, very vigorous indeed. Takes *grip.* Faith, remember? For both of us?"

"I remember," said Cassidy, and picked the tape out of the snow.

The clouds covered them. They must have left the trees without his noticing, and walked blindly into the ambush of the fog. Sightless, Cassidy lost his balance and fell forward. Not even the path existed, for its edges were lost in the downward gust of wet mist, and his hands, grasping the slope before him, were clutching an invisible enemy. He struggled forward again.

"Where are you?"

"Here."

"Pull, lover," Shamus warned. "Keep pulling, lover, or it's shootibangs."

As suddenly as it had descended the cloud cleared and the house stood clean and waiting on its own expensive patch of snowclad hillock, fifteen pounds a square meter, "Mr. and Mrs. Aldo Cassidy" framed beside the bell button and Helen wife of Shamus painted on the balcony.

Painted on the sized, white canvas of the drifting fog, in matt half-tones, a fraction out of register.

Tall, from where they looked up at her; wearing a head scarf of Sandra's; hands set apart on the rail, face turned sharply towards the path, not seeing them but hearing their footsteps in the slush, and perhaps the zigzag echo of their voices.

"Cassidy?"

"She's a bit blue," Shamus warned in a whisper coming up beside him. "Where I belted her. Sorry about that, didn't mean to damage the goods."

"Cassidy?" she repeated, still blind but guessing at the sound.

For a moment longer, she scanned the path not realising they were there beneath her. Waiting, as all women wait. Using her body to catch the sound. Waiting for a ship, or a child, or a lover; upright, taut, vibrant.

"We're just below you," said Cassidy.

The bruise was on the cheekbone, the left one, he recorded; Shamus had hit her with his right hand, a hook probably; a hard wide one from the side, not at all unlike the mark on Sal that evening they had gone to her in Cable

Street. By the time he had opened the door she was in the hall. She closed her eyes long before he touched her, the good one and the bad one, and he heard her whisper "Cassidy" as her arms came gently round him; and he felt her shaking as if she had a fever.

"On the *mouth*," Shamus shouted from behind. "Jesus. What is this, a fucking convent?"

So he kissed her on the mouth; she tasted just a little of blood, as if she had had a tooth out.

The drawing room—it was his own design—was long and perhaps too thin for comfort. The balcony ran the whole length of it, mastering the three views: the valley, the village, and the mountain range. At one end, near the kitchen, was a pine dining recess and Helen had set the table for three, using the best napkins and the beeswax candles from the top left drawer.

"She's a bit thin," Shamus explained. "Because I locked her up till you came."

"You told me," Cassidy said.

"Not *blaming* people, lover? Got to lock princesses in towers, haven't we? Can't have the bitches whoring all over the realm."

Whether she had lost weight or not, Helen's eyes had a defiant brightness, like the courage of the very sick.

"I managed to get a duck," she said. "I seem to remember it's your favourite."

"Oh," said Cassidy. "Oh thanks."

"You do still like it, don't you?" she asked very earnestly, offering him pretzels from the compartmented red plate which Sandra used for curries.

"Rather," said Cassidy.

"I thought you might have gone off it."

"No, no."

"It's only frozen. I tried to get a fresh one, but they just . . ." She dried up, then began again. "It's so difficult on the telephone, all in a foreign language . . . he wouldn't let me out, not at all. He's even burnt my passport."

"I know," said Cassidy.

She was crying a little so he led her to the kitchen, holding her under the elbow. She leaned against him, resting her head on his shoulder, and breathed very deeply, filling her lungs with the strength of his presence.

"Hello hellbeef."

"Hi."

"He just sort of . . . knew. He didn't guess, or suspect, or anything ordinary, he *knew*. What's it called when you mop it up through the pores?"

"Osmosis."

"Well he's got it. Double osmosis. I'm crying because I'm tired that's all. I'm not sad, I'm tired."

"I know."

"Are you tired, Cassidy?"

"A bit."

"He wouldn't let me lie down. I had to sleep standing up. Like a horse."

She was crying a great deal; he guessed she had been crying for several days and now it was habit, she cried when the wind changed and when the wind stopped or when it started again, and this was the *foehn*, it changed all the time.

"Cassidy."

"Yes."

"You'd have come anyway, wouldn't you? Whether he told you to or not?"

"Of course."

"He laughed. Every day you didn't come, he laughed and said you never would. Then in between he got sad. *Come on lover*, he said, *big boy now, where are you?* Then he got loving to me and told me to pray for you."

"I had a lot to do my end too."

"How did the bosscow take it?"

Through her tears he heard Sandra's scream echoing in the stairwell, up and down, like Hugo's magic bouncing ball, between the fine cornice and the flagstone floor.

"Fine. No problem. She was happier, really . . . knowing."

"It was easy here too, really . . . once he knew I loved you."

"I better go back now," said Cassidy.

"Yes. Yes he needs you."

With a little pat of encouragement she urged him on his way.

Shamus was at the long window. He had discovered Cassidy's binoculars and was trying to train them on the bedrooms of a distant hotel. Bored, he tossed them to the floor and sauntered to the bookshelves. The gun was stuck in his waistband; the powder puff dangled idly from his fingers.

"Someone's big on Ibsen," he observed distractedly.

"Sandra."

"I like that lady. Always did. Better than Helen, anyway."

While Helen cooked, the two men played Mark's mouse game. The mouse, which was plastic, was fed into a slide. After it had run about, jumped a gap, slipped through several small holes, it entered a narrow cage and tripped a bell. The bell rang, the door closed, the mouse was caught. It was not a competitive game, since there was no way of losing, and therefore none of winning either, but it was a good game in the circumstances because it enabled Shamus to keep one hand on the gun. They had not had many turns however before Shamus grew restless and, using the poker from the fireplace, smashed the outer end of the cage. After that the mouse escaped, and Shamus became easy again, and even smiled, patting Cassidy on the shoulder by way of encouragement.

"Love you, lover."

"Love you," said Cassidy.

"Shamus has been all over Europe," said Helen encouragingly, emerging from the kitchen with a dish. "Haven't you, Shamus? Marseilles he went to, Milan, Rome . . ." She rehearsed these cities as if they would spark him, much as she might sing the praises of her sullen child, but Shamus remained unresponsive. "And his book is going wonderfully, he's been working *right up to the moment when you came,* haven't you Shamus? Write, write, write from morning till evening."

"Get the fucking duck," said Shamus. "And shut up."

"Cassidy, *wine,*" Helen reminded him with a discreet smile. "We ought to have red I suppose, with poultry."

"I'll fetch it," said Cassidy, making for the door.

"Catch," said Shamus, and threw him a large bunch of keys.

Hard, so that they smashed against the wood beside his head, and smashed again, a second time, on to the wood floor.

Many were duplicates, Cassidy noticed, picking them up. He must have collected them all together when he locked her in the attic.

The oven was the problem. It didn't seem to heat like English ovens, Helen said, it didn't come on inside when you turned the knob.

"It's infrared," said Cassidy, and showed her how it worked.

Nevertheless, the bird was still raw.

"Oh dear," said Helen. "I'll put it back."

Cassidy protested: nonsense, duck *should* be red, that was exactly how he liked it.

Shamus also protested, but for different reasons. No she fucking well wouldn't. If he was going to make history, he said, he wasn't going to be delayed by an uncooked duck.

It fell to Cassidy, therefore, with his finely tuned social instinct, once again to lead the lunchtime conversation. Choosing a theme at random—it was several years since he had seen an English newspaper—he heard himself discussing the rising tide of violence in England, and more particularly the bomb outrage recently perpetrated against a Conservative Minister. He had no use for nihilists, he said. If a man had a grudge, let him speak out, Cassidy would be the first to listen. And what, after all, was the parliamentary system for if we were to be blackmailed by any Tom, Dick, and Harry who held a contrary view to our own?

"I mean what do they want to achieve, for God's sake? Apart from the destruction of society. It's the one question they can never answer. 'All right,' I'd say to them, 'fine: the world's yours. Now tell me what you're going to do with it. How you're going to cure the sick and support the old and defend us against those madmen in China?' Well don't you agree?" he asked, wondering whether he might leave the rest of his duck.

Helen and Shamus had drawn close together, and Helen was kissing and comforting him, smoothing his hair and laying her hand across his brow.

"We've rather been out of touch with English news,"

she said over his shoulder. She was cutting up his food so that he could keep hold of the gun. "Shamus tried your wireless but I'm afraid it broke, didn't it darling?"

"Never mind," said Cassidy generously.

He offered them mashed potato, but they declined.

"Hey, Cassidy," said Shamus, brightening under Helen's care, "what do you think of her cooking?"

"Well, if this is anything to go by, it's excellent," said Cassidy. "But after all, I sampled it in London too."

"Better than the bosscow's?"

"Much," Cassidy lied heartily.

While Helen cleared, Shamus delved in his pocket and produced a small leather-bound volume, which he opened on his knee. It was the size of a diary but fatter, with gold leaf at the edges. Studying it, he appeared to come across passages of particular relevance, for he marked them in heavy ink, using the gun to hold the pages flat.

"It is loaded is it?" Cassidy asked, making his question sound as casual as circumstances allowed.

"Of *course* it is," Helen called proudly from the kitchen. "Shamus never fired a blank in his life, did you darling?"

It's the wine, thought Cassidy, it's lulled him. He had chosen a heavy Burgundy, twenty-eight francs a bottle but renowned for its soporific qualities.

Waiting for Helen again, the two men went on to the balcony for target practice. Ammunition was not a problem, for the pockets of the deathcoat were filled with bullets of different bores and calibres, and though some were clearly too large, quite a number appeared to be suitable.

First, at Shamus' request, Cassidy demonstrated the safety catch.

"It's here," he said, pointing. "You push it away from you."

"Will it shoot?"

"Not when it's on, no."

"This on?"

"No. The other way."

Pointing the pistol at Cassidy's head he pulled the trigger but nothing happened.

"And if I do it this way—"

"Then it shoots. Shamus, shouldn't we wait till the fog's cleared?"

The fog in fact had thickened; beyond it, not far away, he could hear rain falling, and that mysterious grumbling of agricultural machinery which seemed always to fill the valley in times of unseasonable stillness. While they stood there, two skiers, muffled like ghostly abbots, lurched down the trail in the direction of the station and vanished, their skis rasping in the watery snow. Shamus, who was already aiming at them as they disappeared, lowered the gun with an exclamation of annoyance and peered round for other game.

"What's the range of this thing, anyway?"

"About forty yards for accuracy. It'll kill at three hundred."

"It won't fire rapid will it?"

"No."

"I tried to get dumdums but they didn't have any." He aimed the gun again, this time at a chimney on the other side of the path. "She loves you rotten."

"I know."

"And you're equally passionate about her. You pine every minute out of her sight. You can't get to sleep quick enough to dream of her, you can't wake soon enough to come and prise her from my arms. Wife, veg, Bentley are as nothing beside your overwhelming, all-consuming, all-dignifying passion for her?"

Turning his head he gazed at Cassidy over the barrel of the raised gun.

"Poor old lover, what else could we do? Couldn't let you rot out there, could we, all on your own in the cold? Not when we spend our whole fucking lives looking for just what you've found. I mean . . . what kind of man would dig twenty years for gold and not want it when he makes a strike? Eh?"

"No one."

Shamus' gaze had not left his face.

"No one," Cassidy repeated.

"Attaboy," said Shamus, thrilling to him with a sudden brilliant smile.

Taking his arm he led him back to the drawing room.

"Helen," he shouted, still holding Cassidy's arm. "Get ready, you cow! *Courage,* lover," he whispered. "Got to be brave soldier now."

Cassidy nodded.

"Otherwise Papa have to shoot you."

Again he nodded.

"Shan't be five minutes," Helen called from the bedroom.

Together they moved the table into the centre of the room.

"We need *witnesses*," said Shamus from the kitchen. "How the fuck can I be the midwife of history when there aren't any witnesses?" He emerged with a tablecloth, a white damask, part of Sandra's trousseau. "Christ, *those* could do with a rub I must say," he said, looking critically at Cassidy's shoes, which had suffered considerably from the walk from the station. "And what's with those linoleum trousers, then, what the hell are *they* all about?"

"They're cavalry twill," said Cassidy. "They're the best I've got out here."

He had bought them after he committed suicide; the others were ruined by the clover.

"I wish we had *all* the right kit," said Shamus with a sigh.

Helen was wearing a new grey suit, one of Sandra's bought in Berne last year specially for Club cocktail parties; a little old-fashioned for some tastes, but very neat all the same, with flashes of green on the collar and a matching scarf to cover her throat. She came in rather slowly, eyes shining; she had put fresh powder on her bruise and she carried a small bunch of cyclamen heads cut from the plant in the kitchen. Her mouth was stretched tight, probably a smile. The flowers trembled and she was nervous.

"That's her is it?" Shamus asked, as if he had suddenly gone blind.

He was looking out of the window, his back towards them. His shoulders had risen very high. Neither Helen nor Cassidy could see his face, but they could hear him humming in low, flat tones.

36

Shamus had changed colour.

Not blushed or paled, white to red, red to white, according to the supposed laws of mediaeval ballad; simply, his whole person appeared to have taken on the darker, stormy colours of his fervent mood. Watching him, Cassidy dully recognized what he had always known but not till now understood: that Shamus had no physical constancy, no shape or profile to be remembered by; that he was as changeful as the sky outside the window; as blustering, as calm, as light or dark, as driven or as still; and that Cassidy in his mind had spent too long defining him, mistaking his presence for a kind of familiarity; and that he might as well have tried to love the wind as tame this man for the drawing rooms where Cassidy was at home. He had known Shamus when he was six foot tall and had the softness of a dancer; when he was squat and violent, and his shoulders were rounded like a wrestler's; he had known him male and female, child and man, lover and bully; but as a single man he would never know him. That's why he wrote, thought Cassidy, placing him already in the past; he had to make one person of all that army. That's why he was so jealous of God: God has a kingdom and can absorb us all, God rejoices in the variety of his images, God has cathedrals to contain his countless likenesses; but Shamus has only this one body and must drag himself round the world pretending to be one person, that is the penalty of being Shamus, of never surrendering to one place or one woman.

Shamus was also having trouble with the gun.

His new black dressing gown, brought out by Helen, fitted him well, but the cord was not strong enough to carry the weight of such a heavy weapon. Having tried without success to strap it to his hip, he ordered Helen to knot it at the shoulder. But the gun, swinging free, interfered with his sight of the gold-edged book, and in the end he dumped it irritably on the table between the lighted candles.

"Now sit down," he commanded, indicating the sofa. "Close. Hold hands and shut up, both of you." About to go on, his eye caught Helen's beatific smile and he was moved suddenly to anger.

"Stop leering!" he shouted at her, brandishing the gun.

"I wasn't leering. I was loving you."

Replacing the gun, he draped himself in the damask tablecloth, folding it lengthways and hanging it round his neck, so that the two ends dangled forward like a long scarf.

"What the hell's that rumbling?" he muttered, looking towards the window.

"It's the central heating. It goes on and off automatically. The south wind upsets the thermostat."

"Now pay attention," said Shamus, "while I define love."

He held the small book closed in his left hand, the gold-lined pages outward.

"Love," Shamus proclaimed, as they settled nervously to silence, "love is the bridge between what we *are* and what we can *become*. Love is the measure—" looking at Helen "—of our potential. I said stop leering!"

"It's only nervousness," Helen insisted rather pathetically. "I was exactly the same at *our* wedding, you know I was."

"Shamus," said Helen softly. "Shamus."

His eye was on the long window which was now quite blanked out by fog. Raindrops were bursting on the pane like inner actions of the glass, coming from nowhere, held there, not running.

"Lover?" he said, head away from them still, with the alertness of the blind.

"Yes."

"Why did David and Jonathan break it up?"

"I thought you knew."

"I told you—" still to the window "—I told you I never read that stuff."

"Reasons of state I think. They just got divided."

"Shilling off income tax," Shamus suggested.

"Something like that. Shamus?"

"Force of circumstance?"

"Yes. Yes, I think so."

"Not a quarrel about a fifth-rate concubine, for instance?"

"Shamus, we can stop now if you like. There's no need for a service."

"No need?"

"I only mean it doesn't need the formal gesture. None of us is religious, very."

Shamus did not seem to hear him, his gaze was still on the fog, and the motionless raindrops frozen into the glass.

"There *aren't* any fucking circumstances," he said. "There are just people. *Lovely people,*" he continued, in the voice of an American Midwest hostess. *"And if everybody was lovely there wouldn't be any war would there darlings?* I never dreamed you'd make it, Cassidy, that's the truth. I never dreamed you had it in you. I must have been growing cynical. Glad you saved me, lover; no point in bitterness. After all, how often do we meet it: real, total love? Once in a lifetime if we're lucky. Twice if we're Helen."

Turning, he studied her from far away, but his shape was so black against the window that Cassidy could not have told, if he had not known, whether he was facing them or not.

"Jesus," he said, in the extraordinary quiet. "That eye of yours: it's bloody disgusting. Can't you hold a bit of steak against it or something? Cassidy's *very* squeamish."

At this point, the doorbell rang; a three-toned chime not unlike the joyful summons to worship.

"Thank God," Shamus whispered. "Flaherty's arrived at last."

Opening the door at pistol point—note the impeccable fastenings, the hand-sawn hinges, locks lathe-turned—Cassidy saw many people of his acquaintance, beginning with Mark and Hugo, who had made independent travel arrangements, and ending indeterminately with McKechnie of Bee-Line and the Swiss Chief of Police. But the sight of the Eldermans, physical, not imagined Eldermans, laden with parcels, weary from the station path, and iced up round the eyebrows, surprised him very considerably.

I'm *certain* I put them off, he thought. He had telephoned: *John, old man, trouble at the crossroads, can you possibly make it another time or will it break the kids' hearts?* He had written a letter: *Circumstances beyond my control, the chalet has been burnt down, no one is sorrier than I.* He had cabled: *Chalet destroyed in avalanche.* Evidently, however, he had done none of these things, for there they were on the doorstep, the whole tribe of them, dressed in matching woollen hats like a family of softball supporters, the little girls covered in chocolate and the parents carrying the luggage. They stood in the beam of the outside light, smiling expectantly as if he were the photographer, their twelve cheeks red with cold.

"Aldo, old man," said John Elderman.

"We knew you were home from the light," said his wife, nameless once again. And added, using one of her coarse expressions intended to put her on a footing with the Men: "That's why we pressed the tit."

"He's got a gun," one of the children announced, seeing Shamus in the background. "Can *we* play, Mister?"

They were on the doorstep still, and a host has his duties.

"Come on in," said Cassidy with a show of heartiness, and made to help them with their luggage.

Behind him, raised by a head, Shamus was standing on the bottom stair, pressed into a corner, covering them with slow arcs of the revolver while he watched their every movement.

"Who are they?" he demanded, as they crowded in from the icy, wet air.

"A doctor and his family," said Cassidy, forgetting in his confusion Shamus' great hatred of the medical profession. "Friends." And took some luggage from the wife.

"*Your* friends?"

"Sandra's."

"Hullo," said Mrs. Elderman, smiling jovially to him across the hall. "What a *gorgeous* gun. Having a kid's party?" she enquired, noticing also the dressing gown and damask stole. "You look exactly like the Dalai Lama," and gave a most injudicious laugh.

"Piss off," said Shamus.

"That's Shamus," Cassidy explained. "He's staying here too."

And busied himself with roped boxes and the usual luggage of the very mean.

"Hullo old man," said John Elderman with great cheerfulness, climbing out of his duffle coat.

Mrs. Elderman was still staring at Shamus, and neither of them had moved.

"We're a bit crowded just at the moment," Cassidy murmured confidingly, to her husband, aside. "I've had a bit of a visitation. If you wouldn't mind taking over the top floor, just for this evening . . . then tomorrow we'll sort something out."

The very unemotional voice of Mrs. Elderman cut short their conversation.

"Darling," she said, "it's a real gun," and they all looked at Shamus.

"I'm afraid it is," said Cassidy.

The children, experts in sidearms, had also remarked the gun's authenticity. They were standing round it in an admiring group; the smallest was playing with the powder puff. With a disgusted gesture, Shamus waved them back and rose hastily another stair.

"They're foul," he whispered. "They're absolutely terrible."

"Oh I don't know," said Cassidy, embarrassed.

"They'll kill us all, lover. Jesus, lover, how can you *speak* to them?"

"We were having a sort of wedding," Cassidy explained to his new guests. "That's why he's wearing those clothes."

"A *wedding*," Mrs. Elderman echoed, on whom fell all the burdens of the obvious question. *"Here?* At *this* time of day?" And before he had even time to answer, had he wished, "Nonsense. Whose wedding?"

"His," said Shamus, indicating Cassidy. "He's marrying my wife."

John Elderman took his pipe from his mouth. He screwed his infantile face into a creaseless grin.

"But old man," he objected, after quite a long silence, "old Cassidy's married already, aren't you, Aldo?"

"To Sandra what's more," said Mrs. Elderman, and

looked accusingly at Shamus. "Aldo, he's not hijacking you, is he? He looks manic to me."

"Hugo says his Mummy and Daddy are *divorced,*" a larger girl announced, and offered Cassidy a toffee, part used.

"Be quiet," said her mother, and made to smack her.

If Shamus knew fear at all, this was the nature of it, these people its object. Pale and wary, he had taken up a position of extreme defensiveness at the top of the stairs, where he crouched, huddled into the dressing gown, the damask tablecloth thrown round his neck like a college scarf. They were all watching him, waiting for him to order them, but it was quite a time before their attention summoned him to action. Standing abruptly—his legs under the dressing gown were bare, Haverdown legs, and no hint of white among the higher shadows—he made a cursory wave of the gun barrel in the direction of the upper rooms.

"All right. Up here, the lot of you. One at a time, hands on your head, march. *You!*"

"Me?" John Elderman asked, grinning terribly.

"Get rid of that fucking pipe. Not going to have you smoking in church."

And thus within seconds had shooed them, parents, luggage, and children, upstairs to the drawing room. It was not only the gun which won him their obedience; he seemed to know them perfectly: how to command them, how to silence them, what foods to give their children. Within minutes, their luggage was neatly stacked along the landing wall; their children watered, fed, and relieved; and the whole family sat in descending order on the sofa, in the front pew facing the altar.

"This is absolutely disgraceful," said Mrs. Elderman, looking very critically at Helen. "Goodness, whatever happened to her eye? John——"

"Shut up," Shamus ordered her. "Camel driver's gourd! Yahoo! Shut up! You're a witness not a fucking referee!"

John Elderman, seated in the direct line of the gun, seemed disinclined, despite his wife's entreaties, to exercise his calling.

"It's damned odd," was all he would say, in the tone of one making an anthropological study. "It explains a *lot* of things."

He had put his pipe in his pocket.

Helen, meanwhile, left alone, had not altered her posture. She sat where they had left her, wearing an unclouded bridal smile, as if contemplating in the faded posy of flower heads still resting in her hand the sweet shocks of passion which the future held for her. Her other hand lay still and open, awaiting her groom's return. With the entry of the Eldermans she had risen distractedly to greet them, but her mood was reserved and aloof, as became her on her Day.

"Ah yes," she said, hearing the name, "Aldo has spoken about you."

She left the seating arrangements to her husband. Only the children caused her expression to change.

"How nice," she remarked to their mother. "How very sweet."

37

The presence of the larger congregation had had a remarkable effect on Shamus. Whatever doubts had till now assailed him, whatever mysteries and confusions stayed his hand, the unexpected invasion of his enemy, his sworn, archetypal enemy, had swept them all aside. Till now, it had seemed, his pastoral duties hung heavily on him. At moments, even, he had appeared to question his own faith; while his erratic changefulness of style and his frequent recourse to the revolver had much reduced the impact of his words. No more. Now, a fever of activity overtook him. The devil was in the house; Shamus needed herbs, and searched the kitchen cupboards till he came upon a box of thyme which he sprinkled liberally over the improvised altar. Candles, more candles; the Dark One was encroaching, Shamus needed light to hold him at bay. Receptacles were hastily assembled, and while the Eldermans looked on in sullen amazement a box of Price's Household Candles—Sandra's provision against a power cut—was quickly distributed. Soon the room was filled with the smell of burning wax; the dining table a lighted barrier behind which Shamus could take refuge from the terrors and infections of bourgeois mediocrity.

"He's mad," said Beth Elderman.

"Quiet, darling," said her husband nervously. "He may just be overwrought."

"Stop them!" Shamus screamed. "You know their language, reason with them!"

"Please be quiet," Cassidy said politely. "It upsets him."

Outside, the fog had temporarily lifted. In the darkening sky, the revealed peaks of the Angelhorn glittered like giant diamonds. The first lights were going on in the village; but the peaks had their own sun still, and shone with incongruous daylight over the twinkling darkness of the valley.

The thin chimes of a servant's handbell proclaimed the ceremony begun.

—

"Before we *resume*," Shamus began, "I have one or two announcements to make. Sit still," he told a little girl, with a monitory wave of the gun. "Just settle down and stop fidgeting."

Her mother tugged at the child, arranging it hastily, then faced Shamus again, herself more upright.

"First," he continued, in the unctuous, pseudo-intellectual tones of a fashionable West End parson, "let me say how *happy* I am to be able to welcome *children* to our service. It is one of the pleasing signs of the abiding power of religion, that parents"—here an indulgent smile at the Eldermans—"should bring their little ones to *this place*. It does credit to the children *and* to the parents."

He glanced at a piece of paper in his hand. "The next announcement, for those who have not yet heard the tragic news, concerns a holocaust in the neighbourhood of Thailand. Last night, owing to an oversight in one of the American strategic bases, four million Asians were eliminated."

He waited, plate in one hand, gun in the other.

A short, puzzled silence was broken by the chink of a coin as Mrs. Elderman opened her handbag and distributed small change to the girls.

"*Any* currency will do. *Thank* you. *Thank* you my dear. You *are* a Christian, I trust?" he murmured to Mrs. Elderman, accepting her offering.

"As a matter of fact I'm a *humanist*," she replied. "I'm afraid my husband and I find it impossible to accept the existence of God." And stuck out her jaw. "On scientific grounds *and* psychological grounds," she added.

"You obviously have *modern* views," Shamus prompted indulgently.

"Well they're obviously not as modern as yours," said Mrs. Elderman with spirit.

"How long have you known the groom?"

"Ooh, longer than I'd like to say," she squeaked, making a nervous joke about her age, which was thirty.

"Good, good, good, *good*. The third announcement," Shamus resumed, addressing himself to the bridal pair, "concerns your travel arrangements. There's a nine-forty connecting with the night sleeper from Spiez. So don't fucking well miss it. Get that Cassidy?"

"Yes of course."

"Will you all stand?"

Helen and Cassidy were sharing the leather chair, which Shamus had pulled to the centre of the long room in order to make extra space for the newcomers. Helen was on the arm and Cassidy on the seat, but the difference in their levels made communication difficult. This arrangement had not been uncongenial to Cassidy. The extra darkness afforded by Helen's body, the opportunity to imagine himself in other places, had provided him with a temporary ease from which he was now summoned by Helen's hand drawing him gently to his feet.

"Aldo," said Shamus.

"Yes."

"Helen?"

"Yes."

"Before joining you, Aldo, and you, Helen, in holy wedlock, I feel it incumbent upon me to venture one or two *general* observations"—a smile to the Eldermans—"on the service you are about to witness."

In the simple terms becoming to a short address, Shamus briefly explained to the newcomers the difference between *social* marriage, which was the Elderman kind of marriage, rightly devised for the containment of the Many-too-Many, and *real* marriage which was something very rare and had nothing whatever to do with them. He told them about Flaherty and self-appointed divinity, and about the difference between wanting to *die* together, which was New Testament marriage, and wanting to *live* together which was Old Testament marriage. This done, he chanted a few phrases of the *Nunc Dimittis* and bowed several times to the Bartlett print that was hanging over the fireplace.

"The total passion," he announced, in a strong Irish voice, quoting, Cassidy suspected, one of Flaherty's brochures, "demands the total sacrifice—"

About to continue he was interrupted by a whispered "Amen" from Beth Elderman, followed by the higher, obedient whispers of her many daughters.

"*Shut up,*" he told her, in suppressed fury. "Keep quiet or I'll shoot you. Jesus, lover—"

"She didn't mean any harm," said Cassidy.

Picking up the prayer book—it was held open by the weight of the gun—he read aloud:

"*I require and charge you both, as ye will answer at the dreadful day of judgment when the secrets of all hearts shall be disclosed*—which is *now* actually, lover. Not tomorrow, not next day, not in Christopher Robin land, but now—yes or no?"

"Yes," said Helen.

"I'm talking to *him*. I know about you, you whore, be quiet or you'll get another hit. *Him* I mean. Cassidy. Our lover. Will you or will you not have this woman for your illegally wedded wife, whether sick, pissed, maimed, imbecile, however much she whores around? Will you, forsaking all others, including the bosscow, the Veg, the Bentley, and"—he put down the prayer book—"and me, lover," he said, very softly. "Because that's the way it works."

Helen's hand was linked in Cassidy's. From behind him he heard the loose, persistent cough of his French mother and the creak of pews echoing in the vaulted ceiling. Those kids, he thought; the Elderman woman; why don't they *do* something? They're my friends, not his.

"Lover."

"Yes."

"This gun is for shooting defectors, not lovers."

"I know."

"If you say *no*, I shall shoot you for sure, because I hate you quite a lot. That's called jealousy, also an emotion. Right? But if you say yes and you don't want her, believe me that *is* . . . that really *is* . . . not polite."

Helen was looking at him and he knew her look because it was Sandra's look, it covered everything, the whole contract to live and die.

"The point being, lover, that once you drag her off to your cave Daddy won't be there to help you. You can have her, if you want her. But from that moment on you've got to find your own reason for living. I can't do more for you and you can't do more for me."

"No."

"What the hell do you mean: *no?*" Helen demanded, releasing his hand.

"I mean he can't do any more. I agree."

"You see," Shamus explained, "although she's a stupid little bitch, I love her. That's why she's so cheeky. She's got us both. So I'm offering you all I've got and all I want: and naturally, I'll be put out if you reject it. But you've got to decide. Don't let that bitch carry you. Love you, lover."

"Love you," Cassidy replied automatically.

"Then which is it? Yes please or no thank you?"

All this while Shamus had been watching him most intently through the candles, and sweat had formed on his face, which now ran like crooked tears over his shaven cheeks; but his eyes were black and steady, as if neither the pain nor the heat of his torture were relevant to his words. On Cassidy's left, Helen was whispering, urging and complaining, but he heard only Shamus; it was Shamus, most definitely, who held his attention.

"Say yes, you fool," Beth Elderman shouted suddenly from the back, and Shamus raised the gun and might well have shot her if Helen had not intervened. Instead, he came round the altar, took Cassidy by the arm, and led him into the furthest part of the room, to the corner where the table was before they moved it; to a place so dark they could barely be heard.

"She's a heavy eater, boy," he murmured. "Big grocery bills coming up. Dresses, cars; she'll want the lot."

"*Cassidy!*" Helen shouted, furious.

"She can have whatever she wants," said Cassidy loyally.

"Why not just give her the money: you don't have to put up with *her* as well. Five thousand should see her right."

With a quick, conspiratorial glance at the congregation, Shamus had drawn Cassidy towards him so that Shamus' lips were at Cassidy's ear and Shamus' lower cheek was pressed against Cassidy's temple. Coming so close to him so suddenly, Cassidy smelt Paris again, and the drink, and the garbage in the street; smelt the woodsmoke from the fireplace lingering in his dressing gown and the sweat that was on him all the time; and whatever detachment he had found was gone, because this was Shamus, who had once been Cassidy's freedom; and had loved him; who needed him and had leant on him; rested on him in his hopeless search; played with him by the river.

"For God's sake, lover," Shamus insisted. "Why screw up a friendship like ours for the sake of a bit of cunt?"

His lips stayed, their breath trembling on the membranes of his ear. Shamus' jaw was pressed against his head, and Shamus' hands were linked at his neck. Pushing Cassidy gently away from him at last, he surveyed him in his own familiar way, reading (it seemed to Cassidy) his whole life there, all its paradoxes, its evasions, and its insoluble collisions. For a moment, the sky cleared for Cassidy, and he saw the hilltop where they had flown the gliders. And he thought: *Let's go back there. From the hill I can understand it all.*

Then Shamus smiled: the broad, untrustworthy smile of a victor.

"Well?"

"There's no point," said Cassidy.

"What do you mean? *No point?* You're here because there *is* a point! There's got to be a fucking point! I had *you,* and I'm giving you to *her.* I had *her* and I'm giving her to *you!*"

"I mean there's no point in trying to talk me out of it, I love her."

"What was that?" said Shamus very quietly.

"I said I loved her."

"And still do?"

"Yes. More than you."

"More than you love me, or more than I love her?"

"Both," said Cassidy numbly.

"Again, say it again," Shamus urged, seizing him.

"I love her."

"Shout it out! Her name, everything."

"I love Helen."

"Aldo loves Helen!"

"I Aldo love Helen. I Aldo love Helen. I Aldo love Helen!"

Suddenly, without Cassidy understanding why, the rubric, the rhythm of the words took hold of him. The louder he shouted, the brighter, the more excited Shamus' smile: the louder he shouted, the larger the room became, the more it filled and echoed. Shamus was pouring water over him, Lipp-style, a jugful, purifying him in the name of the Few, Helen was kissing him, sobbing and asking why it took him so long. The sound rose; some children were clapping but one was crying, as in the eye of his imagination Cassidy saw his own drenched, stupid body upright in a pool of holy water, shouting love at a laughing world.

"I Aldo love Helen! Can you hear? I Aldo love Helen!"

John Elderman was standing, beating his hands together; his wife was holding her string gloves to her chin, weeping and laughing.

"This is *it*," John Elderman was crying. "My God this is the big league. I'll never aspire to this, never."

"If only more people could see it," said Mrs. Elderman.

But they can, Cassidy shouted, they can. Why don't you turn your head you fool? Sandra's family was packing the pews behind her, Mrs. Groat dressed in fruit and flowers, escorted by her several sisters and lady cousins; Snaps in beige velvet, her cleavage uselessly exposed. From the other side of the aisle came the tearful coughing of the Abandoned One and the plain sobs of Old Hugo, standing beside the empty place for A. L. Rowse. The strains of an organ were filling the room, "Abide With Me" and "Sheep May Safely Graze."

"I Aldo love Helen. I Aldo love Helen. I Aldo love Helen."

"Oh love, oh love," Helen sobbed; she was drying him with a tea towel; her bruise was bright again where her tears had washed away the make-up. "And he didn't stand in our way," she sobbed. "Oh Shamus, darling."

"You see lover," Shamus explained, "you're the only one I ever had. I mean Christ had twelve, didn't he, eleven good, one bad. But I've only got *you*, so you had to be right, didn't you?"

The lights had gone on. Shamus was passing around Talisker. Helen, very proud and quiet on Cassidy's arm, was receiving the congratulations of the guests. Well they had met in the West Country actually, she said; about a year ago; they had really been in love ever since, but they had agreed for Shamus' sake to keep it a secret. The speeches were short and to the point, no one became boring or untimely. Shamus, drinking heartily, the colour high on his cheeks, was the very soul of contentment: if they had children they must be brought up Catholic, he said, it was the only condition he had made.

"He's a *writer*," Beth Elderman was telling the girls, her face flushed with maternal pride. "That's a very special kind of person, that's why he knows *all* about the world. You must never, *never* compromise, do you understand? Sally listen, what did Mummy say?"

"I meet so much of it," John Elderman said shrewdly through his grown-up pipe. "Every blasted day in the surgery, three, maybe four cases, you'd be astonished. So much of it could be *avoided*," he told Shamus very confidentially, "if only they had *help*."

"And of course how he put up with the *other* one for so long," Beth Elderman said to anyone who would listen, "God alone knows. I mean *that* was *total* disaster."

38

The guests gathered on the doorstep, children at the front, grown-ups behind. The festive toboggan lay ready, Mark's again; John Elderman and Shamus had lashed the luggage to the prow. A light, sharp wind had sprung up from the north. The fog had gone for good, the rain had turned to snow, a fine, hard-driven snow that was already settling on the window sills.

For her going away, the bride wore a fitted sheepskin coat which she had found in Sandra's wardrobe, and a charming white fur hat which Mark called Mummy's rabbit's ears.

"Isn't it funny," she said in her excitement, "how everything fits me, just like that?"

Her boots were sealskin, though she did not approve of killing seals. She kissed the girls lavishly and counselled them to be good and kind, and to grow up lovely wives.

"Which you will, I know," she said, crying a little. "I just *know* you will."

To Beth Elderman, she imparted some last-minute domestic advice. The oil system was impossible to understand, the best thing to do was kick it.

"And there's cold duck in the fridge and extra milk on the sideboard. For God's *sake* don't buy the Co-op butter, it's *no* cheaper and it's absolutely foul."

"We think you're doing the right thing," said Beth.

"We know you are," said her husband.

"So long," said Shamus.

He had placed himself, modestly, at the end of the line, in the shadow of the others; he was holding a torch in one hand and a glass in the other; he was barefoot, and the skirts of his dressing gown could have been a curtain borrowed from the window in the hall.

"Is that all you've got to say?" said Helen at last. "*So long?*"

"Watch out for rabbit holes."

"I'd like to kiss you," said Helen.

"Kissin' don't last," said Shamus, in a Somerset accent which Cassidy had not heard before. "Cookin' do."

Rather hopelessly, she turned to John Elderman.

"Don't worry," said the great psychiatrist. "We'll bring him round."

With a somewhat ungainly hoist of the skirts, and a last look at Shamus, she boarded the toboggan, sitting well forward with the luggage so that Cassidy could manage the more responsible rear position.

"Are you getting divorced?" asked a little girl.

"Be quiet," said Beth Elderman.

"Hugo says he is," said the same little girl.

"Aldo," said Beth Elderman, with her plant and rock smile. "Give us a ring. We're in the book." She kissed him, smelling very slightly of ether. "Remember you're a friend as well as a patient," she added.

Her husband gave him a manly hand.

"Godspeed, Aldo. Don't overdo it. We admire you."

About to say goodbye to Shamus, Cassidy appeared to remember something.

"Crikey," he said, all boyish. "Hang on a sec." And darted past them into the house.

Hugo's room was very cold. He tested the radiator. On, but icy. Must be an airlock in the heating. His toys were put away; only a red anorak, the wet-look for this season, hung like a doll's suit from the painted hanger.

Mark's room was lined with pictures cut from magazines, mainly advertisements. The largest was a centrefold spread of a whole family smiling into the camera while they loaded fishing kit into a Range Rover. That's how he wanted us, Cassidy thought, studying the bronzed, untroubled features of the father. Mr. and Mrs. Britain sporting by the river.

"Lost something?" Shamus asked from the doorway, offering him his whisky glass. He was very relaxed. The gun, broken like a shotgun, hung vaguely over his forearm, and he had put the powder puff behind his ear like a Tahitian maiden's flower.

"My watch actually. It must be in the bathroom." He returned the glass, empty.

"Lover."

"Yes."

"Look er . . . I know you're going to keep her in the style to which you're accustomed. But don't er . . . don't let her get her hands on a lot of money. *You* know."

They tried both bathrooms, but the watch was not in either of them.

"And er . . . on the other thing."

"What other thing?"

"The other thing, you know." He bucked his pelvis. "What we did in Paris, *you* know. Watch her. She'll do anything to get pregnant, anything. We'd a flat once up in Durham, we had the builders in. She went through the whole lot of them just on the off chance. Painters, plasterers, masons, the lot."

"I don't believe you," said Cassidy.

They returned to the front door.

"You didn't hit me though, did you?"

"What will you do?" Cassidy asked after rather a long silence. "Now."

"Get pissed. Have a little drink with the Elderberries."

"*Hurry up!*" Helen called. "For Christ's sake, we'll miss the train!"

"You just can't alter him," they heard Beth Elderman say. "He's always been a ditherer, he always will be. He drove Sandra *mad.*"

"That's why Mark's so wet," said the largest girl.

"Great people," said Shamus. "I love them all. Honest, straightforward. Might play Fly with them. Teach the kids."

"And the new book's all right, is it?"

"Finished," said Shamus, without expression. "It's all about you, actually. And immortality. The eternal survival of Aldo Cassidy."

"I'm glad I provided the material."

"I'm glad *I* did."

"*Cassidy!*" Helen called, very angry.

"I've got to go now," said Cassidy, taking Helen's point, "or we'll miss the train."

"Attaboy. Be brave."

"Goodbye."

"Chippie chippie," said Shamus in his poofy voice. "Love to the Bentley. Er lover."

"Yes."

"Not to miss the train but er let us in on something, will you? That waitress down at the station buffet there, the one with the tits."

"Maria," said Cassidy automatically.

"Tell us, does she oblige, do you know? I had the definite feeling yesterday that she was fumbling my hand when I gave her the coffee money."

"Well they do say she's a bit fast."

"How much?"

"Fifty francs. Maybe more."

Shamus' hand was already outstretched.

"It's for when I'm on my own you see. I'm going to need a spot of distraction." Cassidy gave him a hundred. "Thanks. Thanks very much indeed. Pay you back, lover. Promise."

"That's all right."

"And—er—on the general theme."

"Which one?" Cassidy asked, definitely *not* thinking of the train, which he definitely intended to catch, but *definitely*. The general theme of God, perhaps? Of the union of souls? Of Keats, death, taking and not giving? Of kites, or Schiller; or the threat of China to the pram trade? Or something more personal perhaps, such as the slow atrophy of a loving soul worn down to very little any more?

"Money," said Shamus.

At first, Cassidy could not recognise his smile. It belonged to other faces; faces not present, till then, in the worlds which he and Shamus had explored together. Faces weakened by need, and failure, and dependence. It was a smile that accused even while it supplicated; that haunted with its first dawning, imparting without change both allegiance and contempt; a smile from loser to winner, when both had run the same financial race. "Aldo old boy," it said. "Cassidy old man. A thousand would see me right." A shifty, sandy smile worn with a good suit fraying at the cuffs, and a silk shirt fraying at the collar: "After all old boy, we were neck and neck once, weren't we, before you hit it lucky?"

"What do you need?" Cassidy asked. His custom, till

then, had been to establish the minimum and halve it. "We'll have to be quick actually."

"Couple of thousand?" said Shamus, as if it were nothing to either of them really; just a thing that friends arranged between themselves and forgot.

"I'll make it five," said Cassidy, and wrote him a cheque, quickly because of the train.

He did not look at Shamus as he gave it him, he was too ashamed; and he never knew what Shamus did with it, whether he folded it away, Kurt-style, like a clean handkerchief, or read it after the lesson of Old Hugo, from the date to the signature, and then the back, in case. But he did hear him mutter the one word Cassidy was praying to God he wouldn't say:

"Thanks."

And he knew he had seen his first dead body, it stood for all the rest he would ever see; dead dreams, lives ended, no point.

"Just coming," he called to Helen.

"Pay you back one day lover."

"No hurry," said Cassidy, though actually there *was* a hurry in a way because Swiss trains are punctual.

He climbed on to the toboggan.

"It's on your wrist," Shamus called after him, meaning his watch.

He could not possibly have seen it, for Cassidy had pulled his cuffs right down, in the style of Christopher Robin.

"*Whatever* were you up to?" Helen demanded. "I've been sitting here *freezing* for hours. Look at my hair."

One of the children had found a bag of rice, and was flinging it at them in handfuls. The snow was falling steadily, the flakes thicker.

"I lost my watch," said Cassidy.

"I'd have thought you *could* have done without it for once," she said. "Seeing that it's made us miss the train."

The next moment, a dozen willing hands propelled them into the darkness, the children's merry screams of "Good luck" faded behind them, and the happy pair was hurtling ever faster down the hill, already blinded by the icy streams of racing snowflakes.

The station was empty and very cold and the train was quite indisputably gone.

The next one could be late, the guard said, there was a lot of snow higher up.

"There's a lot down here too," Cassidy replied jovially, still brushing himself clean—clean also of the guilt of dawdling—but the guard did not care for jokes apparently, nor was he of the tippable class. He was a big, rugged man, not unlike Alastair a thousand years before him, but his rocky face was set against all pleasantries.

"Well ask him *how* late," Helen told him.

"How late?" Cassidy asked, in French.

The guard made no gesture at all, neither of answering nor refusing to answer. But after staring at Helen for quite a long time, silently closed the hatch on them and locked it from the inside.

"*How late?*" Helen shouted, hammering on the little door. "The *bugger*, look at that."

They had fallen several times on the way down: Cassidy reckoned five. The first time they agreed it was funny; the second time, the suitcase came undone and Cassidy had to stumble like an Arctic explorer through the falling snow, looking for Sandra's clothes. After that, the falling was not funny at all. Helen said it was a lousy toboggan and Cassidy said you couldn't really blame it. Helen said she had thought he *knew* how to drive it, otherwise she would not have consented to come on it; she would have walked and at least remained dry. *Real* toboggans were wooden, she said, she had had one as a child. She hammered again, shouted "Bastard" through the chink, so Cassidy suggested they have a drink and try again in a few minutes.

"We can always go to Bristol," he said.

"To *where?*"

"It was a joke," said Cassidy.

"*Dithering* like that," said Helen contemptuously. "If you'd *wanted* to go away with me you'd *never* have dithered."

But still.

In the buffet, a group of English ladies in blue-banded pullovers was sitting at the English Table. Seeing Helen and Cassidy enter, a beautiful, thin lady with a deaf-aid beckoned them over.

"You old *devil*," she said cheerfully to Cassidy, taking his wrist in her thin, dry hand. "You never even told us you were coming. You're a *devil*," she repeated, as if he, not she, were deaf. "Hullo Sandra, dear, you look absolutely frozen." But men were her preference. "Darling," she asked him confidentially, "have you *heard* what Arnie's trying to do with the Championships this year?"

In a black rage, Helen accepted a glass of hot wine and drank it very slowly, staring at the clock.

"He wants a giant slalom at Mürren, my dear, can you imagine. Well I mean you know what happened *last* time we went to Mürren . . ."

Breaking away at last, Cassidy went back to the ticket office. It was still closed, there was no one in sight, and the snow was falling much harder, masking the village lights and casting a deep silence over the whole white world.

"They say about half an hour," he told Helen, who had moved to an empty table. It seemed inappropriate to give her bad news, so he had invented a small hope. "They're working flat out but at the moment it's almost beating them."

He ordered more hot wine.

"Got your passport all right?" he asked, trying to cheer her up.

"Of course I haven't. Shamus burnt it."

"Oh."

"What do you mean: *oh*. You can get a duplicate. Any consulate or legation will provide one. We can go to Berne. Once the train comes, if it ever does."

"We'll get one tomorrow," Cassidy promised her.

"I'll need more luggage too. All that stuff's *soaked*."

She began crying into her folded hands.

"Oh no," Cassidy whispered. "Oh Helen, please."

"What will we *do*, Cassidy, what will we *do*?"

"Do?" he said gallantly. "We'll do exactly what we said we'd do. We'll have a lovely holiday, then I'll go into politics and you'll be an M.P.'s wife and . . ."

From the English Table, the beautiful lady looked on with great compassion.

"Is she having a baby?" she called pleasantly. "It usually makes them odd."

Cassidy ignored her.

"It's only reaction," Cassidy promised her, holding her hand and fighting to win a smile. "Sorry about it . . . it's not because you're sad."

"Don't *apologise*," said Helen, stamping her foot. "Not *your* fault."

"Well it is in a way," Cassidy insisted. "I got you into this."

"It's not. Love's nobody's fault. It just happens. And when it happens you have to do what it says. There are winners and losers. Like in everything else. We're the winners, that's all. Although we missed the train."

"I know," Cassidy agreed. "We're very lucky." And pressed his handkerchief into her palm.

"It isn't *luck* either."

"Well what is it?" Cassidy asked.

"How should I know? Why did you take so long?"

"What for?"

"To say *yes*. It was *exactly* the same as missing the train. There they were, all waiting, and you being the ardent lover and God knows what and Shamus being so helpful, and all you do is dither while I *sit* there and look a complete fool in front of a *doctor* of all people, and his brilliant wife. Why do you have to know such brainy people?"

Drying her eyes, she saw the guard sitting at a table by the door, drinking schnapps and coffee.

"What the hell's *he* doing there?" she demanded. "He's supposed to be waiting for the train."

Off duty, the guard was quite a different man. "Hallo," he called, raising his glass. "Hallo. Cheerio. Hallo. *Ja. Bonjour.*"

"Cheers," said Cassidy. "You speak English eh? Very good. *Très bon.*"

"No train," said the guard with great satisfaction, as he drank. "Too much snows."

He drank again, as if a little more of the same could do him no harm. As he drank, he walked towards them, bent on conversation; he loomed very large and very drunk, and his eyes were on Helen, not at all on Cassidy. So when the pistol shot came it was almost a relief.

There was no other sound. None. It was not at all a question of distinguishing this bang from conflicting ones:

a door slammed, a car was backfiring; a slate from the station roof. The snow had thrown a blanket over everything; only pistols were exempt. Also, the shot was close. Not in the buffet certainly; but near to it, and it was followed by a chilling howl, midway between pain and fury; a long, baying howl of the kind that by tradition haunts deserted marshes, and ends as this howl ended with a choking, agonised sob, dwindling to nothing; a howl to chill the blood, and arrest drunken railwaymen in mid-movement.

"*My* God," he remarked, with the accent on the possessive pronoun. "They shot the bitch, I think."

He was still laughing at this apposite snatch of Americana as Cassidy raced past him into the station forecourt.

The Russian snow was tumbling crazily through the downbeams of the railway lamps. The line was covered over. A road, a path, a fence, a house, it was already buried by a new generation. *I'm Troy. There's seven fucking civilisations buried in me and each one's more rotten than the other.* Even the nearest buildings were caving in. The newspaper kiosk was on its knees; the eyes of the Hotel Angelhorn were closed and bleeding; in the high street, not a shop or church or ice palace but the remorseless snow was pounding at its doors, blotting out roofs, skirmishing in the forecourts. Wildly, hand to his eyes, Cassidy looked about him. Footprints, he thought; search for footprints. There were none but his own.

"Shamus!" He called loud. "Shamus!" he repeated. "Shamus!"

Using his intelligence too late, he looked back at the buffet window trying to think which way the noise had come from as they sat there. Helen was staggering towards him, wrapped in the sheepskin. Christ, he thought, she actually put it on before she came out to look for him. Behind her, not venturing so far, Rasputin the guard looked on from the doorway, his glass still in his hand.

"Go and look down there," Cassidy told her, pointing down an alley where a very old jeep was sinking slowly into the ground. "Look for footprints, call his name."

"What's he done?" she whispered. "Cassidy, what's he done?"

"Anything wrong?" an English lady asked from behind the porter. "I thought I heard a bang."

"I say," said another. "Did you hear that noise?"

Helen did not move. She was hugging the coat right across her body.

"Go and look for him!" he shouted at her.

Oh Christ she's frightened stiff; that's why she put on the coat, she wanted an excuse for waiting. Seizing her shoulders he shook her; her head fell stupidly from side to side.

"He's hitting her," an English lady said.

"Poor gal, she's pregnant," said the deaf one, as they all advanced into the snow.

"We've killed him," Helen whispered.

Leaving her, he ran quickly down the alley, calling Shamus. He was running directly at the snow now, he had to lower his head to see any distance at all.

He had entered a drift, the snow was in his trousers, his neck, colder than water, colder than fear and his feet were numb. Wading, he came on a pile of logs leaning against a tin roof and the snow was scratched where someone had climbed up. At first he thought the marks were handprints, each finger separate, and he had a crazy vision of Shamus doing handstands while he tried to shoot himself upside down. Then he remembered that Shamus was barefooted, and that he liked impact and a spot of pain; and he saw him sitting astride the station roof, hugging the clock as if it were his latest friend, aiming at him very deliberately, a difficult down-angle shot which mercifully missed.

"Shootibangs," said Shamus.

"Shootibangs," Cassidy agreed.

"I heard a shot! Another shot, a second one!" Helen shouted, tugging at his arm. "For Christ's sake Cassidy, find someone who can *do* something!"

"He's up there," Cassidy explained, pointing. "Shooting at me."

The bullet had passed very close; he had felt the wind of it or something, but the snow made it rather unreal, he was cold and he didn't much care.

Advancing from the buffet doorway, Rasputin the guard was screaming maternal French. Shooting on station property was absolutely forbidden, he was saying; it was doubly forbidden to foreigners.

"Look out," said an English lady to him, "or he'll shoot you too, I can tell."

Helen was scrambling up the log pile.

"Here, let me help you," he said automatically, offering his hand, but Shamus was already coming down. The dressing gown round his waist, he was sliding on his bare behind.

In a bunch, the English ladies withdrew.

"Sorry lover. Couldn't remember what her name was, the one with the tits."

"Maria," said Cassidy.

"That's it, Maria. I needed a whore, you see."

"I understand," said Cassidy.

The guard was still shouting. Irritated, Shamus fired a round at his feet and he ran to the buffet, joining Cassidy's English mothers at the door.

The three of them were standing in the station forecourt, Shamus shivering in the dressing gown, but the snow was so heavy they might have been anywhere; in Paris, in Haverdown, or here.

"Have to make world history some other time," said Shamus.

"That's it."

"What do you mean?" Helen demanded. "What are you saying?"

Cassidy felt obliged to explain.

"It's nothing, Helen. It's just that the main axis is between you two. I'm just . . ." He began again. "Maybe it's between us two, him and me. Only . . . Shamus," he said hopelessly.

"Yes lover?"

"I can't say it, I don't know the words. You're the writer, you tell her."

"Sorry lover. Your world: you end it."

"You mean you don't love me," said Helen.

"No," said Cassidy. "It's not quite that . . ."

"You love the bosscow."

"No. No, it isn't options either."

"He doesn't love *me*," Shamus explained, very simply. "He's gone off me and you're no good to him on your own." He was tearing up the cheque and throwing the pieces over the snow. "Money matter," he explained. "He walked into it with his eyes wide shut. I could shoot him if you like," he suggested to Helen, gallantly.

"I don't mind," said Cassidy. "It's up to you."

"He doesn't mind," said Shamus.

"Cassidy!" Helen cried.

"That match is rained off," Shamus said. "So shut up snivelling or you'll get a kick. I blame myself, lover. I was really going to let you go. I had it all worked out. I was going to train to be a doctor, you see. Elderberry was going to teach me how to do it. Then the bugger said it took ten years. Lover, I haven't *got* ten years. Have I?"

"No, I suppose not."

"Kept talking about the bosscow, what a bitch she was. He's the worst, that Elderberry, a bum."

"I used to hate him too."

"And his wife's a rotten fuck. I can't stand howlers. Ya, ya, ya, all that stuff. Like Swiss porters."

Cassidy nodded. "There was one like that in Paris."

"Here," said Shamus, handing him the revolver. "Souvenir. You might use it some time."

"Thanks," said Cassidy.

Shamus looked down at his bare legs, where they disappeared into the snow. He wore a white crown; a rim of white had settled over his black eyebrows.

"Jesus," he whispered, "we're a long way from home."

"Yes, we are."

"Sorry lover," Shamus said again. "You nearly made it. Come on you bitch," he said to Helen, shaking her without affection. "My feet are cold."

"It wasn't your fault," said Cassidy to Helen. "Please don't feel bad about it. It's all in me, not you."

"Quiet lover. Quiet. Bedtime now."

Coming forward, Shamus kissed him for the last time. When the kiss was over, Shamus turned away. Helen was still holding him. Then Shamus set off, vigorously, hauling her whichever way he wanted her to go, and they had actually started up the hill before she spoke.

"For a while," she said, and began again because she was crying. "For a while you really *did* care."

"Of course I did. All the time—"

"Not about me, you fool. About yourself. You put a value on yourself."

"Helen, please don't cry—"

"Shut up and listen! You put a value on *yourself*," she repeated. "That's something you never did before." Shamus was dragging her; she fell, and half got up. "For God's *sake* do it again," she shouted. "Find someone else. Don't go back into that awful dark."

"Keep trying, lover," Shamus assented, with a last careless wave. "Never regret, never apologise."

The snow had almost covered them. Sometimes he saw them, sometimes there was nothing; it was no longer possible to tell. Once, through a clearing as it were, he made out two uprights, one straight and one crooked, and either they were posts along the fencing or two people leaning together as they struggled with the very deep snow. But as they vanished finally, into the nothing that lay beyond the blizzard, he thought he heard—but could never be sure—he thought, though, that he heard her say "Goodbye, Cassidy," like a whisper alone, as if she were saying goodbye to the old year, to a decade or a lifetime, and then at last his own eyes filled with tears and he lowered his head. As he did so they seemed to go down with him, both together, like two pedestrians in the rain, before the hood of his rich man's car.

Epilogue

The retirement of Mr. Aldo Cassidy, the Founder, Chairman, Managing Director, and principal shareholder of Cassidy's General Fastenings, from active business life was noted with interest in the City press, and with some admiration. A fine example, they said, of a brilliant young businessman who put a lot into commerce and had taken a lot out, and was now retiring to enjoy the fruits. Would the lure of big business draw him back? Would the former whizz kid tire of rural charms? Only history would decide.

Those who knew him best spoke warmly of his great love for the country.

"A perfectionist," a well-known West End Estate Agent testified. "We only ever offered him the best that Britain has for sale."

It was known that the Manorship of Haverdown in Somerset had long been his ambition, not least because of the family connection: an ancient forebear of Mr. Cassidy had rested there with a detachment of Cromwell's horse. "We Cassidys have always been fighters," the Chairman recalled amid laughter and applause, explaining his decision to the shareholders; and accepted with tears in his eyes the handsome canteen of silver which had been purchased by private subscription.

The merger with Bee-Line Accessories Limited had long been in the air: City editors were confident that the inevitable streamlining was in the long-term interest of shareholders. For the new Chairman Meale, nothing but praise: a typical graduate of the tough Cassidy school, they said; a man to watch.

The sale of the house in Abalone Crescent was also noted in the property columns: *A Vision Uncompleted* ran the caption. The knowledgeable named a price of forty-two thousand pounds.

How did they live there, Sandra and Aldo, for the rest of their natural lives? Did the marriage prosper? At first, they talked over their problem with great frankness. Dr. Elderman and his wife were invaluable, coming often and staying long. Sandra accepted that Cassidy had suffered spiritual death, but she was prepared, for the children's sake, to overlook it.

"He should never have had money," she concluded. "If he'd been poor, he couldn't have *afforded* to be unfaithful."

For company, she invited Heather to make Haverdown her permanent home, and Heather, though she had doubts about whether they were just being kind, finally consented to accept an empty wing. When Sandra made pickle, Heather made pickle too. When she ground her liver *pâté*, Heather ground it with her; when she went to country sales, Heather helped her to keep her head; and when she went to London to see how the clinic was progressing, Heather and Cassidy would go to bed together and talk about Sandra's limitations. Sandra was not aware of this practice, and if she had been she would have been extremely cross.

For entertainment, Cassidy browsed at the local library, where young girls attended after school; or he would drive to Bristol on a pretext and visit a dingy cinema in a railway concourse where torrid films were shown to needy peasants. In the early days, attracted by the appearance of shared happiness, he would sometimes flirt with a married couple. The curate had recently imported a plump bride from the North; a pair of Old Etonian antique dealers opened an emporium. But little came of these advances, and with time he abandoned them.

All three political parties considered him for the local council, but specific overtures were never made.

He became a lay preacher but his services were seldom called upon, though he was acknowledged to have a good voice and an agreeably pious nature.

Palominos were bought but the boys were not fond of them and one night they were sold to a gypsy.

Occasionally, in idle hours in his library, Cassidy would try his hand at writing. The spy vogue was high at that time, and he thought he might get in on the market. For a while he even had something quite good going—an idea about deep-freezing a professional assassin, and turning him loose on the leaders of a new age—but gradually the idea died on him and he put it aside. There was something else, too, about the whole process of writing, that disturbed him. The way his thoughts took him in unsavoury directions: back to certain events, for instance, which he had of necessity banished from his conscious memory; or worse still, forward to possibilities that should not be entertained. He realised also what a lonely business writing was, how obvious and yet how tiresomely elusive; and then he would put down his pen and go to the kitchen, where Sandra was making jam. Quietly, he embraced her, usually from behind.

"What's the matter?" she would ask, as if he had a cold.

"Nothing," he said. "I just missed you, that's all."

Sandra slept much, often twelve hours a night.

It was common gossip that the building work at Haverdown would last indefinitely. Within months of their arrival the house was encased in the familiar steel corsetry of Abalone Crescent, and tilers had boarded the roof. What could not be restored must be pulled down and rebuilt for greater permanence. Sometimes the Cassidys said they had a duty to the past, sometimes to the future; the present was not spoken of. A landscape gardener, summoned from Cheltenham to judge the soil, pronounced it sour and advocated sweetness. A second pronounced it sweet, a third prescribed lime. There was much to dig up.

Old Hugo's funeral took place with full parliamentary honours; a Baptist minister spoke at length of a profitable life spent in God's service. But Cassidy was not convinced, and some years later heard that he had opened a new hotel on the Inverness Road, a place called the Ideal Star and managed by a Mrs. Bluebridge.

Of Cassidy himself it was known that he had a great aversion to snow. The Swiss house was not spoken of; probably it was sold.

Mark and Hugo grew up to be increasingly distant. With time they fell in love, and became objectionable.

Did Cassidy ever think of Helen and Shamus? Specifically and by name?

At first, fragments of news came to him, though he never went to look for them. From Angie Meale, *née* Mawdray, with whom he occasionally cohabited on the pretext of attending a heart specialist, he learned that Shamus had an *avant-garde* play running at the Royal Court; but corroboration was not forthcoming. The play was neither reviewed nor advertised. At about the same time a crate of champagne arrived at Haverdown, and a copy of a novel entitled *Three for the Road*. Both appeared to have come from Shamus' hand. He never read the novel, and when Christmas came he sent the champagne to the police station as a small insurance against persecution. "You know young Cassidy of Haverdown?" the Chief Constable was heard to ask of the County. "Remarkable fellow. Flourishing business in London, gave it up, came down here, and sent us all champers at Christmas...."

And in winter, when the fire burned dully in the familiar grate, at dinner perhaps, cut off from Sandra and Heather by the fine silver and old Worcester, he occasionally imagined Helen standing in the chestnut ride in her Anna Karenina boots, staring down the avenue of trees at the lighted windows of the house. Or Sandra would play Beethoven on the piano—she played nothing else these days—and he would remember, through the bone of his unmusical ear, the transistor radio in the pocket of her housecoat as she stole downstairs that first morning to bring him breakfast on the Chesterfield. Occasionally, after such moments of recollection, nightmares assailed him; a stock-whip lashed over his skull; he was being forced to drink high-octane gasoline. Or the streets of Paris had split, and the steams of Hades were belching out of them.

As to Shamus, with time Cassidy forgot him entirely.

Forgetting him became first an exercise, then an achievement.

Shamus did not exist.

Not even on the lonely homeward drives across the moor, when the puffs of mist blew towards him down the long hood of the Bentley; not even when his name was directly mentioned at the dinner tables of County ladies with pretensions to the arts, did Cassidy own to knowing Shamus, the taker and challenger of life.

For in this world, whatever there was left of it to inhabit, Aldo Cassidy dared not remember love.

ABOUT THE AUTHOR

JOHN LE CARRÉ is the pseudonym of David Cornwell. Born in 1931, he attended the universities of Berne and Oxford, taught at Eton and later entered the British Foreign Service. He has been described in *The New York Times* as belonging to the select company of such spy and detective story writers as Arthur Conan Doyle, Dashiell Hammett, Raymond Chandler, and Ross Macdonald. His first two novels were *Call for the Dead* (1961) and *A Murder of Quality* (1962). His third novel, *The Spy Who Came in from the Cold* (1963), was greeted with great enthusiasm and secured his worldwide reputation. Mr. le Carré is also the author of *The Naive and Sentimental Lover*, *The Looking Glass War*, *A Small Town in Germany*, *Tinker, Tailor, Soldier, Spy*, *The Honourable Schoolboy*, *Smiley's People*, *The Little Drummer Girl*, and *A Perfect Spy*.

JOHN LE CARRÉ

"The premier spy novelist of his time. Perhaps of all time," is what *Time* magazine recently called him.

Others echo the praise. But it took John le Carré many years to reach this position. He began his writing career while in the British Foreign Service. Unable to use his real name (David Cornwell) because the Foreign Office forbids its staff to publish under their own names, he adopted the name le Carré (French for "the square") which he claims to have seen printed on a London shop window.

As he states, "When I first began writing, Ian Fleming was riding high and the picture of the spy was that of a character who could have affairs with women, drive a fast car, who used gadgetry and gimmickry to escape." What le Carré has brought back is the realistic spy story.

Call for the Dead and *A Murder of Quality* were his first two novels. It was his third novel *The Spy Who Came in from the Cold* which broke through to bestsellerdom. It features the antihero Alec Leamas, a cold war spy, out to rescue friends from Berlin. In *The Looking Glass War* our hero learns of the double-dealing needed to survive in the intelligence game. A change of pace, *A Naive and Sentimental Lover* follows an unhappy but successful businessman beguiled by a glamorous, wayward couple. *Tinker, Tailor, Soldier, Spy* followed. George Smiley (a minor character in *The Spy Who Came in from the Cold*) is the hero. Head of a British Intelligence department he must ferret out the "mole" who has wasted some of the department's best agents. Le Carré's bestseller *The Honourable Schoolboy* deals with Smiley's attempts to use one of his friends as a pawn to flush out a pair of mysterious Chinese brothers. *Smiley's People* chronicled Smiley's final confrontation with his greatest enemy, Karla. Le Carré's latest #1 bestseller, *A Perfect Spy*, will be published in paperback by Bantam in May 1987.

Le Carré, who has elevated the spy novel to its highest point, is a demon on research. For *The Honourable Schoolboy* he made five trips to Southeast Asia. Pinned down by automatic weapons fire in Cambodia, he dived under a car and coolly noted his impressions on file cards.

Special Offer
Buy a Bantam Book
for only 50¢.

Now you can have Bantam's catalog filled with hundreds of titles plus take advantage of our unique and exciting bonus book offer. A special offer which gives you the opportunity to purchase a Bantam book for only 50¢. Here's how!

By ordering any five books at the regular price per order, you can also choose any other single book listed (up to a $5.95 value) for just 50¢. Some restrictions do apply, but for further details why not send for Bantam's catalog of titles today!

Just send us your name and address and we will send you a catalog!